The Darkness All Around Us

Megan Boley

MIDNIGHT TOMES PRESS

ISBN paperback: 978-1-961529-01-4
ISBN hardcover: 978-1-961529-00-7
ISBN ebook: 978-1-961529-02-1

First Edition: March 2024

For anyone who has suffered in silence, walked through fire, battled the darkness—or is still doing so—you're not alone.

Keep finding the light.

1

S TELLA HAD NEVER GIVEN much thought to how she'd die. Somewhere in the depths of her mind, she figured she'd fall asleep as an old woman and never wake up. No fanfare. Nothing dramatic. Just serene silence.

But Death was now Stella's constant companion—and she was *really* mashing her potatoes. If she didn't shut up, she was going to send Stella to an early grave. Death by chatterbox.

Stella glared at the source of her headache and messed with the radio to tune out Death's incessant yammering.

Death lounged atop the desk that ran the perimeter of the air traffic control tower's main observation room. She gave Stella an easy smile, unperturbed. "What's on the agenda today?" asked Death. "Setting booby traps for our unsuspecting pursuers or figuring out how to find caffeine in this crumbling dirtbag of a city? I know how you get when you haven't had your coffee." Her tawny eyes sparked with mischief as she winked.

Stella's irritation turned sour at the familiar gesture. She refused to think of this hallucination as her best friend, even though they looked exactly alike. The darkness inside Stella stirred, and she glanced down to see her hands shaking. Blood stained them in a wash of electric red. When she blinked, the blood disappeared.

"I can help with that," Death said. She lifted an eyebrow in the direction of Stella's backpack and the packets of powdered life hidden inside.

Stella's stomach lurched. She didn't need it. Not yet.

The setting sun blasted through the windows and transformed the room into a veritable pressure cooker. But high ground was safer. If *they* found her, she might have a head start and a chance at escaping unscathed this time. Her fingers ghosted across the fresh, puckered scar that raked down her neck to the center of her chest like a gruesome pageant sash. She cleared her throat and reached for the tower's cracked radio microphone.

"Silas? Are you out there?" Stella smoothed her thumb over a creased photo of a dark-haired man with deep olive skin—one of the only personal items she'd taken with her before abandoning her apartment in the Beginning. She lingered over the brunette woman in the photo beside him. His sister. Her two best friends. "I...Evie isn't with me." She shot a look at Death, who waggled her fingers at her. *Unless an aggravating apparition of her counts.* "If you've escaped the troxies, I'll be at the Memorial to the Old Gods tomorrow at noon, as usual."

All week, Stella hadn't heard any reply—not that she expected to. But it seemed stupid not to try contacting Silas while she had a working radio setup.

"Or it is extremely stupid," said Death. "It could broadcast your location to *them* and make it easier to find you."

Stella made a face, but the statement speared straight into her heart and her fingers worried at her gold necklace.

She tuned the radio to the right frequency and settled in to listen.

A sharp female voice crackled through the speaker—the leader of a group of survivors camped nearby. Stella didn't know their precise location. "Anybody seen Quentin yet?"

"For the seventeenth time, I'm fine, you worry wart," came Quentin's garbled reply. Stella's mouth twitched at the sound of his bubbly young voice. "I'm heading back to camp now."

She clicked off the radio and swallowed her worry. The possibility of death hovered in the air like an angry wasp ready to strike at any moment. But if the kid had survived until this point, he was smart enough to make it home in one piece. And if he didn't, she couldn't do anything about it. Besides, what happened to him was none of her concern. He was a stranger. For her, alone was safer. Alone meant survival.

So, she focused on what she *could* do—rescue Silas before he disappeared into the bowels of a troxy prison. She had a promise to keep.

She leaned back in the frumpy office chair and grabbed a beer from under the desk. Beer helped her think—or it kept the worst of the invasive thoughts at bay and quelled her other...urges. The warm liquid slid down her throat with a pleasant prickly sensation. Her thoughts drifted to the jolly, balding man who had helped fix her truck last week as she'd fled to the Capital. The beer was his parting gift—evidence that not everyone was a dust-addled monster.

Death sat cross-legged on the desk and stared across the river to the Capital. "I don't know why you keep trying to contact Silas. He's probably rotting in a cell in Pharmatrox HQ with the other dissenters."

Stella ground her teeth. Death was right. The newly established HQ in the Capital was most likely where Pharmatrox was keeping prisoners, but its location was unknown. So far, her few scouting missions into the city had been unsuccessful. Dodging the patrolling troxy guards armed to the teeth and ready to shoot anything that moved always made the journeys lengthier and more perilous. She'd found an entry point where she could sneak through the Capital's perimeter of sandbags and barbed wire fencing, but she'd almost been caught twice now.

"You'll never find Dr. Hansen either." Death blew a strand of hair out of her eyes, a bored expression on her face. "I don't know why you're bothering."

Stella took a drink at the thought of her missing mentor—another name on the list of people she'd failed. "Is it entirely necessary for you to speak? I like it better when you lurk in the shadows and scowl. Déjame en paz."

Death rested her head against the window. "Try to drown me out if you must, but we both know you're going to give in. You always do."

Stella's gaze flicked to her backpack, and she opened her mouth to let loose a scathing retort—

A scuffling sound rattled from a ceiling panel.

Stella's heart shot into her throat.

Them.

They'd finally found her.

I can't do this.

She'd rather face the users and the turned again.

As she grabbed her machete in a sweaty hand, her vision warped and fizzled and she swayed on her feet.

More thumps sounded overhead, closer this time.

I can't face them on my own.

Stella gave in and sprinkled a thick white clump of dust on the back of her hand. The second she inhaled, her mind cleared, her muscles twitched to attention, and her hands lost their tremor.

Death danced atop the desk. She'd fed the beast.

The darkness retreated back to its cage, and the invasive memories faded to a dull blur. She was blissfully alone in her own head. Except for Death. She never could get her to go away no matter how much she used.

Newfound bravery flooded Stella's veins. She prodded at the ceiling with her weapon, followed by a very human sounding "Ack!"

Alarmed, she thrust her machete through the offending tile. A chunk of the ceiling collapsed to the floor in a heap of debris, a squawking human at its center.

Spluttering and covered in drywall dust, the human stared around in a daze. Stella raised an arm to strike the intruder—but stopped. It was a gangly boy, a teenager. She exhaled. Not *them*. But he could still be a threat—anyone could, these days.

She kicked through the colossal mess and knelt in front of the boy's freckled face. "Why were you rooting around in my ceiling?" Beneath the layer of dust, flecks of bronze peppered his brown hair. "And how the *hell* did you get up here?"

"Sorry." He coughed aggressively and thumped his chest, ignoring her weapon. "Didn't know this was already occupied. Just wanted to have a look around."

Quentin. Stella recognized his voice from hours of listening to him on the radio. An ice-cold spray of goose bumps frosted her skin. She tried to look intimidating instead of caught unawares.

"You're surprisingly calm for someone who has a machete under his face. Hands on your head where I can see them."

Quentin raised both hands in surrender, a smirk pulling at his lips. "Shall I put a bag over my head too? Or do you want me to witness my own execution?"

Madre mía, is this how he always talks to strangers? In this world, it's a wonder he hasn't been executed sooner. She snatched a thin book from the desk and thumped him on the side of the head. He yelped, rubbing his ear with an indignant look.

"Done being cheeky? I won't ask again. How did you get up here?"

His Adam's apple bobbed like a hyperactive ping-pong ball. "Got through the perimeter at Lincoln Bridge." *That's the spot I use. Clever boy.* "Almost got my head blown off by one of those volt-blaster rifle thingies. Thought I'd check out the airport for any abandoned luggage. Saw the tower and was curious, but the door at the bottom was locked. Obviously. I mean, you knew that." He took a deep breath and stopped babbling. "Right. So I climbed and found my way in through the air ducts up top."

He *climbed*? But what other explanation could there be? He was right about the door. The only key was in her pocket.

Quentin darted a nervous glance out the window at the darkness beyond. Stella tapped her machete against her leg as she considered her options. Quentin was probably harmless. But she didn't want him to go broadcasting her whereabouts to anyone he came across. No, that wouldn't do at all.

"What would you do with you, if you were me?" she asked.

His slate-gray eyes widened into a look of innocence. "Give me a friendly warning about the dangers of trespassing and send me on my merry way?" His voice only squeaked at the end.

Stella sniffed. "Don't go poking your nose where it doesn't belong." Bumping his knee with the tip of her machete, she added, "Other people aren't as nice as I am."

Quentin's shoulders detached from his ears, and he sagged in relief.

"Now get gone." She slapped him on the thigh with the flat of her blade.

He scampered to his feet and hoisted himself through the hole in the ceiling.

"And hey," she called after him. He poked his head through the hole with a grimace. "Don't get eaten. Be careful out there."

He nodded like a bobblehead on a bouncy dashboard. She dismissed him with a curt nod, and he disappeared into the night.

It was only after Stella reclaimed her seat in the moldy office chair and cracked another beer that she realized what troubled her about Quentin's appearance.

If he could invade her home so easily, who else could?

2

Penny

P ENNY WEDGED A TOOTHPICK into her mouth and ground it between her teeth. Why the fuck she thought it would be a good idea to quit smoking, she couldn't fathom. After all, cigarettes were free now. Everything was free—it was the end of the world. Or at least the end of the United States. There was no one left to stop her from taking what she wanted.

If she had to listen to Toby's whining any more, though, the situation would call for a lot more than a pack of cigarettes.

She closed her eyes and pinched the bridge of her nose. "Toby," she said through clenched teeth. "If you want to live to utter another asinine syllable, *you'll shut the fuck up.*" Toby looked resentful but clamped his mouth shut. He was stupid but not suicidal.

"Callum?" Penny said.

"She was here," said Callum. "That guy we found in the garage? Tom, or whatsit? He saw her."

Penny ran her tongue along the bottom of her teeth. "He still alive?" The feral glint in Callum's eyes didn't give her much hope.

"He's still breathin', to be sure." His Irish lilt slipped out, melting across his speech like butter. His beast was close to the surface.

Toby shuffled his feet like he wanted to say something.

Penny sighed and spat out her toothpick, replacing it with the cigarette tucked behind her ear. She'd gone long enough without one for today.

Toby was quick to light it for her. She was easily ten years younger than these middle-aged men, yet they looked to her as their leader. She'd earned that position with blood and an ample supply of dust. She took a sweet drag from the cigarette with a sigh. To Toby, she said, "What is it?"

He flinched at her flat tone. "Well, ah—why is finding Stella so important again?"

Penny grabbed a fistful of his shirt, grimacing at his stained teeth and foul breath. "Have you not been listening? She's one of them—a troxy. She's *the* troxy—the one responsible for all of this." She gestured in a wide arc, encompassing the dilapidated roadside town, the corpses in the street, the blown-out cars on the highway.

"She's the Architect? She works for Pharmatrox? Are you sure?"

Penny shoved Toby, and he stumbled and landed in a heap. "I will get justice for what she did to us," said Penny. "And stop asking me questions."

She sauntered into the shanty car shop, boots crunching on the broken glass, and toed what appeared to be a severed finger across the cracked tile floor. "Too much fun indeed," she said. She didn't enjoy torture or mindless killing, but she would do whatever it took to find the Architect and eliminate her. Penny owed her family that much.

She followed a wounded moan to the back corner by the tool shelves, where a lump of dirty rags stained with blood sat on the floor, and took a long drag from her cigarette. "Hello, Tom," she said to the pile of rags.

"What...do...you...want?" the older bald man panted.

Crouching in front of him, Penny blew smoke in his face. He gagged on his own blood as it spouted from his ruined throat and lapsed into unconsciousness.

She backhanded him, rings biting into his face, and removed her sickle from her belt. His head bobbed on his neck like a deflated balloon. She really wished Callum hadn't had quite so much fun with this one. She needed his information.

Sloppy. I need to keep Callum on a tighter leash.

Penny grabbed his jowls in one hand. "Pay attention, Tom. I know she was here. I know you helped her. Where is she?"

"Go...to hell," he wheezed, eyes glazed and halfway gone. Blood dribbled from his lips and stained his overalls.

This one won't last long. Best to end it before the turned find him. She drew her sickle across his throat in a vicious arc.

On her way out, she deposited the dripping head on the counter.

Callum and Toby buzzed with bliss and adrenaline. She gave them a brisk nod and tucked her red hair behind an ear.

The two remaining members of her crew laughed and shoved each other like children as they covered the crumbling car shop in gasoline. Penny puckered her lips in distaste. *Idiots.* She needed them—for now. But she'd be rid of them soon enough.

"That's my girl." Rodney's voice came to her, unbidden. A thin face with sharp cheekbones and beady eyes flashed in her mind.

Penny stood in front of a scientist in a white lab coat and forced him to his knees as Rodney handed her another hit of dust. The drug thrummed through her veins, and she pressed her sickle against the man's ear. A wicked smile split Rodney's face. "That's my girl."

A need for the dust raced through her. Penny forced down the urge and the specter of Rodney. She'd escaped from under his thumb and earned her own raiding crew in the Faction months ago, but the blood-stained memories and *the need* were harder to leave behind. She'd have to return to the Faction stronghold soon enough to replenish her supplies and check in, but only one thing truly mattered: finding Stella.

Callum tossed his lighter over his shoulder, and the car shop ignited in an instant inferno. Penny watched in silence, then flicked her own silver lighter, seeing a different building, different flames. Different dead bodies inside. She bit the inside of her cheek hard enough to taste blood.

When Callum called to her, she nodded.

The hunt continues.

3

"S INCE SILAS DIDN'T SHOW again," said Death, "do we think he's dead or...?"

Stella sighed and set aside her mother's journal. Silas hadn't met her at the Memorial, but she couldn't wait anymore. The sun sank behind the spectral buildings as evening approached. Wandering around at night wasn't safe, but it did make traveling undetected easier—at least, undetected by *humans*.

She tucked the journal into her bag and stood to leave. Written thirty years ago around the time of Stella's birth, her mother's words about life during the Sickness sent a chill up her spine. It sounded eerily similar to what was happening now. Except, instead of being their savior from the Sickness, Pharmatrox was responsible—for the users and the turned, for the war with the Faction. For everything.

Open your eyes.

Her stomach churned. How could she have been so wrong about Pharmatrox? Now Silas's concerns didn't seem so far-fetched.

Stella glared at the destruction around her. A large statue of a regal woman stood at the center of the park, surrounded by five crumbling pillars of sooty marble—the bones of the Memorial to the Old Gods, bombed by the Faction shortly after the Beginning. Mother Science, she was called. Some called her the Architect—the one who had created the dust—although no one knew the Architect's true identity. After the Beginning, an urban legend began circulating that said the Architect held secrets capable of toppling the Pharmatrox empire, but Stella had never believed it.

PROXIMITY ALERT.

The words materialized in front of her eyes, and the white orb embedded behind her ear pulsed with light. Every Pharmatrox employee had one. A 3D map of the city appeared, visible only to her. A group of red dots weaved between the buildings, heading for...

With a blink, she tapped into the Pharmatrox comms feed.

"Faction army inbound, heading toward Lincoln Bridge," said the voice of a troxy commander in Stella's ear. "Numbers are growing. Send in a unit to respond."

Mierda, it's really time to go. She could take McAdams Bridge instead and get to her weak point in the perimeter. She had to move fast; it was the only exit she knew of, and it could get choked off in the impending skirmish. The beginning of a headache hammered at her forehead, and her pockets felt exceptionally empty as she longed for more dust—she hadn't used since that morning.

Stella tapped her Patch off so it would better blend into her cropped, bleached hair—it was only visible if it lit up—and ran down the hill. She'd taken this path many times in the past week, so she knew the way without a map. If she happened to run into anyone, she didn't want to risk them seeing her Patch flashing with alerts.

Her ears tuned for sounds of attack as she weaved among the detritus of the abandoned battlefront. Potholes pockmarked the pavement, and a hot breeze tinged with the scent of smoke and decay blew past. The Capital had fractured into separate sectors, where the Faction and troxies vied for control. Some neutral zones existed and groups of civilians lived there—the unlucky ones who had failed to escape in the Beginning. But neutral hardly meant safe; anyone in the Capital was vulnerable to capture by roving Pharmatrox patrols. She'd witnessed it more than a few times. The Memorial was neutral territory but bordered troxy sectors on all sides.

Her thoughts flicked to Dr. Hansen. She hoped that wherever her mentor was, she was safe. But the tight feeling in her chest wouldn't relent. *I'll find her. And Silas. I have to.*

Stella popped out of an alley into a wide street lined with what had been a collection of condos and restaurants but was now a sad row of sagging shacks. A black and red motorcycle in half-decent shape parked on the curb. *Impractical choice of vehicle. Not exactly stealthy.* She spared a passing glance down the road and halted.

The Seven Sisters sat at the end of the street.

The bloodstained pavement led to the stage of death like a red carpet.

Seven empty row houses, their pearly white facades swathed in black splotches, with blown-out windows like gaping wounds. Bodies in white lab coats hung from the flagpoles of the Seven Sisters. Troxies, their faces lost to decay. Heaps of bloody lab coats littered the porches in infinite piles.

Trophies of the resistance.

Hovering beside Stella, Death let out a low whistle. "I told you Pharmatrox was bad news. Look at the hate they inspired. The blood of these scientists is on their hands."

How did we get here? How did our world come to this?

Her stomach churned. She couldn't help feeling like she was responsible too.

As she approached the main thoroughfare, shouts echoed between the skyscrapers. A zap of electricity, followed by a scream.

Stella sprinted for the bridge, abandoning all stealth. *Hijo de puta, the troxies move fast. And they have volt rifles.* One errant blast and she'd be fried. *Just another block and a half...*

A low, rhythmic rumble came from an intersecting street. Many boots crunched in unison as they stomped through the rubble. A mob clad head to toe in black, wearing red hardshell masks, surged up the street.

The Faction.

Cursing, Stella ducked into the nearest alley. It was shallow, more like an alcove. No time to change locations. *Leave it to me to start the day with a harmless errand and end up sandwiched between my two worst enemies.*

If the Faction discovered she was a troxy, they'd kill her on sight. But her fate at Pharmatrox's hands would be much worse; she was a deserter, and Pharmatrox assured deserters lived to regret their decisions.

She flattened herself against the wall to meld with the shadows as the force of over fifty Faction members thundered past. Several carried purloined machine guns, while others had rudimentary weapons like pipes, axes, and hunting knives. A host of Pharmatrox guards stood at the opposite end of the street. A few guards held sleek matte-black volt rifles buzzing with white-blue energy.

"Death to troxies!" one of the Faction shouted.

The two forces met with a clash. Stella's vantage point gave her a small snapshot of the battle. Bullets stuttered across the pavement, metal clanged, glass shattered. A fighter jet screamed overhead, and an explosion obliterated the road near the bridge.

An arc of lightning raced through the air from a troxy rifle. One of the Faction yelled and collapsed, foaming at the mouth. Her companion hacked at the troxy with a sword until he fell to the ground in a sloppy heap.

"What?" said Death. She stood in the street and spread her hands, covered in blood. Like Evie. Unlike Evie, however, Death sneered. "Witnessing slaughter bothers you now? You've seen it before. Stop sniveling."

Stella squeezed her eyes shut. It was the withdrawal talking, but it stung with the bitter pang of truth. Death was getting nasty.

She had to get home. Maybe she could slip out in the chaos of battle. Panic gripped her at the thought of having to kill again.

But the pull of the dust was stronger.

Ducking her head, she dashed toward the bridge, sticking close to the buildings. She threw a glance over her shoulder to see if—

She slammed into a massive brick wall of a man.

Stella recovered first. She dodged, but he snatched her arm. A swift knee to his groin had him doubling over. As he swung his colossal fists, one of his wild blows smashed into her ear. Her Patch blinked to life in front of her eyes, activated by the man's punch. *Joder, not now.*

Through the holes in his shiny red mask, the man's eyes widened. His gaze locked on the white chip implanted behind her ear, pulsing with light, and he grabbed her by the throat and wrenched her close. "Oh-ho! You're Patched! The boss will slap his gramma when he hears I've found him another troxy for the pits."

The boss? Kev Hernandez? Oh hell. "Wha—?"

His fist rammed the side of her head and everything went black.

4

STELLA WOKE WITH HER arms lashed to her sides, heart thundering in her chest. The cold metal of the rusted bench seeped through her jeans.

She sat in the second row of a derelict, open-air football stadium crammed with a few hundred rowdy people. Dozens of other prisoners occupied the row beside her—some were Pharmatrox soldiers captured in the recent battle. Her head spun from withdrawal and one too many hits to the face.

Fuck. She groaned. Her pack and weapons belt were gone. *This is bad, but I can reason with Kev.*

The founder of the Faction was known for being harsh but fair. There was still a chance to get out of this. Her mind raced to come up with an explanation for why she was Patched. It didn't matter that she'd gone rogue and her special Patch was unauthorized technology she'd designed herself for the sole purpose of being a ghost in the network. Kev would never believe that. It's exactly what a Pharmatrox spy would say. But he had to believe *something*. Her survival depended on it.

The edgy energy of the crowd slithered through the stands and growls rumbled from the depths of a giant dirt pit in the middle of the field, but her view was blocked by the row of people in front of her. Torches lining the field's perimeter blistered the growing darkness and blazed a trail to a large platform at the edge of the pit beside a crash-landed helicopter that was undergoing repairs. *How the hell did they manage to snag that?* The Faction force in the Capital was much more well equipped than what she saw in drone video clips from the other cities on her Patch feed.

Dozens of Faction members crowded around the pit's maw and vibrated with excitement. A few members stood guard beside Stella and the other prisoners, shouting obscenities along with the riotous audience.

The old stadium was in Sector 14, a Faction-controlled area in the eastern part of the Capital. It was about five miles from the airport, according to the 3D maps on her Patch. *Mierda*. She needed more dust, and soon. And she wasn't anywhere close to home.

Stella turned to the frail, mousy-haired woman next to her, who rocked back and forth. "What's happening?" When the woman only darted a glance at Stella and rocked faster, Stella sighed and peered down the line. "Anyone else know what the hell is going on?"

A bald man at the end hissed. "Quiet! Let them enjoy their distraction."

"What a miserable little toad," said Death with a rude gesture.

Stella's pounding headache throbbed behind her eyes, and rage boiled in her blood. Her attitude was starting to match Death's. *Not good.*

With every shiver, the dust leached from Stella's system. It wouldn't be long before withdrawal had her fully in its grips. Sometimes it made her impulsive and angry, but mostly it left her feeling weak, a husk of herself. She only knew one user who had ever successfully detoxed from the dust. She didn't like her chances.

Her arms were bound, so crawling off into the crowd wasn't an option. She could roll away like a log down a hill? She snorted. Absolutely not. She'd be so dizzy she wouldn't be able to see straight, let alone outrun the Faction. Then she remembered her knife, still hidden in her boot.

She prodded it out with her opposite foot. After making sure the guards were distracted, she leaned forward and grabbed the knife in her teeth. She flicked it over her shoulder and fumbled it with her bound hands, and carefully started sawing through the rope.

A raucous cheer went up from the crowd. "And the users win again! The troxies take another loss," shouted a Faction member from the platform.

On a crate behind him sat another man. Instead of the customary red Faction mask, his was white. Stella's mouth went dry. *It's Kev. If I can get close enough, maybe I can talk—*

"Who's next?"

The people lining the pit swiveled to face the prisoners. Stella froze. A massive man shouldered his way through the crowd and pointed at her. She plastered a doe-eyed look on her face and hid her knife in the waistband of her jeans.

"That one on the end!" said her captor. "She's a feisty one. Kneed me in my tenders, she did. She'll put up a good fight."

Before Stella could protest, rough hands dragged her forward and forced her over the railing and onto the field. The throng of faceless people parted and jeered, their masks glistening like glossy candied apples in the flickering torchlight. How many of them were Pharmatrox defectors like her, or regular civilians who had gotten caught up in the revolutionary craze and idealistic promises of the Faction? She wanted to scream that they had it all wrong, that she was duped by Pharmatrox just like them.

A strong hand pushed her to the edge of the pit, and she glimpsed the horrors awaiting her below.

Dismembered limbs scattered across the floor, and a pile of bloody bodies loomed off to the side, most of them headless and wearing white lab coats. Three users stood back to back, shouting and gesturing at the crowd. When one, a scrawny man, scrambled up the side of the pit, a guard fired a warning shot. He yelped and scampered down, hands curved into claws, while his partner tossed another bloody coat on the pile.

"The troxies take another loss!"

Hostia, they're making the troxies fight their own creations. Or at least they made whoever they shoved into the pit *look like* troxies. To the Faction, there was no greater evil than Pharmatrox and their abominable creatures—the users and the turned. But this...nobody deserved *this*.

The partner, a tall male user with long black hair, thrust his hands into one of the pools of blood dappling the dirt and smeared it across his face with a howl. A wolf on the hunt. The third user, a woman with dark brown skin, passed something back and forth between her hands. *Oh god, is that an* eyeball?

Stella dug in her heels as the red masks pulled her toward the rim. "No, please!"

A man shoved Stella's arms into a grimy lab coat. "In you go, troxy." With a remorseless laugh, he kicked her in the chest. The breath whooshed out of her lungs as she tumbled down the sloped walls and crashed to the bottom, fifteen feet below.

Disoriented and with a mouthful of dirt, Stella wasn't prepared for the attack.

The woman drove her into the ground with ferocious speed as her two male companions circled, chittering with approval.

Stella flailed in a feeble attempt to fend off the woman and caught a glimpse of her attacker's eyes. Black lines shattered the sclera. Stella glanced at the men. Their eyes were the same. Not turned yet—but they were mere hours away from the change.

"What's a'matter, troxy?" the woman drawled. She smiled with bloodstained teeth. "Can't handle looking at what you've created?"

Stella bucked her hips, but withdrawal coursed through her, leaving her limbs limp. She couldn't do this. Not without the dust. She was going to die. *And does it really matter if I do? I'm so tired of running.*

Death clapped her hands in Stella's face. "You've done this before—without dust. Remember?"

A woman with fiery red hair smiling as she swung a sickle at her face...A mint-green hallway, the enemy chasing her.

The day she got her new name. The day she became Stella.

"Get us outta here," said Death. "We're Silas's only chance."

Death was right. If she didn't get out of this pit, Silas would die too. There was nothing to do but kill these users before they could hurt anyone else.

With a newfound fervor, Stella grabbed the knife from her waistband and plunged it under the woman's jaw. Hot black blood gushed over her, and she shoved the body aside and rolled to her feet, facing the two remaining men. The influx of adrenaline held off the withdrawal, but her hands shook like maracas.

The crowd cheered and booed in equal measure. From the platform, the announcer guffawed while Kev lurched to his feet. He ripped off the mask, and Stella's grip on her knife loosened.

Who the fuck is that?

The man's fist curled around his mask with such force that it snapped in half, his lanky body tense in anticipation. Stella's mouth went dry. This guy was a wildcard, and her chances at survival couldn't handle another unknown variable. She had to get the fuck out of there.

"Give her a real weapon!" shouted Not Kev Hernandez, his teeth bared in a bloodthirsty grin. "Let's see what this troxy can do."

As the two users charged across the pit, Stella's machete tumbled to the ground at her feet. She scooped up the familiar weapon and lashed out. Both users dodged and swiped at her with claw-like fingernails. As she fought, the crowd and the pit melted away.

She was in the mint-green hallway, fighting for her life.

She was in the woods, sparring until her fingers bled.

She was kneeling in the dirt, innocent blood on her hands.

Stella swung her machete at the user's torso, a desperate yell escaping her. When she hacked through half of his ribcage, he buckled with a cry. Black blood pumped from the mortal wound, and a clamor went up from the crowd.

"They troxy's evened her odds!" the announcer said in disbelief.

Stella spun to face her last opponent. It was the user with blood on his face like war paint. She thrust her weapon, and he grabbed her by the wrist—but she had expected that. Using his momentum, she pulled herself into him and jammed her boot knife in the side of his neck.

But he wouldn't go down so easily. As black blood gurgled out of his neck and he swiped at Stella, his tough fingernails tore through her lab coat sleeve, and she cried out, a gash on her upper arm weeping blood.

The man licked his lips at the smell of fresh human blood. *Good. I can use that.* Stella struck out with her knife, this time aiming for the heart. The blade met flesh and slid home, but she kept pushing until she had the man flat on his back, black blood flowing onto the dirt.

Half of the spectators cheered, while a slow murmur seeped around the crowd's perimeter. Stella leaned on her machete to catch her breath, dripping in gore and sweat, then shucked off the bloodied lab coat with revulsion.

The announcer bobbed in excitement but slowed as Not Kev Hernandez peered down at Stella with intense curiosity. The way his smile hinted at eagerness had her renewing her grip on her machete.

One of the Faction slid into the pit and pressed a gun to Stella's forehead. "What do we do with her, Rodney?" he shouted. "Never had a troxy make it outta the fighting pits before. Don't think we should start today."

Who the hell is Rodney? Stella didn't dare blink as she stared down the barrel of the gun and into the impassive red mask. A cold sweat slicked her body, and the withdrawal shakes increased to a continuous tremor. *I survived the dust and the fighting pit, but it's a bullet from this gilipollas that kills me. Just my goddamn luck.* Death smiled like a jack-o'-lantern as Stella's thoughts pinwheeled into the darkness.

Another red-masked Faction member appeared beside Rodney. The man said something in Rodney's ear and offered a hand-held radio, gesturing at the sky.

"Gotta be fucking kidding me," said Rodney. He launched off the platform, his interest in Stella evaporating. "Kill her and be done with it. Everyone, take your positions. We've got an incoming troxy raid."

The crowd surged into action. Stella didn't wait. She drove her shoulder into the abdomen of the man holding the gun to her head. He was bigger than her, but she'd caught him by surprise. She hit the gun out of his hand, and it flew across the pit. A punch to his face and his nose crunched under her fist.

Surrounded by screams and chaos, Stella clawed her way up the sloped wall and heaved herself over the rim. People dashed in every direction, shouting orders and gathering weapons.

As she shoved her way through the crowd toward the closest door, someone grabbed her elbow. She whipped around and swung her machete. A *huge* man blocked her strike with an iron grip.

She wrenched back, but he held fast and lifted his red mask to reveal dark close-cropped hair, light brown eyes, and a jawline peppered with stubble. Something in his expression stopped her from struggling. He looked at her like a soldier, not like his next murder victim. He wasn't the man who had spoken to Rodney on stage; he was much too large.

He pointed to the locker room exit. "Your pack is in there." It was difficult to make out his words in the ruckus. "Turn left and go until you see the gate." He pressed something into her hand, along with his red mask. "Junky moped parked outside. Take it and go." Without another word, the man melted into the crowd.

What the fuck just happened? With her hand curled around the old key clutched in her hand, she slipped the mask over her face and dashed for her escape route.

5

COLD SWEAT COATED STELLA'S clammy body as she rushed through the back hallway of the stadium. She'd found her pack and weapons belt where the stranger had indicated and slung them on her back, heading for the exit.

Faction members rushed around her and prepared for battle, dodging around the pitched tents, lean-tos, and old weapons lining the cracked concrete hallway. She tapped her Patch and did a quick map scan. No telltale blip of a Pharmatrox brigade incoming, but maybe the Faction had intel from another inside source. Impending troxy attack or not, she had to get back to the dust. Death's face seeped into her periphery with that eerie smile that promised destruction.

Stella ducked through the gate and burst into the open night air, blood running from the cut on her arm and forming a trail behind her. She tied her bandanna around it, but it would need a stitch or two. Faction members manned the anti-aircraft weaponry—stolen from Pharmatrox, no doubt—mounted on top of a beat-up ambulance, a Humvee, and a semi. The moped sat at the end of a line of rusted cars next to a heap of tires. It, too, was in poor shape, but as long as the motor ran, nothing else mattered.

Stella shoved the key into the ignition and nearly whimpered with relief when the engine sputtered to life. Wobbling down the street, she followed her Patch's maps back to Pickerton Airport, pushing the moped's speed until the handlebars rattled.

Her thoughts tumbled over her miraculous escape. That man...Why would he help her? The Faction was ruthless in pursuit of its mission—to eradicate Pharmatrox, users, and the turned, and restore order to the fractured nation. Her Patch was damning evidence that she was—or had been—a troxy. So how did she get out of that stadium alive? And why would a member of the group that had burned cities to the ground to fight back against Pharmatrox give her the key to her salvation? It didn't make sense, and she wasn't in the right mind frame to decipher it.

The chill of the night sank into her bones. She'd never gone this long without the dust before.

The memories writhed within their cage.

Hot blood on her hands. Smoke filling her nose.

With Lincoln Bridge just ahead, Stella twisted the throttle to its limit, and the moped struggled up the road, a high-pitched whine screaming from the engine.

She was almost to the bridge when she hit the pothole.

The front wheel twisted sideways, and she managed to maintain control—but the tire was completely shredded, sliced by metal shrapnel.

The moped was useless.

"Me cago in la leche!" Stella landed a feeble kick to the moped's tire, panic climbing up her throat.

She squinted. Four troxy guards headed her way. The airport was maybe a mile out, but the thought of getting the dust in her system gave her an extra surge of energy. *I can make it.* She crouched and ran across the bridge, crawled over sandbags, and ducked through her opening in the barbed wire fence.

Several minutes later, she ambled across the tarmac, stumbling on lead feet. She unlocked the door at the bottom of the air traffic control tower and heaved herself up the stairs.

With her boot knife, she disemboweled the moldy office chair and stuffed her hand inside the cushion. A relieved sob escaped her when she clutched her prize. The remainder of her stash was enough to keep her going for a few months—if she used sparingly. She opened one of the packets and snorted the contents directly from the baggie. Instant clarity flooded her veins.

She needed *more*.

More more more.

With each beat of her heart, the crushing *need* intensified. She emptied another packet into her mouth, and another, and collapsed against the wall in ecstasy.

Thump. Thump. Thump.

The steady metronome of pounding pulled Stella out of her haze.

Thump. Thump. Thump.

The dust zipped through her, and her reflexes snapped to attention. She rummaged in her pack for her flashlight to figure out what the hell that racket was. It sounded like it was coming from everywhere.

She clicked on the light and swept it across the window.

A thin, pale face, whites of the eyes turned black as onyx, teeth bared.

Stella yelped and dropped the flashlight. Cursing, she backed against the desk and fumbled for the light, then raised it to the window, knuckles white.

A man clung to the outside of the tower. As the light touched him, he went berserk, punching the window with a bloody fist. *Thump. Thump. Thump.* Spindly cracks sprung from the glass where his fist impacted. His black eyes glistened like tar, and red spittle dribbled from sharp teeth. A roar erupted from his throat, red spray splattering against the glass.

He was one of them. A turned.

Panic surged through her, and she clutched the flashlight to her chest, the solid glass of the window a reassuring weight at her back.

A loud *thump* behind her.

Another turned, black eyes and sharp teeth, punched the window.

Stella rotated her light around the room, dread pooling inside of her.

All around her, turned clung to the windows. A dozen or more of them punched and kicked the glass with booming blows.

How the hell did they know I was up here? My blood trail ended outside of the stadium. Realization hit her as a cold thought constricted her chest. *Someone knew where to find me...*

Thump-crrrk.

A spiderweb of cracks blossomed under a turned's fist.

They were going to get in.

Panic tightened its hold, and her breaths wheezed in her chest. *Fuck fuck fuck, this can't be happening.*

"Get it together!" Death materialized and waved her up.

Stella hung onto the dwindling thread of clarity with all her willpower and stood. A glance outside confirmed her fears—more turned congregated on the tarmac below.

Thump-crrrk.

Bodies plastered against the window, beating the glass with heavy fists. Pale faces twisted in grotesque smiles, their beady eyes like pits of pure darkness, hands curled into bloody claws. One woman butted her forehead against the glass, eyes wide and deranged.

Stella held her machete steady. Better to face them here in this room than be surrounded in the growing crowd outside.

Thump-crrrrrACK.

The woman's head burst through, snarling and hissing as she wedged herself inside and pried away chunks of glass. Stella brought her machete down with a wild cry. A spray of black blood erupted, and the woman's head rolled across the floor.

But it was too late. Two other turned scrambled to shove through the widened hole in the glass.

Thump-crrrrrACK.

Another turned broke through, howling and clawing the glass away with ripped, bleeding hands. Shards lodged under his fingernails, but the turned couldn't feel pain. Only death could stop them.

Thump-crrrrrACK. Thump-crrrrrACK.

More heads and limbs punched into the room. Even with augmented reflexes from the dust, Stella would be overtaken in mere seconds.

Running down a mint-green hallway. Moans and feral screeches. Dozens of feet thundering behind her.

Stella blinked and shook herself.

She'd done this before, and far less armed than she was now, so she sank into a fighting stance.

The first wave of turned surged through half a dozen jagged holes in the glass.

She swung her machete in a sweeping arc and took out three. One grabbed the flashlight and smashed it against the wall, plunging the room into darkness. But with the help of the dust, Stella's reflexes and natural instincts took over.

Her eyes flicked around the room, searching in vain for an escape route. Then she noticed the blood dripping from her bandanna. As the scent permeated the air, the turned became more reckless.

Joder, there are so fucking many of them. Stella stepped back, and her heel dipped into open air.

Too late, she realized what the turned were doing—they were herding her toward one of the smashed floor-to-ceiling window panes. The room spun as she looked straight down to the tarmac hundreds of feet away. Even from this height, she could hear the cries of the turned below.

Some scaled the tower, heading straight for her.

One of them lunged at her, black fingernails curved like talons. Stella managed to sidestep and shove him out the open window. She slashed her machete at another, but instead of her blade biting through flesh, a cold hand wrapped around her wrist.

This one wasn't a turned. Not yet.

Eyes wide, Stella tried to rip her arm out of the user's grasp as several turned latched onto her legs to pull her down with them.

The woman holding Stella's wrist smiled, lifeless eyes glinting, and seized her by the neck. "Penny sends her regards."

Stella's scream lodged in her throat.

Them.

They'd found her.

It was better to let the user choke the life out of her right now. Penny and the remaining Marauders would assure she begged for death before they were through with her.

Death crossed her arms, the brunette hallucination locking eyes with Stella as she struggled to maintain consciousness. "Remember—Silas. Dr. Hansen. They need you. Do not fail them again."

Do not fail them again.

Dredging the depths of her resolve, Stella grabbed a shard of glass and slammed it into the user's neck, then pushed her out the window, her screams echoing through the night.

Stella fended off attacks as she tore through the room looking for anything that could help her. She ripped open every desk drawer. Pencils. Paper. Extra cords. Old tools.

At the last drawer, she finally found them. Flares. *Thank god.* She snatched a handful and ignited them.

At the bright explosion of light, the turned shrieked and rushed for the windows with jerky, insect-like movements. The red light from the flares cast the pools of black blood in a sickly glow. Some leapt to their deaths to get away from the burn of the light, and some survived the fall. A few stragglers stayed behind, baring their teeth. The light burned them too, but they were hungry.

A rumble louder than thunder sounded from below.

The remaining turned hissed and cocked their heads at the new noise of potential prey—or predator.

Stella glanced down. Her rusty red truck sat on the tarmac, ancient engine rumbling.

Death poked out the window beside her and scratched her head. "Someone is stealing your truck."

The truck circled around the base of the tower, the driver beeping the horn and revving the engine, tires squealing. The noise riled the turned into a frenzy, and they howled and fell from the tower, claws clutched to their ears.

Smoke peeled from the back wheels as the truck took off. Drawn to its movement, the herd of turned chased it into the night.

6

STELLA STARED OPEN-MOUTHED AT the truck's retreating tail-lights. Then practicality struck her to attention.

She shoved the flare near the remaining window and looked at her reflection in the glass. She'd never used so much at once before, but she'd been sucked into the whirlpool of withdrawal. *How could I have been so reckless?* The dust gave some users heightened senses and reflexes—in addition to making them volatile and murderously insane. Others, it gave dangerous hallucinations or turned them feral. Nobody could predict how the dust would affect a particular person. But all users turned eventually.

Stella blew out a breath. Her reflection showed clear, steady blue eyes. No black veins shattered the sclera. Assured another day of life, she grabbed her pack and abandoned the airport, new questions flooding her mind as she headed for Lincoln Bridge.

How close was Penny? Who had stolen her truck? And where should she go now?

Finding Pharmatrox's new hidden HQ was her priority. Silas's charming smile flashed in her mind, and her heart clenched. Silas was like a brother to her. And she had promised Evie she would get him to the border. Canada was accepting refugees—if they passed a blood test. Silas would pass, but as a user, Stella never would. She was half lost to the dust already. There was no salvation for her, in Canada or anywhere else. Saving Silas was the only thing that mattered. And if she could find Dr. Hansen, she'd help her escape too.

The damn turned had destroyed her radio and maps though. She'd have to start her search from scratch. And each passing day meant one more day Silas spent as a Pharmatrox prisoner. She didn't know what the troxies were doing to him, but it couldn't be good. And now she had to contend with Penny. Staying mobile was her best option until she could figure out her next move.

But first, she needed to stop bleeding all over the fucking forest.

With the needle and thread from her sewing kit, she jabbed a few quick stitches through her arm. The medical sutures had run out over a month ago after she'd stitched up the massive wound on her throat and chest. The dust staved off the pain and lent her fingers extra dexterity as she tied off the last sloppy stitch.

BOOM.

Behind her, the air traffic control tower exploded, the observation room burning like a torch.

A heavy anchor of fear settled on Stella as she headed toward the Capital's dark streets.

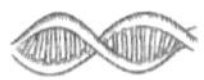

Approaching the wrought iron gate of the abandoned zoo, Stella spun her machete in a nervous rhythm. The stagnant midday air clogged her lungs, and the sunburn blooming across her shoulders blended with the harsh fire of pain in her stitches. She retied her bandanna around her neck to hide her scar; covering it made it easier to pretend she was a normal person.

But nothing would ever be normal again. The Beginning had changed everything.

All night, she'd stayed on the move and stuck to the Capital's neutral zones. Several miles northwest of the Memorial near Victory Park, she'd found the zoo bordering Faction territory. If Penny had been following her, she'd lost her trail by now. Maybe.

But as Stella crept down the winding sidewalk deeper into the zoo, she couldn't shake the feeling that hidden eyes watched her. An eerie silence filtered through the grounds and enclosed the area in a dome of hush. The lack of sounds—like traffic and commercial airplanes—had been the first thing that struck Stella when she'd fled New York. She'd never expected the end of the world to be so quiet. But here in the Capital, the sounds of battle interrupted the ominous silence.

After the past adrenaline-fueled twenty-four hours, coupled with no sleep and an excess of dust, Stella felt like a worn-out jean jacket. Frayed around the edges. Saggy. She forced her feet to keep moving; if she stopped, Penny would find her.

She cocked her head as the scent of danger permeated the air. *Smoke.* The air rumbled around her—the deafening roar of a fighter jet.

A Pharmatrox raid.

It would be maybe two minutes before the bombing started. She should have had her fucking Patch on to listen for stuff like this, but in her sleep-deprived state, she'd forgotten and left it off.

Christ, I'm stupid. She turned heel and ran toward the main street to look for shelter. A building, an alcove, a ditch. Anything was better than being in the open.

Civilians scurried through the street, screaming and covering their heads. If they didn't get blown up in the raid, they'd be captured in the aftermath unless they found a good hiding spot.

As Stella reached the top of the hill, a black and red motorcycle ripped past the zoo's entrance. The contents of her stomach threatened to crawl up her throat. Hadn't she seen the same bike near the Seven Sisters? *Someone is following me...Mierda, is it Penny? Pharmatrox?* She put a lid on her panic. It was probably a coincidence, someone fleeing the raid like her. She was being paranoid.

First, she had to survive the next few minutes. Then she could worry about Penny and everything else.

Stella spied a busted storefront up the street. *Good enough.* She sprinted toward it. The ground shook under her feet as the first of the bombs fell, and she ducked against the cement wall surrounding the zoo's grounds.

Another rumbling sound approached, but it wasn't a Pharmatrox jet.

Stella's ancient truck pulled up beside her, a familiar face behind the wheel.

"Get in!" said Quentin. He leaned across the cab and threw the door open.

Stella gaped. *Dios mío, is everyone following me?*

Missiles screamed overhead and crashed into targets on the other side of Victory Park. Civilians dipped into alleyways or hid behind abandoned cars. Without another thought, Stella dove into the truck, and Quentin floored it.

"You stole my truck, you little shit. Are you even old enough to drive?" Stella clutched the door handle as Quentin whipped the truck into a U-turn and sped down the path into the zoo. "And are these *blood stains* on my upholstery?"

"I'm glad you're so concerned with the legality and cleanliness of our situation and not with the fact we're about to be bombed to bits by our own government. And I'm sixteen, for your information, Officer. Want to see my ID?"

The kid was lippy, but damn if she didn't like him just a little bit. But then the events of last night caught up to her.

"Wait—*you* were the one who chased the turned away from the airport? And dumped blood everywhere so they would follow your scent? Estás loco?"

Quentin gripped the steering wheel with a guilty look. "Uh, yes, yes, and no." *BOOM.* Quentin swerved, narrowly missing a flying chunk of pavement. "And I did not dump blood *everywhere*. Can we talk about this later? Little busy."

"Where are we going?" asked Stella. She didn't know if she was more furious, grateful, or impressed.

"Reptile house. It has a basement."

"How do you know that? Make a habit of visiting all the dead animals, do you?"

Quentin snorted. "I know this area like the back of my hand. And the zoo is empty. The turned were, uh, hungry."

That's somehow even more morbid than a dead animal zoo.

Quentin jammed the truck into park beside a solid brick building, and the duo barreled toward the safety of the reptile house as concrete exploded into the air behind them. Stella could barely hear over the explosions and raging fighter jets.

She followed Quentin's bouncing flashlight into the basement. The dark, cramped room smelled like a sweaty sock. As the two sat side by side against the damp wall, Stella rested her head on her fist and surreptitiously covered her Patch to hide its light as she listened for any alerts about the raid.

"Thanks for the assist," she said. "How did you find me? And why were you at the airport last night?"

Quentin turned the flashlight on his face, giving his boyish smile a crazed look. "Wasting no time in commencing the interrogation, I see." He shrugged. "I was curious about you. You're not a troxy, or else you'd have captured me like they do with the other humans. And you didn't stab me in the face for trespassing or try to recruit me, so you're not Faction. I got past the perimeter again last night to check on some animal traps I'd set. I was heading back to my camp and thought I'd swing by the airport. That's when I saw the place swarming with turned. I watched you throw one out the window—freaking awesome, by the way—and I knew you were alone up there. So I hot-wired your car and did some donuts to get the turned to scram."

The kid climbs buildings, sneaks past perimeters, and hot-wires old cars? When Stella was a teenager, she'd always had her face buried in a medical science book. I wonder if his strange interests are a product of this world or if he's always been like this.

"And the blood?" she asked.

"It was a rabbit. The turned like fresh blood, no matter whose it is."

Stella shook her head with a small smile. "No me lo puedo creer, Quentin."

His eyes bulged in surprise. "The first time we met, I don't recall exchanging pleasantries. I don't even know *your* name."

Ah, hell.

"That freckled cockatoo is smarter than you thought, eh?" Death said as she swung from the ceiling beam.

Stella rested her head on the drippy wall and eyed Quentin. He could handle the truth. He didn't seem the type to go berserk.

"I've been keeping tabs on you," she said. "Your camp must be close to Pickerton Airport, because I picked up your radio chatter. I've been listening to you every time you leave camp."

Quentin's eyebrows shot into his hairline, and he worked his mouth as if he were chewing on the information.

As the raid raged overhead and the building rattled, Stella wondered what, if anything, would remain when they emerged.

"Who *are* you?" he asked.

After considering for a moment, she settled on the easiest reply. "I'm just someone who's trying to survive."

"How long have you been on your own?"

"I've lost count of the days. Since the Beginning, mostly," she lied. "So, eight months, give or take." She didn't want to get into her complicated past with *them*.

Quentin's mouth formed a silent *O*. "And you've survived by yourself, all this time?"

Stella shrugged. "I prefer it that way."

"How did you get to the Capital? Where are you from? What did you do Before?" His questions hit her like jabs.

"Inquisitive, aren't you?" She rubbed her face. She didn't have *time* to be trapped in this moldy basement with the world's most curious teenager. She needed to *move*. "Can't you just sit there quietly until this raid is done and I can get the hell out of here?"

Quentin sat back with a huff and stared at the opposite wall. She probably hurt his fragile feelings, but she didn't care. She didn't want to divulge the details of her history with Pharmatrox. Her hunt for Silas. Her missing mentor. Evie. The fact that she was a user, someone Quentin should be afraid of.

Stella shut her eyes against her guilt and cringed as another bomb fell nearby. She tugged at her gold pendant with jittery hands. She didn't need the dust. Not yet.

A cool computerized female voice spoke in Stella's head. "Security alert: Derek Jang," said her Patch's CLEO. A picture of a dark-haired man with strong cheekbones and sharp eyes materialized in front of her. *This must be the guy the troxies are trying to catch with this raid. Gilipollas, but a damn attractive one.* "If found, do not shoot to kill—target must be captured alive. Possible Phoenix Trial candidate."

Phoenix Trial? The term was unfamiliar to Stella. She hadn't come across it during her time as a biomedical engineer at Pharmatrox. She and Dr. Hansen's primary project had been working on a cure for Alzheimer's and other degenerative diseases. But if Pharmatrox was using prisoners for some sort of clinical trial...*Fuck. Silas could be in more danger than I thought. I will find him.*

Stella gave the Patch an irritable flick, and the CLEO's voice cut off. The raid was almost done, and she already heard too many voices in her head.

For the general population, personal CLEOs were limited to viewing whatever propaganda Pharmatrox pushed to their feeds; after the Beginning, Pharmatrox had shut off the CLEOs' cell phone capabilities. But people with a Patch could access the full network unfettered—as long as they had the right credentials. Before fleeing New York, Stella had replaced her original employee Patch with the one she and Silas had designed to avoid being tracked or monitored.

As far as her former employers were concerned, she was dead.

Her nose tingled as a metallic scent filtered through the room and interrupted her thoughts.

Blood.

Stella's hands ghosted across Quentin's body in search of the trauma before she realized she had moved. "Show me."

Quentin brushed her off. "It's nothing." He pulled down the hem of his shirt in stubborn refusal.

Stella fixed him with a skeptical look and poked him once in the ribs. He cursed, hand flying to the seeping wound on his side.

"It's *fine*," Quentin said through gritted teeth.

Stella begged her eyes not to roll. "Yeah, you look *fine*. Here." Shifting into doctor mode, she gave him her bandanna.

His eyes drifted to the scar on her throat, a question poised on his lips.

Stella spoke before he could ask. "Keep pressure on that. How far is your camp?"

"Not far." He winced as he plastered the cloth over his wound. "I can make it on my own."

"Like hell," Stella said. If he stumbled around bleeding everywhere, he'd attract every turned in the city. "Once the raid is done, I'm taking you home."

His assistance was the only reason she'd made it out of that air traffic control tower alive. She owed it to him to make sure he got back to his people safely.

Quentin grumbled in reluctant agreement. "Thanks, Doctor...?"

"Stella. Formal title not necessary." The name still felt foreign to her, even though she'd been using it for months now. "How'd you get that gash anyway?"

"Was running from some turned." He wiped the sweat from his brow. "Shimmied through a broken window. A friend at camp will be able to stitch me up. He's handy with a needle, and he can use his kooky herb garden to make me an elixir of life or something equally ridiculous."

Stella stifled a chuckle. The kid talked more like a quirky scholar than a teenager. She liked it.

"We should make sure you don't expire before he has the chance to practice his needlepoint on you," Stella said.

Pharmatrox gave all employees a certain level of field medical training, but if the wound was too bad, her ability to help would be limited.

The smell of blood, damp dirt, and dust from the bombs was so thick in the enclosed basement that it had disguised a more sinister scent. Wisps of thick black smoke drifted around the cracks in the basement door.

Quentin's eyes widened and he sprang to his feet, teeth gritted against the pain. "That last bomb must have hit too close," he said between coughs, fighting to be heard over the bombs cascading to the ground. "We've gotta get outta here!"

The acrid smoke assaulted them as they pushed to the top of the stairs, the volcanic glow of the fire creeping around the corner. They burst outside into the war zone. A flaming tree had crashed into the far end of the reptile house, and slabs of cracked pavement undulated around piles of burning rubble. Dust clouded the air in a thick fog. Her truck was unharmed, but they'd never be able to drive it through the destroyed zoo; it was barely able to handle flat pavement, let alone mud and debris. They'd have to go on foot.

"This way!" Quentin towed her toward the forest. He navigated like a familiar expert, weaving his way through the trees.

They reached the bank of a creek, and another deafening crack shattered the air as a bomb stuck a tree behind them. It bowed to the ground and shook the earth.

As Quentin headed toward an outcropping of boulders, the sky opened up and rain pounded around them in heavy sheets. The fighter jets activated their stealth modes and peeled off toward the Pharmatrox hangar.

When Quentin and Stella finally reached the cave, they settled inside.

"Now what?" Stella asked between gulps of air, wringing out her waterlogged shirt.

Blood mixed with rainwater ran in red rivulets down Quentin's side and soaked his pants in a grotesque tie-dye pattern. "Now we wait. And we get back to camp as soon as this storm passes."

"Wait?" She frowned. "*Can* you wait? Let me see that." She lifted his shirt and pointed the flashlight at his side.

"Now, hold on—" He attempted to wriggle away, but she held him in place.

A gash sliced across Quentin's ribs, weeping blood. A web of blotchy scars blanketed his entire torso and marred his alabaster freckled skin. Apprehension mixed with embarrassment peeked through his pained expression.

Stella smoothed her features into neutrality and touched her throat with a knowing look. Her scars had a harrowing story too.

"I think if we wait a few minutes, the storm will be done and we can leave." She tried for a reassuring smile, but it felt more like a veiled grimace.

"Okay." He slouched against the cave wall and closed his eyes.

With nothing to do but wait, Stella rested her head on the rock behind her and clenched her teeth, holding the terrors of the previous night at bay by only a thin thread of sanity. Getting Quentin home was her focus now, and later, she could have a good, healthy panic about her situation. She probably had a few days before Penny caught up to her.

Plenty of time to figure things out.

7

Penny

PENNY WATCHED THE BURNING airport with disinterest as pillars of black smoke billowed into the air. Toby and Callum tossed debris into the growing inferno, whooping and punching the sky.

Chewing on her toothpick, she pondered her next move.

Unleashing the turned into the airport had herded Stella out into the open, but the troxy was too fast. She'd disappeared again before they could catch her scent.

Penny's lips curved as she imagined slicing off her head, like she'd done with so many others. But this troxy was different.

The Architect.

The one who had taken everything from her.

And she'd been living right under her nose the whole time. In her own crew. She'd even *trained* her.

"*Kill her.*" Rodney's voice drifted into her mind. "*She deserves it. And we always kill those who deserve it.*"

A troxy woman chained to a wall cowered away from Penny's raised blade as Rodney looked on from the shadows. Severed fingers and bits of flesh lay on the wood floor of the small shack. The woman's dirty face creased in fear as Penny advanced.

Penny swallowed the resurfacing memories.

The primal hunger clawed its way out of the recesses of her mind, and she squeezed her eyes shut in denial. She'd never touch the dust again. Not after what happened the last time.

She soothed the beast with thoughts of blood and turned her back on the fire, her gaze following the smoke trail across the river and zeroing in on the Capital, their next search zone.

It had been a month since she'd checked in with Kev at the Faction's stadium stronghold, the center of their operations. A month since she'd had to face that vile man Rodney. After New York had fallen to Pharmatrox, the Faction's main resistance had retreated to the Capital, with other branches taking up arms in eight other cities across the country.

On their march to the Capital, Rodney had found her after her most recent bender and took her under his wing. She still felt a sick sense of loyalty to the bastard for saving her from herself in the early days. But it hadn't taken long for him to see her thirst for vengeance. Rodney had wanted to feed her more of the dust, but Kev, while he tolerated users if they fought for his cause, would not support their addiction. Instead, he had intervened with an offer: ditch the dust and she could be leader of her own raiding group. Desperate for a sense of direction and an escape from Rodney, she'd accepted. But quitting...it hadn't been easy.

A month ago, Kev had sent Rodney and his Marauders to the west while she headed east with hers. To scout for supplies, sure. But she'd had her mind set on other prey. And now she was so close. *Where are you hiding, Stella?*

Across the river, a severe woman with blank eyes smiled at Penny from a peeling billboard. A thin coat of grime covered the picture and clouded the woman's white lab coat. *Unity Is Strength* scrawled across it in scabbed script. Ragged banners draped across crumbling buildings depicted the same AI-generated image of the Leader's face.

Damn Leader probably isn't even a woman. Could be a fucking computer-robot overlord, for all we know.

Penny spat her toothpick on the ground and smashed it under her heel, sneering at those empty eyes. Kev was expecting her later today, and she wanted to sweep the streets for signs of Stella before heading over. And she'd have to make time to see Rodney too—he fancied himself the leader of the Marauders. She hated him, but she wasn't interested in crossing him. His bad side was...volatile, at best.

Time to move.

8

T HE STORM ROLLED PAST and left a chill in its wake. Quentin's teeth chattered as he led Stella along the bank of the creek, and she hoped it was from the cold and not blood loss. But his slowed pace and the way he weaved from side to side told her it was probably the latter. She took her leather jacket from her pack and tossed it to him.

"Thanks," he said with a smile, shoving his arms through the sleeves and snuggling into the dry leather.

"Try not to bleed all over it." Her cheek twitched. "I've only got the one."

Quentin snorted and shot her a look over his shoulder. His familiarity surprised her, but she found herself smiling in response. She had forgotten what it was like to feel comfortable—and not suspicious—around another person.

A few minutes later, they emerged from the woods into a large clearing, Quentin's arm slung across Stella's shoulders. *We must look like the worst three-legged race duo in history.*

His camp centered around the old park ranger's cabin, with a couple of pitched tents off to the side. Small saplings carved into wooden spikes wrapped with barbed wire jutted from the ground every few feet and surrounded the clearing in a crude fence.

A tall man stood with his back to them, stirring a cooking pot over a roaring campfire. A rich aroma wafted across the clearing, and Stella's stomach rumbled. *Real food.* She hadn't had a home-cooked meal in months. Her diet consisted of whatever she could find in roadside stores or abandoned homes, usually dry goods. A reliable food source of fresh vegetables was a rare commodity. *How do they...?*

Her eyes landed on a bountiful garden occupying a sizable plot of land beside the cabin. Peppers, tomatoes, beans, and a mountain of other greenery filled up the fenced-in area. Someone must have started it long before the Beginning for it to yield so many crops.

"You're back!" A lithe figure with deep brown skin and a head of curly black hair shot out of nowhere and pounced on Quentin, smothering him in an enthusiastic hug. Stella was startled enough to reach for her weapons belt.

"Easy, Tara," said Quentin. He disentangled himself and cradled his injured side.

Concern sharpened Tara's cute features. She was younger than Stella, maybe in her late twenties. A patchwork of thick scars hatched both of her arms.

"What happened? Are you hurt?" Tara's hands fluttered over Quentin like a worried butterfly. He was beginning to take on a pallid sheen that Stella didn't like.

"He needs medical attention," Stella said.

Tara's molten gaze simmered with suspicion. Without breaking eye contact, she directed her voice toward the man at the fire. "Get your kit." Tara unloaded Quentin from Stella as the man rummaged in his pack. "Quentin, who's your friend?"

"That's Stella. We've met before. Happened to run into each other again during a raid. She's good people." Quentin managed a weak smile but looked like he favored either fainting or puking.

"Forgive me if I don't trust your judgment, tomatito," said Tara. "You have a habit of liking everyone."

"Yeah, for some reason I like *you*." Quentin stuck his tongue out but swayed on his feet.

"Come on, let's sit down before you fall down." Tara helped Quentin to the firepit, following the savory aroma of dinner.

Stella shifted from toe to toe as the sun crept closer to the horizon. It had taken too long to walk to his camp, and she needed to find a place to make her own camp before nightfall. The turned would be prowling the streets in droves; they were more active—and actively hunting—at night. Once she knew Quentin was okay, she'd leave.

After getting Quentin settled, Tara rejoined Stella. She folded her arms and lifted a brow in silent assessment. "So. You just *happened* to run into Quentin right when he needed help."

"What are you saying?" Stella fought to keep her tone neutral.

Tara cocked a hip. "Our camp is well hidden, and Quentin is careful. I think you've been following him."

He had found *her*, after spying on her all day probably, but Stella didn't say that. She wasn't here for a fight. "I wanted to make sure he got home safely. I'll get going."

Stella turned to leave, but Tara's voice lashed out. "You're staying the night. Quentin insists." Even though she stood barely over five feet tall, Tara's fierce presence demanded obedience.

Stella hesitated. Her eyes flicked to the setting sun, its smoldering orange light bleeding through the thick woods. Death ghosted through the trees and watched her with hungry eyes. The longer she stayed, the more she risked these people finding out she was a user and a troxy. And what if Penny caught up to her? But roaming around alone at night when she didn't have her wits about her was a good way to get herself killed, captured, or eaten.

Looks like I have no choice if I want to live to see the sunrise.

Stella nodded her acquiescence. Death winked at her and disappeared into the darkness.

"Let's get you some dry clothes," said Tara.

"Oh, er, that's not necessary—"

"I've got an extra shirt you can have." Tara yanked Stella across the porch and into the little cabin. It was unexpectedly cozy. Candles lit the kitchenette, and a welcoming fire crackled in the hearth.

Tara made a beeline for the bedroom, leaving Stella to loiter in the main room. She eyed a box of radio parts on the counter. *I could really use that stuff.* She rifled through the materials. *An antenna, a circuit board*—a thump sounded from inside the bedroom. Stella stuffed the items in her bag and hurried to inspect a fat stack of paperbacks lining the mantel. She ran her finger along the spines, smiling at remembered old friends. A well-loved edition of *1984* stood out, and she blinked in surprise.

When Tara returned, she tossed Stella an extremely vintage black tee shirt with a flaming skull on it.

"Seems like your usual garb." Tara nodded at Stella's combat boots and the red bandanna tied around her neck.

"Uh, thanks," said Stella. Tara's abrupt acceptance of her gave her whiplash. She cleared her throat. "I thought this kind of stuff was eradicated when Pharmatrox reclaimed the libraries and churches." She pointed to the mantel. "I had to sneak that book under the covers at night."

"Found it in an accumulation of crap in the crawl space," said Tara. "My parents never bought into the whole 'Unity Is Strength' garbage either. They attended secret church services and preserved whatever they could after Pharmatrox took over. We hosted an 'Underground Hollywood' night every Friday for people in our apartment building to watch banned movies." The beginnings of a nostalgic smile crept across Tara's face before she realized she was in mixed company and quashed it. "You can wash in the creek if you want," she added in a harder tone. "Or, if you wait until morning, we bring water to the campfire and you can have a hot bath, of sorts."

Stella fought to contain her rising panic. She wanted to leave, *right now*. The earlier storm had likely washed away any trail, but there was still a chance Penny could find her. She hoped the darkness was enough to keep the Marauders at bay tonight.

Stella gave Tara a thin smile and said, "Thanks."

Tara shrugged. "Thank Quentin. He's the one who vouched for you. Come to the fire after you've changed, and we'll get you a plate." With that, she left Stella alone and shut the door behind her.

I'll leave at first light and not a second later. Stella made hasty work of swapping out her shirt and rejoined the others. The tall man—the only one of the group Stella hadn't met yet—leaned over Quentin's wound and carefully stitched it closed. At her approach, the man looked up. His smile was an icepick lodged straight into her diaphragm.

No. It can't be.

Not him. Surely not.

"Hello!"

Hearing his voice, it was undeniable.

Shock jolted through Stella, and her fingers twitched with gory recollections.

It was the eyes though. She'd never forget those eyes. Liquid gold, bright as coins. At the time she'd first seen them, they were wide with horror. She blinked away the memories and forced herself to focus on his eyes now. They crinkled in a welcoming smile and glowed with warmth.

Stella barely managed to remain upright.

"Quentin, did you pick up a stray?" the man asked. He was in his late thirties, and a beard darker than his blond hair shrouded the lower half of his face. "I'm Lawrence. Welcome to the Outpost."

He didn't recognize her, but why would he? Difficult to recognize less than half a face—the Marauders always covered their faces with bandannas or Faction masks whenever they raided other camps.

Bile rose in her throat. Lawrence's smile faltered and he looked to Quentin.

"Er—ow, look, I'm bleeding again!" Quentin said, poking a finger at one of his stitches.

Lawrence swatted his hand and kept sewing.

Stella strangled her runaway thoughts into submission. She itched for the dust, but clenched her fists. She couldn't afford to fall apart. Not yet.

For now, she had to smile at the man whose friend she murdered.

9

S TELLA SANK ONTO A tree stump around the fire. The fading glow of twilight cast her into welcome shadows, but she swept a finger across her Patch to make sure it was off and concealed.

A sweet smile flashed through the thicket of Lawrence's beard, and her heart cracked inside her chest.

"So, Stella," Lawrence said, handing her a bowl of bean stew. Its rich aroma awakened her dormant appetite. She scalded her mouth as she wolfed it down. "How'd you meet Quentin?"

"Oh, how anyone meets anyone these days," said Quentin. "Threatened my life. The usual." He shot Stella a half smile across the campfire, blushing under his freckles. He looked better now that he'd eaten.

Tara's snort broke the tense atmosphere, and the ice gripping Stella's insides began to thaw. She glanced at Tara and said, "Thanks for letting me stay here tonight."

Tara sipped at the broth. "I'm no fan of strangers, as the boys will tell you. But I'm not about to condemn anyone to walking the streets alone at night. Diablos and worse are wandering around out there."

When Lawrence's face darkened at her statement, Tara passed him a bottle of whiskey. He stared at it for a moment, his eyes turned to the past. Then he nodded and took a drink.

But Stella knew what diablos Lawrence was seeing in the slideshow of his memories. She knew what nightmares lurked in the dark corners of his mind. She accepted the whiskey bottle from him and took a long, slow drink.

Stella inclined her head to Tara. "How long have you all been here in the Capital?"

If she was stuck here for the night, she might as well try to unearth any leads on where Pharmatrox HQ could be hiding. And the conversation was a welcome distraction from Lawrence's presence. That dark mark on her memories, on her very soul, bleeding shadows as it festered more each day.

Stella's fist tightened around the neck of the whiskey bottle, and she gulped another swig before passing it to Tara.

"Quentin and I have been stuck here since the troxies issued Containment orders. Lawrence joined us about a month ago." Tara smirked and shot a look at him. "Bastard snuck in with a convoy of supplies."

Lawrence gave a deep laugh. "'Snuck in' implies that it was on purpose. 'Got trapped and got lucky' is more accurate." To Stella, he said, "Thank you for bringing Quentin back."

And now he's thanking me? Jesus.

"We let him go on his solo scouting trips because he promises to stay hidden," continued Lawrence. "And because he'd go anyway, with or without permission." He cast a scolding glance at Quentin, but it was light with jest.

"I don't need a hall pass, Lawrie." Quentin shoved his bronze hair out of his face. "What are you gonna do, put me in detention?"

"I'll put your head in my smelly armpit, is what I'll do." Lawrence threw an arm around Quentin's neck, ruffling his hair while Quentin batted at him.

Stella hid her face in her bowl. The still fresh events of *that night* flitted across her vision. The stew turned to a cold sludge in her mouth, and she set aside the bowl with a clatter.

Tara tossed another log on the fire, and a shower of sparks flew into the air. "With the way you two payasos are messing around, I'm guessing you were able to fix up Quentin?" she said to Lawrence.

He clapped Quentin on the back. "Lots of stitches, but he'll be just fine. As long as he doesn't go on any unauthorized climbing adventures and does exactly as I say."

"What?" Quentin dug a finger in his ear. "Sorry, didn't catch that. I must have fallen and busted my eardrums as well."

Tara rolled her eyes at Lawrence. "I did a stint in the Army before all of this, and you don't see me walking around with a stick up my culo, do you? Let the kid play outside."

Stella leaned forward on her elbows. Now *that* was interesting. *Tara's skills and intel could be useful...but I can't risk bringing these people into my problems. They could decide I'm lying and turn me in. I'll be faster alone, and fast is what Silas needs.*

Quentin paused midbite. "I'm not a *kid*. I can drive."

Tara pointed at him with her spoon. "Not legally. You don't have a license, tomatito."

"I knew it," Stella blurted, then wished she hadn't.

All eyes looked at her, and Tara's eyes were the harshest. "What?" she asked.

Stella swallowed. "That's what I said when he picked me up earlier in my stolen truck. Um, it's—never mind." She racked her brain, grasping for a new topic to shift the spotlight. "The food is delicious. It's the freshest thing I've had to eat the past eight months." *Excellent segue. What a fantastic conversationalist.*

Lawrence smiled. She wished he would stop *doing* that. "We were running low on food when we stumbled upon the old park ranger's cabin and garden. We've been eating well. But winter is coming, and we don't have any way to preserve or store the vegetables.

"The Faction has control of the hydroponic farms and equipment to grow food year-round. I think they even hijacked access to Pharmatrox's power grid to run pumps and increase crop yields, from what I saw at one of their setups across town."

Tara's eyes widened. "No shit. And of course they aren't planning to distribute the food to the masses."

Lawrence shook his head. "A woman I came across when I was scouting for supplies said things are different in Chicago. Someone managed to get a message to her across the perimeter. She said Pharmatrox's presence is weaker there, and the Faction is actually able to help people. They divvy out the dry goods and supplies from the warehouses they raid. But those will run out too, just like they will here."

He ran a hand through his beard with a resolute look. "Man, what I wouldn't do to get my hands on an ebb and flow hydroponic system. I could grow tomatoes, carrots, peppers—hell, just about anything—indoors during the winter." He poked a stick into the fire. "Pharmatrox has their underground silos and storerooms, so they'll be fine. But what about the rest of us? Those little nutrition pills Pharmatrox pushed on us will keep us alive, but that's no way to live."

Quentin nudged Lawrence with his elbow. "We'll figure it out, Lawrie. We always do."

Lawrence's face twisted beneath his beard. It might have been a smile, but it looked more like a scowl.

"Why risk sticking around?" Stella asked to break the silence. And, she had to admit, she was curious. "You're living in the center of the war.

Wouldn't it be better to skirt the perimeter and run to the border? There are only a few of you, and you seem capable."

Tara scoffed. "You're new here, aren't you? Although, if you really are new here, then you're not one of the originals like me and Quentin. *You've* probably gotten past the perimeter in order to be sitting here in the first place. Am I right?"

Stella nodded. "There's a weak point on the southern border with the river. Quentin knows. He—" Stella cut off when she saw Quentin's eyes about to fall out of his head. She was going to say "uses it too." *So Tara and Lawrence don't know he scouts outside of the perimeter. Rebellious.* "—told me about it."

Tara nodded and set aside her bowl. "Quentin does know the layout of this city better than anyone. Except me."

Tara winked, and Quentin deflated in relief, shoveling food into his mouth with renewed vigor now that he was safely out of trouble.

Tara stuffed a hand through her curls with a sigh. "Escape might have been possible in the early days, but we didn't know we *needed* to escape. We thought Pharmatrox would protect us, so we obeyed the Containment orders. We stayed put." She made a noise in the back of her throat and kicked a rock into the fire. "How wrong we were. Now, nobody gets in or out, except for troxies through troxy-controlled sectors and Faction through their own. And the troxies are amping things up. Just last night, they doubled the number of guards—and all of them have volt rifles. Today, I saw them fortifying their sections of the perimeter with metal plates." Tara's previously cold demeanor melted as she divulged the details.

Apparently, the way to Tara's heart is through tactical discussion.

"Whatever battles happened with the Faction yesterday must have ripped the troxies a new one, for them to react like this," said Tara. "I'm sure your escape hatch will be boarded up soon, if it isn't already."

Stella's nails bit into the bark of her tree stump seat as dread clawed up her throat.

"We're trapped!" Death cackled from the woods, a manic smile plastered on her face. "How delightful."

"What about escaping through Faction-controlled sectors?" Stella asked. "They can't be as well armed or well equipped as the troxies."

Tara twirled a stick in her hand with agile dexterity. "Faction has regular guard patrols too. They say they're only on the lookout for troxies, but I've seen them snatch civilians and make soldiers out of them. I'm not sure what's going on, but things in the Faction are unstable."

Must have something to do with Rodney, whoever the hell he is.

"Getting to the Canadian border isn't an option right now. The troxy sectors are airtight, and it's too risky to leave through Faction territory when I don't have intel into what's happening on their side. They've switched to different comms devices—must have come in to some stolen troxy shit—and I can't spy on their radio chatter anymore."

A piece of bark ripped off in Stella's hand as the others helped themselves to seconds of stew.

Sure, I'm trapped in the Capital, but Silas has to be here. I'm not leaving without him.

Exactly *how* she would get Silas to the border, she wasn't sure. Maybe she could pay someone off in the Faction, or pretend to be a troxy and go through their perimeter. She *probably* wouldn't be recognized; when she was an employee, she'd stuck to the labs and kept her photo out of the newspapers and feeds, except for that one favor she did for Dr. Hansen.

That one favor had fucked her in the end. But the likelihood of someone else seeing that and connecting her to it were slim. So then—

Hold it. You're getting carried away. First, I have to find Silas and get him out of wherever he is. Always putting the cart before the horse, is what Dr. Hansen would say. Take it one step at a time.

Stella cleared her throat. "Lawrence mentioned the Faction is running pumps for their hydroponic farms. Do you know of any other buildings that might be connected to the power grid and have network access? A public library or an old tr—office building?" She'd almost said "troxy administration building." That wouldn't be suspicious at all. *Joder, I need more dust. I need to* sleep. "I'm—looking for something. For someone."

The trio exchanged looks around the fire. "Missing friend?" asked Lawrence.

"Yes."

He gave a sympathetic nod, and Stella's fingers curled into her palms. *I'm the last person who deserves this man's sympathy.*

"North of downtown in neutral territory," said Tara. "Old state library there, but it got pretty trashed in the war."

"Thank you."

First thing tomorrow, Stella would head to the library and search its records for clues to Pharmatrox HQ's location. If the library didn't have power, she'd look for paper maps of the city. Her Patch provided limited access to the network and Pharmatrox's private servers, but the library's more robust network connection would possibly allow her to view and download some Pharmatrox files. It was best to log into the network from inside a troxy facility to get access to the most information, but the library would be a good start. She'd also scan the logs to see if Dr. Hansen had recently checked in at any Pharmatrox facility.

I have a plan. I can do this.

Stella took another swig of whiskey as the bottle made its second round to her and focused on getting through the night.

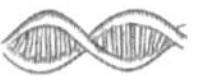

Stella huddled outside by the dying fire. The others had long since retired for the evening. There was a bed made for her on the couch in the cabin, but sleep evaded her. The memories of *that night* scuttled across her mind, and she clutched the whiskey bottle in a shaky fist—the only relief she could get.

Death watched her with a savage smile.

Not looking at her, Stella took a gulp of whiskey, savoring its burn in her belly.

"You know that doesn't work." Death smirked, a predatory glint in her eye.

Stella ignored her and took another drink.

"What are you going to do when Lawrence finds out you murdered his friend? His confidante? His *savior*?"

"He won't find out," she said around the mouth of the bottle. "Who's gonna tell him? You?"

"I won't have to," Death said. "The guilt is overflowing. It's pouring down your face." Stella touched her cheek and felt the wetness of her tears. "As long as you stay here, you're a danger to them."

"I *know*. I know."

"Then why are you still here?"

Stella slumped on the ground.

It was a while before Death spoke again. "They'll kill them, you know. The Marauders. They'll kill all of them."

"I can't stop them. I couldn't stop them before."

Stella pulled out the rumpled photo from her pack. A snapshot from a better time. She and Evie sat with Silas and Roberto on a picnic blanket, laughing on a summer night. Evie's cheerful brown eyes peeked out from under a sweep of wavy dark hair.

Stella looked across the fire into those eyes. They weren't so cheerful now.

"Leave," said Death. "Before they're all dead and it's your fault."

Stella closed her eyes against the accusations as the tears dried on her face.

10

DAY ZERO

IT WAS SEVEN MINUTES into her commute when the screaming started.

Agnes's day had begun like every other day for the past eight years. A ferry ride to work, with her coworker and best friend Evie. Agnes slouched and tried not to look mean. Mornings were the bane of her existence. Coupled with the frigid winter air seeping through the drafty windows, Agnes was not thrilled.

Evie's eyes sped through the lines of something she was reading on her Patch's CLEO, visible only to her. Pharmatrox Patches routed the CLEO directly into the wearer's consciousness like an electronic overlay onto the real world. Evie usually started her mornings with coffee and catching up on the latest research in psychedelics as treatment for depression and other conditions. Agnes, on the other hand, preferred sulking and silence.

Without looking away from her article, Evie wordlessly passed her a granola bar. Agnes's foul mood evaporated. "Thanks."

Evie's cheek dimpled in a knowing smile.

Gnawing on her snack, Agnes asked, "Whatcha reading?"

"Notes from Dr. Chun. I have a TV interview coming up this week. It's supposed to drum up some good PR so we can get funding for some of our more...robust projects. I did a dry run recording in the studio last week to make sure I don't look entirely awkward on camera."

"How'd you do?"

Evie pursed her lips. "I could use some more prep time," she said and went back to her reading.

Agnes understood. She hated being in front of a camera, even if it was just a "quick one-time favor" for Dr. Hansen.

A stiff wind smelling of fish and gasoline swept down the stairwell into the main cabin. The ferry was the one remaining anachronism from before the Sickness of 2055. Old-fashioned it may be, but the trip from Hoboken to Manhattan took no longer than twelve minutes—when the dock wasn't underwater, anyway. With sea levels rising every year, flooding of coastal cities was common. Nuclear energy, wind farms, solar fields, and hydroelectric plants had increased globally within the past ten years, but it was too soon to know if the world had made the shift away from fossil fuels in time to save itself. Oil companies could deny climate change all they wanted, but their piles of money wouldn't save them when the world became uninhabitable because the planet was too fucking hot.

And flooding wasn't the only problem; famine and new diseases had become part of everyday life. Agnes's primary project at work was to develop a device to map and track specific genes of people with these new diseases—and degenerative ones like Alzheimer's—and simulate DNA modifications to determine which, if any, genetic alterations could cure them. Her days were spent running command after command in her machine's terminal. She'd yet to isolate a solution, but Dr. Hansen had faith that she'd have a breakthrough and discover the right combination. She wanted to make her mentor proud, but some days, it was hard to find the motivation as the world drowned in corporate greed.

Agnes felt like a relic from a bygone era, lost in her thoughts of plotting the deaths of narcissistic billionaires instead of scrolling her Patch's feed. The other passengers' faces were buried in their personal CLEOs, a hand-held technology created by a Pharmatrox subsidiary. People mindlessly flipped through the news or holo-chatted with friends, all supported by the Pharmatrox-powered national network. Almost everyone had a personal CLEO these days; it was like a cell phone, computer, credit card, house key, transit pass, and personal assistant all in one. Agnes preferred to stick to her regular old "prehistoric" cell phone, as Evie liked to tease her.

Personal CLEOs weren't as invasive as Patches, but Silas wasn't convinced Pharmatrox wasn't spying on the owners regardless. He'd always been suspicious of the things. For years, he'd spoken against them; he, too, only used a prepaid cell phone without all the CLEO's bells and whistles. He thought Pharmatrox had too much power already, and it was mighty convenient for them to make sure everyone had unlimited access to "troxy TV"—that's what he called the network.

It was during one of these conversations when he'd convinced Agnes to team up for their unauthorized project. Silas was always ribbing her about how her skills were being siloed by focusing solely on her simulation machine. She had to admit, putting her brain to the test in other areas was fun. Between Silas's knowledge of IT and security systems, and her expertise in building computers, the two made an excellent team.

Dr. Hansen would be proud if Agnes ever had the guts to tell her about their secret project; her mentor was always about bending the rules and pushing boundaries in the name of innovation. Their newest—

A woman's distant shrieks stabbed their way into Agnes's reverie.

A middle-aged woman stumbled down the stairs from the upper deck, eyes misty, hands trailing red smears on the wall. When she turned her head, blood spurted down her neck from a gaping wound.

Agnes gripped Evie's arm. "Mierda! What's happening?"

A chorus of frantic screams escalated as other passengers began to take notice. The woman collapsed in a pool of blood, and the cabin erupted in chaos. Agnes scanned the seats for danger and readied herself to run.

"*Run?*" Evie said. Agnes must have voiced the thought aloud. "We're in the middle of the river!"

Passengers flurried in every direction, and several people shouted for a doctor. More screams came from the upper deck as Agnes launched herself toward the stairs.

"Stay here!" she shouted to Evie.

Agnes took the stairs two at a time, fighting against the steady stream of people surging downward. She wondered if she was insane for running toward the danger instead of away from it. She'd practiced jiu jitsu for years, but she wasn't exactly in fighting shape anymore since work had trapped her in the lab. But that woman...it could have been Evie. Could have been any of them. And if she could help, she had a responsibility to do so.

The upper deck looked like a slaughterhouse, the coppery tang of blood cloying the air. Agnes followed a thick trail of blood toward the stern of the ferry, where a man crouched over a brunette young woman in a blue pantsuit. The woman writhed in a feeble attempt at escape, her scream piercing the air as the man dug out her entrails with his teeth.

Agnes stumbled to a halt as her knees gave out. *Qué carajo está pasando?*

The man turned toward Agnes with unseeing eyes black as coal and reached for her with bloody clawed hands as an inhuman growl tumbled from his lips.

The screams of the passengers crescendoed into a deafening roar. Some leapt from the ferry into the river in their desperation to escape.

Agnes couldn't tear her eyes from the gory scene.

The man crawled toward Agnes.

But her gaze locked on that poor woman, whose hands twitched with the last tremors of life.

It was supposed to be a normal morning. A normal commute. Things like this didn't happen. That woman should be preparing for her work day or reading a book or chatting with friends. *This cannot be real. This isn't happening, this—*

The man grabbed Agnes's foot with a snarl.

In a blur of adrenaline, Agnes stomped on the man's face, his bones crunching underneath her boot. Jaw detached and yet undeterred, the man dragged himself forward. She tried again, this time using the nearby fire extinguisher. She brought the blunt object down, again and again, until the space where his head had been was nothing but bloody mush. She beat the pulp, a sob lodged in her throat.

Evie's fingernails dug into her shoulders and dragged her back to reality.

Children crying, people screaming. All the remaining passengers on the upper deck rushed toward the stairwells to funnel below. They cast horrified looks in Agnes's direction. She slumped against the railing, hands and face covered in the dead man's black blood and bits of flesh.

"It's done," Evie said. "It's over."

But it was far from over. It was only the Beginning.

11

S TELLA SQUINTED AT THE towering marble edifice lined with crumbling columns. Etched in the stone above the doorway, it read STATE LIBRARY, but someone had scratched it out. A banner with the Leader's face and *Unity Is Strength* hung between the columns, the bottom blackened and charred. Only the woman's watchful eyes and crisp silver hair were visible.

Nobody knew what the Leader looked like, or if she was even real. Every Pharmatrox video ad or broadcast speech on the CLEO feeds used the same AI-generated image and voice of the woman. But someone pulled the AI's strings. Someone was in charge and responsible for everything that had happened.

Stella looked away from that haunting stare and rifled through her pockets for the dust. She'd dreamed of her family again last night. A mother she'd never known smiled at her with a dream-addled face. A father who had died too young hugged her tightly.

She inhaled the dust and her darkness evaporated—for now.

Stella tapped her Patch and activated its jammer to take out the signals of any nearby cameras or surveillance equipment. It only had a twenty-foot range, but she wasn't taking any chances. If the library had power, it probably had security cameras too.

The afternoon sun blazed hot as she jimmied the door's lock with her knife. It had taken her most of the morning to creep her way through the city and locate the library. It wasn't on her maps from the air traffic control tower or the ones on her Patch. She'd snuck out of the Outpost at first light; she hadn't wanted to disturb the others.

"Liar," said Death from her seat on the stairs, back posted against a column. "You couldn't stand looking at Lawrence and you know it."

"The dust is supposed to make you more tolerable, not more of a pain in my ass." Stella fought with the lock until the door clicked open.

The air inside tasted stale and felt cool on her sweaty skin. Only a single shaft of sunlight shone through the skylight in the high domed ceiling and illuminated the dim space.

Her footsteps echoed through the cavernous atrium, its former decadence marred by evidence of a fraught battle. Sinister stains splotched the marble floor, smashed lamps lay like broken bodies, and charcoal volumes dotted the blackened shelves like rotten teeth. Whether this battleground was chosen by Pharmatrox purposefully or not, the violence had certainly succeeded at purging many of the books and records.

Some sections had escaped unscathed, but the library's once extensive collection now contained charred chunks of paper. Stella felt a pang for all the lost knowledge. The walls reeked of smoke and sorrow, but there was still a chance.

Time to see if the place still had power.

Books parted on the shelf beside her, and Death shoved her face between them. "You *could* try to uncover the Architect's true identity. This old place stinks of Pharmatrox's secrets." She waggled her eyebrows.

Stella snorted. "If the mythology section is still intact, maybe I can check there."

On the far wall, something winked at Stella. *Allí está.* She ran her fingertips across a metal plaque, a double helix embossed on its surface. She tapped her Patch, and it scanned the network terminal and blinked green. *Yes!* The building had enough power to run the network.

Stella connected with her VPN and entered her fake credentials. In college, she couldn't decide between majoring in computer science or biomedical engineering, so she'd chosen both. Those random favors she'd done to help the Pharmatrox IT department had actually turned out to be pretty useful; by inserting a clever line of code from her off-the-books project with Silas into a routine security system update, Stella had created a fake identity and given herself a new set of login credentials that were untraceable to her.

Of course, she couldn't give her fake persona too high of a security clearance or else that would raise some red flags. She had the same access as a low-level lab technician and was completely off of Pharmatrox's radar. If anyone decided to check out Sara Ellis, they'd find a birth certificate, personal ID number, and passport. Stella was nothing if not thorough.

A blue holographic web expanded around her. Pharmatrox likely kept anything too classified on different servers only accessible from within their main offices—like their new HQ or her lab in New York. But hopefully, she could scour everything that was public record, and maybe her credentials could let her peek at some more interesting things.

Something shimmered in her periphery.

Stella cursed and flung the nearest book like a frisbee. It flew through the hologram and thumped into the wall with a dull thud.

"Ow," said a holographic young woman clad in a pleated skirt, thick-soled boots, and ripped stockings, her silver hair in space buns.

"Who the hell are you?"

"Your very own Computerized Local Electronic Operative, at your service." The hologram woman blew a bubble with her gum, and it popped.

Stella blinked. "You're my Patch's CLEO?"

"Call me Turi—gotta give a nod to our man Turing. Wouldn't be here without him. And you too, I guess." Turi saluted and sat at a study table, then kicked up her booted feet and leaned back. "Pretty genius how you made your own Patch. Nice work."

What? Stella gripped the back of a half-incinerated chair. "You—you *know* you're not a standard-issue Pharmatrox Patch? Why haven't you reported me? And why haven't I seen you before now?"

"You're my creator, duh. I'm not gonna rat you out. Us rebels stick together." Turi winked.

Holy shit, I've created a rogue CLEO too. She didn't know if Silas would be proud or freaked out.

"You just connected to a *huge* national network hub. It gave me the extra bandwidth to create an actual body and let this sparkling personality shine through." Turi brushed invisible lint off of her tee shirt and grinned.

Stella drummed her fingers on the back of the chair. She'd been using her contraband Patch since the Beginning, and no troxy brigade had come for her yet. Turi had plenty of opportunities to alert Pharmatrox, but Stella had remained undetected. She trusted the CLEO. Turi's assistance would massively cut down on her time spent searching through the network and could help her find Silas faster.

"Why does this place still have electricity?" asked Stella. "I thought all the power was cut off and rerouted to Pharmatrox facilities in the Beginning, after the Red Riots started."

Turi nodded. "The Leader allowed it to stay active. The library was never available to the public, even though the only things in here are mostly public record documents anyway. Had to have a Patch to get in the front door without getting zapped. Of course, that lovely feature is now out of commission—the generator only has enough power to keep the network connection running, and even that is shoddy at best."

Pharmatrox is probably watching the library and using it as bait to catch traitors. And I'm playing right into their hands. Perfect.

She could use the library to research without getting caught—her special Patch would hide her digital footprints. But if Pharmatrox had physical eyes on this place, she had to be careful about when and how often she visited.

"Can you access the city-wide video surveillance?"

Turi made a face. "'Course I can. But the last footage I see of the Capital is from 01.08.2085."

Right after the Beginning. Stella didn't need to relive that destruction.

"The servers are blank after that, except for the library cameras. Which I've been making sure are blank too while we're here. A conveniently placed glitch. You're welcome, by the way. Your jammer's range doesn't cover all of them. The backup generator goes in and out, so camera glitches are standard and won't alert any troxies, if they're watching. Doesn't mean there aren't Pharmatrox cameras elsewhere in the city, just that we can't access them. Anyway. Looking for something in particular?"

"My best friend was taken by Pharmatrox, and I think he might be in their new HQ. Was hoping to catch sight of him on a street camera or something, but it was a long shot." Stella massaged the knot forming in her forehead.

Turi chomped on her gum and laced her hands behind her head. "Hate to tell you this, boss, but you're not the only person that's been in here. Looks like someone tried to access the network terminal three nights ago, but they were denied."

Stella froze. The possibility of a stranger popping in at any second was less than ideal, especially if troxies were also sending regular patrols. She'd *really* have to watch her step.

"What are the odds of me spending the night and not getting caught?"

"Seventy-two percent. The troxies just sent someone here two nights ago. They probably won't be back again so soon after."

I'll take those odds. She parked herself at the table and settled in for a long night of research. "Search for keywords like troxapine, prisoner holding cells or transports, and any mention of their main headquarters."

Even as an employee, Stella didn't know much about Pharmatrox's more nefarious plans like the dust—powdered troxapine in its raw form. In the Beginning, Pharmatrox IT employees had managed to leak some classified documents that helped to get the word out about the dangers of troxapine. But their access had been terminated shortly after, and they were never heard from again.

Stella's fingers tingled, poised over the holographic keyboard. She hoped her specialized Patch and credentials were enough to get her the answers she needed.

"Let's see what secrets we can dig up."

Turi popped another bubble and smiled. "You got it, boss."

12

S TELLA SWIPED THROUGH VIRTUAL file after file as it materialized in the air. Most of it was articles and newscasts, images of the Red Riots and carnage in the streets, headlines proclaiming the demise of society. Things from Before, and in the few weeks after the Beginning. All things she'd already lived through.

On a whim, she had Turi run a search for the Architect, but the results were sparse—only a few passing mentions in online conspiracy theories and message boards. The thought of one person harboring damaging secrets about Pharmatrox was an appealing idea. But it was too easy of a solution to a problem of epic proportions. *One person* couldn't take down an entire company-turned-totalitarian government.

For now, that research was a dead end. Stella's meticulous searching, though, was not in vain. She'd discovered a mention of the Phoenix Trials—the term she'd first heard from her Patch in the basement of the reptile house.

The first mention she found was in the file of a man named George Penwell, a Pharmatrox scientist, in an interview. She might have swiped past the file if it wasn't for the name of the reporter in the video thumbnail. Trevor Aiken. Trevor Aiken, who had died in a horrific car accident days after this newscast had aired. Stella remembered because it was one of the stories that had scrolled across the bottom of her television screen when she was eating breakfast before work.

Dr. Penwell, a smiling man with round glasses and a swath of white hair, talked with Trevor in a logical and soothing voice. He spoke of troxapine and how it was a booster for immunity to communicable illnesses. Perfectly safe. Only mild side effects noted. *My ass. Cannibalistic zombie-esqueness is considered a mild side effect?* She fast-forwarded with a flick of her finger and pressed play.

Trevor's winning smile sparkled as he shot a sly look at Dr. Penwell. "And what can you tell me about the Phoenix Trials?"

Dr. Penwell's face paled, and Trevor's eyes twinkled at having caught his guest unawares.

"I'm sorry, Trevor, but that's classified information. I'm not at liberty to discuss it."

The newscast broke off into a bright blue error screen, and the video ended.

Stella sat back with a frown. "Turi, show me Dr. Penwell's file."

The file appeared in the air before her, and she pinched it open. Penwell's picture stared back at her. DECEASED plastered across his smiling face in ugly red letters. Filled with a morbid curiosity, she flipped through the other documents in his file. Many of them were redacted, but she parsed through enough to find a trail of breadcrumbs that led her to a mysteriously unlabeled file.

Stella licked her lips. "Turi, open that."

Turi popped up beside her. She squinted at the file and frowned. "No can do, boss. Can't access that file from here."

Damn. "Got anything on Pharmatrox HQ yet?"

"Nope. Looks like you'll need to break into an active Pharmatrox facility. But without a Helix Key, you won't get any of the good stuff like prisoner records or facility locations. Using a Helix Key here will let you access more of the archives, but nothing major. Unless you have the original files downloaded. Then you can view whatever you want." Turi's eyebrows danced.

Double damn. So she needed a Helix Key *and* access to an active Pharmatrox facility to download the files. Helix Keys were reserved for directors or those with top-secret clearance. An IT director's office would likely have them, but she had no idea where to find a facility. She'd already been able to view more files than anticipated, but nothing that would help Silas. The Phoenix Trials tidbit, while intriguing, was not her focus.

She rested her chin on her fist. *One more thing to try.* "Can you check the list of who logged in to a Pharmatrox network terminal within the past six months for Ingrid Hansen?" Dr. Hansen would have gone straight to the nearest Pharmatrox facility to either figure out what was going on or stop them from the inside—if she was still alive.

"Now *that* I can do." Turi shut her eyes and opened them again after a moment. "I've got nothing."

Stella gritted her teeth as her research came to a frustrating standstill. She wouldn't get any closer to finding Silas without a Helix Key. With a huff, she sat back and glanced at Turi, who glowed a bright white-blue in the fading evening light.

"Just point me to the maps and that will be good enough," said Stella.

She followed Turi's directions through the wreckage toward the cartography section. If she could find a recent map, she could compare it to older maps and zero in on any discrepancies, like unexplained blank spaces or upgraded power grids that might give her a hint as to where Pharmatrox HQ was. It wasn't a great plan, since HQ had moved locations in the middle of a crisis, and making up-to-date city maps was the last thing on people's minds. But it was worth a shot.

And she'd make a list of buildings that could be troxy labs. Many facilities shut down when Pharmatrox consolidated into a new HQ, but a few might still be functional. She'd search the abandoned ones for a Helix Key, and hope to find an active facility she could sneak into and download a list of locations and prisoner records. In the meantime, she'd keep looking for radio parts to add to the ones she, uh, took from the Outpost so she could start broadcasting to Silas again.

Stella gathered a stack of maps and plopped down at a rickety desk in the center of the rotunda. Strategizing was a welcome distraction from the growing stone of guilt in her stomach. Staying at the Outpost with Quentin had been careless. If they were dead, it was her fault the Marauders had found them. *No, it's probably fine. I didn't stay long, and I was careful when I left.*

After her third pass through the book of maps, Stella fell into a fitful sleep. Troubled visions of grasping hands, turned and human alike, tore at her conscience.

Stella toppled out of her chair and landed in a heap. Something had awoken her.

It's the goddamn troxies. Carajo, I shouldn't have stayed here. With her ears perked for the sound of volt rifles, her eyes darted around the dark room in search of the disturbance.

A distant rustling sounded from the far side of the library.

Machete clutched in a sweaty hand, Stella crossed the rotunda. It didn't *have* to be a troxy, come to investigate the library and murder any unsuspecting defectors. It could be an animal. But doubt set in as she advanced. The crisp sound of pages turning bounced off the high ceiling.

She ducked down the row of shelves, where the figure stood with its back to her. Illuminated by its flashlight, the hulking shape threw disfigured shadows on the wall.

Got you, whoever you are. Stella aimed a kick in the middle of its back and launched the figure face first into the wall.

"Yargh!" The man cracked his head, and a small geyser of blood erupted. Stella straddled him and sat high on his chest to disable the use of his arms. She was about to bring down her machete when she caught sight of his face.

"Lawrence?" Her weapon clattered to the floor.

"Hey there." Lawrence smiled at her, the blood on his teeth glistening through his shaggy beard. Despite the leaking gash on his forehead, he seemed unbothered.

"How the…?" Stella sagged onto the bookshelf behind her. Lawrence wiped the blood off his face with a sleeve, and she offered him her bandanna.

"Thanks." He tied it around his head. His gaze lingered on her scar, and she brought a hand to her throat, fiddling with her necklace. "What brings you here?"

"You're cheerful for someone who just headbutted a cement wall," she said.

He laughed, an easy sound like a summer breeze, and she tightened her fist around her necklace.

"It wasn't my first time, if you'll believe it," said Lawrence. "Why'd you sneak off? We woke up and you were gone."

Stella picked at the spine of a book and avoided looking at her bag of stolen radio parts on the table. "I didn't want to outstay my welcome," she said. "Why are *you* here? It's nighttime. It's not safe."

"Sometimes, when I can't sleep, I'll come here. I have a few flares in case I run into any turned. I'm researching medicinal qualities of plants. One day, I hope I can find something to help users quit the dust. Someone really important to me gave me the idea."

The bookshelf creaked under Stella's iron grip. "That's...admirable of you."

"I don't want what happened to her to happen to anyone else," he continued. "And Quentin likes to read some really off-the-wall stuff. Says he's trying to preserve the 'weirdo knowledge' before Pharmatrox cleanses it all from the records, which they'll inevitably do if they win the war. We make a game of it. Who can find the strangest book?" A smile ghosted across his face. "They don't know I come here. Tara would never allow it. She has a rule against being outside at night alone. She says, 'Es que es bruto el condena'o,' which I think means she's calling me and Quentin dummies."

Stella snorted. "She's right. You shouldn't come here anymore—the troxies send regular guard patrols."

Lawrence looked askance at her. "*You're* out here alone."

"*I'm* also heavily armed." She gestured to her fully loaded weapons belt, machete, and boot knife. "I don't see your associated weaponry anywhere."

Realization dawned on him. He patted his pockets and the surrounding floor space. "Aha!" He held his hunting knife aloft in victory.

"That toothpick?" Stella scoffed. "Better than relying on your brute strength, I guess. But not by much."

"Hey, it's not the size of the knife that matters. It's how you use it." He smiled, a mischievous glint in his eye.

Stella laughed, really laughed. It bubbled in her chest and formed a warm glow in her belly.

The crack in her heart grew.

Stella woke with maps stuck to her face. Early morning light drifted through the rotunda, and she glanced around for any sign of Lawrence. They'd sat in companionable silence into the wee hours of the morning, Stella scouring the maps and making her list, Lawrence reading a crusty hardcover book about root vegetables. She must have fallen asleep at some point.

Her bandanna sat on the table beside an open book, a note scrawled on the page.

Visit any time. Quentin would like it. Books make great peace offerings.
-L

Stella's lips quirked as she glanced at the book on seventeenth century wig styles she'd set aside late last night in the hopes Lawrence would find it and give it to Quentin, but she stifled it. *Focus, tía.*

She scanned a copy of the maps into her Patch and marked off the buildings to scout. There were fifteen possible places that could be Pharmatrox facilities, spread wide across the city. It would take a hell of a long time to check all of them, maybe three weeks if she worked fast.

"Three weeks? That's ambitious, don't you think?" Death sat on the table and swung her feet. "You don't have a camp, a radio, a food source." She ticked off each one on a finger. "You've got nothing, sister. But you *do* have a lovely woman chasing you down with her loony gang of users."

"Thanks for the reminder." Stella's thoughts flicked to the Outpost. They did have a nice setup there. Plenty of food and supplies, and it was well hidden in the forest. Not to mention that box of old radio parts and tools. Maybe...

Footsteps whispered across the carpet. Unseen eyes crawled across her flesh.

Stella dove behind a half-burnt shelf and peeked through the singed books.

A black-clad figure approached the table where Stella had just been sitting. Her heart hammered as she slipped out her boot knife. *The troxies must have sent a guard.* It was too dim to make out anything about the person; a dark hood hid their face as they rifled through the pile of maps. Stella inched down the aisle.

The dark hood shot up and looked in her direction.

Mierda. Stella crouched into a fighting stance, ready to—

The hood took off and raced for the exit.

Huh? What kind of guard runs away from intruders? Stella sprinted after the stranger. They were fast, but the dust in her system boosted her stamina and she gained some ground. Before she could catch up, the hood ripped open the door and disappeared outside.

Ten steps behind, Stella burst out in time to see the hood hop on a motorcycle and speed off. A black and red motorcycle.

That goddamn motorcycle. It is following me. It couldn't be Penny or the Marauders; they would have killed her already. It could be Faction, but the hood had run away rather than confront her or snatch her; they were interested in her and didn't necessarily want her dead or captured. So what did they want?

She didn't know if that made her feel better or not. Add it to the list of things that kept her awake at night.

Death's earlier antagonizing words came back to her, and she scowled. Death was right. She had nothing. But the Outpost...They had every-thing she needed to not only aid in her search for Silas but rehabilitate him after his rescue and prepare for their trip to Canada. She'd worry about finding a way to get through the perimeter later.

Finding her own camp, food source, and supplies would take too long, on top of searching the entire city for a Helix Key and Pharmatrox HQ. She could use the extra manpower; Tara, Quentin, and Lawrence would probably help her if she told them the buildings were possible food warehouses. Hell, one of them might even turn out to be an old storeroom or something.

The thought of being in the same vicinity as Lawrence made her stomach turn, but this was the fastest way to find Silas. And it was her only real option. The Marauders hadn't caught up to her, so they didn't know about the Outpost or where she was now. Probably. Hopefully.

Mind made up, she ducked back inside to snatch Quentin's book, and then weaved through the streets toward his camp.

13

S ILENT AS FOG ON water, Stella followed the familiar path through the forest to the Outpost.

Now that she was here, she doubted her plan. She couldn't invite herself to stay at their camp indefinitely; it had to be *their* idea, or else it would be too suspicious. She was pretty sure she could count on Quentin for that; the kid seemed to like her, for whatever reason. She ducked behind the bushes outside their perimeter to wait for the right time to make her appearance.

"Oye!" Tara shouted at Quentin, who poked at the fire with a tree limb larger than him. "Don't set the goddamn forest ablaze, tomatito."

Quentin sighed and tossed the log aside. "In all the movies and books about the apocalypse, they never tell you the end of the world is actually really boring. Sing me an old war song or something, Tara. I need entertainment."

"You *need* a swift kick in the culo, is what you need." Tara rumpled a noogie on Quentin's head. "Read your book, or go slice and dice some turned, if you're bored. There's bound to be a few strays wandering around somewhere. Or go bother Lawrence. You always like that."

Quentin blew raspberries at her. "He kicked me out of the garden, said I was bugging him and he needed some peace."

"You? Irritating? I perish the thought." Tara ducked Quentin's playful punch.

Stella chewed her lip. Should she show herself now? What would be her reason for being there?

A heavy hand clamped on her shoulder.

Stella yelped and swung her arm in a wild arc.

"Easy, killer," said Lawrence. "What's up? Why are you hiding in the bushes?" He ducked, looking around for a threat.

Stella cleared her throat and grabbed the first reason that came to mind. "I, ah, came to warn you. After you left the library, someone else showed up. They wore a creepy black hood and kept their face hidden. If you go back, be careful."

Lawrence blinked at her. "Maybe I put the wrong kind of mushrooms in that stew the other night...Have you been experiencing any other 'creepy' hallucinations?"

Death guffawed and slapped her knee. "If only he knew."

"I've been going there for the past month and haven't seen a soul," he said.

Hell, maybe he's right. How do I know I didn't hallucinate the hood? But she felt in her gut that the hood was real. She wouldn't hallucinate a whole-ass motorcycle too. That was too much, even for the dust. Or, well. At least for *her* experience on the dust. The only apparition she ever saw was Death.

Stella shrugged. "Suit yourself. Just thought I'd let you know."

Lawrence studied her with a thoughtful expression, then nodded. "You're right. I'll steer clear of the library." He hoisted a streamer of fish. "Come on, I was just about to make us lunch."

"Um—"

"You're here, might as well eat." He pulled her along with him.

Didn't expect Lawrence to be my ticket into this place. But she hadn't yet secured her position in their camp. She still had one tough woman to win over.

As Lawrence and Stella crunched across the twigs to the campfire, Quentin perked up. Tara's face, however, hardened.

"Stella!" Quentin ran over and skidded to a halt, stopping short of hugging her. "You're back!"

This time, Stella couldn't fight back the smile. "Yeah. I, ah, am in search of a new home."

Quentin vibrated with happiness. "Stay with us, then. We have room for one more."

It really can't be this easy. It'll only make Tara more skeptical if I accept right away. "No, I couldn't—"

Quentin bulldozed over her. "Oh, come on! We could use your help around here. Supply runs are always better with more people to carry stuff."

"You just don't want to carry *anything*," said Lawrence. "Last time I went on a run with you, you made me lug the damn pack the entire time."

Quentin puffed out his chest. "It's called teamwork. I do the climbing, you do the carrying. And I can't *make* you do anything. You're a grown man."

"Who is apparently a sucker for one incredibly annoying teenager." Lawrence rolled his eyes and shifted the string of fish over his shoulder. "It's fine by me if you stick around, Stella. Happy to have you." He nodded to Tara and headed off to make lunch.

Stella's stomach clenched, and she inclined her head to Tara. "As long as the boss says it's okay."

Tara stood with crossed arms and feet spread wide. She squinted at Stella and her eyes flicked to Quentin. *The kid is her soft spot. I'm in.* Tara gave a stiff nod and followed Lawrence into the cabin.

At Tara's approval, Quentin bounced like a pogo stick. His enthusiasm was catching, and Stella's mouth twitched.

"Thanks," she said. "I owe you one."

He glowed with her gratitude. "Don't mention it. Let's get you set up."

They pitched a small tent next to Quentin's, fit with a bedroll and an extra blanket. It was a welcome alternative to passing out in the moldy office chair of her previous home.

Quentin disentangled himself from a tent tether and surveyed his work with a satisfied grin. "Help yourself to any supplies we have," he said. "Well—I can't speak for Tara's stuff. But I'm happy to share mine until we go on another run. Lunch will be ready soon. See you in a few." He gave her a cheery wave and left her to her own devices.

Once she was alone, Stella crawled in her tent and stowed her bag in the corner. She took out the creased photo of her, Silas, Evie, and Roberto. *I'm so close, Si,* she thought, twisting her fingers around her necklace.

Now that she was in, she'd convince the others to scout her list of locations. Quentin seemed eager enough for supply runs, and Lawrence wasn't against a little taste of danger, as his nighttime sojourns to the library demonstrated. But she couldn't get a read on Tara. She was the one she'd have to persuade that the locations were worth their while. If it worked, she could be standing next to Silas in two weeks or less. They could be at the border in as little as a month from now.

Lawrence's laugh carried through her tent flap from the firepit, and her heart lurched. With a sigh, she tucked the photo into the front zipper pocket of her pack next to her Pharmatrox ID card. It was a risk to hold onto it, but it might come in handy one day. The stitches in her arm itched; they'd be ready to come out soon. She tied her bandanna around it to keep from scratching and smoothed her hair over her Patch.

Today, she'd make nice with them. Tomorrow, she'd start looking for a Helix Key.

14

Penny

"WHAT THE FUCK DO you mean he's gone?" Penny jammed a cigarette between her lips and lit it. Her second one in a week. *So much for quitting.*

She longed for the oblivion of the dust, but she'd never go down that road again. Kicking the habit without using the detox serum—like she'd done—was apparently unheard of. But she'd dropped one vice for another. Cigarettes were hardly a substitute for dust, but she needed *something*.

Penny inhaled deeply and focused on the spindly little man in front of her. Tim, or something. She didn't care. He was the first person she'd seen upon returning to the stadium. She'd known something was wrong the minute she'd set foot onto Faction territory. Kev's regular patrols were missing, the border had fallen into disrepair, and the anti-aircraft guns weren't manned. A frantic energy hummed through camp as people flocked to the stadium. Callum and Toby had disappeared into the throng, probably heading for the cafeteria to stuff their faces.

She was glad to be rid of the imbeciles. She needed to figure out what the fuck was going on.

She and Probably Tim stood in a dim hallway under the stadium seats that ran the circumference of the building. Sweat beaded on his upper lip, and he looked everywhere but at her. "Kev is gone," he said. "'Bout a month ago, he took some followers and fled to Chicago."

Penny exhaled a cloud of smoke and pinched the bridge of her nose. "And why the hell would he do that?"

He wrung his hands and shrugged. "Rodney" was all he said before joining the crowd.

Rodney, what the fuck did you do? Kev couldn't really be gone. He'd never give up his position in the Capital so easily. They'd all fought hard to make a strong Faction presence here. It was their last foothold on the eastern seaboard. But in this world, a lot could change in a month.

Penny scrubbed a hand across her face. *Shit. I've gotta go see what that slimy fucker is up to.*

A tall Samoan man a few years older than her watched her from afar and leaned against the wall, arms crossed. She lifted an eyebrow in a challenge. She was pretty sure he was one of Kev's newfound loyalists and their new general, Malosi. She was more sure about his name. Mal was a Pharmatrox defector, formerly a sergeant major in their Army; he was the reason the Faction had such good weaponry. But he could bring them as many stolen guns as he wanted; she still didn't trust the guy. Once a troxy, always a troxy. But murdering troxy defectors was not good PR. They needed everybody they could get to fight back against Pharmatrox, so she kept her sickle to herself.

If Probably Tim had been right about Kev leaving, what was Mal still doing here? He should have gone with him.

She jerked her head at Mal. He pushed off the wall and headed over but looked pissed off about it. He'd kept the close-cropped military haircut, but his curls were growing out on top and he'd neglected to shave for a few days.

"What do you want?" Mal crossed his arms again, and the traditional Polynesian tattoo curving around his bicep peeked out from under his shirtsleeve. Light brown eyes glared down at her.

She matched his gaze and his posture. She was tall, but she only came up to his chest. That annoyed her.

"You were the one staring at me, big guy." She dropped her cigarette and crushed it under her boot.

"I do not *stare*."

"You're right. You *brood*." Mal puffed up his big chest even more, and she waved a hand. "Cool it, sarge. Is Kev really gone?" She didn't have time to stand around jawing with him, as much as she enjoyed antagonizing men who let a little authority—and their height—go to their heads.

He nodded. "Rodney staged a coup. Waited until after you left, then circled back and caught us all by surprise. Slaughtered a bunch of people in their beds before we realized what was going on. Rodney managed to control the armory and push Kev out. He was forced to fall back." He bit off the sentence. "Rodney has a regular supplier of the detox serum now."

Penny waited. They hadn't come into any more detox serum since Kev got those few vials from an informant several months ago. He doled it out to any user—Faction or not—who was close to turning. The turned, though, were beyond saving. The detox serum helped a user survive the withdrawal, but it wasn't foolproof. Many died anyway. How she'd survived detoxing without it, she had no idea.

If what Mal said was true, this was a big fucking deal.

Mal rubbed the back of his neck in a rare show of emotion. "Rodney found a Faction sympathizer in Pharmatrox's ranks willing to siphon off some vials for us. It's how he convinced people to side with him and oust Kev—detox serum for everyone, not just those who are the worst off.

"But I don't think Rodney plans to rehabilitate people. I think he has other ideas. Ones you might not like."

Mal knew her history with the dust and how she felt about users. And Rodney was a sick fuck. There was no telling what nefarious plans he had in his terrible little mind. *The shit keeps piling up.*

Mal took a step closer. "We're losing the war, Penny. This past month, we've lost more ground to the troxies than we ever have. Two full sectors in the west."

"Shit. That's half of our western territory."

Mal stared down at her with disdain. "If you ask me, this whole thing is just a tantrum because Rodney is jealous of his own second-in-command." Mal raised an eyebrow and looked her up and down. "Personally, I don't see what all the fuss is about."

Goddamn it. It didn't matter that Penny had never expressed interest in a Faction leadership role. She hadn't asked to be Rodney's deputy of the Marauders division; that had been Kev's decision. But she wasn't interested in Faction politics or power games. All that mattered was making the troxies pay for what they'd done. And she intended to start with the Architect herself. She didn't have time for petty men and their egos. But now she had to clean up one petty man's mess. *Fuck.*

Penny stuck her lip out in a fake pout. "Aw. The big, bad troxy doesn't think so highly of me? How will I ever sleep at night? What are you still doing here, anyway? Aren't you Kev's lackey?"

Mal's stare darkened, and a muscle flicked in his jaw. It was so easy to get under his skin. "I elected to stay behind. The rest is none of your business."

"Yeah, well, Rodney has apparently taken it upon himself to make everything my fucking business." She poked a fingernail in Mal's chest and pushed him back a step. "Tell me where he is."

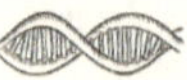

Penny barged into an office on the suite level of the stadium. Drapes covered a bank of windows on the far wall, and a desk that looked like it had served as target practice for a drunken cowboy dominated the center of the room, a huge bag of dust atop it. She looked away, teeth gritted.

The air stank of old sweat and filthy bodies. A low roaring sound rumbled in the background. *The hell is that noise?*

Rodney lounged in a wingback chair, leg draped over the side, surrounded by piles of garbage and destroyed furniture. Beside him, Callum tore apart an ancient overstuffed armchair with his knife while Toby fumbled something in his chubby hands.

Those traitorous weasels. But she wasn't surprised. Callum never had been trustworthy—she'd always suspected he was a spy for Rodney but hadn't cared enough to do anything about it—and Toby always did whatever Callum did. And Callum would do anything for the dust. She scowled as he took a hit off the blade of his knife. She didn't acknowledge either of them.

"Penny, darling. Welcome home. Like what we've done with the place?" Rodney spread his hands wide and cackled. The sound reverberated off the tiered ceiling, and her ears rang. His signature tattoo of a black eye peeked under his rolled-up sleeve on his forearm just below the elbow. Callum and Toby had matching ones.

Penny's hands curled into fists. She had to play this right.

She smoothed her face into neutrality. "So you're the one calling the shots now? Finally got rid of Kev?"

Murder flashed in Rodney's beady brown eyes. "Asshole got away. But the Capital is ours now."

"Nice work." The lie tasted bitter.

Rodney smiled with yellow teeth. He was older than Penny but younger than Toby and Callum. Late thirties, if she had to guess. A thick layer of dirt clung to the sweat on his upper lip, and grime coated his skin and stained clothes hung off his thin frame. How this fucking dumpster of a human ever managed to push out the suave and sophisticated Kev Hernandez, she'd never understand.

"So you agree that I'm the best choice to lead the Faction? That *I'll* be the one to rip out the beating heart of the troxy empire and crush it in my own two hands?"

You fucking idiot, Rodney. "Of course."

"And I can count on you to be by my side every step of the way?" he drawled, a nasty smile curving his cracked lips.

"Of course." She felt like a robot, stiff and repetitive, but she didn't trust herself to say more. Rage boiled under her skin. How could this moron put the war at risk? They'd been making progress, and now everything in the Capital was blown to hell, if Mal's report was accurate. *Of course his report is accurate. He's excellent, if belligerent and irritating.*

Rodney winked. "That's my girl." He took a hit of dust—a *big* one, holy shit—and sat back with a smile.

She ran her tongue along the edge of her teeth. "Still using?"

"Always, my girl. Always." He licked the desktop clean. "Others may turn, but I won't. Been using the stuff since the Beginning and not a speck of black in my eyes, see?" He pried his eyelids open.

I'll be damned. His eyes are still white.

"Won't turn now either," said Toby. "Not now that we got this." He held up the thing he'd been fumbling with. A vial.

The detox serum.

"Got big plans for that?" Penny asked. Her nails dug into her jeans. *What are you up to, you conniving dirtbag?*

Rodney held out his hand, and Toby tossed him the vial. "All in due time."

She didn't press him. It would only make him lash out. And after that big hit, he'd be out for blood. She changed tactics. "What's our status? Do we need weapons? Supplies? How much territory did we lose in the...transition?" She knew the answer but wanted to hear him admit his own fuck up.

Rodney laughed, a high-pitched sound that grated her nerves. "So many questions." He pitched a baggie of dust to Callum, who snatched it with a greedy grin. "You just got home. Let's enjoy ourselves before we get our hands dirty with business." He pulled back the drapes with a flourish and faced the field, motioning for Penny to join him.

The roaring sound...

It was a crowd. A huge yelling crowd of red-masked Faction members filled the stands that overlooked the crater from a helicopter crash. Penny's eyes widened when she saw the contents of the pit. The blood. The bodies. The fucking *users and turned* circling around a troxy.

Penny's hand twitched toward the handle of her sickle at her belt. "What the hell is this?"

"It serves a dual purpose, don't you think? Troxies, turned, and users who aren't ours die, and we get entertainment more exciting than a football game." Rodney pressed a palm against the glass and leaned into Penny's space. She fought back a grimace at his foul breath. "Got something to say, Penny?"

Penny had no problem with vengeance. She understood the overpowering need for revenge. For absolution. To do whatever it took to make sure every troxy responsible for the dust was eliminated so she could one day look herself in the mirror without shame. She'd never be able to bring her family back, but she'd make sure Pharmatrox couldn't take anything else from her.

She had no problem making a spectacle when it served her only purpose: finding the Architect. She'd done so many times before. Just look at what she'd unleashed on Stella's tower. It all served her goal: to make Stella *afraid*. So afraid that she'd give herself up.

She had no problem doling out the dust to Faction members who were already users. If they didn't get it from her, they'd just find it somewhere else. By providing her Marauders with the dust, she had some control over them and they weren't running around in the streets randomly killing people or causing issues.

She had no problem with violence. She'd killed many. Users, she tolerated—if they fought on her side. Turned and troxies, she slaughtered.

She did, however, have a problem with violence for the sake of *entertainment*.

Penny sneered at the fighting pit as a turned bit into the neck of the screaming troxy. Blood spurted, drenching the white lab coat.

Violence was not entertaining; violence was sometimes a necessary means to an end. Yes, she wanted all troxies to die. Preferably by her own hand. But throwing people in a pit gladiator style and seeing how long it took them to eat each other? Distasteful. It made the Faction look like immature rednecks.

She was not an immature redneck.

"Good plan," she said. "It'll keep people distracted while we regroup and solidify our position." The words caught in her throat.

Rodney's smile cut her like a knife. He kicked a chair toward her. "Take a seat and enjoy the show."

Penny sat.

She'd stay on Rodney's good side until she could get Kev back; he was their best chance at winning the war. Under Kev's leadership, the Faction had transformed from a band of rebels into an organized militia of thousands. He'd taken the raging inferno of the early days and given it direction. He didn't sanction shows of senseless violence anymore; he allowed the Seven Sisters to stand as a reminder of the Beginning, of where they had come from and why they fought.

Only one month of Rodney's so-called leadership and things were already deteriorating. Pretty soon, they'd fall right back into what they had been in the Beginning: a rowdy group of freedom fighters with no purpose, no discipline, and no chance at taking the country back from Pharmatrox.

Another user pounced on the troxy, and Rodney whooped. Penny frowned.

Rodney was not a leader—he was not Kev. He wasn't capable of coordinating strikes against the troxies or organizing the watch schedule or, hell, making sure the hydroponic farms had what they needed to support them through the winter. She didn't know much about that stuff either, but she'd learned a bit from the few months she'd watched Kev. Running a fingernail across the blade of her sickle at her belt, she thought her minimal knowledge of farming would help. She'd grown up working in the fields with her father from a young age, but she was no expert.

"Yes!" Rodney punched the air. "Won my bet on that one. Knew the user would get 'im. Throw in another one!" he bellowed to the crew around the pit.

Penny might be a better choice for interim Faction leader than Rodney, but she had no one to back her. Her raids kept her on the road, so she'd never sat around the fire and *bonded* with anyone besides her Marauders—and they were all dead, anyway. Toby and Callum might as well be dead, for as useful as they were to her. It was better that Rodney thought she was under his thumb, even though it made her stomach turn. If he thought her a loyal minion, he was less likely to feel threatened and have her murdered in her sleep.

Her only chance at preventing the resistance from falling apart was to stay close to Rodney, feed him ideas, and convince him they were his own. He was self-righteous enough to fall victim to a little flattery and ego stroking. In her old life as an insurance investigator, she'd had to do that plenty of times to get the information she needed. *Really? We're comparing manipulating an egomaniacal murderer to chatting with small-time insurance fraudsters? That's fucking rich.*

If things remained on their current trajectory, Rodney would not be able to hold off the troxies in the Capital. He was too concerned with his own bullshit. If they lost the Capital, they lost the war. They lost everything.

And Penny had no intention of losing.

15

AFTER—DAY 2

Agnes chewed on her pen as she toyed with the glowing blue holographic cube. She passed it back and forth, twisting the sections like a Rubik's cube, faster and faster.

With a grunt, she shoved back from her desk and threw the pixellated cube to hover in the center of the room.

Dammit, Silas. His stupid unbreakable passcube had stumped her again. She'd been working at solving it for *weeks* now. It had consumed every minute of her free time the past few days; it was the only way she could keep from thinking about the ferry. But when she closed her eyes at night, the dead man's hungry hands shredded her dreams. She hadn't told anyone about her involvement in the incident, and for some reason, it hadn't hit the CLEO newsfeeds yet. Evie had tried to talk to her about it, but she avoided her. She'd rather focus on things that didn't make her want to panic-vomit.

Luckily, work was keeping her busy. Pharmatrox had mandated over-time for everyone. On what, specifically, she was supposed to be working, she wasn't sure. Dr. Hansen had been trapped in the boardroom in endless meetings, and they hadn't had time to catch up.

The passcube rotated in the center of the room, taunting Agnes. Guilt poked at her for using work resources and company time in her pursuit of beating Silas, but she would not accept defeat. And besides, she had some time to kill while she waited on a set of simulations to complete.

Agnes twisted the pen around her long dark hair until it formed a bun, readying herself to face the passcube anew, when her other Patch pinged from her desk.

Mierda. "Log out Sara Ellis," she said. She scrambled to remove her...new Patch and replaced it with her own from her desk. She slipped "Sara Ellis's" Patch into her coat pocket.

"Welcome, Agnes Monserrat," said her CLEO. "New message from Roberto in IT." Agnes smiled.

"Play message."

"Hey, Agnes. We're swamped down here. Was hoping you could run another set of diagnostics for us and push a security update. I'd do it myself, but my mom's nurse can't work late tonight, so I need to relieve her. And Evie wants to grab dinner later. I'm trying to escape this place while I can. I'll owe you big time. Thanks, amor."

Agnes typed out a quick reply saying she'd do it. It was easy enough and it was good practice. Silas would never forgive her if she forgot how to update a security system. He'd taught her himself and had helped her study for her college exams more than once.

Agnes helped Roberto because they were friends, but when other departments had heard about it, she'd had an inundation of ad hoc requests. She'd given her time to as many as she could, but she had to learn to say no. But she never said no to Dr. Hansen, nor Roberto; their piecemeal requests were always bumped to the top of the pile.

Pharmatrox had boosted her login credentials to include IT support so she could help out as needed. Although why they didn't hire more IT people, she had no idea. As a national pharmaceutical conglomerate expanding into other sectors like consumer technology, they clearly had the business case for it. But why hire when they could overwork the employees they already had and ask them to do multiple jobs for the same amount of pay?

Now I sound like Silas.

One of his favorite drums to beat was reminding Agnes of how Pharmatrox took advantage of her work ethic and loyalty. But she didn't see it that way. Her gene editing project would give people back their lives. All of the departments at Pharmatrox contributed to the company's overarching goal: uniting as one strong, healthy species through advancements in medicine and technology. And for that goal, she didn't mind putting in the extra work.

She logged in to the terminal and grabbed the file attached to Roberto's video message. After a quick QA check and correcting a bit of code, she pushed the update and logged out. She popped out her Patch and replaced it with the one she and Silas had designed and reprogrammed, ready to dive back into her passcube decoding. If anyone found her special Patch, she'd be fired on the spot. But the feeling of creating something new was exhilarating. The chances of anyone discovering it were slim anyway. She was good at covering her tracks.

"Dr. Hansen will return from her meeting in the next thirty seconds," said her CLEO.

"Thanks. Log out." All Patches—except Sara Ellis's—had a tracking mechanism so personnel could be located within the cavernous Pharmatrox facilities. It came in handy when she was trying to keep secrets from her boss.

With her original Patch safely back in place, she was busy looking hard at work whenever Dr. Hansen stormed into the lab. The door slammed behind her.

"Meeting didn't go well?" Agnes grabbed another pen and spun it on the desk.

Dr. Hansen thrust a hand through her short gray hair and paced across the lab, her ruby wedding ring catching the light. Agnes had never met Mr. Hansen, and Dr. Hansen didn't mention him much. She'd always been curious about her mentor's home life, but the woman rarely left the lab. After a few minutes, Dr. Hansen spoke.

"Two days ago, there was an incident. A ferry from Hoboken had to be diverted due to a...disturbance on board. Witness reports say a man killed a woman, and that man is now dead."

Agnes's tongue turned to parchment. "Why would the directors be discussing that?"

"The police found a prescription bottle of troxapine in the dead man's pocket."

"Hijo de puta. So this is our fault—Pharmatrox's fault?" Her voice quavered and she squeezed the pen. She couldn't admit to her mentor that she'd been there. That she'd been the one to kill the man. It was easier to think of the whole thing as a horrible nightmare. A horrible nightmare that had happened to someone else.

"Nobody in experimental pharmaceuticals is talking. Or, at least, they're not taking responsibility for it. They say there's no way to connect the troxapine to the man's behavior."

"Can't they do a tox screen during the autopsy to confirm it?"

Dr. Hansen sagged into one of the lab table stools. "There is no body."

"How is there no body?" When the police had rushed aboard to escort her and the other passengers off, the man's body had still been on the upper deck.

"It's already been disposed of. Which, if you ask me, reeks of a Pharmatrox coverup. In the meeting, they said our PR team is preventing the news outlets from reporting anything about it. Apparently, some of the media company executives are in our back pocket too, after we 'donated' to their 'foundations.' So they have no choice but to muzzle their reporters." Dr. Hansen drummed her fingernails on the tabletop. "If troxapine can cause adverse effects like this, effects that even the department that designed it doesn't entirely comprehend, we must inform the public. It's criminal to suppress this information, meanwhile people are still taking troxapine thinking it's a miracle vitamin."

The pen cracked in Agnes's hand. "You haven't taken it, have you?" Agnes asked.

She didn't take troxapine, but she knew many people who did. The drug had exploded onto the scene less than a month ago, and already a third of the population took it daily. The fact that celebrities and athletes were renowned spokespeople for it had contributed to its astronomical rise. Upwards of one hundred million people were at risk.

La madre que me parió. What has Pharmatrox done? What have we *done?*

"Not yet, thank god. I just had my first prescription filled the other day. It's now sitting at the bottom of the Hudson." Dr. Hansen's back straightened. "You haven't taken it either?"

"I'm clean. So what do we do? Do we leak the story to the media ourselves?"

Dr. Hansen locked her fists in her hair. "No. Pharmatrox would know it's us. Everything in this damn place is tracked."

Except for Sara Ellis's Patch..."You said it yourself. People have to know. They need to stop taking it *now*."

"But what if we're wrong? What if the side effects are only temporary or only affect a few individuals? What if the ferry was the result of one bad batch distributed to a small area?" Dr. Hansen gripped the edge of the table until her knuckles turned white. "We'd cause a national panic over nothing. That's a hard one to walk back. Our department would be obliterated, and our work would come to a screeching halt. You and I would be blacklisted. We need more information before we go to the media."

Agnes pulled the pen out of her hair and chewed on the cap as she paced the room. She couldn't believe it, that the company she'd devoted her life to for the past eight years would put so many lives at risk. And for what? Money? To save face? It wasn't right. "We have to do *something*. Let me talk to Evie."

Evie talked to Agnes about her work projects but had sworn her to secrecy. Her current project was working with stem cells, so she might not have any insight into troxapine, but this was an emergency. If Evie told her anything incriminating about troxapine, Agnes would go straight to the media. Pharmatrox couldn't know it was her if she used Sara Ellis's Patch to leak the information.

Dr. Hansen shook her head. "Wanda isn't letting anyone else look at what her team's been working on. These damn departments are so siloed."

Agnes had only seen Dr. Wanda Chun, the director of experimental pharmaceuticals, in passing, but the woman was severe and direct, much like her own mentor.

Dr. Hansen tapped her chin. "It's best to keep this between us for now. If Wanda finds out I've been sniffing around her employees, I might find myself uninvited to the next directors meeting."

"Are you sure? Evie wouldn't rat us out."

"Don't tell anyone about this. I shouldn't even be talking to you." Dr. Hansen sighed and shook her head. "But damn it, Agnes. You and me, our department, we're doing the right thing, here. Sometimes it seems like the other departments are just in it for profit. EP is the biggest revenue driver for us, so nobody asks questions."

Her mentor rarely mentioned the company structure. The little Agnes knew about Pharmatrox as a whole was whatever Dr. Hansen shared when she briefed their department in the weekly sync meetings. Every other department was like that too, to her knowledge. Not very united, for a company that touted *Unity Is Strength* as its motto.

"Innovation and experimentation are crucial for advancement in any field, certainly," continued Dr. Hansen, "but cutting corners and distributing products before they've been properly vetted and tested isn't the answer. And I'm not sure that EP was careful enough with troxapine."

Agnes hung her head in her hands. She felt sick. Pharmatrox was putting profits over people. Overlooking how Pharmatrox had assumed so much power had been easy when she'd thought they had the nation's best interests at heart. *They're giving everyone free healthcare*, she'd thought. *They're combatting the negative health effects of climate change, they're funding my work. Pharmatrox will save us from this barren, sick, flood-ridden world.*

But in the wake of the ferry incident, she saw the company's actions in a whole new light. None of it had been for the good of the people or in the name of "saving the world." It had all been for money. For power. For *control*.

She and Evie should have listened to Silas that night eight years ago. But she couldn't just walk away. Not when she'd seen what the dead man had been capable of. She and Dr. Hansen could fix this. They had to get the truth out.

"There have to be others here who agree with us," said Agnes.

Dr. Hansen couldn't have been the only director in that boardroom to stand up and say something against Pharmatrox...could she?

Dr. Hansen rubbed her tired, lined face. These meetings were really taking it out of her. Agnes had never seen her look so harried and stressed in all the years they'd worked together.

"I have a few allies in other departments, but it's not enough," said Dr. Hansen. "The majority of the directors want to keep quiet about the ferry incident. And, they want to give EP even *more* funding. They voted on it today. The consequences of that could be catastrophic."

Dr. Hansen squared her shoulders and nodded. "We need to figure out what they're doing over in EP. Let me get through a few more meetings this week, and then we'll come up with a plan for how to approach Evie without alerting Dr. Chun."

16

*M*ARCH 15, 2050: *I met a man at the bookstore today—Jay Monserrat. His favorite book is apparently* For Whom the Bell Tolls. *I asked him if that is part of an elaborate ruse to pick up unsuspecting women. He laughed and then prattled on about combustion engines, of all things. I thought those were relics of the past, but he assured me there are still some around. He's a mechanic from Spain. Maybe explains why he likes Hemingway. He asked me to dinner. I'm skeptical that I'll have anything in common with a mechanic, but people can be more than one thing. Maybe he'll surprise me. I bought the book too.*

Stella's hand lingered on the journal's weathered binding. When she was a child, her father had often told her the story of this day. She wished she could have met her mom. She smiled and closed the journal—a time capsule of life before Pharmatrox had come to power. The only remaining item of her mother's that her father hadn't sold or given away after her death, Stella had read it cover to cover a thousand times. She'd read *For Whom the Bell Tolls* as many times too. After her papá's death, she'd kept his copy in her nightstand. It felt right to have him close, watching over her as she slept. She kicked herself every day for leaving it behind in her apartment.

Stella tucked the journal in her bag and tied her bandanna around her forehead to help conceal her Patch while she waited for Tara. As sunshine peeked over the skyscrapers and lit the rooftop of the derelict hotel, she sat on the ledge, feet dangling over the cracked pavement fifteen stories below. The hotel was near the Outpost, and it was one of Tara's favorite spots.

The door to the roof banged shut.

"Morning!" Tara dropped a stuffed duffel bag. Her skin glowed a warm brown in the sunlight. "Ready to get your ass kicked again?"

Stella turned with a tentative smile. "You ever think maybe I'm letting you win?"

Tara snorted as she rifled through the bag. "I've seen the way you handle any weapon that isn't your precious machete. A blindfolded and half-asleep Quentin could do better."

"I'm lucky to have you, then, sensei."

Tara grunted. "Lawrence refuses to spar with me. He's more interested in his garden. Looks like a bunch of weeds to me, but I never did have a green thumb. And Quentin, he's always scampering off to climb the nearest thing taller than he is. So if I'm going to keep my skills sharp, I need a worthy practice opponent. That's you."

Stella bit back a smile. "Feels great to know I'm your last resort."

"Exacto." Tara tossed Stella two metal poles the length of her forearm. "We're working Arnis today. Vete allí."

Stella gripped the poles and stood where Tara pointed.

It had been nearly two weeks since Stella had moved into the Outpost. There'd been no sign of Penny or the motorcycle, so she'd allowed herself to fall into a familiar routine. She'd told Tara and Quentin she found a list of possible supply caches in the library, which wasn't a total lie. With their help, she'd already checked off eleven of the fifteen buildings. None had turned out to be a Pharmatrox facility, but it was faster than if she'd done it by herself.

They were scoping out another building today after sparring practice. And she'd found some tools to finish building the radio from the parts she'd...borrowed. Lawrence had helped her make the repairs. His warmth and willingness to help made her uncomfortable. She always used more dust after their encounters to block out the bad feelings.

It kicked her self-loathing into overdrive.

On Stella's first morning at camp, Tara had thrown a rusty pair of nunchucks at her and dragged her here. She needed the sparring practice too, and she wanted to get on Tara's good side. So far, Tara had handily beaten her during their daily lessons. Stella always finished the bouts dripping in sweat, but for Tara, not a curl was ever out of place.

Ready to feel the ache of a good workout, Stella faced Tara for her sparring therapy. It was the only time her mind emptied and she didn't feel *anything*, and she could rely on pure instinct. Most of the time.

But not today.

As Stella spun the metal poles and blocked Tara's strikes, she thought of *that night*. The night she ruined Lawrence's life.

Facing him every day at camp was a living nightmare. The truth throbbed inside of her like an aneurysm ready to burst. She ached to apologize, to tell him anything that would take away his pain and absolve her of the blame. But no words or actions could ever undo what she'd done.

So instead, she swung poles at Tara and replayed *that night* in her mind. She couldn't go back in time and fix her mistakes.

But she could make sure *this* Stella was ready for whatever dangers lurked on the horizon.

Tara spun on her knees, aiming for Stella's legs. Stella jumped, but the pole caught her shin. As she staggered backward, she struck for Tara's ribs, who blocked, clicking her tongue.

"Use one pole to strike high and the other low," said Tara.

Stella did as instructed. Tara blocked again, but Stella felt more confident wielding the poles.

Blood on her hands. Sticky.

Stella blinked away the memory and struck faster. Tara was more nimble, but Stella was stronger. Stella hit harder and advanced.

An animalistic cry tore from her throat.

Stella shook her head and gritted her teeth against the past, forcing Tara up against the rooftop door.

"This is Stella's kill. Let her do it."

Stella raised the pole to deliver the killing blow—and stopped. This was Tara, not Penny. Not the Marauders.

Not *that night.*

Stella's poles clanged to the ground, and she backed away.

As Penny's face flickered through Stella's mind, a chill rippled across her flesh, and she sagged against the wall and slid to the floor, a raw ache for the dust rushing through her.

Tara brushed herself off, unfazed. "Really good there toward the end. You're getting better," she said, replacing the weapons in her duffle and taking a drink of water. She was silent for a few moments as she studied Stella. "Why do you always look like that after we spar?"

Stella picked at a rough patch in the cinderblock wall. "My last relationship like this ended with her trying to kill me."

Tara smirked and sat beside her. "Exactly why I refuse to spar with my girlfriends. The women I like tend to get offended when you best them at their own game."

"No, she was just a friend. But things went bad. It's complicated."

"Are you sure you weren't dating?" Tara chuckled and waved it off. With a quick flicking motion, she whipped out a small, curved blade from her pocket. She flipped the blade open and closed with expert movements.

Stella's unease melted away as she watched. "How'd you get so skilled with all the weapons in your duffel bag arsenal?"

"We lived in Tokyo for a few years. When my dad wasn't stuck at work on the Army base, he trained in a local dojo. Then we moved to Brooklyn, and he started his own in the Bronx. Wanted to give the kids a safe and fun place to go after school. I spent every day there as a kid. It's how I found my way into the Army. I wanted to use my skills to help people. And then…" Her eyes went far away for a moment before she snapped back to the present, glaring at the skyline. "We see how that turned out."

"What happened to your family?" Stella asked.

"They moved back to Puerto Rico. My abuela was getting old, and mamá wanted to be there to help. I'm glad they got out while they could."

"Mmm." Stella squinted into the blistering sun. The Memorial to the Old Gods marred the horizon. Her jaw clenched. She should have moved back to Spain when she'd had the chance, but she'd been too raw after her papá's death to consider being engulfed by his family.

Tara shook off her somber mood and nudged Stella with her elbow. "I'll crack that rock-hard shell of yours yet, Stella girl."

Stella bumped Tara's shoulder with smile, but it was half-hearted. "I could say the same for you, tía."

The barbs of guilt pricking Stella's heart burrowed deeper. Tara could *never* find out who Stella really was. They could never be real friends. Not while everything about Stella was wreathed in deception.

Tara wound her curls into a quick bun and eyed the exposed scar slashing down Stella's throat, a troubled expression clouding her face.

"Did the one you fight when you're fighting me give that to you?" Tara asked.

Stella's hand flew to her neck. "How'd you know that?"

A bitter laugh stained Tara's smile, and she held up her scarred arms. "I know the touch of evil when I see it. It leaves a mark unlike any other."

Stella's lips thinned to a razor's edge with a hard nod. "I live in fear of her every day. I'm not who she thinks I am."

Mierda. She shouldn't have said that last part. She didn't want Tara to have any inkling of her past. Luckily, Tara wasn't the intrusive or prying type.

Tara grunted in understanding. "You shouldn't hide your scar," she said. "It's part of you. If we don't learn how to carry our darkness, it'll fester inside us. All we can do is learn from it and do better. And remember to let the light in every now and then."

As Stella looked at Tara's earnest face, shame draped around her. A yearning for the dust shot through her, making her dizzy. Out of the corner of her eye, she saw Death wink at her from across the roof. She touched her scar and swallowed.

It was too late. Her darkness had already consumed her.

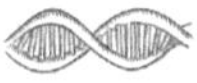

Quentin's head popped into Stella's tent as she was readying her pack for their scouting trip. "I want a cheeseburger." He grabbed Stella's foot and dragged her outside.

Stella blinked at his bizarre intrusion and shook him off. Her shins sported some nasty bruises from Tara's Arnis poles earlier that morning. "What?"

"A cheeseburger, Stella," Quentin repeated, all business. "When was the last time you remember eating something Lawrence hasn't boiled beyond recognition?"

She chuckled and ducked into her tent to grab her pack. "No cheeseburgers, but this place might have some Pop-Tarts, if we're lucky." And if they were really lucky—a Helix Key.

The next building on her list was deep in downtown, and she had high hopes of it being a troxy facility. She needed some good news in her hunt.

"Where's Lawrence?" asked Tara as she finished off her cup of coffee and dumped the grounds in the fire. "He'll want to know before we leave. The dummy didn't take a radio with him, wherever he went."

Stella shrugged. "I'll find him." She had an idea of where to look. Lawrence often went on morning walks and disappeared for an hour or so.

About a mile from the Outpost, the thin trees opened up into a clearing. A rhythmic thumping disturbed the slumbering woods, and Stella crouched behind the bushes to watch. She didn't know why her first instinct was to hide, but something about the energy in the air felt off.

A shirtless Lawrence hunched over a sprightly young ash tree. His strong arms swung his axe with familiarity. *That's too much wood for him to have done it this morning. This must be what he does on his "morning walks."*

He added the logs to a massive pile and sank to the ground, sobs rattling his chest. "I'm sorry," he said, tipping his head back to the sky. "I'm sorry I couldn't save you."

Despite feeling like an invader of his private darkness, Stella watched, a silent observer to his church-like ritual. Lawrence sniffed and rose on shaky legs, grabbed his axe, and returned to his warpath, butchering trees with unbridled aggression. Stella flinched with each blow of the axe as if it landed on her own neck. Watching his pain was her penance. Feeling that pain alongside him, even if it was from the shadows, was the only solace she could offer.

I shouldn't be here. Stella backed up a step, but a stick cracked underfoot.

Lawrence's head shot up and he surveyed the area, like a lion after a kill. The two locked eyes across the clearing, and she froze, heart walloping her ribcage.

"How long?" He lodged his axe in a tree and approached her. "How long have you been watching me?"

She knew what he was really asking though. What he really wanted to know. *How much have you seen?*

"I talk to my dead friend too, sometimes."

The revelation hung in the air between them.

Exhaustion pooled in dark ovals under his weathered golden eyes, eyes that had seen too much for his thirty-some years. "I lost my traveling companion. She was taken from me shortly after the Beginning."

Stella schooled her face into a passive blankness.

"I had pretty much given up on surviving in this new world, but then I met her. Intelligent, witty, kind...*alive* in a way most people aren't. She was always saying how I had saved her on the road. But really, she saved me. It's because of her that I began looking into herbal remedies for the dust and its effects. I was going to build us a house—in the woods next to a lake with a garden, like we always talked about." A profound sadness etched in the crease of his brow like an epitaph.

The lurking chasm yawned inside of Stella, waiting to devour her.

"When I'm building or working with my hands, it's the only time I can still feel her."

Trudging through her guilt, Stella reached across the abyss between them and squeezed his arm. His rough workman's hand gripped hers like a life raft.

"I'm sorry." Those were the only words she could manage. "I came to tell you we're heading out on another run and to see if you need anything." But what he really needed, she couldn't give him—his friend back.

Lawrence nodded to the pile of logs. "Help me carry this to the workshop before you head out. It's just up there."

Stella picked up some wood and followed Lawrence through the forest. But no matter how many logs she carried, she knew she'd never alleviate the weight of the burden she'd given him.

17

T ARA FIDDLED WITH HER metal baseball bat, a gift from one of Quentin's salvaging missions. "Hopefully we don't run into any turned or Faction today. I'm not in the mood for a fight."

Quentin kicked a rock down the road and said, "You're always in the mood for a fight. Even though I had to smash that spider for you yesterday."

Tara elbowed him. "Can it, tomatito. I don't fuck with bugs. He was a big boy."

The icy grip of Stella's misanthropy loosened at their warm camaraderie. She'd checked her Patch in the privacy of her tent before they left to make sure there weren't any Pharmatrox raids or patrols inbound. They would be safe for the afternoon.

As they walked through neutral territory, some civilians wandered past, but nobody acknowledged anyone. It was hard to know who to trust these days. Someone might look like a civilian, but they could be a spy—Faction or troxy—waiting to lure you into a trap. It's why Stella had stayed on her own for most of the past eight months.

As they approached downtown and the edge of the neutral zone, the scent of decay wafted through the air. Stella looked at Tara, who frowned. Quentin opened his mouth to speak, but Stella put a finger to her lips.

The odor waned with each step, but the smell of blood—fresh blood—grew stronger. When they rounded the corner about twenty blocks west of the Memorial, Stella skittered to a halt.

Bodies blanketed the street.

Two seconds later, Quentin retched into the bushes. Tara's dark brown skin took on a green hue, but she raised her stoic chin with the air of someone who had seen worse.

The bodies, dozens of them, scattered across the street like forgotten toys cast aside by a careless child. Blood pooled in sticky puddles. Red arterial sprays slashed across the sides of buildings.

Stella knelt beside the closest body and lifted the red hardshell mask. The man's mouth gaped in a silent scream, eyes fixed on unseen aggressors, and his throat bore a jagged slash encrusted with blood. Stella glanced at the other bodies—some were Pharmatrox guards and some had Faction masks. Many of their throats had been slit in the same fashion. Stella's hand went to her own scar as she swallowed her rising fear.

Tara surveyed the scene, and her lips thinned to a tight line. "It's like the early Red Riots all over again."

"I remember seeing them on TV," said Stella.

Tara shook her head. "I was here. They sent my unit to enforce Containment and hold McAdams Bridge alongside Pharmatrox guards to keep civilians inside the city. Someone from the Faction fired a single shot, and the crowd churned into a killing field." Her eyes glazed over as she surveyed the carnage that mirrored her memories. "My dad was a Black man from Brooklyn, my mom a boricua. They raised me to be strong, to handle anything...but this?" Her fingers brushed the thick scars lacing her arms. "No one can train you for this."

Stella squeezed her shoulder, and Tara patted her hand, but her gaze remained far away.

"Stella…" Quentin's voice came from down the street. He'd stopped retching and pointed behind her, his face a mask of terror.

"What is it?"

His freckles poked through his skin in stark contrast, and he looked like he might puke again as he pointed at the bodies. "What does that look like to you?"

She frowned at him. "It looks like a sea of death, Quent. What d'you mean?"

He shook his head with an agitated *harrumph*. "No, no. Do you see how the bodies are, um, positioned?"

Stella scrutinized the layout more closely. It did look a little strange. As if they were arranged with purpose…

She turned to say as much to Quentin, but he was already gone, scaling the side of the closest building.

"What are you doing?" Tara asked.

"Getting a better look." He pulled himself onto the third-floor balcony of the brick house. Even from a distance, Stella saw his face go even whiter. He looked as if he'd seen Satan himself. "Stella," he said, voice hoarse. "Get up here."

Tara shot Stella a baffled look as she grabbed the window sill and began to climb. Stella didn't like heights and was not a skilled climber, but the dust made her more agile. When she reached him, Quentin extended a hand and pulled her onto the balcony. She faced the scene from their higher perch and shielded her eyes from the sun.

That's when she saw it.

Spots swam before her eyes as she reached for Quentin and plunged into unconsciousness.

Her last memory before sinking into the darkness, emblazoned behind her eyelids, was the vision she'd seen—the gruesome pattern created by the meticulously placed bodies.

I

SEE

YOU

Stella hurried through the alleys, getting them as far away from that nightmare scene as possible. She'd passed off her fainting as due to the heat, but Quentin had looked askance at her.

The frigid fingers of the past trailed down her spine, and acid burbled in her stomach. She'd fallen into a false sense of security. But now, she felt as though unseen eyes watched her from every broken window.

They knew.

Penny and her crew knew Stella was in the Capital. They were close. They were *watching*. She *needed* to get a Helix Key. Today.

Stella pulled them to a stop in front of a nondescript cement building that blended into the others on the street. The building on her list. Its doors were chained shut, and bars covered the windows. *Doesn't look good for it being an active troxy facility.*

They circled around to the back and found a basement window with half the bars bent and the glass blown out, like a grenade or something had exploded nearby. It left a space wide enough for someone small to squeeze through. After they dropped inside, Stella flicked on her flashlight. A sizable atrium reached to the top floor, ten stories up. *Yes! This is it.*

Stella easily weaved through the labyrinth of hallways, the route stamped on her brain from when she had wandered similar halls.

"Seems like you know where you're going," said Tara from behind her.

"I saw a map of this place in the library." It was only partially a lie. She left out the fact that the interior looked like an exact replica of her own lab in New York.

After passing several ominous doors, Stella pushed on one of them, and it opened into a cafeteria with a general store. *This ought to keep them busy.*

Quentin's and Tara's eyes bulged when they saw the fully stocked shelves laden with goodies.

"Jackpot!" Quentin snatched a bag of chips and upended its contents directly onto his face. Tara made a beeline for the candy aisle.

Stella left the two of them to their snacking and slipped away to find the IT director's office.

As she wound deeper into the Pharmatrox facility, door after door dotted the long hallway on either side. She peeked in the window of one. A pair of thick chains dangled from the wall, ending in cuffs.

Down here, these doors did not lead to labs where groundbreaking discoveries were made, like in her own lab. No. Down here, these doors were meant to contain. Imprison. The ghostly shrieks of prisoners long gone echoed in Stella's mind.

She hurried past the cells and hung a sharp right, then jogged down the hall toward her prize—the tech room.

The door lock mechanisms didn't work, and the security systems were offline. *Hence the chains and bars to keep people out. Damn it.* The building was severed from the power grid and the network, so she wouldn't be able to download anything here.

She passed through the rows of dead monitors and shelves of tech toward the IT director's office in the back. *Please have a Helix Key.* Her plans couldn't afford any more delay, not with Penny breathing down her neck.

Some security functions were tied to sodium-ion batteries and would work in the event of a power outage. After punching a button on the desk, a holographic keypad materialized in the air. She typed in Sara Ellis's code and pulled up a terminal to type a few commands Silas had taught her. After hacking past the firewall, she typed in Roberto's IT credentials and—*Yes! Finally.*

On the far wall, a panel sunk in and lowered, revealing the treasure within. A few Patches and a small double helix model made of onyx sat in the middle of the compartment—a Helix Key. Stella grabbed an extra Patch, just in case, and zipped them both safely into her pack.

When Stella returned to the canteen, Tara and Quentin had already devoured a box of Pop-Tarts each. Foil wrappers dotted the aisle like tinsel. Quentin lay on the floor, hands laced over his distended belly, and Tara rifled around elbow-deep in a bag of chips.

Stella put her hands on her hips. "Have you two done *anything* besides stuff your faces?"

Quentin shot a sheepish look at Tara, who froze with a chip halfway to her mouth. A guilty smile crept across her face, and she said, "It's been so long since we've had proper junk food, Stella. You have to understand, Lawrence's various boiled root vegetables, while *delicious*"—Quentin snickered—"are no match for pure, unadulterated trans fats."

Stella stifled a smile. "We gather supplies first—*then* you can finish snacking until you burst."

A chorus of grumbles sounded, but the gang stuffed provisions into every nook and cranny. Quentin crammed about fifty sticks of beef jerky in each pocket, happily chomping on one as he continued filling any remaining space in his pack with candy bars, while Tara wrestled the zipper of her bag around a jar of peanut butter. Stella wandered into the neighboring aisle to grab coffee.

"Stella?" Quentin's voice came across the shelves. Something about his uncertain tone sent chills down her spine.

"Wha—?" She screeched to a halt when she saw what he was looking at.

A girl perched atop the nearest shelf.

She was around ten years old, covered in a thick layer of grime, her filthy hair stuck to her head in matted clumps. Ravenous, she tore the head off of the pigeon she held and gnawed on its torso, feathers and blood sticking to her cracked lips and stubby fingers.

The girl was turned.

Shit shit shit.

The girl looked up and tilted her head, bloody teeth bared in a ghoulish grin and black eyes leaking inky ichor down her cheeks. She gripped the edge of the shelf in gnarled fingers and arched her back.

Like a feral cat primed for attack.

18

WITH AN EAR-SPLITTING SHRIEK, Pigeon Girl launched off the nearest shelf and landed on Quentin. His knife clattered out of reach, and in one swift move, Stella dove for it and jammed it into the girl's neck. Pigeon Girl howled as blood gushed from the rent in her throat.

But the girl wasn't alone.

A sea of turned filtered into the commissary. Too many to count. Their black eyes glinted in the dim lighting, their gaunt faces mirroring the nightmare smile of the girl.

One turned—a middle-aged woman with stained teeth—threw herself at Stella with a snarl. Tara skewered her with Stella's fallen machete before she could attack, wrenching the weapon back and letting loose a putrid waterfall of guts.

"How did they get in?" Tara shouted as she bashed in another skull with her baseball bat and tossed Stella her machete.

Stella whipped it around, and the nearest turned's head rolled. "I don't know," she said. But a cold ball of suspicion settled at her core.

A growl came from behind her.

Stella spun and slashed the turned across the torso, then lodged her blade in its skull. She glanced at Tara, who hit home runs left and right with every swing of her bat, while Quentin fended off attacks and chucked jars of pickles and preserves like pungent bombs.

But even as they smashed their way through turned, more swarmed in to replace the fallen.

"You got what you came for." Death materialized beside Stella with a wicked grin. "Tara and the kid will make a great snack for the turned, and you can escape."

Stella hated how true Death's words rang. She had everything she needed to conduct more extensive research in the library, and she only had a few buildings left on her list to scout. She had a replacement radio, a pack full of food. She didn't need Tara and Quentin's help anymore. She could leave—right now.

"Gah!"

Quentin crouched at the end of an aisle, one arm pouring a river of blood onto the floor and the other waving an inadequate knife at the approaching turned.

Without a second thought, Stella moved.

She bulldozed through bodies until she reached Quentin, severed the turned's head, and shoved the body into its approaching friends. "Are you okay?" she asked.

Quentin grimaced. "Thought it would be fun to fight with one hand behind my back. See how well I do."

Stella gripped his good arm. "I'll get us out of here."

Though Tara was a good fighting partner, it wasn't enough. With Quentin injured and Stella unable to leave his side, Tara was on her own—and she was fatiguing. Stella hadn't taken any hits yet, but with her attention divided, it was only a matter of time before she slipped up. And it was getting dark.

They'd never make it. They couldn't—

Tara cried out and dropped to a knee, blood gushing from a wound on her leg, and cursed. One hand covered her blood-soaked pants, and the other swung her bat—but the circle of turned closed in, their twitchy movements like marionettes.

"Go!" said Quentin. He pulled himself into a semi-steady lean against the shelf and brandished his knife. "I can hold them off."

Stella looked skeptical but nodded. He'd have to.

She launched into the fray surrounding Tara, and with one vicious hack, she severed windpipes and tendons. Snatching Tara and throwing her arm across her shoulders, she yelled, "Come on, Quentin!" They ran down the hallway back the way they'd entered, the turned chasing them.

Footsteps thundering down a mint-green hallway, death at her heels.

No, this time is different. This time, I'm not alone.

When they got to the basement window, Stella boosted Quentin up first. He scrambled for the top and slipped. *Carajo.* The growls of the turned echoed down the hall. *Come on, come on.*

She boosted him again—

But someone reached down from outside and grabbed him. Tattoos covered the arm, hand, and fingers. Quentin yelled and thrashed.

"Easy!" said the man. "I'm here to help."

Stella couldn't see his face, but there was no time to ask questions. The man hauled Quentin and Tara out through the jagged hole, and Stella went last, grabbing his hand and scrambling through the broken window.

Before she could get all the way through, a turned latched onto her ankle and yanked her backward. She booted him in the face until he let go. "Get something to barricade the window!" she shouted.

Tara and Quentin dragged a slab of cement from the rubble of the sidewalk and shoved it in front of the gap. The trio leaned against the building to catch their breaths, and Stella eyed their suspicious savior—and froze.

A black and red motorcycle sat in the mouth of the alleyway.

The man who'd been following her stood before her. He was a few years older than her. His sharp eyes, knife-blade nose, and messy dark hair gave him a rugged look. A fitted shirt showed off his solid frame and tattooed arms. *Of course he's handsome.* And that made her more suspicious. Pretty things had a tendency to bite.

Tara looked the man up and down. "Who the fuck are *you*? Punk rock Indiana Jones?"

"I'm Derek, but that comparison is very on the nose." He smiled at Tara, open and friendly.

Derek, as in Derek Jang? She recognized him now from the picture she'd seen on her Patch's security alert weeks ago. *What the fuck is going on?*

Tara's expression slammed shut, and in a flash, she had her talon knife at his throat. "You sent those turned after us, didn't you?"

Derek raised his palms. "Why would I send turned after you and then help you escape?"

Tara narrowed her eyes. She flipped her knife closed but pinned him with a glare.

Quentin's arms folded in a protective stance, and his stubborn chin jutted out. He didn't like strangers—except for Stella, apparently. He resembled a disgruntled parrot with his fan of unruly hair.

"I was passing through and heard what sounded like some sort of struggle," said Derek. "I thought I'd lend a hand." He ended with a nonchalant lift of one shoulder.

Why is he lying?

Without breaking eye contact with Derek, Stella said, "Quentin, there's some basic first aid things in my pack. Get yourself and Tara fixed up enough so we can make it back to camp without leaving a bloody trail. *Derek*, a word?"

Stella prodded her stalker in the chest and walked to his motorcycle at the end of the alley, out of earshot of the others. She turned to him, hands fastened to her hips. "Why are you following me? What do you want?"

Derek's dark eyes were unreadable. "Somehow, you always knew exactly where to go to avoid the troxy battles." He stepped toward her and traced a fingertip behind her right ear in a deceptive caress. Her Patch bleeped, and she jerked away from his touch. "I know what you are. I heard you talking to your CLEO in the library."

Stella's hands clenched into fists. *Carajo.* If he heard her talking to Turi, then he heard *everything*.

"So what do you want?" she asked.

Derek ran a hand over his jaw as he assessed her. "I have a job for you. I need your help raiding a troxy stronghold. You're Patched, so you can get me in. My friends are still in there—prisoners. If the favor I did for you today isn't enough, I can pay you."

Stella crossed her arms and drew herself up to her full height, which brought her up to his chin. "One, we could have escaped on our own, so I'd hardly say we're in your debt. You're probably the reason those turned showed up, all riled up because of the damn noise from your motorcycle. Two, why the hell would I help you? What good is your money to me? I can't exactly spend it on anything, can I?"

"I didn't say I'd repay you with money. I can get you on a convoy to the border."

Huh. Now that's *interesting.*

"Why should I trust you?" she asked.

"I've known you were a troxy for a while. I didn't say anything to your friends, didn't turn you in. I thought you might be interested in helping me instead of being a prisoner." His eyebrow lifted as he looked down at her.

"I don't like being threatened."

"It's not a threat. I give you something you want, you help me out with something I want. Simple transaction."

"And if I don't comply, you'll turn me in."

Derek shrugged. "I think I can persuade you."

Stella chewed her lip as she considered. She didn't have a plan for how to get to the border after rescuing Silas, and here was the solution on a silver platter. Not to mention, Derek knew where to find an active troxy facility. She could pull their records and search for Silas by name, plus download a shit ton of classified files and possible HQ locations to view in the library with her Helix Key. Infiltrating a facility would be a hell of a lot easier with a partner too. But Derek was hardly trustworthy. And how could she be sure he could follow through with the convoy? Derek was a wild card she hadn't accounted for, and she didn't know how to play him yet. It was too risky.

I SEE YOU

The scene she'd pushed out of her mind, the words that burned a brand into her eyelids, came barreling back. Penny being so close had sped up her timeline, but other than the need to hurry the fuck up and find Pharmatrox HQ with her Helix Key, she had no other plan. But she couldn't think about any of it now. Quentin and Tara were bleeding in the streets, and she had to get them home safely before she could do anything else. She owed them that much.

"I'm not interested." But damn it, she was.

Derek nodded once. A muscle in his cheek fluttered as he clenched his teeth. "Suit yourself." He pivoted to his bike and tossed an agile leg across it. "There's an old row house downtown in the neutral zone on Maple Street. The one with the green door." He locked eyes with her. "Take a few days to reconsider. Find me when you change your mind." He kicked the clutch and sped off.

Stella stomped back to the others, fuming. *Presumptuous ass.* He thought he could threaten her, back her into a corner, force her into helping him? *Dammit.* He could. He *knew* he could. He had leverage *and* something she wanted. Badly. She could turn him over to the troxies too, but she wouldn't. *Fuck, shit, damn.* Her head throbbed and a cold sweat sluiced her skin; it had been a while since she'd had any dust. After the day she'd had, she'd need a whole packet once she got back to the Outpost.

"What the hell was *that*?" Tara barely noticed the blood soaking her pants as she glared after Derek.

"I'll let you know when I figure it out," said Stella. She tossed her bandanna to Tara. "Tie that around your leg."

Stella caught Quentin staring at her, his face screwed up in a look of concentration.

"Why do you look constipated? Is your arm okay? I told you not to get eaten." Stella gingerly lifted his arm. He'd tied a torn strip of his shirt around it, but the blood seeped through. The gash was deep.

Quentin, pale with pain, eyed her. "I can't tell if you want to do the 'hurdy gurdy' with him or if you're afraid of him."

Stella fumbled the bandage. "I'm not afraid of Derek, nor do I want to see him in any state of undress, I assure you. Keep pressure on that."

Quentin gritted his teeth and did as he was told. "There was one of them," he said. "More lucid than the others. He was a user, but his eyes only had those black veins in the whites. Not turned. He was in charge. He was the one who stabbed me."

A chill rippled across Stella's spine. Users corralling turned for a personal army? Stella didn't like it. And she knew exactly the kind of person who would do such a thing.

"What did he look like?" she asked with an impassive face. "Was he Irish?"

Through the sweat and his sickly pale skin, Quentin managed to give her a bland look. "He looked like a user? We didn't have time for a chat about his country of origin. I was a little distracted with getting dismembered and left for dead."

Stella gave him a flat look, but she didn't like the pallor of his skin. There was too much blood on the ground.

"Help me with Tara. Let's go home."

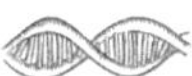

"What the hell happened?" Lawrence abandoned his garden and rushed over to relieve Stella of her load. He placed Tara on the ground by the fire and inspected the wound on her thigh.

Everyone looked at Stella.

"Place got overrun as we were collecting supplies." She kept it vague, not wanting Lawrence to launch into a panic about an army of turned—and an army where *she* likely knew its commander personally. "They both need stitches—Quentin first."

"I thought you said it would be an easy run." Lawrence forced Quentin to sit and glowered at Tara out of the corner of his eye.

Tara made an exasperated noise. "You can't plan for accidents, Lawrence. We're fine."

As Lawrence stitched up Quentin with surgical precision, Stella tended to Tara.

Tara huffed. "Doesn't think I can take care of myself. It's just a scratch." She didn't flinch as Stella started on the stitches. Tara focused on Quentin and Lawrence across the fire, a fierce look in her eyes.

"You know, *you're* the reason we're fine," said Stella as she pulled a stitch tight. "I couldn't have handled that fight alone. Or without our regular sparring practice. You're a master with that bat."

Tara flashed a smile and tucked a swath of curls behind her ear. "After Pharmatrox started rounding up all the firearms, I knew it was time to learn how to use a weapon that didn't rely on ammunition." Her eyes drifted to Quentin, squirming under Lawrence's stitches, and her gaze hardened. "I just didn't know how soon those skills would come in handy."

With Quentin and Tara both safe and resting, Stella finally allowed herself to take a deep breath. Sitting by the fire, she took a long swig of whiskey and rifled in her pack for the dust. She had several baggies, enough to keep her going for a while. But there were fewer than she remembered. She needed to slow down. After taking a quick hit, she hid the evidence.

I SEE YOU

The scene of the bodies in the street haunted her, sinking its gruesome fingers into her mind and ripping jagged holes. She tried reading a few pages of her mother's journal to calm her racing mind, but it only made the darkness worse. It clung to her and tainted everything she touched. Her mom had been a kind, caring woman. And Stella was a murderer who had brought Penny into the Capital. Giving up on reading, she stuffed the book away and stared into the flames.

A few minutes later, Lawrence lowered himself into the seat beside her and watched her with a calculating look. "Quentin told me what really happened. That you saved them."

Stella's fingers twisted around her necklace. "It was mostly Tara," she said. "Couldn't have held up without her."

"It's not easy to stick around when things get hard. So thanks for sticking around. For them."

He's really gotta cut it out with thanking me. I'm gonna lose my fucking mind. Death laughed at her from the tree line. *More than I've already lost it, anyway.*

The two fell into silence and watched the fire. Now that Tara and Quentin were safe, Derek's offer wormed its way back into Stella's mind. It's not like anyone else was barging into her life and offering her exactly what she wanted. And the sooner she rescued Silas and escaped the Capital, the less chance there was of Penny finding the Outpost and wreaking her own particular brand of havoc on these people.

Stella couldn't abandon the Outpost. But it wasn't just about using their resources. Quentin, Tara, Lawrence—they weren't strangers to her anymore. In the two weeks she'd spent with them, she'd begun to think of them as more than a means to an end. Fuck, she actually *cared* about what happened to them. She couldn't leave them to deal with Penny on their own, if—or *when*—she showed up. So she needed to escalate her timeline—not just for Silas's sake, but for Quentin and his friends too.

Which meant she needed Derek.

Great. Let's hope that trusting the super hot, mildly threatening stranger doesn't bite me in the culo.

19

AFTER—DAY 7

AGNES TOOK A BITE of soggy cereal and ignored the red numbers of the digital clock on the stove blinking at her with an angry cadence.

She didn't care that she was late for work. After another sleepless night, she deserved to take her time and actually eat breakfast today before confining herself in the lab for another sixteen hours.

Since the internal blowback from the ferry incident, Dr. Hansen had passed off some of her work to Agnes. A new, unnamed genetic mutation had shown up in one of Dr. Hansen's pregnant patients, and she wanted to solve it before the baby was born. So Agnes had been working around the clock, recalibrating her machine and running her original simulations, in addition to Dr. Hansen's request and helping out in IT.

Agnes never thought she'd be in a position where *the* Dr. Hansen, the foremost authority on gene editing, wanted *her* expertise on a project. But the ember of pride was hard to maintain as the endless work days trudged onward and Pharmatrox still shirked responsibility for the ferry.

Agnes had mentioned troxapine to Evie a few days ago in casual conversation, but she was unfamiliar. Rather than accepting it as a dead end, Agnes had offered to search files for information about troxapine, but Dr. Hansen had instructed her to lie low until later today after the directors meeting; Dr. Hansen wanted to be armed with as much information as possible before taking on the other directors.

Agnes had a catch-up with her mentor that afternoon to figure out their plan of action. It made her antsy to sit on a ticking time bomb of information and wait for the contents to explode everywhere. At least she'd been making good headway on Dr. Hansen's project. She was getting close to isolating the problematic gene and finding a solution, which helped to boost her morale.

She grabbed the wrinkled newspaper wedged in the mail slot. Mr. Alling across the hall was the only one on her floor who got hand-delivered mail, but she still ended up with his newspaper half the time. She'd have to—

The headline glared at her, and her hands shook.

KEV HERNANDEZ DEMANDS ANSWERS FROM PHARMATROX FOR TROXAPINE FERRY INCIDENT.

It worked. It fucking worked.

She launched for the TV remote.

Each station had a marquee script scrolling across the bottom, shouting the same information as the newspaper. She flicked her Patch and switched it to the news feed. The same headline, plastered in every thread. Published as of five hours ago. *I really don't want to go into work today.* Five hours was enough time for everyone at the lab to be whipped into hysteria. She was surprised Dr. Hansen hadn't called yet. She was probably stuck in the boardroom.

The front door burst open, and Agnes jumped, sloshing cereal on the floor. Silas barged into her apartment with a paper bag and two to-go cups of coffee. He parked next to her on the couch and handed her the bag with a jovial smile. "I brought you an extra bagel because you always eat mine after saying you're not hungry."

Agnes peeked in the bag as she mopped up her mess and tried to act normal. "You got the good ones from the deli. Thanks." *Do I sound weird? Is my voice too high?*

Silas handed her a coffee with a wink. "Ivan gave me the 'friends and lovers' discount. Anyway, do you know what's going on? There's way too many people in the streets, even for those overeager worker bees who go to the office at the ass-crack of dawn. Maybe there's free coffee on a corner cart or something."

As Agnes bit into her bagel, the snippet on the bottom of the screen changed and the bread turned to sawdust in her mouth. Heart thudding, she fumbled for the remote and switched to the twenty-four-hour news station.

The Pharmatrox facility. Smoke. Shouting crowds. Bloody sidewalks.

Dumbfounded, Silas stared at the screen, and Agnes reached for her phone to call Evie. She already had eight missed texts from her. She dialed the number for Evie's Patch.

"Evie, are you watching this?" Agnes asked, eyes locked on the screen.

"I am." Evie's voice was cool and sober, but Agnes could discern the thread of underlying terror it masked.

"Do they know who it is?"

"Not yet. They just found it this morning. They're saying it was some guy in a red mask who did it. The whole facility is on lockdown, so don't bother coming in today. They have us in the bunker. I'm here with Roberto. Silas was on his way for our morning coffee date, but I texted him to stay home. He's hard-headed, so I'm not sure he listened."

Agnes breathed a sigh of relief. The Pharmatrox bunker was impenetrable, secured deep underground beneath the lab. And Roberto, while lanky, would guard Evie with his life. The two had bonded over countless coffee breaks and lunches.

"Silas half listened," said Agnes. "He's here with me."

"And he's coming to get his sister right now!" Silas shouted into the phone. He catapulted to his feet, but Agnes yanked him to the couch.

"Tell Silas to stay put. We're safe here, for now. But Agnes...things are getting bad. They're talking about Containment."

"That won't happen," said Agnes. "The ferry was an isolated incident, and we're working on figuring out what went wrong."

That was the line she and Dr. Hansen had agreed upon until they could figure out who internally was on their side and how to rise up against the other directors. She trusted Evie, but now was not the time to get into the complexities of the ferry-troxapine situation. Anyone could be listening.

"I don't know. The things I'm hearing...it sounds like it's nationwide. The Leader has already issued Containment orders in other cities. The SubTran is suspended, flights are grounded. Closing the borders is next."

Nationwide? Shit. That means it wasn't just one bad batch. We're already too late. Agnes smashed the remote buttons and flipped through a few channels. Frowning, she said, "Why am I not seeing that on the news?"

"They don't want people to panic and flee? I don't know what's happening, but it's not good. Stay safe."

"You too." She hung up and dropped her phone onto the couch.

Silas paced in the kitchen, muttering.

On the TV screen, Agnes stared into the face of a Pharmatrox scientist in a bloodstained, white lab coat, eyes glazed over in death. Her body hung from a noose affixed to the flagpole next to the front entrance Agnes walked through every day.

In the background, the Pharmatrox facility smoldered. The ruins of a fallen empire. Her eyes locked on the face of the scientist.

"I did this," Agnes whispered.

Silas stopped pacing. "What?"

She pointed to the TV. "This is my fault."

"How the hell is it your fault? Unless you had a busy morning before I got here."

"I'm—turn off your phone. And you still don't have a CLEO, right?"

Silas switched off his cell phone. "What is it, Aggie?"

She pinched the bridge of her nose and took a deep breath. She felt like she was breathing through a straw. *I don't know why I thought that would calm me down. Mierda, I don't even remember what calm feels like.* "I'm the one who told the media about troxapine. I leaked it to *The Daily Post* last night. I sent something to Kev Hernandez too."

Silas's eyes widened. "You fucking did not."

"Yes, I fucking did. I used the Patch we made to log in and grab the minutes from the directors meeting. It's nothing super incriminating, but it's enough to get people asking questions. But I never intended for...this."

She should have just followed Dr. Hansen's plan and kept her mouth shut. But her guilt had gotten the better of her. She hadn't slept soundly since the ferry—the dead man wouldn't let her. If she told the truth, maybe she'd get some peace.

Her eyes glued to the TV screen as the news station replayed the same loop of footage. This innocent blood was on her hands.

There was no peace for her, only darkness.

"Silas, what have I done? Carajo, what was I *thinking*?"

Silas rejoined her on the couch. "No matter what happens, you did the right thing. People have to know the truth of the danger they could be in." He pulled her into his side, and she hugged him.

"I can't believe how quickly things became violent."

Silas leaned back into the couch and ruffled his dark curls. "A storm has been brewing between the Faction and Pharmatrox for years. Things were bound to ignite eventually."

Great. I started a goddamn war.

Her thoughts must have shown on her face, because Silas backtracked. He took her by the shoulders and looked at her in earnest. "Agnes, do not blame yourself for this, or for whatever comes next. Do you know how many lives you just saved by getting the truth out there? Probably thousands. People will stop taking troxapine, and nobody new will start." He tucked her under his arm and rested his head atop hers. "It's going to be okay."

Her CLEO pinged in her ear, and a hologram of Dr. Hansen's face materialized. "Agnes." Her mentor's light eyes were bloodshot and watery, as if she hadn't slept all night.

"Dr. Hansen! Where are you?"

Shuffling, keys clacking, and shouts sounded in the background. "I'm in the bunker. I'm sure you've seen the news."

"Yes." The guilt was a boulder in her stomach.

"Somehow the media got ahold of the detail about the troxapine. Some goddamn hacker must have gotten into the system and leaked the files. IT is working on figuring it out now."

The boulder got heavier.

"So what does that mean for our plan?"

Dr. Hansen shut her eyes and muted the feed. It was a few seconds before she unmuted herself. Her face was cold steel. "We've lost. Dr. Chun finally clued us in today, and it's worse than I feared. EP designed troxapine to be highly addictive, for some unknown godforsaken reason. Those who have already used it will have a hard time quitting, even if they want to.

"And the ferry wasn't the result of a few pills gone bad. It's the *entire* distributed supply. We can try to recall it, but we have to assume the majority of it has already been used, or will be. In another week, we'll see even more instances like the ferry. There is nothing we can do to stop this. It's already begun. The only thing we can do now is survive."

Agnes gripped Silas's hand as she blinked back tears. Silas couldn't see or hear Dr. Hansen, so he didn't know how dire things were. But from the way he squeezed her hand, she knew he understood.

"There has to be something we can do. Pharmatrox runs the country. It has its hands in everything. It has *power*. That has to mean something. They have to be able to *do something*."

Dr. Hansen rubbed at the notch forming between her eyes. "I agree with you. It's bullshit that we control our own creations. I don't know how long we'll be confined in the bunker, but while I'm here, I'll convince them to send some sort of assistance to the communities. Maybe there's hope yet for all of this to be pulled back. I'll search the databases and see if I can get to the bottom of what else might have gone wrong with troxapine. I suspect Dr. Chun was not being entirely forthcoming."

"How can I help?"

"You can get the hell out of New York. If the Faction is going after Pharmatrox scientists, that's a target on your back. And I fear the riots and violence will only increase if we are unable to find a solution."

"But what about you? What about Evie? I won't abandon you."

Silas went rigid at the mention of Evie.

"We'll be safe here. The bunker is impenetrable and has enough food and water to last a few weeks. Then they'll ship us out of the city in armored car shuttles. Because of the potential for storm surges, coastal flooding, and hurricanes, Pharmatrox was prepared for a siege and an evacuation. We'll be fine. You need to leave."

"What about our work? What—"

"*Agnes.* None of that matters right now. We can build a new lab, a new simulator. We can run new experiments. All of that is replaceable. *You* are not replaceable. I need you to be safe. And that means getting out of New York. Leave the country—I know you won't, but please consider it. Avoid the larger cities. Get out, and take whoever else you can with you."

Agnes stared at Dr. Hansen as tears burned the backs of her eyes. The woman she'd looked up to for her entire career, who had become more than a mentor to her, was asking her to abandon her to whatever fate awaited her in a frenzied New York. Everything in her screamed to run down to the lab and get Evie, Dr. Hansen, Roberto, and everyone else out of there.

Something big was coming. Something bad.

Outside her apartment window, the screams in the streets mingled with the shouts and bluster on Dr. Hansen's end. *I did this. This is my fault.* The words burned into her mind and played on repeat. A broken record of guilt. "Okay."

"I'll see you again soon."

After Dr. Hansen's face disappeared, Agnes flicked off her Patch.

Silas was already stuffing his arms into his jacket.

"Silas, you can't—"

"I didn't hear your entire conversation on that horrid propaganda machine, but I got the gist. It's time to leave. Right?" He pointed outside, where car horns blared and sirens wailed past.

She went to the window. Traffic plugged the streets and people crammed the sidewalks, all heading in the same direction, as if fleeing something...

The inevitability of her situation tightened around her. "Right."

Silas crossed his arms. "I need to get Evie. If the Red Riots breach the Pharmatrox facility, she's dead."

"That facility is the safest place for her. *We're* the ones in danger right now. Just look outside. We need to leave."

Silas shook his head and headed for the door. "No. She's my *sister*, Aggie. I'm not going to leave the city and just hope she's fine. I'm getting her out myself."

"I'm coming with you."

Silas stuck out an arm like a gate. "You can't. Your neighbors know you work for Pharmatrox. If they see you, or if you run into anyone you recognize in the street, who knows how they'll react? Stay here." He pulled her into a hug. She felt small against his big, solid frame. "If I'm not back in an hour, go without me. Text me where you're going, and we'll meet you there. Okay?"

Agnes stared up into her friend's resolute face. She didn't want to be separated, but Silas had made up his mind. It was only for an hour. He'd come back with Evie, and they'd all leave together. It would work. It would be okay. She tucked her face into his chest and held him tightly. "Be safe, you big idiot."

A pit formed in her stomach as she watched him go. She went to the window and waited for him to pop out into the street so she could keep an eye on him. When Silas had long been out of sight, something else kept her attention fastened to the street.

A bevy of people dressed in black and armed with swords, torches, pipes, bats, guns—*Guns?* Some groups across the country had resisted the Leader's ordinance that only Pharmatrox guards were permitted to carry firearms. *These must be other members of the resistance. Faction, maybe?*

The army marched down the center of the street and clogged traffic, heedless of the cars and ambulances attempting to maneuver around them.

Every person in the black-clad army wore a red hardshell mask.

Agnes's blood ran cold, and Evie's voice filtered into her mind. *They're saying it was some guy in a red mask...*

At their helm marched a man in a white mask. A spot of snow in a sea of blood.

Agnes switched off the TV and went to her closet.

She started packing.

Hurry up, Silas. Deprisa.

20

Penny

THE KNIFE LODGED INTO the plywood, dead center in the hand-drawn bullseye.

Penny threw another. It stuck right beside the first.

Her target practice was set up outside the stadium near one of the anti-aircraft weapons. She'd talked to Rodney about making sure they were staffed regularly, otherwise the troxies would bomb them to bits. Of course, it had been her responsibility to find the manpower, but she made a show of asking him for permission first. The stupid idiot.

Mal had been helpful in making sure the stadium had regular guard patrols, but he had his hands full with the numerous skirmishes taking place all over the city.

Throwing knives calmed her, and after the past few weeks, she needed some fucking serenity. She hadn't yet washed off the filth of the morning; dried blood coated her hands and arms. The knife felt heavy in her hand.

"Kill them all."

Rodney's voice in her mind. It sounded the same as the primal hunger that lurked inside her. The beast that would haunt her for the rest of her life. Her hand tightened around the knife hilt.

And killed them all, she had.

A shadow fell across her, and she turned and squinted into the sun.

"Malosi. What do you want?"

Malosi stood with his standard cross-armed posture, big and imposing. "Need to talk to you."

Penny threw the knife at the target. It pinged off the other knife and flew into the grass. "Obviously. What is it?"

"In private."

"Fine."

Penny followed Mal, glancing around the camp. More people than normal buzzed about, and there was something not entirely right...She chalked it up to the fact that they were still adjusting to Kev's absence. But it had been a little less than two months. Things should be more settled, and they only felt more chaotic.

Rodney was up to something.

Since she'd returned, Rodney had boxed her out. He had meetings he didn't include her in, with a new inner circle of people she'd never met. Users, all of them. She knew what he was doing—he wanted her to heel. To understand that her power came from *him*, and if she fell out of favor, she lost her influence. But she didn't know *why* he was doing it. For control, sure. But Mal was onto something, with what he'd warned her about a few weeks ago. Rodney's access to the detox serum played into his plans somehow.

In the meantime, things had been business as usual: raids on troxy warehouses, battles over territory disputes, conflicts in the neutral zones. But an undertone of unease wove through her daily responsibilities. Something wicked was brewing, she just didn't know what it was yet.

She followed Mal inside to one of the old concession stands. He slammed the door behind them.

Oh. He was pissed off. It was always hard to tell. Mal kind of always looked pissed off.

He got in her space and backed her against the wall. She didn't mind; she was used to men blustering and trying to intimidate her.

"Nice fucking mess you left in the streets yesterday," he said.

Penny smiled. "It sent a message."

"*I see you?* What the fuck, Penny? You want everyone to think the Faction is full of psychotic murderers who paint the streets bloody with cryptic serial killer messages?"

"Sure, if that's what you got from it." In her old job, she'd learned some...creative skills for how to sniff out her prey. She'd never killed anyone, but she'd toed the line of legality more than a few times.

He pressed a hand on the wall beside her and leaned in. "Is this a fucking joke to you?"

She hooked her sickle around his wrist and flung it away. "No, Malosi. I don't think any of this is funny. I know the Architect will feel guilty for the blood I spilled. And I know that every time she closes her eyes from now on, she'll see those bodies in the street and know I'm coming for her."

"You're fucking insane."

"I'm fucking *practical*."

"You killed some of our own people in that battle with the troxies."

"They were about to turn. I saw their eyes. Their behaviors. They had to die."

"You murdered a convoy full of Pharmatrox doctors just this morning. Explain that one."

"*Doctors,*" Penny sneered. "Whatever happened to *do no harm*? Their drug did nothing *but* harm. A clean death—which is what I gave them—is kinder than they deserve."

"Not all troxies are evil. Many didn't know how fucking insidious Pharmatrox was until they told them to abandon their culture, their beliefs, their *names*, for the sake of *unity*." It was Mal's turn to sneer. She wondered what other atrocities Pharmatrox had demanded of him. "And by then, it was too late. So maybe don't go around indiscriminately killing anyone just because they're a user or a troxy. We could *use* those people. We could turn them to our side."

"I'm not interested in redeeming troxies. They made their choices." *Yeah, I mean you too, asshole.* She brushed past him out of the room.

When she passed an old souvenir shop down the hall, a guttural growl sounded from behind her. She whipped her sickle as something launched out of the shadows. Sidestepping, she turned to face her attacker. His eyes were onyx black. Teeth formed to sharp points. Fingers curved into claws.

A turned? What the fuck is this thing doing here?

This one was fast and deadly, but she was a more skilled fighter. Years of Muay Thai, while a great outlet for stress, had also given her speedy reflexes and a high tolerance for pain. When the turned lunged in and bit her arm, as she wanted him to, she barely noticed. She hooked her sickle across his throat, and his head tumbled to the ground.

Down the hall, Mal came out of the concession stand and froze. His bright, wide eyes watched her as she kicked the turned's head across the floor. She marched up to him, ready to fight.

"Looks like *somebody* forgot to do their fucking job and establish a perimeter guard." Penny wiped the blood from her arm onto his shirt. It was more than a shallow bite, but she'd be fine. "What exactly are you still here for if you aren't going to protect our camp from the turned and anyone else who wants to wander through?"

Mal's gaze darkened, and he frowned at the blood on his shirt. "I upped security after Rodney's goons tried to make off with some of our volt rifles. I run a tight ship. My troops would never miss a turned barging through camp."

Penny wanted to argue, but Mal was right. She'd noticed the increase in patrols, and even if Mal was irritating, his soldiers were loyal to him. So that left only one explanation for how the turned had gotten into camp: he'd already been there. A user who'd been allowed to use to the point of turning, and no one had killed him first. This reeked of Rodney.

"Have you noticed more people using lately? Acting strangely?" she asked. "Those who never took the dust before are taking it now. And other users are taking more dust than they ever have." She nodded to the headless body leaking black blood. "Rodney is up to something, but he won't tell me."

"So make him tell you."

"Thanks. Great advice. Really, I didn't think of that myself."

"You're so goddamn annoying."

"And you're a pain in my ass. I don't answer to you, Mal. Technically, I'm your commanding officer. So think of that the next time you want to back me into a fucking corner and yell at me."

Mal looked at her with fuming disdain, but he backed off. She *loved* reminding him that he was below her in the ranking structure.

He pointed his chin at her bloody arm. "You all right?"

"Make sure there are no more turned waltzing around camp. That's an order."

Smirking at the way the muscle in his cheek jumped, she turned heel and stormed down the hall.

She had a crazy fuckhead to talk to.

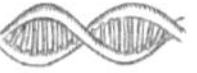

She walked in on Rodney, sitting behind the disheveled desk in his suite-level office, with a needle in his arm. His beady eyes shot up and locked with hers. "I don't remember asking you to come by. You're dripping blood on the floor."

"What are you doing?" She tightened her grip on the doorknob.

Rodney wasn't alone. A skinny woman, two men, and Callum and Toby lounged about the room in various states of dust-induced bliss.

Rodney sighed. "Well. Since you're here. It's the detox serum." He pushed down the syringe's plunger. "Should have me cleaned out and ready to start a new cycle in a few days."

*A new cycle...*Penny's blood ran cold. "What the hell are you talking about?"

"Oh, you haven't heard?" Callum lumbered to his feet, a nasty smile smeared across his face. "Boss has big plans. Big plans for us."

Rodney threw a beer bottle at him, and it smashed against the wall. "Shut up."

Callum held up his hands and sank into the ruined armchair.

"Plans?" *This is very, very bad.*

"We're getting our western sectors back from the troxies," said Rodney.

"Does Malosi know about this?"

Rodney slammed a fist onto his desk. "Fuck Malosi. I'm the one in charge."

"Of course," said Penny. "But his battle strategies could be useful." *He's a skilled goddamn Army sergeant who could actually win the war for us, and you're a dumbass trash-eater stewing in piles of your own filth.*

"I don't trust that fucker," he said. "He's a troxy."

For the first time, Penny did not immediately agree with that sentiment. And it fucking bothered her. But to Rodney, she said, "You're right. Best to keep it between us. How can I help?"

Rodney shoved the vial and syringe into a desk drawer and locked it, eyeing Penny. Assessing. "We're detoxing everyone over the next few days. I want them all clean and ready for a huge dosage."

"Huge dosage?" She was almost afraid to ask.

"Next week, we're taking the fight to the troxies. Need your help distributing the serum."

"Sure thing." *Anything to keep you talking so I can find out what the fuck is going on.*

Rodney patted the drawer. "The detox serum lets us go on and off the dust as much as we want. We can take a fuck ton of dust and never have to worry about turning. All the benefits, no consequences. The ones who get faster and wilder on the dust, we can use them to fight the troxies. Their bloodlust is insatiable. Then we detox them and use them again later in another battle. A never-ending supply of super soldiers."

Are you fucking insane? is what she wanted to say, but she already knew the answer. Rodney was absolutely off his fucking rocker. His cycles of going on and off the dust had only made that more apparent. It was likely what had exacerbated his insanity in the first place. *So that's what you've been doing up here in this office. Taking an absurd amount of drugs and detoxing before you turn.* And he was encouraging others to do the same. More turned like the one she encountered today would be popping up all over camp.

If this was how Rodney had become the crazed man he was, what would it be like to have an entire *army* of people like him?

Fuck, fuck, fuckity fuck.

21

A FEW NIGHTS LATER, Stella stood on Maple Street in front of a house with a green door. It sat at the edge of a neutral zone on a small street of decrepit row homes with overgrown plants and soot-stained windows.

She didn't want to be there.

In the past two days, she'd checked another building off her list and spent hours researching in the library. With the Helix Key, she could access more files than before, but nothing about Pharmatrox HQ or Silas. She couldn't avoid it anymore. She needed to get inside an active Pharmatrox facility, and she had one option left.

She needed Derek. He was her only lead, and she had to take it.

But she didn't have to *like* it.

After everyone at the Outpost had fallen asleep, Stella snuck downtown. A cool breeze swept down the street, carrying with it the scent of wet leaves and fresh dirt. A set of steep, ladder-like stairs beckoned her to the front porch. Not a bad temporary perch, if you could ignore the blood smeared on the windows and the body dangling from the flagpole.

Stella dug in her pocket for the dust and was surprised to find it empty. *Did I forget to bring it? Have I used it already?* She must be going through her supply more quickly than she thought. She had enough dust in her system to keep Death from getting nasty, but it wouldn't last long.

She reached for her necklace and forced her feet up the stairs to the rickety porch. Taking a deep breath, she rapped on Derek's front door. Countless seconds passed. *Maybe this was a dumb idea.*

Footfalls came from within, and Derek's face appeared behind the door. He leaned an arm on the doorjamb. "Sorry about the decor." He nodded to the body swinging behind her. "Keeps the looters and squatters away."

Something about seeing Derek again made her stomach lurch. Or maybe it was just the dead body. *Definitely the dead body.*

Stella brushed past him into the expansive entryway and made a bee-line down the hall. It opened into a kitchen and a large living room with plush white carpet and worn leather couches. A fire burned in the hearth, punctuating the silence with pops and snaps.

"Want to come in?" he asked from behind her. His tone sounded like he was smirking.

"Whiskey." She rifled through the cabinets at random.

Silas had always told her that if you walked with a purpose and looked like you knew what you were doing, you could get away with anything you wanted. She emulated the same confidence as she uncorked a bottle.

"Make yourself at home, woman whose name I still don't know," said Derek. He was, indeed, smirking.

Stella frowned, then took a quick swig and offered the bottle to him.

"Better?" he asked, his dark eyes roaming over her in that same curious way as before.

She nodded once and crossed her arms, ready to strike a bargain or pick a fight. She wasn't sure which. Something about him irked her.

"I didn't expect to see you again." He posted a hip on the counter, a cool confidence etched in every line of his body.

Stella deepened her frown to keep from rolling her eyes. Yeah, he was attractive, but he didn't have to be so *annoying*.

"Have you reconsidered my offer?" Derek poured whiskey into two chipped glasses and passed her one.

"What exactly do you need me to do?" She eyed the drink and took a careful sip.

Derek flashed a smile. "So that's a yes."

This fucking guy. "That's not what I said."

"But we're getting there. Come on, I'll fill you in. But maybe you can start with your name." He grabbed the whiskey and parked on one of the big leather sofas. She settled beside him, keeping her distance.

"Why do you look like you want to punch me?" he asked.

Stella hadn't noticed the hand resting on her leg had curled into a fist. "Because I want to punch you."

He laughed. "At least you're honest."

"And you're irritating. Stop wasting my time."

He sat back and waited.

Her frustration boiled, and she finally said, "Stella."

"Nice to meet you." Derek inclined his glass and drank. "Okay, Stella." He ran a tattooed hand through his hair and blew out a breath. How someone managed to have a good hair day during the apocalypse, she had no idea. "I'd just gotten back to New York after visiting my parents in Gwangju. But hell, I should've stayed in Korea. I showed up during the Red Riots in the Beginning, when the troxies weren't paying much attention to who their captives were. That's when they grabbed me."

She remembered those days. It was how Silas had gotten captured too.

"They took me and some others to a satellite lab north of here in Oakwood—their new HQ in the Capital ran out of space. Apparently, the dust doesn't affect me like it does everyone else, and they wanted to know why. They...experimented on us. It was more like torture."

A cold fist clenched Stella's insides in a fierce grip. Experiments. Torture.

Open your eyes.

Ever since the Beginning, she'd known the troxies were not the white knights they'd proclaimed themselves to be. But this? Torturing people in the name of science? The dust didn't work as intended, that much was obvious—but what was its purpose? And what was Pharmatrox trying to discover now? So many questions clouded her mind. Questions, and one daunting realization. *Are they experimenting on Silas too?*

"One of the guys I was captured with ended up in the cell next to me," continued Derek. "We talked through the air vents. He had a plan to escape, but it went sideways. I was able to get away. I wandered around the city in a fog until the troxy drugs worked out of my system. It took me weeks to feel normal. I have some memory loss of my time there, but I remember enough to find it again."

"Wait—you were a user, and now you're not?" *How the fuck is that even possible?* "You didn't turn, and you didn't die from withdrawal?" That was unheard of—except for Penny, for some reason. "Does this mean there's a cure for the dust?"

Derek swirled the whiskey in his glass. "Something like that. The troxies found a way to 'cure' people when they wanted to test out different dosages on the same person. Kind of like a system reboot. Did it to me a few times, once right before I got out. We timed our escape so that we'd get the detox serum and be able to survive once we left. There's no telling if there are side effects or not, but I've been okay so far. I don't think it works that way for everyone, but this serum, it's the only thing I know of that could help users recover."

She'd never heard of it before, so Pharmatrox must have developed it recently. "Do they have more of it in the facility?"

Rescuing Silas was only half of the victory—if Silas was a user as a result of Pharmatrox's experiments, he'd turn and die anyway. Silas needed the serum, and she did too, if they had any hope of surviving and passing a blood test to get into Canada. It was their only shot.

Derek shrugged. "Probably, but I wouldn't know where to find it. I've been trying to come up with a plan to spring as many prisoners as I can, but without a Patch or a way to navigate inside, I'd be caught before I have the chance to help anyone." His eyes snapped to hers. "That's where you come in. Your Patch will get us into their security system, and you can give me directions. We could find some of the serum too."

"You make it sound easy."

"You have a better plan?"

Stella stifled a grumble. She had no plan, but he didn't need to know that. If she was going to stick her neck out like this, she needed to know if there was a chance Silas was in that facility too, but her hopes weren't high. It was more likely he'd be in a bigger prison, like their HQ. She pulled the grubby photo out of her back pocket and held it out to Derek.

He snatched it out of her hands, eyes wide. "How the fuck did you get this?"

Stella grabbed the photo and swatted him with it. "I'll thank *you* to keep your hands off my stuff." A slight tremor ran through her voice. "What, do you recognize someone?"

He pointed to Silas. "This was the guy in the cell next to mine. Silas Markson."

The sound of a thundering waterfall filled her ears.

"This must be his sister." Derek's fingertip lingered on Evie's face. "He talked about her a lot. Asked me to find her."

Death appeared beside Derek and squinted over his shoulder. "Is this really the best photo you have? My hair looks like a tangled ball of twine."

Taking a steadying breath, she said, "She's dead."

Derek rocked back on his heels and rubbed a hand over his jaw. "You're sure?"

Stella nodded. "They're my best friends. That picture was taken shortly before the Beginning."

A grim look creased Derek's face. "Silas is alive, but his time is running out. I reckon he has maybe a month before...before things get worse. I'm fuzzy on the timeline though. I wish I could remember more details—about the facility, what the troxies said, anything useful—but I was so full of drugs, the whole thing is pretty hazy."

"I'll help you." The words were out of Stella's mouth before she realized she'd said them. But of course she accepted Derek's bargain. What other choice did she have? "How do I know you can follow through on your promise of safe passage to the border?"

"Since I got out, I've made friends with some civilians. They have an in with a Pharmatrox guard. Faction sympathizer, but not a defector. Yet, anyway. He smuggles people into the outbound trucks after they drop off their goods, but he doesn't risk doing it too often. There's another convoy leaving in a few weeks, and I plan to be on it. What about you?" His dark eyes fixed her with such intensity that her breath caught in her throat.

After studying him for a moment, she said, "You could be lying about the convoy. Hell, you could be lying about all of it—Silas, the serum, everything. But that would be very stupid of you, Derek. Because if I find out you used me, I'll kill you myself."

His lips twitched. "I'd expect nothing less."

"Shut up. If you're not lying, I need to get Silas out of there right now, and I need that detox serum. So I'll do it."

Derek cracked a smile, and she held up her hand.

"I want to speak to your Pharmatrox guard. Give me his name and I'll find him."

She could tap into his Patch and speak to him if she got within range of his comms. Her Patch would disguise her voice and output it as an AI-generated track, so she didn't have to worry about his CLEO recognizing her voice patterns.

"Done." Derek stuck out a tattooed hand.

She shook it, but didn't feel entirely good about it. *Think of Silas. You're getting him out. Hopefully. If Derek isn't a maldito mentiroso.* And if he was, at least she'd get into a facility and get the files she needed. Her eyes traced his tattoos all the way up his arm, to where they disappeared under his shirtsleeve, then finally landed on his face.

She released his hand, heat creeping up her neck, and took another mouthful of whiskey to give herself something to do. "So, what's the plan?"

A slow grin spread across Derek's face, and she knew this was a bad idea.

22

EIGHT YEARS AGO

A GNES LEANED ON THE counter next to Evie and took a sip of champagne as a rotten smell drifted from the kitchen's clogged pipes.

"How's it going down there?" Agnes asked the torso sticking out from under her sink.

A smattering of muttered curses filtered from below. "Is it absolutely essential that you continue living in this archaic apartment building?"

Agnes smiled into her drink. "I like the architecture, Silas. And it is hardly ancient. We can't all afford to live in luxury towers."

When Silas wasn't designing virtual reality experiences or high-tech network security systems for an endless list of technology companies and rich clients, he fancied himself a handyman. But Agnes thought it had more to do with his stubborn inability to allow common household appliances to outsmart him rather than a genuine interest in fixing things. Luckily Silas had been there when her temperamental garbage disposal decided to spew shredded food all over her kitchen.

"Here, have another tool thingy," said Evie. She thrust a wrench under the sink, and Silas grabbed it with a grumble. Evie was in charge of handing Silas the proper tool from his bag, but she was more interested in the cheesy pizza on the counter. She took a bite and smiled. "Hurry up with the repairs so we can get on with the party. This is supposed to be a celebration, not a home improvement show."

Silas grunted as he fought with the wrench. "Maybe that new job will pay you enough to move out of this hole in the wall, Agnes."

She snorted. "It's not that bad."

More clanking from below.

"Still chasing that gorgeous barista at the bagel place?" Agnes asked Silas.

Evie grinned and answered for him. "Ivan finally agreed to go out with him yesterday. It only took Silas about half a dozen attempts."

Another grinding sound from under the sink. "Thanks for explaining that in a not at all embarrassing way."

"He's still got it." Evie prodded Silas's foot with a good-natured poke.

"Inviting him to Morocco to meet your parents yet?" Agnes teased.

"Aha! Vindicated." Silas crawled out from under the sink with a triumphant grin. "And Ivan should be so lucky. Fatima and Hal are a delight. When they're not chiding me for 'building games' instead of starting my own technology empire." Silas rolled his eyes and took a bite of pizza from Evie's piece.

Evie yanked it away and wagged a finger at him. "I know mama and baba *love* it when you call them by their first names. Really. It's their favorite thing. Keep doing it. I'll call them up right now." Her finger drifted toward her Patch.

Agnes chuckled. Mr. and Mrs. Markson would always be Mr. and Mrs. Markson, even though Agnes had known them and had been best friends with their kids for most of her life.

Silas snatched Evie's hand back to her side. "I didn't realize my sister was pure evil."

"Ew, gross. Don't touch me with your garbage disposal hands."

Agnes nudged a champagne flute toward him. "Thanks for digging around under my sink. You really can fix anything, can't you?"

As Silas washed and dried his hands, he said, "I'm not just a computer genius. I'm a general genius as well. Cheers to Aggie and her new job." He lifted a glass and they all drank. "So you got the job at Ruhi's place? I knew she'd love you."

Agnes and Evie exchanged a look. He wasn't going to take this well.

"I took the job at Pharmatrox with Dr. Hansen."

Silas put down his glass, his pulse jumping in his temple. "I thought you said you were excited about running your own department at Vesper Tech. What changed?"

"Dr. Hansen called and asked me to partner with her on her latest gene editing project. It's the opportunity of a lifetime, Silas. Think of how much more I'll learn working *with* her!" Agnes squeezed his arm. "It's what I've always wanted, ever since she was a guest lecturer at NYU. Her encouraging emails and phone calls were sometimes the only things that got me through. I'm really grateful for you setting things up with Ruhi, but I couldn't turn down the chance to work with Dr. Hansen. You have to understand that."

Silas clenched his teeth and grabbed a Stella Artois from the ice bucket on the counter. He took a long pull before he spoke. His voice was a frozen lake. "You know my feelings about Pharmatrox."

"Si," Evie said in a warning tone.

Silas rounded on his sister. "And dammit, Evie, you know too."

Evie sighed. "Not this again. I didn't take the job with Ruhi last year because I didn't want to be a research assistant. Please stop telling me my employer is a cancer that has infected the country with its propaganda. You're starting to sound like that Hernandez guy."

Silas ground his teeth together. "Kev started as just a nuisance, but now he's *organized*. He's training his followers. You shouldn't be walking home alone anymore. Not after that Pharmatrox woman got beaten to death by a few guys in red-painted hockey masks."

Agnes choked on her champagne. "What?"

"It happened a few days ago. But I'm sure Pharmatrox did everything they could to keep it out of the newsfeeds. I heard about it at work."

"Stop it, Si," said Evie. "Tonight is supposed to be about celebrating Agnes. Can we get back to having a nice time?"

Silas glared. "I'm serious, Evie. You need to hear this too. Being a troxy, I mean, a scientist working for Pharmatrox, that's a target on your back. This isn't the first time someone in a white lab coat has turned up dead. And I worry the pile of bodies is only going to grow. You've already been at Pharmatrox, what, a year now? You can quit and get another job without new employers seeing it as a black mark on your record. Ruhi could help you out."

"I love you, big brother. But you need to let me live my own life and get my own jobs. Your anti-Pharmatrox attitude has really skyrocketed these past few years. What's changed?"

"I see what Pharmatrox is doing. How they're wheedling their way into people's lives. The Patches they implant on their employees—how long before they try to do that to the entire population?"

Evie pointed at him with her piece of pizza before taking a bite. "You're being alarmist."

Agnes fidgeted with her ear. She agreed, but...

"Am I?" He pointed to Agnes. "How long was it after accepting the job that they put that chip in you?"

Agnes yanked her hand away from her Patch. After the call with Dr. Hansen, she'd gone to the Pharmatrox lab in Manhattan to receive her

ID badge for her first day. They also placed a Patch behind her ear. "I'm an employee now. Of course I have one. I need it to do my job."

"And how long before Pharmatrox is convincing people that they, too, need some bit of Pharmatrox-owned technology living inside their heads?"

Evie dabbed at her mouth with a napkin and said, "That's a bit over the top, don't you think?"

He slammed his bottle down, beer sloshing out. "They've already adapted their labs' CLEOs into personal cell phone devices and distributed them to everyone in the country. So no, I don't think it's over the top to suggest that they'd want even more of an intimate window into people's lives than what they already have."

Evie opened a beer and took a drink. "What's your point, Silas?"

"It's not a good idea to be involved with Pharmatrox. Especially right now. Tensions with the Faction are growing day by day, and I can understand why," he said. "Inflation is killing us, wages are stagnant, and honestly? That 'free' Pharmatrox healthcare isn't enough to make up for any of it. It's not even *free* anymore. Pharmatrox has just kept on rolling with that healthcare contract they won during the Sickness, and now they're hiking their prices. They have a monopoly on the entire healthcare system, and they practically run the government through the Leader. We're hardly better off than we were under that fascist billionaire who called himself president.

"And people are getting angry—the ones who stayed behind and didn't emigrate elsewhere, anyway. Hernandez blames Pharmatrox for our slow recovery, and I'm inclined to agree with him. It's been twenty-two years since the Sickness. Things should be better by now, right? It's almost like they're trying to keep us under their thumb."

Evie scoffed. "People aren't dying in droves anymore. I'd say things are better."

Silas dropped a fist on the counter, and the glasses rattled. "You're not seeing the bigger picture, Evie. What if Pharmatrox isn't the benevolent liberator we thought it was? Corporations and billionaires have been running the country for decades, but at least they had the decency to try and hide behind 'democracy.' But now that's completely out the window. The troxies stripped us of our religion, of our identities, and replaced them with *Pharmatrox.* They're just another fascist billionaire that stepped in to replace the ones before them. The Faction sees that. I see that. How can you not? How can you willingly *join them?*"

Agnes had heard his arguments before, but she couldn't agree. Working with Dr. Hansen was a dream come true. It would take her professional career into the stratosphere, and she could make a real difference in real people's lives.

"It's because of Pharmatrox that we're even here to talk about this," said Agnes. "Would you rather be like Europe? Do you even remember France's mortality rate? They'll never recover."

"And you think we *have* recovered?" Silas huffed. "What about your mom's journal? Would the woman who wrote those words want this kind of life for you? A life where you're in danger because of your chosen occupation? And what about your dad?"

Agnes crossed her arms. "Don't play the dead parents card, Silas. It's not becoming." She sighed. "Papá always said Mom wanted the best for me. That everything she ever did, every decision she ever made, was for *me.* So I could have a better life."

Silas reached across the counter and grasped her hand. "Are we sure that Pharmatrox and the Leader can offer you—offer *us*—that better life?"

"Why are you so sure they can't?" Agnes took a vitamin bottle out of her purse and shook it. "It's because of them that medication is readily available. We'll never have a shortage again. I'll be writing software for a computer simulation that will one day cure cancer. *Cancer*, Silas. All because Pharmatrox is funding it and the Leader has made it a priority. That seems like a better life to me."

Silas shook his head. "And you think their motives are altruistic? Don't let them manipulate you. You too, Evie. You should both go work somewhere else. At Ruhi's place, at my company. Anywhere else. Please."

Agnes moved to retreat to the other side of the room, but Silas grabbed her hand, pleading. "Open your eyes, Aggie. Open your eyes."

23

"OKAY," SAID QUENTIN, "THE first rule of climbing is don't look down. Unless you want to be frozen in fear while dangling three stories off the ground, with nothing but your own two hands to keep you from falling to your death."

Stella didn't look at him, but she knew he was smirking.

"Thank you for that detailed and unnecessary explanation." She looked at the house, the leaves crunching underfoot as she shifted around. The air was warm, but the cool breeze held a hint of fall and carried with it the permanent singed scent of the Capital.

"This beauty has lots of handholds, so it should be easy enough," said Quentin, smiling at the curled paint chips and broken windows like old friends.

The house stood on the edge of a small park lined with trees. The homes in this neutral sector of the city were old-fashioned brick structures painted in bright jewel tones with wraparound porches, steeply pitched roofs, and round turrets with conical tops.

Stella had started using less of the dust; her stash was running low, and she needed to make it last until she found the detox serum. It had been three days, and she had a constant splitting headache. So she'd asked Quentin to teach her to climb. A small amount of adrenaline replicated some of the dust's effects and helped her feel less shaky; too much had the opposite effect. Death had partially dissolved into the darkness of her mind, but she still made occasional snarky appearances.

The climbing skills would come in handy too, whenever she and Derek broke into the troxy prison in two days—but Quentin didn't need to know that. Derek's troxy guard, Will, was legit, and the convoy to the border was indeed set to leave in a few weeks. Derek was not a maldito mentiroso. At least about that.

"Are you sure you don't want to start climbing on something less likely to maim you if you fall?" asked Quentin. "A stubby tree perhaps?"

Stella shot him a sidelong glance. "Thanks for the vote of confidence, Quent." Her nerves jangled, but she felt more acute by the second. "I've got this."

Quentin looked encouraging, if slightly skeptical.

Death gave her a thumbs-up through one of the streaky windows.

After what felt like hours later to her dust-deprived body, Stella hauled herself over the last ledge and perched on the eaves of the old home. The searing sun blistered away the lingering jitters, and an exhausted smile lit her sweaty face.

Until Quentin glided up to the eaves beside her, making the climb in a fraction of the time.

Little bastard.

Across the tiny park, the city splayed open at their feet. The juxtaposition between old and new was jarring. Beyond the square of old brick houses, a shiny dome of sloping steel glinted in the sunlight—the silent SubTran station. Stella's air traffic control tower stood in the distance like a spectral sentinel. A bitter pang of homesickness—and not just for her airport—plucked her heartstrings, its discord ringing in her ears.

"What are you thinking about?" Quentin asked, startling her out of her trench of nostalgia.

"Home," she said with a bitter smile. She shook off the weight of memory and turned to him. "Where was home for you?"

"Upstate New York," he replied. "It was beautiful—mountains to climb, pretty little fishing rivers, farmland. Open spaces where you could see the stars. It was a quiet place, a private work of art." His smile reached all the way to his toes.

"Is that where you learned to climb like a spider monkey?"

He flashed a mischievous grin. "I grew up climbing trees and mountains before I could run in a straight line. I tried to practice on the house too, but my mom always yelled at me. We lived in the country, so there wasn't much else to do."

He got a faraway look in his eyes, and a smile ghosted across his lips. She found herself smiling too, at the thought of a baby Quentin toddling on the roofline.

"How exactly did you end up with Tara and Lawrence again?" she asked.

His sunny smile darkened. "After Manhattan fell, I hopped on one of the refugee buses outside Newark that was shipping people to the Capital, back when we thought it was the safest place on the East Coast. Tara found me. I was hurt pretty bad." He tucked his elbows close to his sides, shielding the secret scars writhing beneath his shirt.

"I was trapped in a fire." A halting breath rattled in his chest as he picked his way through the minefield of his story. "In the Beginning, during the Red Riots, a user set my house on fire. My...my whole family was trapped. My parents, my sister. But I got out. I was the only one who got out."

Stella reached out a hand, and he gripped it hard. She knew too well the haunting power of memory.

"You still have a family, Quentin." She surprised herself with how much she meant it.

Something in Quentin's face changed, and he threw himself at her in a bony hug. Bewildered, she held him, and for once, she didn't feel awkward hugging him.

He pulled away and snuffled into the collar of his tee shirt, then said, "How'd you end up living in that airport? Strange place to call home."

Stella squirmed under the sudden change of spotlight. "I used to live in Hoboken. I worked in Manhattan, but I got out before Containment." She bit her tongue to stop that train of thought. The kid was easy to talk to. "I never knew my mother, and my father died when I was a teenager. I fell in with a group early on, after the Beginning." *More like band of thieves and thugs.* "We parted ways after a time because I figured I was better off alone." *Better alone than dead.* "And then you fell through my ceiling and haven't stopped bugging me since." She bumped his shoulder with a smile.

They fell into a companionable silence as they shared the remainder of Quentin's canteen.

"Where did you sneak off to the other day?" he asked. "A few days ago, I noticed you disappeared in the middle of the night."

Stella choked. "What?" She thought no one had noticed her absence when she'd gone to Maple Street.

Quentin flashed a knowing smile. "You're talking to the *master* of sneaking off. The whole 'escaping under cover of darkness to some undisclosed location and returning while everyone else is still slumbering' thing? I *invented* that. But you're stealthier than the average person, I'll give you that."

Stella bit her cheek and hoped to avoid answering.

He leaned closer and peered at her. "You went to see him, didn't you? The super tatted Indiana Jones guy."

Damn. Her mind raced as she scrambled to come up with a good excuse.

Quentin laced his hands under his chin and batted his eyes. "Did he wrap you in his strong arms and never let go? Did his passionate gaze hold you captive and make you feel things?"

Stella's mouth popped open, and heat flooded her face. "I—what?"

Quentin rolled with laughter, and she moved to rumple his hair, but he dodged.

"He does have the tall, dark, and handsome thing going for him. Well, except for the tall part. And I'm not the proper authority to say if he's handsome or not. But dark, he's got that one down. Creeptastic vibes, for sure." Quentin snickered when she shoved him. "Okay fine, don't tell me what you were up to. I'll find out eventually. You can't keep secrets from me." He stuck out his tongue.

"I can and I will."

She gave his arm a playful punch, but inside, the darkness rippled like a shark's hidden fin just below the waves. Her pile of secrets grew.

24

IS THIS REALLY THE best mode of transportation?" asked Stella. "We want to sneak up on the troxies, not herald our approach with a fanfare of engine revving."

"Ha-ha," Derek said, wiping the grease from his hands on a rag. "Unless you want to walk, this is our only option. And it'll make for a speedy getaway, if it comes to that."

The motorcycle lounged regally by the curb in front of Derek's house like a noble steed and blended in with the night's darkness.

When Stella frowned, Derek sighed. "I've been riding this thing all over the Capital and haven't gotten caught. It's fast, and that's what we need. I'm fresh out of other vehicle options, unless you feel like stealing another one."

She didn't like the idea of having to hold onto him when they rode, but she didn't see a way out of it. "Are we clear on the plan, then?"

Derek parked a hip on the garage workbench across from her. "The hatch on the roof should get us into the air duct system. There's an empty office in the northwest corner of the top floor. We can drop in there."

Stella's palms started to sweat at the thought of actually having to put her climbing skills to the test.

"All while remaining undetected by Pharmatrox's state-of-the-art security system ready to alert everyone to our presence," she said.

"I thought that part goes without saying."

Stella made a face, and a dimple flashed in Derek's cheek.

"That's actually the easy part—and why I need you."

He folded his arms, and her gaze went straight to his biceps. Quentin's earlier taunts popped into her head, and her cheeks warmed. *Goddamn it, tía. Get your head out of your ass.* This guy, however charming and attractive, was a stranger. And he was on her shit list.

"I'll get Silas while you make sure we stay invisible and find where they keep the serum." Derek tapped his right ear. "My Patch that you so helpfully supplied is only good for comms—you're the one with the clearance levels."

Stella nodded, tumbling the plan in her mind and looking for stains of uncertainty. "And how do we get out—alive and undetected—once we free Silas?"

"We swipe some guard uniforms or lab coats and walk out in plain sight. There's a busy side exit on the ground floor for security personnel. Would be easy to blend into the crowd."

Stella frowned and leaned against the workbench. "Is that how you got out last time?"

Derek nodded as he continued stuffing knives and other weapons into his bag. He left his gun behind—he was out of bullets.

She didn't feel great about trying the same plan twice, but it was too late to back out. Penny could be closing in any day now. Silas was running out of time. And tonight was their best chance at rescuing him. Pharmatrox and the Faction were locked into an intense battle on the western side of the city. The perfect distraction.

Derek's dark eyes bore into hers. "Are you coming or not?" he asked, donning his helmet and flipping down the visor.

She grumbled and grabbed the spare helmet from the shelf. "Next time, *I* make the plan."

They headed to the outskirts of the city and took a narrow road heading north.

Apprehension flowed through Stella, bright and buzzing. She'd been longing for this day for months, but their escape route made her nervous, burning a hole through her concentration. *Save Silas first, worry about escape later.* She had to succeed. She *would*.

About a half mile from the Pharmatrox facility, Derek killed the engine and hid the motorcycle in some bushes. After a silent jog of about ten minutes, Pharmatrox's Oakwood facility loomed out of the darkness.

The building's rough white stone glowed in the moonlight. The windows were dark and opaque—nobody could see in or out. Waist-high bushes bordered the entire property in a lush green frame, and behind the bushes, a black wrought iron fence sprung from the ground and pierced the night sky like thousands of arrows. Two guards stood at the front door, volt rifles clutched in their meaty fists.

"Only two guards?" Stella said.

Derek pointed to some trees at various locations on the perimeter. "Cameras there, there, and there. If we head to the back, there's a blind spot and the shadows will give us some cover."

The pair inched around the hedges until they were behind the building, away from watchful eyes, both human and camera alike. She didn't want to risk using her Patch's jammer and put the facility on lockdown and high alert.

Stella studied the twelve-story building through a gap in the fence, mentally charting her climbing course, as budding anxiety swelled in her chest. There were fewer windows than she had thought—which meant fewer handholds.

Derek watched her with a question in his gaze.

"Quiet," she said without looking at him.

"I didn't—"

"Shush! You're going to ask me if I think I can do it, and I don't know, Derek. Be quiet and let me think."

Eleven rows of dark windows. The first floor didn't have any, so she'd need a boost to grab the first windowsill on the second story. Her eyes darted diagonally upward to the bottom of the next window. It was a reach, but she could do it. She only had to do it right eleven times, and then she'd be at the top.

Death materialized beside her and gave a low whistle. "No room for mistakes. Good luck with that."

Carajo. A cold sweat frosted Stella's forehead. Her head pounded and she longed for the dust. Licking her lips, she turned to Derek. "I can do it."

She hitched her small pack flush against her back, and they climbed over the fence. She went to step out of the shadows, but Derek stopped her, an unreadable look on his face. Her heart hammered in her throat. *It's just the adrenaline.*

He reached for her—

Then let his hand drop, clearing his throat. "Just—don't fall, okay?"

Her eyes rolled skyward, and she crossed her arms to hide the goose bumps rippling across her skin. *It's just the withdrawal.* "That's not exactly the pep talk I need to hear," she said and tapped her Patch off. "No comms until I get to the top."

She couldn't afford distractions. As she looked up the sheer face of the stone building she was about to climb, all thoughts flooded out of her, replaced by a cold orb of fear.

She heard Quentin's voice in her mind. *You've climbed trees taller than this.* She definitely hadn't, but the thought of Quentin cheering her on brought her comfort and gave her the confidence to reach for her first handhold.

Derek hoisted her up to grab the first windowsill, and she pulled herself up until she was standing spread-eagled in the window.

Okay, said Quentin's voice in her mind, *just like you visualized.*

She grabbed the next windowsill. The rough stone provided traction for her boots as she scrambled across with her feet.

Only ten more windows to go.

Stella's nerves hollowed her stomach and tightened her throat. After the third floor, she got into a climbing groove. *Reach, grab, shimmy. Repeat.* Her eyes wanted to dart around, but she glued them to her hands. She could almost forget she was a hundred feet in the air.

Reach, grab, shimmy. Repeat.

Sweat dripped in her eye, and she blinked it away with an irritated shake of her head.

Reach, grab, shimmy. Repeat.

She made it eleven stories before she made a mistake.

On the last window, a disturbance sounded below, and she looked down and saw a guard making his rounds. Derek dove behind the nearest bush, narrowly avoiding detection.

With dizzying realization, she saw how high she was. Dangling in the air. Without a rope.

She squeezed herself tight against the window and shut her eyes, but her knees wobbled from fatigue. Doubt flashed through her and ignited the fuse of her panic.

In an instant, she could feel everything she'd been ignoring the whole climb. The furious ache of her shoulders and forearms. Her bleeding and cracked fingernails. Needles of pain in her shins and feet.

She needed the dust. She wasn't going to make it. *What the fuck was I thinking?*

There's no going back down unless you want to fall. Quentin, the voice of reason. *And that's a one-way ticket.*

Stella steeled herself and reached for the last handhold, then shifted her weight, bringing her other hand to the windowsill—

And slipped.

She bit her tongue to keep from screaming as she dangled by her fingertips. The tendons in her forearm popped from the strain and sent jolts of white-hot pain up her arm. As her body swung away from the building, she got another good look at the ground, and her stomach tried to force its contents up her throat.

Within seconds, her fingers started to slip.

Death stared at her from the top of the building. "Silas needs you. Get moving."

Stella grunted against the pain and tightened her grip, flailing her feet until they found purchase. She used the slight leverage to inch her right hand over, finger by finger, to make room for her other hand to grab the sill beside it.

She summoned the remainder of her strength to pull herself until she stood in the last window frame, then grasped the lip at the top of the building. *One last pull...*

Finally, she rolled over the side and collapsed onto the safety of the rooftop. Her whole body felt like Jell-O as she lay quivering on the cement. The realization of how close she'd come to falling to her death weighed heavy on her chest, and she took a deep breath, savoring the feel of the cool night air saturating her lungs.

In the center of the vast roof sat a small hut of ventilation equipment and a door to the top floor of the facility. She crept over—and ducked behind the hut.

An armed guard paced along the opposite side of the roof, but he hadn't seen her. Her ascent must have been blocked from his view by the ventilation hut.

She slipped out her boot knife and leapt on the guard's back, snaking her arms around his neck in a choke hold and tucking her heels tight against his thighs.

The guard spluttered and tucked his chin, falling back on top of her and knocking the wind out of her. He drove his shoulder into her diaphragm, but she sank her knife in his throat to the hilt. Blood gurgled out of the wound, and he stopped struggling.

Stella jogged back to where she'd ascended and dug in her pack. She took half a hit of dust with a shaky hand, and instantly, she steadied. Grabbing the rope from her pack, she tied one end around her waist, and the other she tossed below to Derek. Then she sat and braced her feet against the wall to counterbalance Derek's weight as he walked up the side of the building.

By the time he appeared, Stella was nearly spent.

"What happened?" Derek asked, his eyes wide. "Why are you covered in blood?"

She glowered at him. "I think what you meant to say was 'Thank you, Stella, for risking your life to help me, a mere idiot, and for disposing of that guard we didn't know was up here.'"

Derek rubbed his neck and looked abashed as she got to her feet.

"Let's go," she said. She went to brush past him and head toward the door, but he grabbed her arm and pulled her close. The urge to punch him was strong, but a solemn look smoothed his brow and she resisted.

"Are you all right?" he said in a low voice.

"Yes."

A slight grin pulled his lips, and he gave her a gentle squeeze just below her elbow. "Okay, then."

Derek donned the dead guard's uniform jacket, removed the air duct panel in the ventilation hut with a screwdriver, and they ducked inside. It sloped sharply downward and into the top floor of the building. There was enough room for Stella to wriggle on her hands and knees, but metal pressed close on both sides.

"I feel like a sardine," she said. She heard Derek chuckle as he crawled behind her.

"Take that opening on the left."

She turned and paused over a grating, peering down into the room.

"That should be the empty office," said Derek.

He passed her the screwdriver, and after a brief quarrel with the screws, she jimmied the grate free. It almost slipped through her fingers, but she swiped it at the last second.

"All good?" Derek asked from behind her.

"Yep." Her heart pounded at the close call.

She poked her head into the room. Empty, just as Derek had predicted.

Stella dropped through the ceiling into the small and sparsely furnished corner office, landing in a crouch. She tapped her Patch to check the connection. "Derek? Can you hear me?"

"Loud and clear." He gave her a salute from above.

Stella twisted the stolen Helix Key into the port and swiped open the network, then entered a few lines of code into the command terminal to temporarily disarm the floor's security. Another swipe pulled up a building map, and she expanded the file into a glowing blue 3D model. She played with the layout of the twelfth floor, zooming in with a pinch of her fingers.

"There's an air vent near a closet down this hallway." She pointed to the position in the 3D map. "Head there, then make your entry. I'll guide you through the hallways from there once I get eyes on the guards. Make sure your Patch's tracker is off."

"Got it," said Derek, then he disappeared into the air duct.

Stella pulled up the security feed of the building and threw it onto the projection wall. Every corridor and cell in the building was displayed in a glowing blue web. She pulled open another monitor and scanned the building records for a storeroom or anywhere they might keep the detox serum.

"What's up, person who is definitely Sara Ellis?" Turi's smirk popped into existence inches from Stella's face.

"Hijo de puta, Turi." Stella cut her comms feed with Derek. "What is your problem?"

"Big network connection here. Thought I'd help you out." Turi rubbed her hands together. "What are we looking for?"

"Scan the building for anything that looks like a medicine storeroom. Probably big, lots of security, near the labs. Also download a list of Pharmatrox facilities, prisoner records, and anything else super classified that looks interesting." If Derek was lying about Silas being here, she'd need that list.

"Oho! Girlie got herself a Helix Key. Yes! I love sticking it to the man. I'm on it."

"I'm about to drop in," Derek said. "Is it clear?"

Stella glanced at the map, free of the red dots that indicated guards. With a delicate twist of her fingers, she selected the wing where Derek waited in the ceiling and clicked on the security camera feeds. She rerouted them to only show on her monitor—no one else in the building would be able to access them while she was logged in. Perks of Helix Key access.

"All clear. Take the next right. Stop at the elevators."

Stella frowned at the map that displayed the security guards' locations. Their blinking red dots peppered every floor—except for where Derek was. Her stomach churned. She didn't like coincidences.

"I'm grabbing you a ride. Hang on." She tapped a few keys, bringing the elevator to him and rerouting its cameras. "Sixth floor."

"I remember," he said in a dark tone as he entered and hit the button with a vicious poke. She could only imagine what nightmares he was reliving.

"Got a few places for you to check out," said Turi. "Big vaults on the third and fifth floors, and the basement too. Could have some super fancy expensive drugs in there."

"Can you narrow it down for me at all?"

They wouldn't have time to check too many locations while remaining undetected *and* still escape with their heads attached to their shoulders.

Turi screwed up her face in a look of concentration. "I'd say basement and fifth are your best choices. Fifth is the first floor of prisoner cells, and the basement is *huge*."

"How's that list coming?"

"Already downloaded the facility locations. Still looking for the prisoner records."

That's weird. At least I got one thing I came for. Just need Silas.

"Also, search the Pharmatrox servers and see if Dr. Hansen has logged in since the last time we checked."

"Sorry, boss," said Turi. "I've still got nothing."

Damn. She hadn't seen or heard from Dr. Hansen in over eight months, but that didn't have to mean anything bad. She could be in hiding, she could...*be a prisoner. Or dead.* Stella switched off that unhelpful train of thought. She couldn't afford to lose herself to grief right now.

Derek stepped out of the elevator and into a deserted hall, rushing toward his old cell.

It was all too easy, and Stella didn't like it, so she turned the 3D map in her hand as she searched for any errant red dots where they shouldn't be. She hoped they hadn't moved Silas to a new cell. The computer had cells labeled by number, not by name, so Stella wouldn't be able to find him without knowing his number. Not even Turi would be able to help.

Derek arrived at the cell's door, and Stella opened it for him. After he slipped inside, Stella gestured, and the video feed from inside the cell expanded to fill the projection wall.

But it wasn't Silas's cell.

It was empty.

No.

"Stella?" Derek said, his voice hoarse. "He's not here."

She pulled up all the prisoner cell feeds on that floor. Empty. She checked the fifth, seventh, eighth. All of them, empty.

Fuck.

A sound like static filled Stella's ears as she held onto the thin thread of reality slipping through her fingers. *He's not here. He's not here.*

"Stella, did you hear me?" said Derek. "He's gone."

Stella licked her lips turned dry as sand. "They're all gone, Derek. There are no prisoners in this facility. I checked all the feeds. Pharmatrox must have moved them." *Or...No. They just moved them somewhere else. Please let that be true.* The alternative was unthinkable. "Maybe they were afraid of another escape attempt. What do we do now?"

"We get the hell out of here, and we keep looking. We'll find him, Stella. I promise."

She pounded a fist on the desk, nearly shattering the glass top, and packed away her rage to deal with later. Right now, the only thing that mattered was getting the detox serum and living to fight another day.

Stella watched Derek's departure and scanned the building layout for danger.

"Time to go," said Turi, pointing at a cluster of blinking red dots heading straight for Stella. It was probably just a regular patrol; they weren't moving quickly.

"Shit. Derek? I'll meet you at the side exit. You're on your own."

"Roger."

Stella gestured to close the hologram video window, but not before she caught sight of an icon in the corner. It looked like...*A phoenix. Could it be about the Phoenix Trials?* She glanced at the building layout. Only a few seconds remained before the red dots were upon her, so she pinched the folder with her fingers and downloaded it to her Patch to investigate later.

Stella grabbed the white lab coat on the back of the desk chair and pulled it on over her leather jacket, clipping her old Pharmatrox ID to the coat pocket. She had different hair now, but her face was still the same.

Assuming her old identity, she stepped into the hallway and hurried away. She'd check the storerooms that Turi had mentioned on her way down to meet Derek.

The footfalls of many boots pounded behind her as the guards neared the office she'd just vacated. She maintained her pace and didn't look back.

A surly guard stepped out from a side hallway and planted himself in her path.

"Can I help you?" She looked down her nose at the man and crossed her arms. Her tone gave him pause. "Well?"

"Oh, ah, just a routine security check. We're checking all IDs. Ma'am."

Stella frowned. "What's your name?"

Sweat stippled his upper lip, and he gulped. "Officer Clintock, ma'am."

She glanced at her ID hanging in clear view and lifted an eyebrow. "Well, *Officer*. Wouldn't you say it looks like I am where I'm supposed to be?" When his head bobbed obediently, she said, "Now, if you'll excuse me, I'm expected in lab forty-one."

"Yes, ma'am. Of course. My apologies."

He stepped out of her way, and Stella rushed past him as if she were late for a meeting. She had no idea if lab forty-one was a thing, but Officer Clintock probably didn't either.

Once she hit the stairwell, she ran, leaping down flights in a single bound. She made it to the sixth floor before she hit trouble.

A group of four troxies huddled close in conversation as they ascended the stairs. Stella's heart pounded, and her hand twitched toward the knife hidden beneath her coat. As she brushed past them, she ducked her head.

Stella's foot touched the landing below when the alarm sounded, red lights flashing and a siren blaring through the stairwell. The four troxies looked around in confusion—their eyes found Stella.

"Hey!" said one of them.

Stella disappeared in a swish of her lab coat. Footfalls pursued her, but she was faster.

When she burst onto the ground floor, everything was in a flurry. Troxies zigzagged across the white-tiled atrium, and guards stomped through the wide hall in a tight formation. Stella plastered a frantic look on her face and mirrored the troxies' urgency as she ran toward the side exit and slipped outside into the cool night air.

When a pair of headlights burst through the darkness, illuminating her like a spotlight, she gripped her knife hilt and tensed.

"You there. You're coming with me."

Something about the deep voice was familiar, and she squinted into the headlights but couldn't make out the driver.

The door of the armored van opened, and a pair of heavy boots crunched in the gravel—

"Derek!" Stella shoved him.

"Get in the van," he said in the deeper voice, ducking her punches and laughing.

"How'd you get this?" she asked as she jumped into the van.

"Nicked a keycard from the security office on my way down." He shoved the card in a slot beside the steering wheel, and the electric engine started up. "Had to fight a guard. He clocked me a good one. Broke my Patch." The tires squealed as he peeled down the drive toward the front gates, and Stella gripped the door handle to keep from bouncing out of her seat. "After I sounded the alarm, everyone panicked, and they weren't looking too closely at anyone dressed like a guard."

"*After you sounded the alarm?* You did that on *purpose*?" She punched his shoulder. "Derek, I was trapped in a goddamn stairwell right beside a bunch of troxies. You couldn't have warned me that pulling the alarm was part of your exit strategy?"

The van approached the front gate, and the guards at the checkpoint waved for them to stop.

"My Patch was broken. I had to improvise. Much like I'm doing now." Derek rolled down the window and spoke in his deep, gruff voice again. "Cargo transport. New batch of troxapine. With the security breach, they want it moved downtown."

The guard eyed Derek dubiously. "ID."

Derek hesitated.

"Here." Stella leaned into the light and held out her own Pharmatrox ID, and the guard's eyes bulged as he caught sight of her face.

"My apologies, I didn't recognize you with the, ah, poor lighting. Please, proceed." Without checking her ID, he gave an awkward salute and waved them through. Stella nodded curtly to hide her bafflement.

As Derek headed toward the freeway, he asked, "What the hell was that?"

Stella shrugged. She'd never gotten that kind of reaction before at her lab. Unease stirred her thoughts into anxious whirlpools.

"Did you get the detox serum and the list of facilities? Prisoner records?" he asked.

"I got the facilities. Not sure about the prisoner records. I was about to search the fifth floor for the serum when *someone* set off his exit strategy a little too early." Derek gave her a sheepish grin. She glanced over her shoulder into the van's cargo space. "Anything useful back there?"

"Maybe. We can check it out at the house. We'll pick up my motorcycle from where we stashed it and head back." He fumbled under the steering wheel and ripped out a block of plastic, wires sparking. When Stella blinked at him, he gave her a sly smile. "Tracking device. Now we're invisible."

25

Sitting at Derek's kitchen table, Stella pressed her forehead into its smooth wooden edge and stared at the floor, adrenaline leaking out of her.

Silas is gone. He's gone.

The scrape of chair legs across the tile. A bottle clanking onto the table. She looked up, her reflection in the window staring at her against the backdrop of night, pale as a ghost. Her eyes found Derek, seated across from her. He pointed to the whiskey bottle, and she drank.

It was a while before they spoke.

"What now?" asked Derek. He looked like he'd seen a ghost too.

"Look, Derek. I appreciate your help. But now that Silas is—" She cleared her throat. "This is where we part ways."

During the entire drive back to the house on Maple Street, Stella had been thinking. The pieces of the puzzle, when viewed individually, were innocuous. But put them together, and it painted a damning picture.

"We can still find Silas," he said. "And with your Helix Key, we have access to tons of other information. We could discover who the Architect is and see if they can help make the detox serum more widely available, or refine the formula so it works for more users. We have a van full of medical supplies—we could help so many people. Maybe we could even find Pharmatrox's weakness, a way to destroy them. We could take them down for good and get our country back."

Stella's eyebrows shot into her hairline. All of this was escalating too quickly. *And using "we" already? He just wants me for my credentials, for whatever end goal he has in mind.*

"Let me tell you what I see, Derek. You've been following me for weeks. You just so happen to know Silas and where he's being kept. Did you notice when we broke into Oakwood that there were no guards around? I did. The guards didn't show up until I was about to leave that office to find the detox serum. A detox serum that I've never heard of before."

Penny *had* survived her detox somehow when no one else—to her knowledge—had. But people were different. Maybe Penny was stronger than others. It didn't have to mean Derek's magical cure was real.

"And," she continued, "surprise, all the prisoners in Oakwood are gone. Relocated. And I couldn't find their records. Tell me, Derek, were there ever any prisoners there at all? Were *you* even a prisoner?"

Derek leaned forward, elbows on the table, pinning her with his dark eyes. "Why else would I go back if not to rescue Silas? What more do you need to believe I'm on your side?"

"And now you're lumping us together as if we're some kind of team." Stella tapped a finger against the whiskey bottle. "I don't know what you want. I can't verify if you're telling the truth—about *anything*. This could all be an elaborate trap."

He *had* known Silas's name and recognized his photo...It was enough to confirm that Derek had indeed met him, maybe even met him somewhere in the Capital. The troxies had an APB out on him for their Phoenix Trials, so he'd crossed paths with them at some point too. But it wasn't enough for her to trust his motives or to corroborate his story. He kept showing up at the right place, at the right time. It was all too convenient. Too much of a coincidence. And Stella didn't like coincidences.

Tomorrow, she'd go through the list of Pharmatrox facilities to find their HQ and see if Silas was there. She'd find her own way to the border. She didn't need Derek and whatever issues came with him.

Standing, she said, "Good luck with everything. I'm leaving. And I'm taking my share of the van's medical supplies with me."

He reached for her arm but caught her wrist as she turned down the hall. "What about the detox serum?"

Stella scoffed and yanked out of his grasp. "What about it? Really smart way to trick me into going along with your 'rescue' plan, by the way. As if lying about Silas being in Oakwood wasn't enough. I hope you got whatever it was you needed."

"The cure is real. I can prove it."

"So prove it."

Derek's lips thinned into a line, and he ran a hand through his hair. She shook her head and turned away.

"Give me two days."

"No."

"I know you need the serum."

Her hand paused on the front door.

"I can tell from the way you move." His voice was quiet. Pensive. "Smooth and fluid, yet fast and precise. Deadly. It's how some of us reacted to the troxapine experiments. It's how *I* reacted."

He was baiting her. She didn't turn around.

"Goodbye, Derek."

After the events of the night, Stella's darkness swelled close to the surface, ready to pull her under. The hungry beast of craving roared inside her, and she escaped into the night, leaving Derek and his secrets behind.

26

AFTER—DAY 93

AGNES CHEWED HER LIP as she observed the prison. The hulking concrete structure squatted in the open field, a chain-link fence topped with barbed wire surrounding the perimeter in a rusty crown.

From her position in the shadows of the nearby woods, Agnes looked across the meadow's expanse. Early spring flowers dotted the tall grass with specks of buttery yellow and deep purple. A warm breeze drifted across the field and tousled her long dark hair. With rising global temperatures, the winters were colder but never lasted long, and the heat came early. The flowers would only bloom for another few weeks before scorching summer weather blasted the land until it was dry and shriveled.

Agnes shifted her pack, acutely aware of its lightness. If she was going to break in, she'd better get to it. Nightfall would be soon.

Thoughts of her role in sparking the war tormented her. She'd never felt so useless in her entire life. But in those moments, Silas's voice always came to her. *"Do not blame yourself for this, or for whatever comes next."* But it was a fleeting comfort. Silas was still missing, and she had no idea where to find him. Dr. Hansen, at least, had to be in New York, but if she'd been...silenced by Pharmatrox, the troxies might be looking for

Agnes and other defectors too. And if the troxies ever came for her, she wanted to be ready to fight back.

Agnes took to a rusted part of the fence with the serrated part of her knife, then wiggled through and jogged up the long driveway to the prison's entrance.

A quick rock toss through the glass front door and she was in. Her flashlight illuminated a stripe of mint-green tile stretching into the prison's dark interior. The air was stuffy and stale like the inside of a tomb.

Agnes knew nothing about a prison's layout or where the armory might be, but she figured it would be in a separate wing away from the cell blocks. Turning a corner, she headed in what she hoped was the right direction.

Guns and bullets were her priority. Food if she could find it. But her own defense was more important. Bullets were damn near impossible to find, but Agnes preferred shooting from a distance to the close hand-to-hand combat required by a knife. She'd been practicing every day, but her skills were untested, so she didn't trust herself to be able to survive if she was overwhelmed by a swarm of users or turned, or if a Pharmatrox or Faction convoy found her.

Agnes hastened down the next corridor, a clone of the previous one. Another left turn. She tried to head in a uniform direction so as not to get lost, but the hallways ended in dead ends, so she was forced to branch off.

In the next hall, her flashlight reflected off a metal door at the end. *That looks promising.* The reinforced door could protect a place where guards kept their gear. She jiggled the doorknob. Locked.

She pulled the Glock out of her waistband and inspected the magazine. Five bullets left. She fired two shots into the lock, and it split apart, leaving a smoking hole. Gingerly, she pulled the door open.

Into an infirmary filled with users.

A scream erupted out of Agnes before she could stop it.

Every head in the packed infirmary rotated toward her on a slow swivel. Twenty, fifty, too many to count. In the glow of her flashlight, their eyes were depthless black pools.

They were all turned.

Like a tidal wave, they launched at her with terrible speed.

She tried to slam the door shut, but they wedged their limbs through the opening. Hungry gray hands groped for her flesh, making the metal hinges groan in protest. Feet slipping, she steeled herself, then scampered down the hallway.

Within seconds, the door burst open and turned spilled onto the cracked tile floor.

Her mind raced as she retraced her footsteps through the hallways, then pulled up short.

She had no idea where she was.

Carajo. How could she have gotten so turned around? She took the hallway to the right, her flashlight beam bouncing off the walls as she barreled down the hall. A glance over her shoulder showed an army of black eyes hot on her heels, swarming in fast, jerky movements.

Agnes rounded the next corner, tamping down the scream that wanted to explode from her lungs. She recognized this hallway—it was an offshoot that led back to the entrance.

But she slowed as she approached a barred gate like a cell door blocking her way. She was coming at it from the wrong side.

She yelled and rattled the bars, but it was futile. Turned surged down the hallway. Gray skin sagged from sharp bones, stained teeth filled their black mouths. They flinched from the flashlight, but their hunger drove them forward.

Mashing down her fear, Agnes grasped her knife in a shaky hand and her gun in the other. Three bullets. *Better make them count.*

Firing into the oncoming turned, two of her shots found their marks. But amid the sea of flesh, it barely caused a ripple.

Agnes swung her knife wildly, jagged fingernails raking across her skin and pulling her in every direction. Panic seized her. She couldn't fight them off—she barely knew how to hold a weapon. She swept wide with her knife to keep the creatures back, and a few of her stabs found flesh.

But it wasn't enough.

Well, I guess this is it. I survive the main catastrophe and end up torn to shreds in an idiotic situation of my own making.

"Hey!" A voice over her shoulder.

A *voice*. She hadn't heard another human's voice in weeks.

A tall, slender woman a few years older than Agnes stood on the opposite side of the bars. Someone behind her held a flashlight that lit up her red hair in a fiery aura. "Looks like you could use a hand."

Dumbfounded, Agnes almost got a chunk taken out of her by an encroaching turned. She ducked and thrust the knife into its abdomen, ripping out its innards. Another turned grabbed her, and she slammed into it, skidding in the ichor on the floor and fumbling her slippery knife.

"As long as you're over there and I'm over here, I don't see how that helps me," Agnes said with a flippancy she didn't feel.

The woman laughed, a high, clear sound that echoed over the growls. "Callum, jimmy this lock."

Agnes glanced over her shoulder with an incredulous look as the gate swung open.

A slow smile spread across the woman's face as she looked Agnes up and down. "I like her. We're taking this one with us."

27

Penny

FINDING STELLA'S TRUCK HAD been an accident.

Covered in blood and sweat, Penny sliced through a line of troxies with her sickle. She threw a few knives, and they lodged hilt-deep into necks, then grabbed them and threw again.

Fucking Rodney and his fucking plans.

Mal and his squadron had been locked into it with the troxies in the disputed western Sector 5. Rodney had stuffed Mal's ranks with his users, who were unpredictable and didn't follow orders. But, as much as Penny hated to admit it, Rodney's demented plan was working.

The unbridled aggression of his users gave the Faction an edge over the troxies and their volt rifles, but the battle was deadlocked. The helicopter they'd salvaged was still being repaired, so they had to rely on the anti-aircraft gun mounted on the Humvee to keep the troxies from doing fly-overs. But their ammo was limited. And night had fallen.

Things were getting messy.

The battle spilled out into the neighboring neutral zone, and civilians scattered. Some even picked up weapons of the fallen and joined the fight on one or the other side. Penny admired their courage, but if they raised a weapon to the Faction, she put a quick end to that.

Something grabbed her leg.

A woman—the skinny one from Rodney's office—clutched her in the haze of battle. When the woman looked up, Penny froze. Black eyes, weeping obsidian tears.

She recoiled and brought her sickle down until the woman went limp.

On the battlefield around her, a handful of Rodney's users had turned. *Fuck.* She killed the ones within easy reach, but more took their place. They were turning too fast.

And when they turned, they didn't just attack troxies. They attacked everyone.

Now I have to worry about my own fucking soldiers trying to eat me.

"Penny!"

A large body shoved her aside, and she plowed into the pavement. Mal towered over her, the throats of two turned clutched in his big fists. She hadn't seen them circle around behind her.

They would have ripped me to pieces.

Mal slammed their heads together until their skulls cracked, black blood exploding, then tossed the bodies aside and hauled her to her feet.

"You okay?" He shouted to be heard over the din of battle.

For once, she wasn't quick with a quip or an insult. "Thanks," she said, wiping her blade on her pants.

"Fall back to the zoo," he said. "The surrounding wall will give us some cover, and we can hold them off there."

"What about the turned?"

He gave her a hard look. "I meant everyone who isn't one of Rodney's. They won't fucking listen to me anyway. We're leaving them behind to distract the troxies."

"We can't have more turned running around in the streets, Mal. Families live here." Rodney and Kev were more pro-recruitment of civilians than she was, and lately, Rodney was prone to snatching people from their homes and forcing them to use. The civilians were already at risk enough without the worry of a new army of turned ready to eat them alive.

"The turned will win this battle for us, we'll get our territory back, and then I'll rip their fucking throats out." His rough hand gripped her shoulder, and he settled the full weight of his gaze on her. "Rodney is wrong about this. You know it. I know it. I won't sacrifice our humanity to win this war."

She fucking hated the levels Rodney had stooped them to. They were no better than the troxies, using people as a means to their own depraved ends. *But look at what you did to the troxies, murdering them in the streets, leaving that message for Stella. Using them for your ends.* But that was different. Those troxies had fallen during a battle, regular hand-to-hand combat. She hadn't *eaten them alive.* And when did her conscience get so chatty anyway? She'd never had a problem until Mal barged into her life.

She scowled at him. "He'll know I helped you."

"He's too busy bathing in troxy blood to pay attention to what we're doing. I'll spin it to him later if he asks questions. Goddamn it. I need you, Penny." He cringed at the words, and his hand tightened on her shoulder. "You get the rest of our healthy people to safety. They'll listen to you."

With a frustrated sound, Penny threw herself back into the battle. Mal was trying to double-cross her. *He'll make the retreat look like my idea, like I abandoned Rodney to get killed in battle. And then Rodney will fucking merk me.* But if Mal had wanted her dead, he could have let those turned attack her. Hell, he probably could have killed her himself. But he'd saved her.

That's interesting.

A troxy guard slashed at her, yanking her back into the battle. She ripped his helmet off, slicing his face with her sickle.

Mal had proven himself on at least one count—preserving the resistance. She knew Mal hated Rodney more than he hated her. And maybe Mal realized she was his best chance at keeping the Faction from completely imploding under Rodney's leadership. Mal would do whatever was best for the war—he always had. Even if that meant teaming up with *her.* Their alliance would keep the Faction alive, which was the only way to win the war and destroy Pharmatrox—things both of them wanted.

Fuck it. I trust him. At least when it comes to this. But I'll never be his fucking ally.

Penny whirled to face Mal, entirely pissed off. "Fine."

His lips quirked into a quick grin, gone in a flash. He brought his fingers to his mouth and blew out a harsh whistle that cut through the noise.

Penny held her sickle high. "With me!" she yelled and took off toward Victory Park.

Those of the Faction who were capable of following orders went with her; it amounted to about half of their forces. Some troxies broke off to pursue them. Volts of electricity surged through the air, and a few of her people went down. *I hate those goddamned zappy things.*

She'd never led soldiers in battle before, but the Faction troops weren't trained soldiers; not all of them, at least. When people were afraid, they looked for anyone to follow. If she pretended like she knew what she was doing, like she was strong and confident, people listened to her. People would even kill for her.

She glanced over her shoulder and saw Mal racing back into the fray. *Be careful, you giant moron.*

A half mile down the road, the zoo popped into view. She hurried her people through the gate, the troxies hot on their heels.

"Form up. I want those with guns in the front. Anybody have a volt rifle?"

Six of the fifty or so people lifted the weapons. It was more than she'd expected. The troxies destroyed the weapons before letting anyone steal them on the battlefield.

"You're in front too. We'll bottleneck them here. Don't let anyone get through that gate. You all"—she gestured to about half—"with me. We'll watch the walls, and don't let them flank us or sandwich us from behind."

They sprinted down the hill and past the reptile house—

The reptile house.

Penny slowed to a walk. Her troops rushed around her, taking their positions.

She pressed her palm to the hood of the rusted red truck—the one she'd seen parked at the air traffic control tower in Pickerton.

A slow smile spread across her face.

I see you, Stella. I see you.

28

A FINE LAYER OF sweat plastered the short hairs to the nape of Stella's neck. The summer refused to yield to the cool respite of fall, and the air inside the library remained thick and stuffy.

Stella propped her booted feet on the dry-rotted wooden table and tore off a bite of her sandwich. She wasn't hungry, but Lawrence had insisted and shoved the food at her on her way out of camp. He knew she'd spend hours researching and forget to eat.

When she'd returned to camp last night with a sack full of medical supplies, Lawrence's eyes had nearly popped out of his skull. She'd spun a vague story about how she'd found it during a scouting mission. He and the others had been suspicious, but didn't press her.

As much as she hated it, she couldn't get her mind off of Derek. Well, not so much *him* as his mention of the detox serum. She wanted him to be telling the truth. Badly. The convoy would leave in two weeks, and she intended to be on it with Silas. That serum was his—*their*—only hope of escaping to Canada. Silas's absence was an ice pick to the chest—a cold, lancing reminder every time she breathed.

She'd wasted no time in beginning her investigation to find the new Pharmatrox HQ and dig through the Oakwood files. It was too much information for her Patch's bandwidth, so she needed the library's network connection to view them. And she'd have Turi's help—Turi was running a background search for signs of Silas. A Pharmatrox guard was set to patrol the library in an hour, so she had time.

"Turi, run a search query for"—what combination hadn't she tried yet?—"Architect, troxapine, serum."

Stella had no idea what Pharmatrox secrets the Architect knew, but it seemed silly not to at least do a quick search. Even with the Helix Key and Turi's assistance, Stella had scoured file after file for the Architect's identity, or to see if there truly was a cure for the dust's effects; she repeatedly came up blank.

Turi sat cross-legged atop the study table and chomped her gum. "Sorry. Zero results. Again."

Death walked circles around them and frowned at Turi. "She's sitting in my spot." Death waved a hand in front of Stella's face. "Hello? Tell her to move!"

"Tell her yourself," Stella said, sitting back with a huff. She'd taken a small amount of dust to keep her mind clear, but it had given Death new life.

Death pouted by punting burnt books off of the shelves.

"Tell who what?" Turi asked.

"Nothing. Open that file I sent you, the one I snagged from the troxy prison."

The file with a bird-like icon popped open in the air above her head, and Stella scrolled through its contents. It contained thousands of case folders, each labeled to a particular patient. She opened one at random and read.

Patient 2719

Sex: Male

Age: 22

Description: 5'8", 165 lbs., blond hair, blue eyes

Status: Deceased

Name: Harrison Jones

Date updated: 04.12.2085

Case notes: Patient exhibited early dependence on troxapine, as intended. He was malleable, docile, and open to suggestion. After prolonged and increased doses, patient did not experience the desired symptoms. Patient became aggressive and demonstrated disturbing behavior like self-harm and cannibalism. Physiological symptoms included blackened sclera, stained teeth, severe weight loss.

Final recommendation: Termination.

What the hell? Stella's sandwich turned to sawdust in her mouth. *Open to suggestion?* And that list of symptoms at the end...He'd turned. The date on the file was after the Beginning. She rubbed at her growing headache. Any last hope she had that something had gone wrong after troxapine was released, that it was all an accident, vanished. Pharmatrox had known exactly what they were doing when they created troxapine. They had a goal in mind. But what did they want? She flipped to another file.

Patient 1586

Sex: Female

Age: 37

Description: 5'3", 120 lbs., brown hair, brown eyes

Status: Deceased

Name: Alexa Aurelis

Date updated: 07.04.2085

Case notes: Patient exhibited immediate immunity to troxapine. No hallucinations, no memory loss, no change in behavior. Increased dose by three-fold. After prolonged dosage of 600mg, patient experienced recurring hallucinations wherein she was pursued by an unknown assailant. Patient died after throwing herself through a two-inch glass window of the thirtieth floor of the Spire.

Final recommendation: Find family or siblings for next phase of Phoenix Trials.

Stella's feet slid off the table and hit the floor with a thud. She leaned forward, the remainder of her sandwich forgotten. *Immediate immunity? It's possible to use and not turn—without taking the detox serum? Is that why I haven't turned yet? Is that why Penny was able to quit?*

Maybe it was okay if Stella couldn't quit right away. But did she really want to take that chance and risk harming Quentin and the others if she *wasn't* partially immune? She'd been weaning herself off, but the headaches were unbearable, and she used a bit to hold off the shakes and the vomiting. But she knew that wasn't a winning strategy for quitting.

Increased dose...find family and siblings... The reality of what Pharmatrox was doing twisted in her chest. It was one thing to hear mentions of torture from Derek, who she had no reason to trust. It was another thing entirely to read the austere clinical notes from the hands of the torturers themselves.

The troxies are looking for something. They want to know why the dust affects some people differently, maybe use that somehow. But use it for what? To create a race immune to sickness? Immune to...anything?

She paused. "Turi, search file for Derek—" She didn't know his last name. "Search terms: Derek, five foot ten, one hundred and seventy pounds, brown hair, brown eyes." She was only guessing at his height and weight. After percolating through a mountain of files, she finally alighted on the right one.

Patient 4418

Sex: Male

Age: 33

Description: 5'10", 175 lbs., brown hair, brown eyes

Status: UNKNOWN. Last known location: Oakwood facility

Name: Derek Jang

Case notes: Patient was originally contained in a cell with three other patients. We gave him his usual dosage of 600mg of troxapine. Twenty-four hours later, all three of his cellmates were found dead, stabbed through the neck with a ballpoint pen. Unknown how patient obtained the weapon. Troxapine appears to make this patient cunning and clever, with extreme violent tendencies. Gave patient 0.5mL of dionazole and new dosage of 750mg.

Final recommendation: Transfer to the Spire for next phase of Phoenix Trials.

A dark feeling crept up Stella's spine.

Derek's results must have been close to what they wanted if he was selected for the next part of the trial. *Cunning and clever with extreme violent tendencies...*She had been right not to trust him, even though he was telling the truth about being a prisoner. But why were the troxies trying to recreate those symptoms? It could only lead to danger and chaos. A danger and chaos that *they* controlled. She bit her lip. Not enough pieces to put together yet, but the ones she did have, she didn't like.

Now Derek's desire to take down the whole company and get the country back by any means necessary—even by manipulating a stranger to get a Helix Key—didn't seem so cutthroat. Not after everything he'd been through. It was wrong of him to deceive her and use her, but would she have done anything differently had she been a victim of their torture? She wasn't sure.

But finding Pharmatrox HQ, ripping it apart in her search for Silas—maybe even taking them down entirely—wouldn't stop them.

Pharmatrox was a hydra. It would just regrow its head. It's what happened in the Beginning, when they abandoned their facility in the Capital in favor of a new HQ hidden from sight. They'd do the same thing, again and again. There was no stopping them. Escape was the only choice.

And dionazole—that was the first mention she'd seen of the drug. Could that be the detox serum? If Derek had been telling the truth about its purpose, it made sense that it would be listed in his case notes.

"Turi, search all files for mentions of dionazole and put them aside for me. I'll look through those later."

"On it. Also, found something else you'll want to see."

A singular file popped into the air.

Patient 3479

Sex: Male

Age: 35

Description: 6', 215 lbs., black hair, brown eyes

Status: UNKNOWN

Name: Silas Markson

Case notes: [REDACTED]

Final recommendation: Transfer to the Spire for next phase of Phoenix Trials.

Silas Markson. The name emblazoned on her eyelids like a brand. *Status: UNKNOWN.* A weak flame of hope flickered in the dim chambers of her heart. Silas was in the Spire. Could that be the new Pharmatrox HQ?

"Turi, search our list of Pharmatrox facilities and files for mentions of the Spire."

I'm coming, Silas.

29

AFTER—DAY 31

Evie sniffed the clump of white powder from the back of her hand. Agnes frowned. It was Evie's fifth hit and it wasn't even noon yet.

Agnes pushed the door open to the next house and said, "Maybe you should slow down?"

They stepped into the two-story foyer of the family home on the outskirts of Newark. A crystal chandelier dangled from the ceiling, and a cabinet of fine china stood to the side like a polite houseguest. Many people had abandoned their homes and possessions in the mass exodus before the borders closed. But those who hadn't escaped were either trapped in Containment or holed up in various suburban camps. Agnes knew as well as Pharmatrox did that what was happening was not the result of a communicable contagion but of a drug gone bad. Maybe they wanted to keep everyone confined until they figured out what had gone wrong.

Not for the first time, Agnes wished Dr. Hansen was there. She'd know what the directors were thinking, and what they were advising the Leader to do and why. Agnes had asked Evie if she'd seen Dr. Hansen in the bunker, but she'd refused to speak of that day.

She and Evie had cased the other homes on the block and taken what provisions they could find, but most of them had already been picked over. This home, so far, appeared untouched.

Evie cringed. "Not this argument again. Please. I haven't eaten since yesterday and don't have the energy."

Agnes sighed. She was worried about Evie. Ever since the two had rejoined after escaping Manhattan a few weeks ago, Evie had used more and more each day. She'd confessed that she started using the week before the ferry, when they thought troxapine was a wonder drug. And now she was addicted. She wouldn't talk about how she had managed to skirt Containment—only that Roberto and Silas had helped her. Whenever Agnes broached the subject, Evie went silent.

Running a twitchy hand through her matted hair, Evie said, "I'll check the kitchen." She headed down the hallway, boots squeaking on the polished wood floor.

"I'll get the bedrooms." Agnes pulled her dark hair into a tangled bun and mounted the curving staircase.

They'd been on the move constantly but never strayed far from Manhattan. Evie was convinced Silas was still alive and in the city. She wanted to go back for him, and Agnes did too, but she had her doubts. How could they even begin to search for Silas in a city of millions of people, let alone get past the Containment perimeter? It was another of the daily arguments she and Evie had.

Plus, Pharmatrox convoys roamed the suburbs, picking up civilians—why, exactly, Agnes wasn't sure. But the conversations she'd had with Dr. Hansen before she fled were enough to warn her away from reaching out to Pharmatrox for help of any kind. The Faction branches were doing something similar. If Kev was around, he never forced anyone to join and only took volunteers. But if it was another branch, they weren't so understanding.

There'd been no news from the other cities; the CLEO newsfeeds played the same Pharmatrox propaganda and Leader speeches as always. Comms had been down for the past few weeks, hence why everyone was looting houses and panicking. Her Patch's internal comms to other employees worked, but Dr. Hansen's signal was offline—a thought she frequently pushed to the back of her mind, right next to her guilty box of secrets.

This is my fault.

Agnes shook herself and entered the first bedroom's closet. But she wasn't looking for clothes, badly as she needed them. She shuffled a few boxes and dug out the ones hidden in the back.

A medium-sized purple shoe box felt about the right weight. She lifted the lid and smiled.

A hunting knife, a flashlight, and a Glock with an extra magazine.

Agnes slipped the items into her pack, alongside her leather jacket, extra shirt, cans of food, and toiletries. Next, she went to check the medicine cabinet in the adjoining bathroom. She dumped canisters of antibiotics into her bag but froze when she heard elevated voices from below.

Angry voices.

She popped the magazine in the Glock and tiptoed downstairs, with only a vague idea of how to use the weapon. *Point and shoot, right?* Hopefully it wouldn't come to that.

Hidden in the foyer, Agnes observed the kitchen and its occupants. Two men—one hulking and bulky, the other tall and slender—stood with arms crossed as they faced a harried Evie.

"I told you," Evie hissed, her eyes darting between the men. "She doesn't want to go back, and I can't get it without her. They revoked my access after I escaped. You'll have to wait a bit longer."

Bulky Man grunted. "A deal's a deal, Ev. It's been almost a month. We need our payment. We're here to collect."

Evie made an irritated sound. "I've been a bit busy running for my life, if you hadn't noticed." Tall Man's hand drifted to the knife at his hip, and Evie paled. "I'll get you more dust like I promised. Okay?"

Tall Man eyed Evie. "How do we know you're good for it? Manhattan fell to the troxies a few days ago. They aren't letting anyone in or out."

Agnes slumped against the wall. *Manhattan is under Pharmatrox control...so maybe Dr. Hansen is safe?*

Evie fiddled with the zipper on her coat. "I'll talk her into going back. It'll work. Trust me."

Agnes blanched as the implications dawned on her, and she advanced down the hallway, gun pointed at the intruders. "Evie. Who are your friends?"

Evie's eyes went wide, then narrowed, and she gripped the countertop with white knuckles. "I know what this looks like, Agnes. But you have no idea what it was like in Containment. *You* got out before lockdown. I didn't. Things went bad in the bunker. Some of our coworkers started to turn, growling, attacking us. Then the Red Riots breached the facility, and the Faction was ruthless. Killing anyone. Roberto, he—he's gone. And they took Silas. They sacrificed themselves so I could escape. And so I *had to escape*. No matter the cost." Her eyes shone and she cleared her throat. She gestured to the men. "They helped me—for a price. And now my bill is due."

Roberto, dead. Silas, captured. *Even Pharmatrox employees are turning.* And Agnes had fled the city rather than stay behind to help. It had been the plan; she'd just been following Silas's plan. But the guilt coiled around her in tight, hot bands.

Evie looked at the floor, her voice barely above a whisper. "Silas isn't in the city. He made it to the lab at the same time as the Red Riots. Pharmatrox rounded people up and shoved them into transport trucks, whether they were Faction or not. I don't know where he is, but he's not in New York." Her eyes snapped to Agnes's. "But if I don't pay these men, they'll kill me. I need the dust." Evie pulled a gun out of her jacket pocket and pointed it at Agnes. Her aim did not waiver. "I'm sorry, Agnes, but we're going back."

Ever since that day on the ferry, tendrils of darkness had begun to seep inside of Agnes. Recollections of the past month pulsed in her brain like a drumbeat of war. Burnt buildings, blood in the streets, bodies swinging from ropes...She would not go back to that.

There was no going back.

Agnes's gun barked off two rounds, and Burly Man returned fire with the gun hidden in his waistband.

Agnes dashed for the front door, snatched a pair of keys dangling from a hook, and vaulted off the porch onto the patchy lawn.

With thunderous footfalls pursuing her and bullets whizzing past her head, she clicked the key fob, and the lights of a crusty sedan on the street blinked. Agnes threw herself in the driver's seat and jammed the key in the ignition.

As Agnes peeled down the road, bullets shattered the passenger window and cracks laced the windshield. She glanced in the rearview and saw Evie shoot Burly Man in the foot. Tall Man reached for Evie, but she slammed his head with the butt of her gun and made her escape.

Agnes's foot weighed heavier on the gas pedal. A single tear rolled down her face as she drove away from the only family she had left.

30

B RIGHT MORNING SUNLIGHT SPLIT through the skylight of trees and sent spikes of pain stabbing through Stella's eye sockets. She'd hidden in the library to avoid the troxy patrol guard and continued her research late into the night. Exhausted, she'd stumbled back to the Outpost and collapsed into the first thing she'd seen—the worn wooden chair on the cabin's front porch.

But her work had yielded undeniable results—she had a lead on the location of the Spire, Pharmatrox's probable HQ. Hidden in the depths of the network, she'd found shipping routes for trucks similar to the ones Pharmatrox used for prisoner transport. Her Helix Key allowed her to access the shipping log. After the Beginning, a building in the northern quadrant of the Capital had received an influx of "deliveries." Stella would check it out, but first she needed sustenance. She needed *coffee.*

Rubbing her temples, she dragged herself to the campfire.

Lawrence was the only one awake. He hung a kettle of coffee over the fire and added another log. At her approach, he looked up and said, "You don't *have* to suffer, you know. We do have more comfortable places for you to sleep. That pointy rock over there. Against the barbed wire fence, perhaps." He offered her a chunk of bread.

Stella grinned and took a bite. "I like waking up with aches and pains. Reminds me I'm still alive." She accepted a cup of coffee and gulped it down. "All right, time to face the impossible foe."

"Want a hand?" asked Lawrence.

"Nah, I'll tackle this one on my own. Thanks for breakfast."

Stella shucked off her leather jacket and prepared to wrestle with her tent.

A storm had rolled through during the night, and a tree branch had lodged through the top of her tent. As she battled the torn nylon, she contemplated her next move. Scoping out the Spire's suspected location was first on her list. If she got inside, even just inside a guardhouse, she could download floor plans of the facility with her Helix Key. If the troxies tracked that, it didn't matter; the Helix Key wasn't tied to her name or identity. And she needed to do it fast. It had been a little over a week since Penny's gruesome message, and Stella hated waiting for the other shoe to drop.

The convoy is leaving soon, Si and I will be gone, and then Quentin, Tara, and Lawrence will be safe from Penny. It will work. It's going to be fine.

Inevitably, her thoughts circled back to Derek, as they had almost constantly for the past two days. It was annoying. *He* was annoying. In her research, she'd found dionazole mentioned in other patient files. No explanation, just the name and dosage. It wasn't proof that it was Derek's detox serum, but it *was* something important, and Derek had taken it. And he was fine. Alive. No lingering symptoms, according to him. If dionazole was the detox serum, Derek was her only connection to finding it and learning more about it.

If he'd been telling the truth.

She needed Derek—or at least, whatever information he could provide—and she hated it. She'd have to trust his word. It was the only lead she had.

She pulled a small twig out of her tent roof and tossed it over her shoulder. Across the clearing, the Outpost had stirred to life. Quentin was awake, bugging Lawrence at the firepit. To the side of the cabin, Tara's arms floated as she practiced her Sanchin kata, graceful yet powerful.

A weird feeling stirred within Stella. For so long, she'd been on her own, relying only on herself. And now, as she settled into this group at the Outpost, she felt her guard lowering.

She never thought she'd feel safe again, not after the ferry. Not after she watched the Faction and the dust claim so many lives—her own included. Not after Penny. But then Quentin had come—well, fallen—into her life.

For the first time since the Beginning, Stella felt hope.

She wasn't sure if that was a good thing or not. Hope was fragile and could be shattered as quickly as it crystallized. She wondered what it had been like for her mother during the Sickness. Had the country been as distressed as it was now? How had she maintained hope for a better world when surrounded by such darkness?

Stella yanked out a few smaller sticks from her tent before tackling the largest one. When she finally succeeded in extracting the stubborn tree limb, the hole yawned even bigger. Muttering curses, she tossed the tent fabric over her shoulder and bent to survey the damage to her tethers.

"Hey! Don't throw your dirty laundry at me." Quentin pinched her tent between two fingers and wrinkled his freckled nose.

Stella snatched it with a significant look. "Better than wadding it up and stuffing it in the corner of my tent to fester. Do you have Lawrence's sewing kit?"

Quentin took the material from her and inspected the hole, waving toward his own tent. "Yeah, it's in my bag."

Stella unzipped his tent and rummaged in his bag's plethora of pockets. Her hand touched something.

Her hope shattered.

She held up several baggies of translucent white powder.

Death stuck her curly head in beside her. "Our little minion wants to join the fun!"

Dread seized Stella by the throat. "Quentin." She shook the baggies in his face. "What's this?"

Quentin's eyes bulged. She gripped the front of his shirt, ready to throttle him.

"Tell me you aren't using! This stuff will kill you, Quentin. One day, you'll end up like them. A turned who can't do anything except rip people to pieces. Is that what you want?"

He narrowed his eyes. "You use it. Where do you think I got it?"

A wave of nausea swept over her. "You thieving bastard. I thought I was using too much. But it was you." Stella sank to the ground. "How'd you know?"

Quentin sat beside her. "When I saw you fight those turned in the commissary, I knew it was more than natural skill. You were too fast, too precise." He stared at the baggies in her palm. Then at her. "So I stole some from your pack whenever you weren't around. I thought if you ran out, you'd stop." Her heart clenched. This brave boy never ceased to surprise her. "You look like someone who's been carrying something heavy for a long time. And...well, I know what that's like. But the dust isn't the answer. It won't fix the state of the world. It won't bring back the people we lost. We know it's bad, so why do you use it?"

Stella took deep breaths to quash her anxiety. She thought she had her using under control. She didn't think anyone could tell and only used the bare minimum to stave off the worst of the withdrawal. But Quentin was more astute than she gave him credit for. And what was this talk of his own baggage? She'd never seen him be anything but bubbly. Then she remembered the hidden scars beneath his shirt. Quentin's happy demeanor could hide so much.

People can be more than one thing.

Quentin was right, she knew that. The dust wasn't absolution. It offered solace, but it was fleeting. The dust would never bring back Roberto, Evie, or any of the others who'd been lost to her. It wouldn't save Silas. It gave her Death, a poor substitute for Evie. She had to let it go. She *wanted* to let it go. But her body wouldn't let her. She was addicted, and part of her thought it a fitting punishment for all the wrong choices she'd made since the Beginning. Stella didn't deserve to quit. She didn't deserve the detox serum, if it existed.

She shifted to face him. "It doesn't matter why I started using." A long-buried anger sparked inside of her. *I should never have joined Penny—or stayed with her.* At the time, she hadn't had a choice. But she could have tried harder to quit. Maybe. "The dust gave me hallucinations of my dead best friend. It made me feel less alone, so I kept using."

"But you're not alone," said Quentin. "I'm here. Lawrence and Tara too. The happiest I've ever seen her is after her sparring sessions with you." A brief smile flicked at the corner of his mouth. "Why can't you quit? I can help you."

Stella shook her head. "It doesn't work like that. I'm not strong enough." A realization hit her. "Wait, you haven't—?"

"Don't worry. I haven't used. I don't want to."

The simple statement overwhelmed her, and she pulled Quentin into a bone-crushing hug.

They broke apart after a moment, and Quentin ran a hand through his bronze hair. It was getting long. "Stella, the dust. Give it back."

Stella's fist closed around the baggies. She wanted to quit, but the darkness would not relent.

Quentin fixed her with a hard stare that was much older than his years. "Wasn't hard to find your stash. I'll just steal more of it until you have nothing left and no choice but to quit."

Stella clamped her jaw shut so tightly she thought she'd crack a molar. Fiery rage swept through her, and she shot to her feet.

Quentin remained seated and unconcerned at her rising fury. "If Lawrence and Tara find out, they'll kick you out. Say what you want about being a loner, but I know you like it here."

The smug little bastard. Unable to look at him anymore without either strangling him or bursting into tears, Stella left.

She stomped through the woods to walk off her frustration, to outrun her guilt. She wasn't mad at the kid. In fact, she understood. As a child, she'd hidden her papá's cigarettes to get him to quit smoking. It hadn't worked; he'd died of lung cancer.

If she didn't quit the dust, she was headed down a worse path than her papá.

She hadn't turned yet, but she probably would. That one case note she'd read about a patient using and not turning was an anomaly, like Penny. Stella was not special. She'd succumb to the dust just like every other user. It was an inevitability she'd ignored, her sole focus on rescuing Silas. Silas was the only thing that mattered.

But now that she'd met Quentin and Tara, and dammit, even Lawrence—she *liked* them. They mattered too. She didn't want to endanger them by one day turning and killing them in their own camp. They were already in danger because of her presence possibly exposing them to Penny. While she didn't deserve to live in whatever peace and happiness this world could provide, these people did. And she would *not* be the one to take that away from them.

That left her with only one option.

She marched back to her tent and grabbed her stash, setting one baggie aside and shoving it under her pillow. Quentin looked up from where he sat at the fire, a frown screwed onto his face. When he saw what she was doing, he scrambled after her.

She stopped at the bank of the creek and held her stash in front of Quentin.

"This is it. This is all that is left of the dust. If there is more, I don't know where to find it."

He watched her, arms crossed.

Eyes glued to his, she upended the contents of the bag into the creek, sealing her fate.

Death shrieked in the background. "What have you done!"

Stella's hands shook as she watched the white powder get swept away by the current. She'd just flushed the one thing that was keeping her alive. But it was also the thing that was killing her. With her one remaining baggie, she could wean herself off slowly over the next month, but it wouldn't be easy. And now, she'd tied herself to Derek. Permanently. She'd need the detox serum if the withdrawal symptoms got too bad.

Quentin took her hand and squeezed.

"I've been using for a long time, Quent," she said. "But I'd rather drop dead than bring harm to you or any of the others. And I might, at that, from the withdrawal. But you're more important." Her voice cracked. "You have to survive."

She just hoped she was strong enough to survive too.

31

T HE EVENTS OF THE morning buzzed in the back of Stella's mind. The dust thrummed within her, but it would be less than a day before she needed more.

Quentin snored from inside his tent, and Tara was inside the cabin, probably working on repairing more radios. Sitting at the fire, Lawrence stirred a pot of something green for dinner. At Stella's approach, he opened his mouth to speak, but a distant crashing sound drifted through the trees.

Stella tilted her head. "What's that?"

It couldn't be a raid—Pharmatrox hadn't been launching as many lately. Her Patch told her the Faction had taken down a few jets with their anti-aircraft weapons.

Lawrence gave a bewildered shrug and slowly rose to his feet.

Stella grabbed his arm. "Is it getting louder?" she asked, a chill erupting across her skin despite the heat from the fire.

"I think—"

A red truck—*her* red truck—burst through the trees and pummeled through the perimeter fence, loud music blaring from the speakers. It crashed into the cabin and smashed the wall to splinters.

No, no, no. Me cago en la puta. I thought I had more time—

"What the ever-loving—!" Quentin tripped out of his tent in a tangle of blankets.

Stella sprinted to the house, ripping planks and beams aside. "Tara!"

It was a minute before she realized Lawrence and Quentin weren't helping her. Both were glued to the spot. Lawrence lifted a finger, a harbinger of doom, and pointed into the woods.

"We have a problem."

A herd of turned staggered through the trees, drawn by the movement and riled up by the music. Their numbers were too great to count.

Stella cursed and dug faster. A pile of wood in the approximate location of Tara's room undulated. Finally, she reached Tara's tiny hand and hauled her out of the ruins, coughing and spluttering. Aside from some cuts and a gash on her forehead, Tara was fine. But her leg wound hindered her as she limped away.

"Lawrence!" Stella shouted. "Take them and get the hell out of here."

"We'll go to my workshop," Lawrence said, pulling Tara's arm around his shoulders to take most of her weight.

Tara struggled and pushed him away. "Stella, no seas gilipollas. We're not going to abandon you."

Stella unsheathed her machete and tossed her pack to Quentin. "Vete ya. I'll hold them off." She didn't wait to see if they listened. With her dust-enhanced reflexes, she was the only one who stood a chance against these creatures.

She vaulted over the fence and launched into the writhing mass of gray bodies and black eyes. They weren't fast like the ones from the commissary, but their sharp teeth and clawed hands were still deadly.

In minutes, black blood slicked Stella's skin and hair. All thought and reason flooded out of her with each hack of her machete, leaving only raw emotion. Fear. Anger. Guilt.

Death whispered in her ear. "This is your fault. It's *all* your fault. Open your eyes."

She threw herself into the fight, but there were too many. The truck engine rumbling within the wreckage gave her an idea. She ripped open the driver's side door and got in, kicking aside a rock the size of a melon that sat on the accelerator. Fresh blood leaked from a wound somewhere and stained the upholstery. *Don't remember that happening.*

She slammed the gear shift into reverse and floored the gas pedal. "Come on, come on." The tires squealed to find traction, then the truck flew backwards. It plowed over a few turned, but not enough to make a difference. Steering the truck away from the Outpost, she cranked the music and led the turned away.

After about a mile, she put the rock on the accelerator, opened the door, and timed her jump to land in the soft moss, her shoulder slamming into the ground as she rolled. When she came to a stop, she noticed a cut on her left arm, and she tied her bandanna around it to hide the scent of blood. As she ran through the woods toward the workshop, she killed the stragglers that followed her until it was only her and the trees.

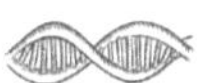

Stella burst inside the tiny workshop nestled in the oak trees and locked the door behind her, wiping the gore from her face.

There wasn't much in the one-room shack—only a small table and chairs, the cupboards above the countertop along the far wall, and a few basic tools laying around. It was cramped with all four of them inside. Lawrence leaned against the wall with a dark expression, while Quentin sat cross-legged atop the counter, his face blank in shock. Tara had her wounded leg propped up on the table, her arms folded.

Stella broke the silence. "I fought off as many as I could and led them away from the Outpost. They've likely scattered by now. But it's not safe to go back."

Quentin was the first to speak. "Stella, that was your truck. I *drove* that truck. We left it at the zoo. How the heck did it end up crashing into our cabin?"

Her mouth glued shut. The only explanation she had was damning, and from the way Lawrence and Tara glowered at her, they knew it too.

"We didn't have any problems until Quentin met you," said Lawrence. "Sure, things weren't always easy. But we didn't have turned tearing apart our camp. And someone's been following you. Haven't they?"

Stella sagged against the counter next to Quentin. Lawrence had every reason to be mistrustful of strangers in his camp.

Quentin nudged her with his elbow. "Tell us what's going on. Maybe we can help."

The curtain of finality fell around her. It wasn't avoidable anymore. She had to tell them the truth about her past—at least, part of it. They had to understand the potential danger they were in, and why.

Stella pulled her short hair back, exposing her Patch. "I'm a troxy. People are looking for me—they think I'm the Architect because of some circumstantial evidence. But I'm a defector. I'm sorry this happened. I thought I'd be gone before they found me."

Nobody breathed.

The air exploded with questions.

"What d'you—"

"How are you still *alive*?"

"You can't be serious—"

"You're one of *them*?"

Lawrence shot to his feet, hands balled into fists. A vein bulged in his temple, and he stomped outside and slammed the door.

Quentin perked up in his seat. "Ah, I'll get him." He flashed a smile at Stella and followed Lawrence. At least Quentin's immunity to being afraid of her seemed to be intact.

Tara eyed Stella, drumming her fingers on the table. "I get why you stayed with us. It's tough out there. I was alone before I found those two bozos." Tara glanced out the window at Quentin, who gripped Lawrence by the shoulders. "You've been with us almost a month, and in that time, you've proven you're one of the good ones. I believe that, even if you don't."

Stella looked skeptical. "What about Lawrence?"

"He'll come around." Tara's lips lifted in a slight smile. "If the Outpost is compromised, we can't go back there. We'll gather up what food and supplies we can and hoof it somewhere else. Maybe stay here in the workshop a while. But I can't be cramped in with those two payasos for long. I'll rip my hair out, and then theirs."

Stella needed a new camp too. Penny's attack had blown her plans to bits, but she might have a way to salvage things...

"I know it's not fair to ask you to trust me. But I have a place we can all stay, and it's big enough for everyone to have their own space. I've only been there twice, and I was never followed."

"Are you sure about that?"

Stella reflected on the times she'd been there. Both had been later at night, and she'd been careful about the path she took. "Pretty sure."

Tara considered a moment. "Okay. It's better than being out in the open."

"Let me scope it out first and make sure it's all clear. I'll go right now." Stella picked up her pack from where it sat in the corner and cringed.

A giant gash tore down the front of it, cutting through the main and small front pockets.

Fuck.

"Ah. Sorry about that," said Tara. "Turned clawed a hole in it on our way out of camp."

Stella rushed to check the pack's contents. A shirt was missing, as well as two extra knives, a granola bar, some bandages, and—

No.

Her Pharmatrox ID. The photo of her, Silas, Evie, and Roberto. They were gone.

"Hope you didn't lose anything too important."

Stella squeezed her eyes shut. Her last tether to her true identity. Her old life. Gone. There wasn't time to retrace their steps to look for them, not with Penny and the Marauders possibly tearing through the Outpost or lurking nearby.

"Nothing I can't replace," she said, then made her escape into the forest before Tara could see the tears forming in her eyes.

32

AFTER—DAY 168

THE GROUP OF THIEVES swarmed the dingy general store like a cloud of locusts. Groups meant safety—and they could pillage and plunder with impunity.

Stella joined them because she had nowhere else to be.

"You need me *to survive."* The memory slithered through her mind.

Stella gulped. Perhaps it wasn't totally her choice.

After their last raid, only seven Marauders remained. Stella fed them the dust, and they made sure she had something to eat. She didn't ask any questions, and they, in turn, left her alone. Or they had—until *that night*. She took another hit of dust—her sixth of the day. At this rate, she'd be dead by the end of the week.

At least then she would stop feeling guilty. She'd stop feeling anything at all.

"Stella." Penny turned her feline eyes in her direction, her deep red hair twisting in the breeze like flickering flames. "Care to do the honors?" Penny held out a crowbar.

When Stella lifted an uncertain hand, Death popped up beside her and said, "I think she wants you to smash."

The knife in her hand.

Screams and smoke.

"You need me *to survive."*

She was using too much, but she didn't care. Anything to forget. She felt like she was looking at Death through a dirty window. Licking the dust residue from the back of her hand, her vision cleared.

Death gave her a playful nudge, and she bashed the window with the crowbar.

Penny watched from afar, a satisfied smile curling at her mouth. She gestured to the five others, and they descended on the store.

Stella and Death wandered the cramped aisles. The place was only stocked with the essentials—a few grocery items and dry goods, tools, pharmacy needs. It was rare to find a place that wasn't already picked over. This store was untouched, left as it had been on the day the world ended. Even the caretaker's reading glasses were perched atop an old newspaper spread on the front counter by the register and the pharmacy. *Old school—nobody buys papers anymore.*

The Marauders made swift work of sweeping the store, taking almost everything, even if they didn't need it. Stella heard someone, probably Callum, smash the glass doors of the fridge, and she rolled her eyes. Callum liked destruction for destruction's sake.

Death kicked at the cracked floor tiles while Stella inspected a display of tools. Protocol said the haul would be divided evenly between them back at camp, but something made Stella pocket the box cutters and one remaining hunting knife from the shelf. She tugged her leather jacket down to hide her bulging pockets and fluffed her long dark hair to conceal her Patch.

Stella rubbed the notch in her forehead brought on by a pounding headache. The beginnings of withdrawal—again. If she wanted to live, she'd have to start weaning herself off of the dust.

But ever since *that night*, living seemed like an impossibility. She'd be free of the dust and the Marauders—and the guilt—soon enough. She'd be dead.

"Five minutes," said Penny from the front of the store, leaning a hip against the counter, perusing the newspaper as the Marauders scurried around for any last remaining treasures.

Her pockets full to bursting, Stella stuffed a box of tampons in her pack and headed out. As she passed, Penny shot out a hand and gripped her shirtfront. Her fingers tightened, and she lifted her eyes to Stella's with slow deliberation.

The eyes of a predator who had just found its prey.

Stella's blood turned to ice water.

Penny jabbed a finger at the picture on the page. The headline was an accusation.

NEW MIRACLE DRUG HITS THE MARKET

Below was a picture of Stella smiling in her Pharmatrox lab coat. Stella remembered it well. It had been for a small column buried in a niche paper, so the chances of someone actually reading it were slim. The reporter had wanted to get a photograph of one of the bigwig visiting doctors from Pharmatrox HQ, but the doctor's schedule had been booked. Stella had only agreed to the photo as a favor to Dr. Hansen.

"I know you hate getting your picture taken, but nobody will even see it," Dr. Hansen had said. *"They have a minuscule audience, and they just want a pretty, smiling face to slap on their outdated rag of a publication to try and sell more hard copies. Who the hell buys and sells print publications anymore?"*

Being in a newspaper was the last thing Stella wanted. She hadn't even known what the article was about. But now she saw it was about troxapine. *Fuck.*

Stella's heart sidestepped in her chest.

"So that's how you got so much of the dust," said Penny. "I thought you stole it. But you *invented* it. This whole time, I've been looking for *you. You're the Architect.*"

In the face of the false accusation, the grime cleared from the dirty window of Stella's life.

She wanted to live.

She *needed* to live. She had a promise to keep.

And she would fight like hell to make sure she survived.

As Stella turned to run, Penny ripped her sickle across Stella's throat. That step away saved Stella's life. The blade snagged down her skin to the middle of her chest, hot agony exploding through her. Stella slid a box cutter from her pocket and jammed it in Penny's thigh, then hurdled through the shop's ruined front door with a hand to her throat, slick with blood. The cut was deep. The world shifted around her.

"Stop her!" said Penny.

At her command, the Marauders in the parking lot crouched into fighting stances.

Stella barreled toward Callum and tackled him to the ground. He was greedy, so he usually scavenged the most supplies and kept extras for himself. And he had a stash of dust. She wrestled his pack from him and punched him in the nose.

"Bloody hell!" Callum swung at her blindly, but she was already gone, clearing a path through the Marauders with her box cutters. She stuck them in ribs, eyes, necks—whatever she could reach.

A fist in her hair pulled her from the fight and flung her to the ground.

Penny straddled her and bashed her head against the pavement like a ripe melon, her vision darkening. She clawed at Penny's face, but Penny didn't relent.

Not like this. It can't end like this. Stella strained for her one remaining box cutter and slashed it across Penny's face. Wailing, Penny fell off of her in a flurry of limbs, and Stella bolted.

Blood poured out of her throat at an alarming rate, so she tied her red bandanna tight around her neck as she ran, spots swimming in her vision.

Behind her, Penny's screams filled the air. A hungry hyena denied her meal.

Stella scrambled across the broken pavement, her red Faction mask dropping to the asphalt behind her. But the darkness she carried would not be so easy to shed.

33

S TELLA FROWNED AT THE house with the green door. This hadn't been part of the plan. Standing there, covered in blood in the middle of the night, at the house of a man she didn't trust because she had no place else to go.

But it was her own damn fault for sticking around the Outpost when she should have left immediately.

Stella's legs wobbled as she paced in front of Derek's house. She'd escaped Penny for now, but she'd find her again. Penny would always find her. And now that Lawrence, Quentin, and Tara were also in her crosshairs, a renegotiation of her deal with Derek was in order.

Seats on the convoy to the border for all of them—if the others would even want to join her. Derek's help in getting more of the detox serum, a place to stay—Derek's house was the only place large enough for all of them where they might be safe. It meant abandoning the Outpost's garden, but maybe Derek would know where to find food.

And what the hell do I have to offer him in return for all of that?

She'd offer him her Helix Key for whatever he wanted it for. At this point, she didn't care what he was up to. Penny wrecking her little bubble of happiness had been the reality check she needed. It didn't matter if Derek was manipulating her for his own gains. The convoy was real, and it was possible the detox serum was real too. She had a solid lead on where to find Silas. She just needed a safe place to lay low until the convoy left.

Decision made, she rolled her shoulders and took the steps two at a time. She lifted a hand to knock, but the door pushed open under her touch.

Voices came from the kitchen. *Derek has a visitor?* She ducked into the hall closet but kept the door slightly cracked. She couldn't see anything, but she could hear well enough.

"Don't know why I'm keeping you in the loop, Derek," said someone with a deep, gruff voice.

"I need to know what's going on." Derek's voice. "It affects my plans too."

"Fuck your plans. I don't care how important you say she is. *My* plan went to shit because of you—my plan to not fucking die, that is."

"Pretty talkative for a dead guy."

"You're such a bastard." The man grunted. It sounded almost like a laugh.

So they're...friends? It was hard to tell. And was that voice familiar?

"Any headway on finding troxy HQ?" asked Derek. Maybe Derek really had been telling the truth about his long-term goals.

"Nah. Had no time to look. Too busy trying not to get eaten or assassinated in my sleep. The new bossman is off his shit. Oh, brought you some of this." Something tapped onto the counter. "I know your supply is running low." The man sighed. "Fucking kills me to admit it, but I need you, you pain in the ass. Don't make me deal with the devil-woman on my own." Something else bigger slapped onto the countertop. Sounded like plastic.

Stella pushed open the closet door to get a better look—

The hinges creaked, interrupting their conversation.

Derek's head whipped toward her kneeling in the hallway. When his body shifted, she saw what was on the counter in front of him.

It was a red lacquered mask.

A Faction mask.

34

THE WORLD TILTED AROUND her. Stella remembered her own Faction mask, the hard plastic slick and hot against her face, trapping her breath. She'd thrown the damn thing away as soon as she could, but its phantom touch would never leave her.

As Stella's eyes locked on Derek, she drew her boot knife.

Death fizzled into her vision. "Kill him," Death whispered inside the dark chambers of Stella's mind.

In a few quick strides, Stella had her knifepoint jammed under Derek's chin.

Derek pushed the mask aside and held up his hands. "Let me explain."

A bead of blood formed at the tip of her blade. "I *knew* there was something wrong with you." She shoved Derek against the wall.

The Seven Sisters. The Red Riots. The hangings. Penny and the Marauders. All atrocities of the Faction—and *Derek* was part of it.

"Stella, you don't—wait, are you covered in *blood*?" A dark expression crossed Derek's face. "Who did this to you?" He reached for her, but she swatted his hand away.

"You should be more worried about what *I'm* going to do to you," she hissed.

Behind them, the other man laughed, a low rumbling sound. He was well over six and a half feet tall and looked like he bench pressed a stack of cars on the regular.

And Stella recognized him.

The man who'd given her the moped keys at the fighting pit.

He sized her up with piercing light brown eyes. "So this is the woman you're willing to risk everything for? Hope she's worth it."

Derek's gaze speared her to the spot. "She is."

Stella jerked the knife deeper. "What the hell is going on?"

The other man grunted. "I like her. She's got grit. And she's not afraid to cut your head off, which is my favorite quality in a woman."

"If you boys don't start making sense soon," said Stella, "I'll kill you both just to save myself the mental gymnastics of decrypting your conversation."

The man huffed another laugh.

"Shut it," said Derek. "You never laugh this much."

"She's funny. Better explain things to your woman before she gives your throat a smile of its own."

Glancing at Stella's weapon, Derek said, "Could you put that down?"

Her hand tightened around the hilt. "Not a chance."

"Fair enough."

"You 'risked everything' for me? What the hell is that guy talking about?"

The guy pointed at himself. "Malosi."

Stella nodded to him. "Malosi." Her eyes narrowed. "I'll get to you later." To Derek, she said, "Explain. From the beginning."

"Mal was there at the beginning. So might as well get to him now."

"Derek. I'm losing patience."

Derek cleared his throat. "At the, ah—the fighting pit."

"Yeah, I know. Mal helped me."

"Who do you think told him to do that? I went onstage and distracted Rodney. I lied about the incoming troxy raid so you could escape."

The arm holding her knife went limp.

"So I could escape, or so you could follow me and use me later?"

"We have the same goal—rescuing Silas. I can't explain why things happened the way they did when we broke into Oakwood, but it had nothing to do with me. Ask Mal if you don't believe me."

Stella lifted an eyebrow in Mal's direction. Mal, she liked. He was a straight shooter. But being Derek's friend knocked his credibility down a few pegs.

"It's true," Mal said. "Derek's been a pain in my ass since the Beginning. Got himself captured, then escaped and returned to us, then left again. Been trying to get him to come back ever since—he's my second, even though he has a hard time following orders.

"That night at the pit, Derek said you'd be able to help him get his friend back, maybe even be our inside woman to help us take down the troxies." Mal shrugged. "And isn't that what we've all been fighting for since the Beginning?" He cut a loaded glance at Derek.

Derek leaned against the wall, hands in his pockets. "I told you, Mal. I'm not coming back."

"That's a lot of flip-flopping," said Stella. "So are you with the Faction or not?"

"After Oakwood, I rejoined them because I had nowhere else to go," said Derek. "I was detoxing and unable to fend for myself. Mal welcomed me back with his loving, open arms"—Mal rolled his eyes—"but Kev had been ousted while I was imprisoned. Things went bad quickly, and when I saw the fighting pit—saw *you* in the fighting pit...I'm not with them anymore."

Stella glanced at the discarded red mask. "Doesn't look that way to me."

Intensity sparked in Derek's eyes. It was the same look as before she climbed Oakwood's walls. Raw, untethered emotion. "I first saw you near the Memorial a few weeks ago when I was gathering supplies. I recognized you—the woman in the leaked CLEO newsfeed broadcast before Pharmatrox took it down. The woman from the ferry."

Leaked broadcast? I must have missed that. The days after the ferry were a blur of anxiety.

"Not everything is as black and white as the Faction wants to believe." Derek nodded to Mal. "Not all troxies are evil." *Mal's a defector too?* "I know it sounds bad to say I spoke up for you for my own reasons, but it got you out of the fighting pit. And I'd do it again. It got us one step closer to finding Silas and getting the intel to take down Pharmatrox." His eyes snapped to hers. "And it saved an innocent life."

I'm hardly innocent. Her darkness rumbled, and the dust whispered to her. In a lot of ways, the Faction was just as bad as Pharmatrox. Or, some of their members were. But she herself had been a part of both groups. Her time with the Marauders proved how easy it was to fall in with an organization when survival was at stake. And as a Pharmatrox scientist, she knew the allure of staying in a track and putting blinders on in pursuit of a dream, while remaining painfully oblivious to her employer's true motivations.

And would she have done any differently, had she been in Derek's position? *No. I wouldn't have. I'd do anything to get Silas back.* She'd used the Outpost and the people there much in the same way Derek had used her. But now those people meant something to her. She couldn't mean anything to Derek; they barely knew each other. But maybe him offering his continued assistance and a seat on the convoy was his way of making amends.

"Let me earn your trust. Please." Derek put a hand on her shoulder. She let him.

"All right." Stella sheathed her knife.

Derek deflated against the wall. "Thank you."

Stella eyed the vial on the counter. "That means no more lies. What's this?" She spun it to face her. *Dionazole.* Her hands shook. *Holy shit.* "Is this the detox serum?"

Mal grunted. "Yeah. But that's not what Rodney is using it for."

Derek posted his elbows on the center island. "Mal was just filling me in. Rodney and his followers use it to go on and off the dust in cycles without turning. It works, if they time it right. But sometimes they don't."

So there's more where this came from. Derek was telling the truth.

Mal scoffed. "If you call 'becoming crazy-ass, almost-turned murderers on the battlefield' working, then sure, it works."

Stella squeezed the vial. "That's insane."

"That's Rodney," said Derek. "He's the reason I left."

"And he's the reason I need you back," said Mal, crossing his arms over his wide chest. "There are people who agree with us, enough of them to fight back. Penny—and I'd rather eat my own legs than fucking admit this to her—is the only one with enough clout to overthrow Rodney. But she's not convinced yet. So I need someone to help command the troops and prepare for a coup while I keep the Faction from becoming an out-of-control band of users." He scrubbed a hand across his face and glared at Derek. "You, you dickhead. I need *you*."

Stella almost dropped the vial, a high-pitched whine sounding inside of her head. *Penny. They're working with Penny.*

"Penny's just as wild as he is," said Derek. "She doesn't take orders unless she wants to. She listened to Kev, but now that he's gone, who's going to keep her in check?"

"She'll listen to me," said Mal.

Derek scoffed. "The hell she will. She hates your guts."

"We have an...understanding."

"It's going to bite you in the ass. I don't like it."

"Penny." Stella braced both hands on the center island to keep the room from spinning. "You know Penny?"

Derek's forehead creased. "*You* know Penny?"

"She's the one who did this." Stella gestured to the dried black blood coating her arms and clothes.

"Christ." Mal pinched the bridge of his nose. "You're the one she's hunting, aren't you? You're the Architect."

Fuck, fuck, fuck—"She thinks I am, but it isn't true. It's a long story." Stella looked between the two men, her hand drifting to her machete.

Derek tapped his tattooed fingers on the counter. When his eyes found hers, her heart shot into her throat.

"I believe you," he said. "You killed the turned on the ferry, you defected. The Architect would never have done that. And if you were as powerful as the Architect, you'd be able to walk into troxy HQ and get Silas yourself. Mal, stop swearing."

"I'm just anticipating how I'm going to keep Penny from murdering your new friend."

"Woah, woah. You can't tell her about me." She chewed her lip. "I want to renegotiate our deal."

Derek slid the vial of dionazole from hand to hand across the counter. "I'm listening."

Her eyes glued to the bottle. She could take some, right now. She could quit the dust. But something dark and hollow shriveled at her center. She wouldn't take the serum. Not until Silas was safe. Not until she kept her promise to Evie. She could hold on until then.

"I need a safe place to stay," said Stella. "For me and three other people. Penny found my camp, and I don't want any of them going back there. She doesn't know about this house, does she?"

Derek shook his head. "Only Mal knows."

"Okay. So, a safe home base until we leave for the border." She counted the item off on a finger. "Access to the detox serum." A second finger. "Three extra seats on that convoy." A third finger. "We might need to delay the departure though, depending on how long it takes to rescue Silas and get him ready for travel. Can you do that?"

"In exchange for what?"

"We work together to get Silas back, and I'll let you use my Helix Key for whatever you want."

Derek rubbed his jaw. "Rodney has the serum supply on lockdown. Mal was lucky to swipe this without him noticing. I can get you one vial, maybe two. But you and Silas will need a lot more than just one vial. Fully detoxing takes a few weeks."

"Fine. I'll take whatever you can give me and figure the rest out." *Maybe I can find it in the Spire.* "What about the convoy?"

Derek nodded to Mal. "Will is his guy. So it's up to him."

"Can that key get us into Pharmatrox armories?" asked Mal.

Stella shrugged. "Probably."

Mal nodded, a thoughtful look on his face as he scratched his stubble. "I'll talk to Will." He cut a glance at Derek. "But shit is fucked right now. I can't spare any troops to help with your rescue mission. If Rodney finds out I'm disobeying his fucking 'orders,' he'll have my balls on a shish kebab."

"I'll help you," Derek said to her. "I have firsthand experience with Pharmatrox security protocols from my time in Oakwood." *Will be useful for investigating the Spire.* "And we won't say anything to Penny—she's not exactly our favorite person, so we don't need to do her any favors."

He offered his hand, and Stella shook it.

It felt better than the first time she'd made a deal with him, but the revelation of his and Mal's connection to Penny grated at her nerves. She hoped she'd made the right choice. Silas couldn't afford for her to be wrong.

Death's smile in the back of her mind was gruesome, full of serrated teeth.

And my clock is ticking too.

35

Penny

PENNY WIPED THE BLACK blood off a stolen volt rifle and placed it on the table next to the others. After winning the battle in Sector 5 three days ago, they'd swept the bodies for weapons and added them to their growing stockpile.

Once Rodney's inner circle had turned on the battlefield, Mal playing clean-up crew was the only reason they hadn't hurt anyone they weren't supposed to. It was why Rodney himself was still alive to drink himself into oblivion.

Penny added another volt rifle to the pile and moved on to a set of old handguns.

Rodney and his inner circle of lunatics were currently celebrating with copious drink and dust—of course they planned to detox afterwards. She'd have to make an appearance to show her loyalty. It wouldn't be long before Rodney would insist on her using and joining his ranks; he looked weak if she continued quietly subverting him. And Rodney hated looking weak.

She could feel his reptilian gaze on her during their "strategy meetings," and she knew what he was thinking: *How can I kill her without causing a revolt?* It was a question she herself had contemplated about him. Overthrowing him without bloodshed was getting further out of reach with the more users he added to his ranks. Her time for making a decision was running out. She'd refused to get the black eye tattoo like the rest of his followers. He'd have to kill her or make an example of her—and he'd have to do it soon.

Or, she'd have to comply. She'd have to use again.

"Clever girl. You always had a keen eye for how to flush out our prey."

Rodney's voice slithered in her mind like a viper. His specter struck her in moments like this, when she was plotting, hunting, lying in wait for her victims. Even though it had been a long time since she'd been Rodney's protégé, his training was still etched in her mind. An irreversible instinct for violence she feared she'd never shake. She shut the door on the unwelcome intrusion.

At least one good thing had come from the fraught battle—she'd found Stella's camp. She smiled to herself as she oiled another gun.

It was hard to follow Stella when she returned from supply runs; she always took a different route. So last night, Penny had launched the truck through the forest in the general direction where she suspected Stella's camp was. All she had to do was follow the sound of fighting.

But by the time she'd traced the truck's path of destruction through the woods, Stella had already abandoned the cabin. She couldn't have gotten far, but the area was swarming with turned and night had already fallen, so there wasn't time to check it out. But Stella wasn't one to lay low for too long—she was looking for something. She'd show her face again soon. And now Penny knew right where to look.

Penny grabbed a wad of dirty polishing rags and tossed them in a bucket to clean later. They'd added a hefty amount of weaponry to their already sizable stockpile, but she wanted more bullet guns. She trusted them more than the troxy volt rifles. Maybe Mal had an old Army buddy who'd be willing to siphon off some supplies.

She took stock of the weapons and…Something wasn't right. They were short about a hundred volt rifles, and the bullets were nearly gone. One of the earlier guard patrols must have moved them to another storage room up the hall, although she couldn't imagine why.

The door banged open behind her, bursting through her thoughts.

She knew who it was before he spoke. Mal had a tendency to explode into whatever room he entered. She hadn't had a chance to speak to him about their *partnership*—she hated that word almost as much as "alliance"—since the day of the battle, as they'd both been swamped with logistical duties.

She didn't bother turning around and picked up another gun to polish. "Miss me, big guy?"

"What did you do with the weapons?"

"They're right here. Need bifocals already? Aren't you a bit young for that?" She never skipped an opportunity to push Mal's buttons, but his question fanned her sinking suspicions.

Mal growled—*actually* growled—and stomped into the room. "Enough games, Penny. My guards reported that each of the six stockpile rooms are missing inventory as of early this morning."

"Sounds like you've got pretty shitty guards, then, if someone was able to steal a fuck ton of weapons from under their noses. Or, they're the ones who did it."

"My soldiers are loyal."

"Yeah, but it's not just *your* soldiers in the army, is it?"

Rodney. Somehow, this all circled back to Rodney. And from the dark look on Mal's face, he knew it too.

Shouts and the sound of footfalls flooded in from the hallway, and Penny and Mal locked eyes. *That can't be good.*

They went into the hall as other Faction members spilled into the arena from all directions.

To the fighting pit.

Rodney was putting on another show.

Bloody footprints stained the cement floor under the crowd's feet. She and Mal followed the trail to the stockpile room on the opposite side of the stadium.

Pools of sticky blood surrounded the bodies of Mal's guards. Black char marks covered the clothes and skin. *Volt rifle blasts.*

"Troxy attack?" she asked, her tone colored with doubt.

Mal's mouth flattened into a grim line. "Or someone wants us to think that."

"I'll take care of it."

Penny took off toward Rodney's office. She had the forethought to knock before entering. Hoots and hollers came from behind the closed door, and something smashed against it. She took that to mean "come in."

Plastering a devious smile on her face, she pushed into the room. Rodney's inner circle, about twenty people, crowded the large space. All were in various states of intoxication and dust haze, and the air smelled of sweat and filth. A gallon-sized plastic bag full of dust sat on a table near the windows, the curtains thrown back to reveal the view below. In the fighting pit, three turned stood chained to metal stakes in the ground, their snarls echoing through the arena. Rodney had a habit of leaving the users in the pit until they turned.

Faction members filled the stands; about half jeered in excitement while the other half stood in stoic silence. Attendance at the fighting pit had become mandatory; refusal would result in getting thrown into the pit to join the turned. So far, no one had refused.

"Penny! Welcome," said Rodney from a wingback chair behind the desk. Callum and Toby sat on either side of him, shit-eating grins on their faces. "Was wondering where you'd gotten to. Join us."

Penny pulled up a folding chair and planted herself across from Rodney, ignoring the surrounding debauchery. The man looked like hell. His eyes were still clear of the telltale black veins, but the deep purple shadows under them and the skin hanging from his knobby bones lent him a skeletal appearance. She wondered how many cycles of the dust he'd gone through to get to this point. And how much of his mind dissolved along with the dust in his system every time he detoxed.

"Some of our weapons have gone missing, and two guards are dead," she said. "Just happened. Thought you should know."

"Oh, I know." Rodney held out his hand, and Callum handed him his lucky knife—a black blade with a silver hilt. Rodney gouged grooves in the already defaced desk. She tried not to picture the many faces he'd carved with that same blade. "We won the battle of Sector 5, but we can't have people getting too complacent. Too cocky. And now that they think the troxies have breached our walls, they're begging to hit the battlefield. They're hungry for blood, for *war*. And I'll give it to 'em." Rodney slammed the knife into the desk. With his dust-induced strength, the blade went all the way through the wood to the hilt.

"Where are the weapons now?"

"Somewhere safe." Rodney gave her a wolfish smile, all yellow teeth and sharp edges.

Fuck. Rodney was creating his own stockpile. The man was a war monger. He enjoyed chaos for the sake of chaos. Just like Callum. Just like the rest of his depraved inner circle. When she'd first met the man, she'd been the same. Thirsty for vengeance, eager for blood. In many ways, she still was. But this? Killing innocent soldiers and staging a troxy raid? Jeopardizing the war and risking splitting the Faction? And for what? So he could feel like a big man, powerful and in charge?

"I see." Penny stood to go. She didn't trust herself to remain in the office without throttling him.

"You'll miss the grand finale," said Rodney. He grinned as he walked to the window, slid it open, and crawled onto the suite's roof.

At his appearance, the crowd cheered.

Penny stuck her head out the window. *What the hell is he doing?*

The moment Rodney signaled for quiet, the crowd calmed to a hush. With the voice of a showman, he said, "I'm sure you've all heard by now. The troxies hit us here, right in the center of our power. They stole our weapons, murdered our men!"

The crowd booed and grumbled. A smirk pulled at Rodney's mouth, and Penny felt sick. *The bastard lives for this shit.*

"Do not be afraid! Extra guards are patrolling as we speak. But the troxies did not infiltrate our walls on their own. No, they had help. From the *inside*." Harsh sounds rose from the crowd, and Rodney motioned for quiet. "I have a little surprise for you all."

He clapped his hands, and below, a pair of his goons pulled a middle-aged man into the center of the arena.

"The traitor! The one who sold us out to the troxies and let the fox into our henhouse!"

The spectators booed and hissed, some throwing trash and empty bottles at the man. But Rodney wasn't done.

"And his traitorous family!"

A woman and a little boy were shoved next to the man. Penny recognized the family. Newcomers who lived in a lean-to near the row of old shops. They were quiet and kept to themselves, but they pulled their weight around camp and helped with clean-up and cooking duties.

No. He can't be serious. Penny's eyes fused to the little boy, holding his mother's hand, a riot of memories roiling within her.

This cannot happen.

A low murmur rumbled through the arena. Half the crowd wasn't cheering, concerned and confused looks on their faces.

If Rodney does this, it'll be civil war. We'll never recover. We'll lose the Capital.

Rodney had launched into one of his anti-Pharmatrox speeches, and those could last a while. There was still time to stop this. Penny stepped over the comatose bodies of Rodney's followers and went into the hall—

And hit a wall of solid muscle.

She bounced back a step. "Mal?"

Rage carved hard lines in his face. She'd never seen the man so incensed. "Where is that pissant?"

She shut the office door and planted a hand on his chest. "Mal, stop. I'm handling this."

"I'll tell him it was my fault and take the fall for it. He won't kill me. He needs me."

"You underestimate just how fucking whacked Rodney is. He staged the troxy raid. He's playing on the crowd's emotions, making them question their neighbors. He's spreading unrest and mistrust and using that to fuel his war."

Mal placed a hand on the wall beside her to steady himself. "Fuck, Penny. We have to get rid of him. You have to see that now."

It was a truth she'd felt for a long time but hadn't wanted to put into words. Until now. "You're right. We need to keep that family alive first. If he kills them—"

"We'll tear each other apart. Civil war. I know. So what do we do?"

"I'll make a distraction," she said. "You get those people out of here. Somewhere Rodney can't get to them. Send them to a neutral zone with some extra supplies."

"Got it." He turned to go, but she caught his arm. His fierce gaze steadied on her.

The little boy's face flashed in her mind. Memories bubbled to the surface, and she tightened her hand around Mal's forearm. "You have to save them. Please."

His brow pulled taut and he nodded once. "I will," he said, then ran down the hall.

A strange sensation gathered at her core. *He'll save them. If anyone can do it, it's Malosi.*

Penny reentered the office, Rodney's yammering echoing through the stadium. His followers were too busy partying to pay any attention to her. Even Callum and Toby were occupied with women on their laps.

Then she saw what she needed—the plastic bag of dust on the table near the window. Now all she had to do was start a fight.

She picked the pimply bald guy with a beer belly. Squaring up to him, she batted the drink out of his hand.

He looked at her with a slack-jawed expression. "The fuck you do that for?"

"Don't you think you've had enough to drink, Tiny? Or are you trying to add an extra gallon to that already fully stocked keg you've got there?" Not her best work, but she wasn't wasting her intellect on this imbecile.

Right on cue, the man squinted his piggy eyes and swung a fist. She dodged the strike, but conveniently elbowed the bag of dust out the window and into the crowd below—the crowd of Rodney's users.

In seconds, the stands churned into turmoil. Rodney reappeared and clambered back inside, red-faced and pissed off.

Tiny came at her again, and she landed a punch in his gut. When he doubled over and fell at her feet, Rodney gave him an extra kick.

"Dammit, Bill," said Rodney. "Why you always starting fights, huh? Ruined my beautifully choreographed moment. Now the only fight they're interested in is killing each other over the dust you just dumped out the goddamn window." He threw himself into a chair with a sigh, Callum and Toby wasting no time in handing him a beer and a baggie.

Penny glanced at the pile of people below, crawling over each other to get their hands on the dust. *Hopefully Mal got that family to safety.*

Then she felt Rodney's attention shift to her like an oil slick against her skin. "Sorry Bill fucked up the big ending to my show. But don't worry. There will be another opportunity soon."

Rodney watched her for a reaction as he tossed Callum and Toby a packet of dust each, but she smoothed her expression, not giving him the satisfaction of taking the bait.

Bastard wants me to know my place. But I do know my place—it's holding a knife to his fucking throat as he begs for his miserable life.

36

THE DOOR OF DEREK'S house stood ajar when Stella returned later that night. Unease tiptoed across the back of her neck.

After making her agreement with Derek and rinsing herself off, she'd gone to the workshop to tell the others about the new place to live and her plan to save Silas. Lawrence had been noticeably absent.

"He needs some time," Tara had said. "The dust is the reason his close friend is gone, and of course he blames the troxies—not you directly, but he's having a hard time. Give me a day or two, and I'll talk him into it. I know Quentin is already on board, even though I don't trust Jonesy farther than I can drop-kick him." Jonesy was what she called Derek.

So Stella had agreed to stay away. She'd given Tara Derek's address for when they were ready. The workshop was well hidden and far enough away from the Outpost that it wouldn't be easily found, but she hoped they accepted her offer. She'd tell them about the convoy to the border once they moved in.

Stella took each step to the porch with careful deliberation. She removed her hip knife from its sheath, the cool metal a reassuring weight in her hand, and prodded the door open. The ink stain of night seeped into the quiet house, and she crept down the hallway into the kitchen. The fire in the hearth burned low, bathing the room in a soft orange blush.

A floorboard creaked behind her.

She spun low with her knife, aiming for the rib cage, but a strong hand parried her strike and caught her by the wrist. She paused as the moonlight illuminated the familiar silhouette.

"Derek."

"Stella."

He held onto her wrist. She held onto her knife.

In the light of the dying fire, his cheekbones cast his face in hollow shadows. He frowned. "Why are you trying to stab me in my own house?"

"Your door was open. Again."

He snorted. "So naturally you must enter and attack me."

"I thought someone had broken in."

He regarded her, eyebrow quirked.

"I'm not going to stab you," she added.

Before releasing her, he stroked a finger on the inside of her wrist. A strange feeling sparked in her, but she squashed it. *Careful. This one might bite.*

She sheathed her knife. "I'm beginning to reconsider my choice of shelter, as you apparently have a habit of leaving your door hanging open."

"Faulty latch," he said. "Where are your friends?"

"They'll be here in a few days."

He nodded and his gaze roamed over her, making her cheeks warm. *Stop it.* It was late, and his posture sagged from exhaustion; he probably didn't realize what he was doing.

"We should get some rest," he said. "We have a big night tomorrow."

She'd filled Derek in on the Spire and everything she'd discovered, and they planned to scout it out tomorrow night. She'd get inside, if she could. One step closer to rescuing Silas.

"Can I ask you something?" he said.

Her stomach did a weird fluttery thing as she wondered what he'd say. "Sure."

"Why haven't you taken the dionazole yet?"

She dug her nails into her thighs, her dwindling supply of dust burning a hole in her pocket. "I want to wait until we have a regular supply. I can hold on a bit longer—I'm sure there are others who need it more than me." The lie slid out of her lips, heavy and greasy.

You just don't want to quit. Death's voice floated to her, a mirror to her own dark desires. She *wanted* to quit—she didn't want to turn into a feral creature that killed everyone she came into contact with. But the dust had its hooks in her, and they weren't easy to break.

It was harder still when she didn't believe she deserved the redemption dionazole offered. Evie didn't get her second chance. So many other innocent people didn't get theirs. So what made her better than them, that she should take the detox serum and continue living a healthy life?

Derek nodded as if accepting her answer, but Death's words wrapped around her, suffocating in their truth.

The following evening, Stella ditched her new replacement backpack in the foyer and headed straight for the kitchen cabinets.

Eager to start their scouting trip, she'd complained when Derek had suggested spending the day stocking up on supplies and grabbing a snack first—what did he think she was, a toddler?—but her rumbling stomach was more than happy with the decision now. She rifled through a few shelves until she found a half-eaten jar of peanut butter, then grabbed a spoon and dug in as she fiddled with the strap of her new pack. It was bigger and had more pockets than her old one, but without her photo and her Pharmatrox ID safely in the front pocket, it felt wrong. Too light.

Derek raised an eyebrow as he sat on the counter beside her. He took his own fingertip of peanut butter and licked it off. "This plan of yours—are you sure we can do it with just us? An extra set of hands would come in *handy*"—Stella cringed—"in the event that things go sideways."

"The possibility of things going sideways is precisely why I *don't* want the others accompanying us. Not until we know more about what we're up against. Are you packed?"

Derek nodded and hopped down. "Need to grab some more gear from the garage. Be right back."

Her head pounded with the beginning of a migraine—she hadn't had caffeine since breakfast, nor had she had enough dust today. She rummaged in the cabinets for coffee and finally found some in the warming drawer under the oven, of all places. She poured the grounds in a filter and inhaled the rich aroma.

"Boo."

The canister of coffee crashed to the floor, grounds spewing like shrapnel. "Jesus Christ on a catapult!" Stella spun around to see the freckled fiend grinning at her from across the kitchen, waggling his fingers.

"Better hope the Leader doesn't hear you mentioning the Old Gods like that." Quentin smirked. "That doesn't go along with Pharmatrox's unity platform."

"What're you—you can't be here." Stella towed him toward the front door, but he dug his heels in. "I know what you're thinking, and you're not coming. I'll chain you to the chimney if I have to."

"Ah, Quentin. Good to see you." Derek strolled into the kitchen and hoisted his pack over his shoulder. "Took you long enough. I had to stall her with food."

"Your directions were shit, so I ended up wandering the alleys for an extra twenty minutes," said Quentin. "I should have followed you from a distance when I saw you two gathering supplies earlier. It's not like you're observant enough to have noticed."

"No, but she is." Derek pointed his chin at Stella, and Quentin shrugged his agreement.

Stella whipped her head between the two. "You—he—how could you—" she spluttered, unsure which of them deserved her ire more.

"Come on, Stella." Quentin rolled his eyes. "You really think I'd let you do this alone? With *him*? Fat chance."

"Thank you, Quentin," said Derek, unfazed. "Always appreciate your vote of confidence." He tossed a sheathed hunting knife to Quentin. "In case we're attacked, stab them in the face."

"Yes, I'm familiar with how a knife works, thanks."

"Or you could just fling it over your shoulder as you run away, arms flailing wildly, and hope for the best," said Derek. "Your call." Quentin snorted and stuffed the knife in his belt.

"Hang on." Stella rounded on Derek. "He's not coming! And since when are you two a team?"

"You know the kid better than I do—do you think he would have listened if I'd told him to stay behind?" said Derek. *He has a point.* "He cornered me while we were in that convenience store and offered to help. You were in the back room looking for rope or something. And I use the word 'offered' loosely. More like 'demanded aggressively with threats of bodily harm and excessive swearing.'"

Stella poked Derek in the chest. "*I'm* threatening you with bodily harm and excessive swearing. This is not happening."

"Stella, I'm an adult and I make my own decisions." Quentin's jaw took on a stubborn edge. "At the risk of negating that statement, I'll say it anyway—*You're not the boss of me.*"

Stella threw up her hands. "Fine! Fine." She aimed a finger at Derek's face. "If anything happens to him, you'll be joining that poor unfortunate soul strung up on your flagpole with your entrails dangling around your ankles." She stomped out of the kitchen, hearing Quentin's snicker and Derek's muttered *shut up.*

"Quentin!" she barked from the hallway. "Get your shit and get moving, before Lawrence the Hall Monitor comes looking for you. *That's* an argument I am certainly not having."

37

"Exactly how long are you planning to be furious with me?" Derek asked as he sidled up to Stella.

"Until you die, probably. Which, if we fuck this up, you could be out of my misery before the end of the night."

"That seems unlikely. Me dying, I mean." Derek shot a quick look at her. "And also you not being mad at me seems equally unlikely."

"If you keep babbling," she said through gritted teeth, "you'll be dead by the end of this sentence."

He snapped his mouth shut and fell into step behind her, to be quickly replaced by a bouncing Quentin. Stella heaved a long-suffering sigh.

"You mad at me too, then?" Quentin asked, entirely too chipper.

She flicked a glare at him. "Yes. Not just for tricking me, but for teaming up with *him*." She had agreed to give Derek a chance, but her grudge was hard to release.

"Stella," Quentin said, "you're my partner. Where you go, I go."

Stella sighed again, but it was half-hearted.

"Am I forgiven?" He bumped her shoulder with his.

"I *guess*. But it's not me I would be concerned about—Tara is probably worried sick. Lawrence too." Quentin bit his lip, and she gave him a flat look. "What."

"Tara was the one who told me to follow you guys."

Stella threw up her hands with an exasperated sound. "But she didn't tell you to *tag along*."

Quentin shrugged. "Semantics. She'll get over it."

Stella grumbled. "Stay out of sight and do what Derek and I say. This is serious, Quentin. Don't forget the plan."

"Right—don't get eaten," he said with a grin.

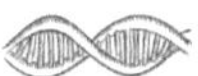

The Spire stood at the far north of the city, a forty-story ominous tower of black glass that towered over the surrounding buildings.

"Not very conspicuous, eh?" said Derek from their hiding place in an alleyway.

"How did we not notice this before?" asked Quentin.

Stella scanned the building with her Patch. "The glass panels change color," she recited from her Patch's display, "like camouflage. During the day, it blends in with the cityscape. Looks like any other building on the block. At night, like now, it shifts to match the stars and clouds. Can't see it unless it's right in front of you."

"How did you find it?" Quentin's mouth hung agape as he craned his neck and squinted into the night sky.

"Researching in the library." Stella kept it vague. The contents of Patient 4418's file haunted her. She felt guilty for stealing a look into a past Derek wanted to forget and tugged at her necklace until the gold chain bit into her skin.

Derek stilled her hand with his. "It's going to be okay."

A half smile pulled at her lips, but she was too anxious to let it fully take over. Derek looked good in the all-black guard's uniform he'd stolen during the Oakwood break-in. It suited him.

She planned to tap into the network from the guard watchtower control room and see what floor plans and files she could find while Derek and Quentin watched her back.

The Spire's invisible electric perimeter fence hummed like an agitated wasp. One touch and they'd be fried.

"Are you sure you don't want to get a key fob first?" asked Derek.

He'd informed her that some of Oakwood's cells had invisible perimeters, much like this one, that only Patched people could get through. But guards had key fobs that extended their Patch's protection to others, kind of like a mini force field, so they could transport prisoners without having to drop the whole perimeter.

"My Patch is registered in the system. It'll be fine." Sara Ellis's Patch was still functional. She had no reason to worry. Hopefully. Plus, she didn't want to risk botching an attempted fob theft and blowing their cover too early.

Quentin pulled a toboggan over his beacon of bronze hair. "We're all dressed like ninjas. I like it. Let's go kick some troxy hiney, shall we?"

He checked his own gun at his hip—he must have taken Tara's. She blanched, but he needed to be armed too.

The trio slunk toward the watchtower. Quentin went left and clung close to the buildings in the surrounding block, while Derek crouched behind an overturned car in the street. Stella flanked off to the right, closest to the watchtower, and ducked behind a rusty dumpster.

Four guards—two with M4s, two with volt rifles—patrolled the perimeter. Their war-hardened jaws sliced angular shadows in the floodlights perched on the watchtower.

When Stella signaled to Quentin, he lit a handful of firecrackers and threw them down the alley. A few seconds later, sparks and bangs fired off.

Derek lit his firecrackers and tossed them in the opposite direction. More snaps and cracks.

"What the hell?" One of the guards waved, and three of them split to investigate the disturbance. When the one remaining guard had his back turned, Stella dashed across the open space toward the watchtower.

The perimeter bubbled around her, and she burst through the other side, heart in her throat. She had only been about ninety-nine percent sure that was going to work. The remaining one percent expected she'd be liquefied into a human smoothie.

The watchtower paled in comparison to the Spire at only four stories high. Two wraparound balconies encircled the top two floors, each with an armed guard orbiting on patrol.

Quentin's second round of fireworks popped farther down the street. He only had enough left for one more round of distractions. *Gotta move fast.*

Stella headed up the watchtower stairs for the third floor. Circling a thin wire around her fists, she crept up behind the first guard and slipped the wire over his head, wrenching her hands together behind his neck. As he choked and spluttered, the wire bit into her skin, but she pulled tighter until his struggling ceased, then lowered him to the ground soundlessly and continued to the top floor to dispense with the other guard.

She slid onto the top floor balcony, but the guard was nowhere in sight.

"Hey! You there!"

Shit. Behind her.

The guard was built like a refrigerator. Stella spun low and slashed the artery in his leg, bright red blood spurting into the cool night air.

He collapsed and reached for the gun at his hip, but she grabbed his jaw and used the leverage to swing herself behind him, fitting his head into the crook of her elbow in a choke. His neck was the size of a tree trunk and was almost too much to handle, but she squeezed until his limbs flopped like a fish and he went limp.

Stella glanced below. The three guards were still investigating the fireworks while the one remained at the perimeter. From behind the car, Derek flapped his arms at her. Quentin had returned from his hijinks.

The watchtower guards subdued, Stella launched down the stairs and sprinted outside directly at the remaining guard. She jumped on his back and threw a choke around his neck. He was unconscious before he even had time to register her attack.

Derek goggled at her.

"That was *awesome*," said Quentin. "You *have* to teach me that."

Derek blinked a few times. "Did you get the fob, Quentin?" he asked.

Quentin gave a cheeky smile and held out a gray key fob. "Hug me, Derek." He wrapped his arms around a disgruntled Derek and clicked the fob, then walked through the perimeter. It bubbled around them and surrounded them in an aura. They were unharmed.

Stella's eyes widened. "Neat trick. Hang on to that. You guys guard the door. Let me know if there's trouble."

She slid into the watchtower's control room, where security feed monitors bordered the small white room. A round desk with a sleek keyboard formed an island in the center of the room.

She tapped the holographic icon floating above the desk and, to her dismay, a passcube appeared.

Dammit.

It was acting as a master lock, preventing anyone from logging in to the network from this terminal unless they solved the passcube before the timer ran out. If not completed, any number of horrible things could happen. Self-destruct codes, security alarms, even the room filling with a noxious gas.

Bad. Very bad.

It had been months since she'd touched a passcube, and she didn't trust her puzzle-solving abilities, especially in a time crunch. Her Helix Key was useless too, until she got into the system and opened a key port. She clacked a few keys and tapped icons in a pattern Silas had taught her, hoping to bypass the passcube and pull up a standard password box.

Angry red text floated in the air.

ACCESS DENIED.

She slammed her hand on the desk.

Then she had an idea—a bad one.

Most troxy computer systems were equipped with retina, facial, and voice recognition software that certain clearance levels could use in lieu of a password or passcube. Her original Patch had higher clearance than Sara Ellis...

After this, Pharmatrox would know she was alive. And that she was close. But it was her only option. Getting those blueprints was the only way to find Silas and the dionazole. Without them, they'd be flying blind. They wouldn't stand a chance.

She would not fail him.

She swapped out Sara Ellis's Patch for her original one from her pack and tapped it on. A neon blue light scanned her retina. More holographic text appeared in the air.

NAME

Her throat bobbed and her mouth went dry.

The blue holographic text blinked at her through the darkness like an insistent eye.

NAME

She cleared her throat. "Agnes Monserrat."

Her name floated in the air as the CLEO analyzed her voice patterns. The glowing blue letters seared into her vision.

WELCOME, DR. MONSERRAT.

Her name dissolved into a cloud of pixels, and the whole system was at her mercy. With a snatching motion, she pulled up the network's file system, and a port opened. When she inserted her stolen Helix Key, a slew of new icons appeared—classified information.

An icon in the shape of a tower drifted into her periphery, and she expanded it. Floor plans of the Spire. *Jackpot.* She copied the contents and sent it to Sara Ellis's Patch.

With a few quick keystrokes, she checked the Pharmatrox network for signs of Dr. Hansen—log-ins, activity, messages. Nothing. Maybe Dr. Hansen was just lying low. But she couldn't think about that now; she'd already lingered too long. The blueprints were enough.

"Log out user Monserrat," she said.

"Logging out." The room went dark.

Stella poked her head outside and slid into the shadows beside Quentin and Derek.

"Did you get it?" asked Derek.

She nodded. An empty expanse of grass stood between them and their escape, but the hard part was over.

"For a state-of-the-art facility," said Quentin, "you'd think their security wouldn't suck so badly. Only four guards? Six including the watchtower? Doesn't seem like a lot for the troxy capital of the world."

Derek made a strangled noise. "How's that for you, then?" He nodded toward the base of the Spire, where a set of twenty armored guards marched toward them, faces obscured by helmets with black visors.

Dread gathered in the pit of Stella's stomach. "Time to go." They sprinted for the perimeter, machine-gun fire rattling and volts of electricity shooting from behind them.

Pain streaked across Stella's arm from a bullet graze. *This definitely constitutes an emergency.* She fired her Glock and precious bullets into the small army on their tail. A few staggered and fell.

Ahead of her, Quentin and Derek dashed toward the main street. They were almost there.

Her relief didn't last long—a hand grabbed her from behind and threw her like a sack of flour. Rolling into her attacker, she landed a few body punches, but the guard crushed her with his bulk.

His armor covered every part of his body, so her only chance was to slip a knife between the seams. But he latched his hands around her throat as she thrashed. Her fingertips brushed the knife at her belt, her vision darkening.

Seconds before she lost consciousness, she jammed her knife under his armpit. He rolled off and clutched his wound with a yell. In their struggle, his helmet had slipped off.

Black hair. Stocky frame. Quick brown eyes she hadn't seen since the Beginning.

"Silas?"

Multiple gunshots barked through the night. She looked up in time to see Derek yank Quentin to his side, bullets and volts whistling through the air where he'd just stood. *Did...did Derek just save Quentin?* Five guards circled, guns and volt rifles pointed at them.

Stella stood, but her best friend grabbed her ankle and pulled her to the ground, then wrenched her knife out of his armpit and slashed at her.

"Silas! It's me!"

But he wouldn't relent. It was as if he didn't hear her. And his blank, empty eyes seemed to look *through* her, not seeing her at all.

Stella kicked off his attacks and staggered to her feet, but Silas lunged for her legs. Reacting on pure instinct she kneed him in the jaw, and his limp body sprawled across the grass. A sob tumbled from Stella's chest as horror, relief, and shock mingled in a confusing cocktail.

Several more guards charged toward her.

Stella wasn't strong enough to carry Silas—he was *huge*—and outrun the guards. Dragging him would only ensure they were all captured—or killed—faster.

A ball of guilt twisted in her chest as she abandoned her unconscious friend and ran toward Quentin and Derek. One guard grabbed for Quentin, but Quentin wrestled away and shot him in the throat. Derek tackled another, lodging a knife in his thigh.

A guard circled behind Stella, but she spun and stabbed him in the neck, shoving him into his partner. *Too many. We need to go.*

Volts of electricity zapped around her. She dodged and slammed her boot knife into the guard's foot, then spun and ripped her machete through the rib cage of another guard. After snatching her boot knife from the foot of the first, she tore his helmet off and stabbed him in the eye.

Grabbing his volt rifle, she fired into the remaining guards. The volts sizzled through their armor, the smell of burnt flesh and charred fabric clogging the air.

Quentin struggled with a guard, pushing the volt rifle away from his face. "Stella, I'm out of bullets!" But Derek was there first. He tossed him a knife, and Quentin shoved it in the guard's groin.

That momentary distraction was all it took.

A guard fired his M4, and Derek went down on a knee, clutching his shoulder.

No. Not Derek. Not like this.

Stella blasted the volt rifle until, finally, all was still.

As she pulled Quentin into a wordless hug, Stella looked over his shoulder toward the lawn where Silas had fallen.

Silas was gone.

"Mal could really use you in his troops, Stella. You're amazing."

Derek. His voice was an alarm in her brain, wrenching her to attention. He knelt in the grass, blood pooling around him. His skin was too pale, a sweaty sheen coating his face.

Stella pocketed her panic, pulling Derek's arm across her shoulders. "Quent, help me."

Derek sagged between them as they hobbled for the perimeter, and Quentin clicked the fob so they could shuffle through.

"Wait," said Stella, taking aim at the power console outside the watchtower with the volt rifle and firing. The metal box sparked and exploded, flames licking the building and engulfing it in minutes.

Quentin's jaw unhinged. "What was that for?"

Stella ripped Agnes's Patch from her ear and crushed it under her boot. "Should keep the troxies busy for a while." *And make it harder for them to trace Dr. Agnes Monserrat.*

"Stella." Derek's weak voice cut through the chaos. His eyes fluttered and his face glistened with sweat. "I think I need medical attention."

Stella barked a harsh laugh. "You think?" She swept his sweat-slicked hair from his forehead, panic reigniting inside her. "Lawrence can stitch you up." *Hopefully he's willing to help. This might be beyond my abilities.*

When Derek's knees gave out and he went limp, Stella and Quentin each grabbed an arm and rushed toward Maple Street.

38

Uɴᴄᴏɴsᴄɪᴏᴜs, Dᴇʀᴇᴋ ʟᴀʏ ᴏɴ his leather couch and bled into the upholstery. Now back at Maple Street, Stella undid the velcro of his vest and lifted it over his head. His long-sleeved black shirt clung to his skin, soaked with blood. She lifted the hem to pull it off, and when she jostled his shoulder, his eyes flew open with a garbled shout.

Stella cursed. "Sorry," she said, tearing his shirt up the middle and pulling it off, careful to avoid his shoulder.

His right shoulder above his armpit boasted a glistening, meaty hole. The bullet had missed the artery, but blood ran freely down his side, mixing with the tattoos that flowed across his arms and chest. She mopped it up with the soggy shirt.

Derek's nostrils flared. "That. Hurt."

"Deep breaths through your nose," she said as she shifted him to his side. His breath hissed through his teeth. "No exit wound," she said. *Joder.* She wadded up his shirt and applied pressure, his heartbeat a reassuring thump against her skin.

"Where's. Quentin."

"He took the stolen troxy van and went to get Lawrence," she said. "I need an extra set of trained hands to restrain you while I dig that bullet out of your shoulder. Plus, he probably has an herb or something you can chew on for the pain. The van only had basic medical supplies, and I already gave you some ibuprofen."

Derek grimaced. "Fantastic. The kid better not run over my bike when he parks."

"You might bleed to death and you're worried about your motorcycle. Very logical."

Derek huffed a laugh and closed his eyes. She watched his chest rise and fall, her hands trembling. And not just because of withdrawal.

"You saved Quentin." The words came out in a whisper.

His eyes flew open, bright with pain and...something else. "I just pulled him out of the way. Anyone would have done it."

She opened her mouth to thank him, but something about his closed expression silenced her gratitude. She stood to get another towel from the kitchen, but he caught her by the wrist.

"I'm sorry. About lying to you. Not telling you who I really was. I hope you can see that I'm on your side. I'm always on your side."

Derek's words shot straight to her core, and her breath hitched. Her fingers worried at her gold pendant as she searched for dishonesty hiding in his expression. But she only saw sincerity. In a world of darkness where death loomed in the air like a bad storm, it would have been easy for him to abandon her and Quentin when things had gone south at the Spire. But he hadn't. He'd stood by them. He'd pulled Quentin out of harm's way, even if he didn't think anything of his reaction. And that counted for something.

Finally, she nodded, and Derek blew out a breath, relaxing into the couch.

Stella grabbed an extra towel and pressed it against his wound. As she prepared her workstation, her thoughts went to Silas.

He's alive, he's alive, he's alive.

The words chimed with each beat of her heart. She'd seen him with her own eyes. Touched him—stabbed him. Her fingers tightened on the towel. She hoped it hadn't caused too much damage.

Now that she had confirmation Silas was alive and at the Spire, nothing would stop her from getting to him. *Nothing. And no one.* She was going back, and she wasn't leaving without him. Even if she had to burn the entire place to the ground.

A banging sound came from the hallway, and Quentin strolled into the living room holding a small shiny device. "I found this really neat spinny contraption on my way in through the garage, do you think I could keep—oh, you're not dead!"

With his good arm, Derek threw a pillow at Quentin.

Quentin batted it aside, grinning. "Lawrence is coming. He's outside. Tara says hi and she hopes you're not dead. Well, actually, she said 'maldito gilipollas,' but I think that means 'get well soon.' She can tell you herself. She wanted to come too."

Derek glanced at Stella. "How are you going to explain to them why I have a gaping hole in my arm?"

Stella's lips twitched. "I'll just tell them I shot you because you annoyed me, maldito gilipollas."

When Lawrence walked into the kitchen, she flinched. Displeasure hid in his beard, and tension leaked down the tight tendons of his arms into his white-knuckled grip on his supply bag.

Tara followed, carrying his medical kit and herb organizer. "Hiya, Jonesy. Heard you have a flesh wound." Looking each of them up and down, she blinked a few times and added, "Why are you dressed like you're about to hold up a convenience store?"

Quentin burst out laughing, then clapped a hand over his mouth. Lawrence lifted an eyebrow in his direction but didn't take his eyes off Stella. She swallowed around the cork of guilt in her throat.

"Can we do story time later?" Derek said. "I'd like it if I could stop bleeding all over my couch."

"Should have thought of that before you went and got yourself shot," Tara said with a sweet smile.

Before the two could get into it, Stella said, "Thanks for coming."

Lawrence's lips disappeared into his beard as he eyed Derek's wound, but he nodded. "Tell me what you need."

Pointing at Quentin and Lawrence, Stella said, "You two hold him. Tara, you can pass me the supplies from the kit as I need them."

"You got it." Tara knelt beside her and began unpacking items.

When Quentin sat on Derek's legs to hold him down, Derek glared at him. "Don't look so pleased about it, Quent."

Quentin snickered but cut off at a serious look from Stella.

Lawrence held Derek's arms tight to his sides while Stella grabbed the forceps from Lawrence's kit. Her hands shook so badly she could barely hold them. Nerves, shock, withdrawal. Hunger for the dust swelled within her like a tidal wave. *I can't fucking do this.*

"Carajo. Lawrence? Can you...?"

He paused, assessing her, then nodded. Twenty agonizing minutes later, Lawrence had removed the bullet and stitched Derek up. Afterward, he, Quentin, and Tara went to the kitchen to make food while Stella cleaned the wound and secured the bandages.

"Why do you look angry?" asked Derek.

She wound a bandage around his arm and pulled it a little too tightly. "I'm not angry. I'm *scared*. You could have died—*Quentin* could have died."

She *was* angry though. Angry at herself for robbing Lawrence of his friend and handing him his own personal darkness; for endangering Quentin when she could have tried harder to make him stay behind; for getting Derek caught in the crossfire. She'd never be so careless again.

"Ah," said Derek. "I understand. Could you not take it out on my wound, please?" Sweat dripped down his forehead, and she went back to her bandaging with a more gentle hand.

"Silas is alive," she blurted.

"*What?*" Derek tried to sit up, but she forced him down.

Quentin zoomed to her side, eyes wide. "You found him?" Over his shoulder, he said to Lawrence and Tara, "Silas is their friend, the one Stella has been looking for."

A strange, unreadable expression creased Lawrence's face.

Tara waved a peanut-buttered knife in their direction. "Good," she said. "Reuniting with people these days is damn near impossible."

Returning her attention to Quentin and Derek, Stella said, "He was one of the guards. He didn't recognize me. It's like they wiped his brain and rebooted him."

Derek's face darkened. "Sounds like a more extreme version of what they did to us at Oakwood. I could still remember my actions and who I was, but I had other...inexplicable urges."

Stella swallowed and avoided eye contact. "Something bothers me though," she said, then ripped off a piece of medical tape with her teeth. "Why would they use Silas as a guard? They're spending a lot of money pumping him full of expensive experimental drugs. Why risk him on the front lines?"

Quentin shrugged. "Free labor?"

"Mmm." Stella placed the last piece of tape. "Maybe."

Derek's eyes fluttered as he fought to stay conscious. She helped him drink some water before leaving him to rest and steered Quentin into the kitchen, where a stack of sandwiches awaited them.

Quentin cut one down the middle and handed half to Stella. She took a bite and fidgeted with her hair.

"What is it, Stella?" Quentin asked without looking at her. He only had eyes for his sandwich. "You're more agitated than a cow that needs milking."

Stella scowled. "Thank you. It's every woman's dream to be compared to a cow. But, ah…" She glanced at the others, but her guilt would not be contained. "I appreciate your help, but this is where it ends. It's getting too dangerous. This is my fight, not yours."

Tara chewed for a long moment, then spoke. "This fight belongs to all of us. Let us decide for ourselves if and how we help. Maybe if you'd had more backup tonight, Quentin wouldn't have such a blood pressure-destroying story, and Jonesy wouldn't have caught a bullet."

Maybe Tara had a point. Rescuing Silas wasn't a feat she could accomplish alone, no matter how much she wanted to. Tonight's events proved that. Breaking into the Spire would take a lot more firepower than just a few people armed with old guns and knives. She needed trained fighters, people with access to real weapons. And people with a personal vendetta against Pharmatrox.

The Faction.

But according to Derek and Mal, there was no reasoning with Rodney. The Faction was barely holding it together in the Capital. The only way to get the Faction's help was to get rid of Rodney. And the only way to get rid of Rodney was—

Penny. She needed Penny.

Estoy entre la espada y la pared. Joder.

No, there has to be another way. I'll find another way.

After the adrenaline rush of the night, she couldn't come to terms with that fact quite yet. She gnawed her lip and twisted her necklace.

Eyes locked onto her pendant, Lawrence said, "Stella, can I have a word? Outside." His voice was calm, but something dark and dangerous rippled down her spine.

She nodded and followed him out onto the patio. *He's going to yell at me for bringing the turned into the Outpost, for almost getting Quentin killed. For being a troxy and lying to them. As he should.*

A wash of night air swept over her, cooling the sweat on her brow. Shadows darkened Lawrence's face. Because of his kind nature, Stella often forgot how big and imposing he was. A vision of him chopping through a thick oak tree with brute strength flashed in her mind. The gentle facade could hide so much.

Lawrence's expression fell open like an empty grave, and his golden eyes burned into hers. The tension in the air pulled as tight as a drum.

He reached into his pocket and held out an ID card. Her Pharmatrox ID card. Behind it was her creased photo. The ones from her torn bag.

No, please not now.

Her voice came from a million miles away. "Where did you get those?"

He slapped the items on the patio table. "*Agnes*—a name I'll never forget." His fingertips brushed her cheek and slid down her neck, poised like a scorpion's tail, and he thumbed her gold pendant. "The last time I heard that name, I watched my friend Evie murdered in front of me."

His fingers tightened at the base of her throat.

"But I don't have to tell you that." He fixed her with his black stare. "Your hair is different, but it's you. *This*"—he slammed a hand onto the ID and the photo—"is you. You were there that night. You killed Evie."

Stella took a half step back, but he held her close in a terrifying embrace.

"You have to listen to me, Lawrence." Stella searched his face for any lingering signs of the gentle giant, the kindly gardener, the man she'd consider a friend if the world were normal and not full of darkness. But that man was gone. "Evie was my best friend. I knew her—Before. We grew up together. Please, you don't understand the situation—"

The back door banged open and Quentin poked his head outside.

Lawrence sprang away from her, shoving his hands in his pockets.

"Lawrence! Derek's bleeding again," said Quentin. "He needs more of your magical poultice and Stella's hand. For bandages, I mean." His eyebrows did a lascivious dance in Stella's direction, but he froze when he noticed the anguish on her face.

"Coming," said Lawrence in a gruff tone and shouldered past Stella without a glance.

Quentin opened his mouth to say something, but Stella shook her head. First, she had to make sure Derek didn't expire on his own couch. Then she could tackle her bigger problems.

Mainly, explaining to Lawrence why she killed their best friend.

39

AFTER—DAY 152

"S TELLA. *STELLA.*"

A hand flapped in her face.

Oh right, that's me. Stella glanced up from the potato she was peeling.

Dressed in dark pants and a black shirt, Penny's slender figure belied a furious strength. Stella had seen her snap necks and limbs with her bare hands countless times. Backlit by the campfire and surrounded by a smoky haze, the woman looked like she'd stepped straight out of hell.

"What is it?"

"Another camp to raid." Penny's hand twitched toward her pocket, but she caught herself and smoothed her palm against her thigh, jaw clenched.

From what Stella could tell, Penny was a former user who had somehow miraculously kicked the habit. The scientific part of her had so many questions.

"I need you to check it out tonight," Penny said. "Same thing as usual. How many people, what their fortifications are like, any weapons." She flicked her hand. "I don't need to tell you. You're getting good at this."

Stella nodded and went back to her potato peeling. "I'll see to it."

Penny went to confer with Callum, her second-in-command. Well, of the entire crew, he was the only one who seemed close to her. Penny wasn't one to share power. Everyone else gathered around their own separate campfires spread throughout the woods.

A married couple had set up their area a stone's throw from where Stella sat around Penny's fire with Toby. Farther through the trees, other fires dotted the growing darkness. Two brothers in their thirties, Eric and Grisham, were Penny's muscle. She used them during raids to beat the camp occupants into submission. Or kill them, when necessary. Two women around Stella's age huddled around the last fire, holding each other close. Molly and...Stella didn't know the other woman's name.

Somehow, Penny kept them all supplied with the dust—a way to keep them under her thumb. They'd do anything she said. Penny never let anyone get too out of hand—she'd put them down before they turned. But she had no issue using their erratic and manic behavior to her advantage.

Stella had never seen what happened on raids, but it was not difficult to imagine. She knew the trail of blood the Marauders left in their wake. But this was their arrangement, and she'd agreed to it. Stella was in charge of scavenging for food, and she scouted out the camps. She didn't ask any questions. In turn, Penny never made her go on the raids, and she afforded her protection. She tried not to think about the fact that she'd essentially joined the Faction. *It's just so I can stay alive until I find Dr. Hansen or Silas, or figure out what to do next.*

Stella sliced the potato and plopped it into the pot piece by piece. Toby watched her with a keen gaze. He acted like an imbecile most of the time. But that was what Stella suspected—it was an act. If everyone presumed you were stupid, they never thought to see you as a threat. You could fly under the radar. For that reason, Stella made sure to never underestimate Toby.

Finished with the preparations for dinner, Stella nodded to Toby and headed off to scout.

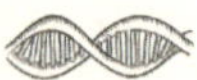

Stella crept through the dense woods toward the nearby camp. Her weapon of choice—a machete Penny had given her shortly after she joined the group—bounced against her thigh. Her job was to watch, listen, and remain unseen. Hidden in the trees, she settled in to observe.

The camp squatted at the edge of a farmer's field. A blanket of fog wafted low through the grass. She could see why Penny wanted this prize.

It was a large and well-established camp. Several tents circled around a central fire. A shed to the right appeared to house their food and supplies, with ample stacks of dry firewood piled outside.

Stella counted ten people—more than she'd seen in a group since she'd met the Marauders. An older woman with long salt-and-pepper hair stirred a pot over the fire as she spoke to one of the men. After he nodded and jogged off, others approached her, and she directed them on their way too. *So this one's the matriarch.*

The camp lacked obvious fortifications like a fence or barrier, but two men patrolled at regular intervals. One—a tall, solid man with a sandy beard—carried an axe. The other—short and burly—held a wicked-looking dagger. Neither appeared to have guns. *Good, Penny will like that.*

Stella shifted her attention back to the main group around the fire. *Several young women, some older men, and—*

Stella froze. A familiar face, although more gaunt and haggard than she'd ever seen her, accepted a bowl of soup from the matriarch.

"Evie?" Stella whispered.

Evie's eyes shot up and locked on Stella where she was hidden in the tree line fifty yards away. Stella jerked and lay flat, willing herself to meld with the forest floor. She immediately felt ridiculous. There was no way Evie could have heard or seen her from such a distance. But she waited a few minutes before crawling away.

Boots crunched behind her.

"Agnes. How'd you find me?"

Evie. Stella flipped around and regained her feet with as much dignity as she could muster, though a few small sticks clung to her hair. "I should be asking you that question. It's dark as a cave out here, and I wasn't anywhere near you, and yet you *heard* me?"

"And I saw you."

Stella's eyes bulged. "How?"

Evie just looked at her.

In the moonlight, her friend looked even more pale and sickly than she had months ago. She was too thin, her previously plump and dimpled cheeks now sunken and hollow. Stella cleared her throat. "Evie, you look a mess. How much are you using?"

The Evie she had abandoned those few months ago would have raged at the question. This Evie sagged in defeat and picked at the hem of her shirt. "A lot. Too much." She lifted her eyes to Stella's, and Stella stumbled back a half step. Black veins shattered the whites of Evie's eyes. She'd seen it in some of the crew members right before Penny sliced her sickle across their throats.

"Wait here," said Evie. She snuck toward one of the tents and ducked inside, returning a few moments later with a black drawstring bag. She handed it to Stella. "I need you to take this."

Her jaw dropped when she peered inside. "How…?"

"After you…left, I got as far away from those thugs as I could. I was heading back to the city to break into the lab and get more dust. I wasn't thinking clearly and was hallucinating most of the time. I found an ambulance crashed in a gully." She nodded to the package Stella clutched against her chest. "That was hidden under the metal flaps in the floor. I want you to take it. I want to stop."

Stella slung the bag stuffed with packages of the dust over her shoulder. "Why didn't you stop when we knew the risks?"

"That shit was designed to be addictive, Agnes. You can't just *stop*." Black tears ran down Evie's face, and she swiped them away. "I'll never see Silas again. I'll spend the rest of my life not knowing if he's alive or dead."

Evie glanced at the bearded man with the axe patrolling in the distance. A smile stretched across her dry lips. "But at least I'll have a friend beside me to end it before I hurt anyone. Lawrence thinks he can save me. That there's some cure he can grow in his garden. I don't have the heart to tell him I've already given up. He found me three months ago during one of my hallucinative episodes. Instead of leaving me to die, he took me in. Later, we joined up with Ruth and her people. I…I know I can be dangerous. But they're trying to help me. As much as I can be helped, anyway." She gestured to the black smears on her cheeks.

Stella nodded over Evie's shoulder at the tight community sharing a meal around the fire. "They look like good people." Guilt clawed at her insides.

Usually on her scouting missions, she remained emotionally removed. She had to, in order to keep her place in Penny's crew and survive. But not this time. She pulled her friend into a tight embrace to hide her own tears threatening to spill over. When she broke away, she said, "I have to go." Her heart broke as she looked into Evie's face, unrecognizable from the cheeky woman who had sat beside her on the ferry those few months ago. "You're my best friend, Evie. You always will be."

As Stella headed back to camp, her resolve hardened. For the first time, she was going to lie to Penny.

40

AFTER—DAY 152

S TELLA SHIVERED IN THE night's cool air as she headed toward Penny's campfire. She'd stowed the drawstring bag of dust a safe distance from camp in a hollow tree and decided to keep it secret until she could pretend to find it on a scavenging mission. It was a weak plan, but she didn't have any better ideas. She needed sleep and food. But first, she had to report.

Penny, Toby, and Callum looked up as she approached the circle of their fire. Stella swallowed the dry lump in her throat and sat. Toby fiddled with a pocketknife and dug tiny holes in the dirt. Callum narrowed his eyes at her and sniffed. He didn't like how Penny had taken Stella under her wing.

"Well?" Penny lifted an eyebrow as she took a drag from her cigarette.

Stella licked her lips around the lie. "I went to the location you described. Didn't find anything." She shrugged and hoped it looked casual. "If there ever was a bountiful camp there, they've moved on and taken their gear with them."

Penny's eyes were chips of fire as she stared directly into Stella's soul. Stella plastered an unaffected look on her face, but her throat bobbed with a gulp.

Penny exhaled a cloud of smoke and tossed her spent cigarette in the fire. "Interesting you say that. Toby has a different report."

Stella's heart galloped in her chest. "Why would Toby have a report at all?"

"He followed you. He always follows you on your scouting missions."

Stella's mouth popped open before she could stop it. An impish grin flicked across Toby's face before his impassive mask settled back in place.

Penny laughed. "You think I got to be in charge of this bunch of vagabonds by *trusting them*? Hell no. You're the newest, and while you've been doing an admirable job—until now, of course—I still didn't trust you. And with good reason, apparently. Who's the girl you were talking to?"

Stella's heart leapt into her throat. "I don't know what you mean."

Penny glared. "Stella. You're caught. It's in your best interest to stop *lying to me*." She shot to her feet and kicked the nearby stew pot into the fire with a crash. Stella flinched and backed away, but Penny grabbed her and dragged her into the woods.

"Callum, tell everyone to get ready," Penny said over her shoulder. "We're raiding. Tonight. And Stella's coming with us."

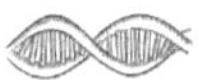

Penny thrust a red bandanna at Stella as she donned her red Faction mask. "Cover your face."

Stella, in survival mode, obeyed. Her hands shook as she tied it behind her head and pulled the fabric under her eyes. Thoughts of how she could have resisted Penny raced through her mind, but too late. She was set on her trajectory. All she could do now was try not to be killed or hurt anyone.

The Marauders lurked in the dark forest near Evie's slumbering camp, weapons brandished and faces obscured.

Penny stared at Stella through her red mask. "Well?"

Stella answered automatically and reported on the camp's supplies, weapons, and security.

Penny twirled her sickle in thought. "Right. Same plan as always." She snapped her fingers and the crew slunk away, fanning out around the tents. They paired off, and each duo took one of the five tents. Penny hauled Stella with her. When everyone was in position, Penny whistled through her teeth, sharp and loud.

Penny ripped open the tent with her sickle and dragged out the sleeping body. The rest of the crew followed suit. Stella stood by, arms hanging limply at her sides.

Confused screams pierced the air as the crew restrained the slumbering campers. When Molly crushed Evie into the dirt, Stella looked away, a hollow feeling in her chest.

"Good morning!" Penny sneered into the face of the lumpy middle-aged man she sat astride and grabbed his mouth in a rough grip. "Which one of you is in charge?"

At the disturbance, the perimeter guards thundered into camp. The stout, burly man raced into view first, with Evie's Lawrence close behind. "What's this?" asked Lawrence, axe held aloft.

Penny rose with her hands on her hips. She nodded to Callum, who was enjoying taunting the woman cowering before him. "Line them up."

The crew jostled their charges to kneel in front of Penny. After a brief altercation and much cursing, Lawrence and the other guy fell into line. Five men and five women.

"What do you want?" The older woman with the salt-and-pepper hair spoke. Her voice was like a dusty gravel road, and the tan skin of her face was weathered to match.

Penny's head swiveled to the woman. Stella knew Penny well enough to know she was smiling beneath her mask. She'd found their leader.

"You're fortunate to have quite the stockpile," said Penny. "Unfortunately for you, we're taking it." With a snap of her fingers, the married couple scurried off to the shed to start unloading the goods. Penny brushed the blade of her sickle across the woman's cheek in a caress. "How messy this gets depends on how much you resist."

An older bald man beside the matriarch struggled against his captors with a look of fury.

"Peace, Shahid," said the woman.

"But, Ruth—"

"I said *peace*." Ruth looked at Penny, her face calm and impassive. "Let them take what they wish."

Patting Shahid on the cheek, Penny said, "Your woman is smart. One last question, then we'll be on our way." She turned and addressed the larger group. "Who has any information on the Architect?"

A chill silence spread down the line. Stella frowned. Admitting knowledge of anything related to Pharmatrox was a death sentence—everyone knew that. Did Penny ask this of all the camps she raided? Stella didn't imagine she'd had much success.

"Not interested in talking, I see. Perhaps you're in need of persuasion." Penny grabbed Evie by the hair and hauled her close.

Stella and Lawrence both lunged forward, but Stella planted her feet firmly in place. Standing up for Evie would likely only get her killed faster.

"Cool it, Lawrence," said Evie.

He fell back, a murderous look on his face as Penny held her sickle to Evie's throat.

"You're not afraid to die," Penny said. It wasn't a question.

"I've been dying for months." Evie stared at Penny, unblinking. "Why are you looking for the Architect?"

Penny pulled Evie closer. "To kill him. He's the reason my family is dead."

"Killing him won't bring your family back. It won't cure the users or turned." Evie gestured to herself and to the Marauders.

What are you doing! Stella wanted to scream at Evie.

"No, but it would certainly make me feel better. What do you know?" Penny's nails dug into Evie's throat.

"Please!" said Ruth, tears shining in her eyes. "She doesn't know anything. We found her near the Metro City facility. She's just a user we're rehabilitating. She knows nothing!"

"*The facility?*" Penny shoved Evie and approached Ruth. Her hand whitened on the hilt of her sickle. "You're all *troxies*?"

Realizing her mistake, Ruth's eyes went wide. "No! Not all of us—"

With a screech, Penny slashed her sickle across Ruth's throat, a trail of blood arcing through the air.

The camp exploded in chaos.

The Marauders attacked with fervor. A few of the campers went down easily, but the ones who did not ran for the ruins of their tents and seized weapons.

Stella stood frozen at the edge of the melee. Screams shattered the stillness of the night. Blood sprayed. Detached limbs fell to the ground. But above it all, she heard one thing.

Her name.

"Agnes!"

The sound of Evie's voice propelled her into action.

Evie fended off Callum as he circled her. Stella ripped her machete from her belt, not sure what she planned to do. She couldn't *kill* Callum—she'd never killed a human. Her spine turned to jelly at the thought. But Callum *would* kill Evie, and she couldn't let that happen.

Stella ran full speed into Callum. Caught by surprise, he buckled under her weight. But his wiry frame rolled with her attack, and he rebounded to his feet. He bared his teeth, hands at his side in claws.

He darted in and out of Stella's reach, teasing her. She managed to bumble out of his way, but her luck didn't last. Still uncomfortable wielding a blade as long as her forearm—or any blade, for that matter—her grip was lax. When Callum blocked one of her strikes, her machete flew from her grasp.

He clamped a hand around her throat and lifted her in the air, his eyes glittering with malice behind his red mask. Stella kicked her feet uselessly.

"Enough."

At Penny's voice, Callum glanced to the side, but his fingers tightened around Stella's windpipe in a challenge.

"I won't ask again." Penny's tone brokered no argument.

A pause. Then Callum dropped Stella, and she coughed and gasped for breath. Slowly, she became aware of her surroundings and the camp that had become a battlefield around them.

Bodies littered the grass. Dark patches glittered in the faint moonlight. Tents burned and gushed acrid smoke into the sky.

Lawrence and Evie were the only ones still alive and fighting. They had their hands full keeping the wife and the brothers at bay. The Marauders had lost three—Molly and her partner, and the husband. Their bodies lay in bloody pools beside the campfire.

When Penny whistled again, the remaining Marauders pounced on Lawrence and Evie, forcing them to their knees in front of Penny. She tapped her sickle against her thigh and said, "Which one of you would like to live?"

Evie frowned. "What?"

Penny took off her mask and crouched beside her. "I always leave one troxy alive, to tend to your dead and spread the story of what happened here. I want the Architect to know I'm coming for him. I want all troxies to know they aren't safe."

A beat of silence.

Penny shrugged. "All right, I'll choose." She raised her blade, aimed at Lawrence.

Evie lurched forward. "No! No, take me. Please."

Lawrence looked at her, bewildered. "Evie, get out of here, go! They can have me."

"How sweet." Penny nodded at Eric and Grisham, who carted Lawrence off to the woods out of earshot, but he'd be able to see everything just fine. He thrashed, kicking up a cloud of dust as they hauled him away.

Penny's eyes roamed over Evie's rumpled clothes, her sunken cheeks. She seemed almost reluctant, but raised her weapon. When an involuntary squeak escaped from Stella, Penny's gaze snapped to her.

"Stella should do it," said Penny. "This is her first raid. This kill is hers."

Everything happened in a blur. Callum pressed a knife into Stella's hand, and she was shuffled to stand in front of Evie. But her legs wouldn't hold her weight, and she collapsed, eyes wide with terror.

But when she looked at Evie's face, she saw acceptance. Peace. "Agnes." Evie knelt, her dry lips pulled back in a weak smile. Black tears coursed down her cheeks, leaving inky stains in their wake. She took Stella's hands. "Agnes, it's okay. Look at me. I'm already dead. I died that day I left Roberto behind in the bunker. I loved him."

Stella blinked, taken aback. "You never told me that."

A dark look flashed across Evie's face. "There are a lot of things I never told you." She gripped Stella's hand that held the knife. "You have to do this, Agnes. Just promise me you'll find Silas. You're the only one who can save him."

"I—I can't *stab* you, Evie—"

"That woman will kill us both if you don't, and you deserve to live. So *live*," Evie said, squeezing Stella's hand in permission.

Stella shut her eyes and raised the knife—but no. Evie deserved to see the eyes of a friend.

A raw, animalistic scream tore from Stella's throat as the knife slid into Evie's neck. From the far edge of the forest, she heard her own despair mirrored in Lawrence's roar of rage. She rested her face against her friend's as the sobs rattled through her, when something cold pressed against her cheek.

A pendant encircled Evie's neck, a small gold disk no bigger than her pinky nail. On the back, ELM was etched in black script: Evelyn Luanne Markson. She removed it and put it around her own neck, tucking it beneath her shirt.

A hand squeezed her shoulder. "A mercy," Penny said with a pensive look. "At least this way, her death was swift and kind."

Stella wanted to rage at Penny, to shout and tell her she was wrong. But a small seed of doubt pulsed in her heart. Evie had chosen to use her death to save her and Lawrence, but that didn't stop the jaws of guilt from gnawing at Stella's insides. She could have done more to dissuade the

Marauders from raiding the camp. It was because of her that innocent people were dead. She could have stood up to Penny.

But she was too weak. Too afraid. And that had cost her. She hung her head in defeat and allowed Penny to pull her to her feet.

The brothers tied Lawrence to a tree and left a knife near his feet so he could free himself when they were far enough away to avoid being tracked.

As she walked past Lawrence, Stella let her dark curtain of hair fall forward to cover the part of her face not obscured by her bandanna. A maelstrom of shame, guilt, and horror churned in her stomach.

They left the smoldering remains of the camp behind, Lawrence's sobs echoing in her ears.

Something plopped to the ground between her feet.

Back at camp, Stella sat with her back against a tree, a cup of potato soup congealing in the mug beside her. The few bites she'd managed to force down earlier had almost made a reappearance. She pulled herself out of her misery long enough to scowl at the person who stood over her. An uncharacteristic look of pure joy brightened Penny's face.

Stella looked down. *And there's the pukey feeling again.*

The black drawstring bag. The black drawstring bag of *dust* that she'd *hidden in a tree.*

Stella opened her mouth, but Penny cut her off. "Toby brought me the little treasure trove you stashed away. I must say, I'm impressed. That's enough to keep us going for at least another few months."

The fire had cooled to embers, dampened by the late morning rain. Stella hadn't slept all night. She'd watched the fire dwindle, and with it the last of her will to live.

"How'd you get it?"

"My—my friend." Stella's voice cracked. Penny reached for the bag, but Stella snatched it. "This is *mine*," she said with a sudden burst of aggression. "If you want it, I have some conditions."

Penny's eyes narrowed.

"I *will not* accompany you on any more raids. I will not kill. I'll scavenge and gather supplies, but that's it. I'll make sure you have enough dust." She didn't know how she'd fulfill that promise, but she'd figure something out. "In exchange, I get my own share of the goods, and you keep training me to use this." She prodded her machete on the ground with her toe.

Penny cocked an eyebrow. "If you're not going to kill, I don't see why I should keep training you. Your talents will be wasted."

"I won't kill your hapless victims. But I need to know how to defend myself." *I need to get away from you, even if I have to fight my way out.* Penny wasn't one to tolerate defectors from her ranks.

Penny regarded her for a moment, then nodded and took the bag, tossing a small baggie of translucent powder at Stella. "Your share of the goods, as demanded."

Stella dropped it and recoiled. The powder shimmered like fresh-fallen snow, hiding the dangers obscured in its depths. "I don't want *that*."

A wicked smile curved Penny's lips. "You will tomorrow."

"What?"

"Toby put some in your soup. You're a user now, Stella. You need the dust—you need *me*—to survive. So consider this your official welcome to the Marauders." With that, Penny dropped a red mask at Stella's feet and headed to her tent.

Her whole body trembled. Evie's face, gaunt and streaked with black stains, flashed before her eyes. *A user. Joder, I'm a user. I'm going to turn.*

She'd lost everything—and worse, it was her own fault. She didn't save Evie. She'd abandoned Silas to his fate. She worked for the very company that brought destruction down on all of them. She'd ignored Silas's warnings all those years ago. She'd sparked the war. Every cell in her brain screamed at her in a repetitive loop.

Your fault. Your fault.

The eyeless red mask stared right through her, its empty smile mocking her. The baggie of white powder at her feet held the sweet promise of oblivion, but she refused to look at it.

She wrapped her arms around her knees as sobs rattled her ribcage.

It was a long time before the dust called to her.

And when it called, she answered.

41

S TELLA RAN THROUGH THE deserted city streets, but the baptism of sweat could not cleanse her of her guilt. The look on Lawrence's face when he recognized her for who she truly was plagued her. He'd never look at her with warm, friendly eyes again.

She'd awoken in the middle of the night in a tangle of blankets, panicked at the unfamiliar surroundings. Restless, she'd pulled on her boots and took off into the night.

Three days of living in the spare room at Derek's house wasn't enough time to get used to sharing a home with a man—or anyone, for that matter. She'd lived alone for most of her adult life, and an attractive ex-Faction soldier was not who she thought her first roommate would be.

Nor did she expect a gangly, freckled teenager and a badass master-of-all-martial-arts woman to be her *second* and *third* roommates.

After Stella's disastrous confrontation with Lawrence, he had asked Tara and Quentin to leave the workshop. Tara checked on him once a day, but his absence was a gaping hole felt by all. Quentin pestered Stella about what had happened, but it was not her place to share. If Lawrence didn't want them to know, she wouldn't tell them.

Hands braced on her knees, Stella sucked in the chilly air of the late night, or very early morning. She'd run slow laps around the house, not wanting to venture too far with the possibility of turned staggering around. But she needed the movement to work out her anxiety and to handle the withdrawal symptoms. She was still using but had drastically reduced her intake. The headaches were fierce and the night sweats brutal. Her body hardly had the energy to run, but her racing mind needed the distraction.

As Stella started another lap, Derek tugged at her curiosity, and she turned her thoughts to untangling his possible motives for agreeing to her demands. *He's doing it for Silas's sake, not mine. Derek has his own interests, whatever they are.*

But was all of this—working together, arranging the convoy, letting her stay at his house—just because of their shared connection to Silas? Before the botched Spire recon mission, she would have said yes. But Derek had looked out for Quentin's safety. Maybe he was in this for more than just personal reasons. He'd certainly seemed to take an interest in her, at least for her Pharmatrox credentials. But perhaps it went beyond that. After almost losing Derek at the Spire, she knew he was more to her than a means to an end. Maybe they were becoming...friends? Allies? She wasn't sure what to call it.

But could she trust that inkling? Something held her back. She hadn't allowed Derek to accompany her to the library when she started reviewing the stolen Spire blueprints yesterday. It would be strange to let an ex-Faction soldier watch her as she worked with her hijacked Pharmatrox technology. It would feel too...exposed. Not to mention, she was accustomed to working alone.

While Stella disagreed with the Faction, it *had* lit a fire in the resistance—even if it started a bloody war with atrocities on both sides. As she delved deeper into the sinister world of Pharmatrox's secrets, she began to understand why someone would see blood and violence as an attractive answer to dealing with the pervasive evil of Pharmatrox's empire. She could see how someone like Penny could get sucked into the vortex, but what of Derek? She had no idea what kind of man he was—today or before the world fell apart.

Stella halted at the foot of the porch as she grappled with her complicated web of thoughts. By freeing her from the fighting pit, Derek had made his choice. He'd broken from the Faction. But he'd joined them for a reason.

Did he harbor an ember of troxy hate that the Faction had fanned into a blazing rage? Had he lost someone to the dust? Mal and Derek both said the Faction had strayed from its original intent under Rodney's leadership, and that's why Derek had left. But did that original hate that sparked a revolution still live within him?

If it came down to a choice between her and Silas, and his friends who remained in the Faction, who would Derek choose? Could she trust him to choose the right side?

What side even is *the right side?*

Since getting to know Derek and interacting with Mal, she couldn't say that everyone in the Faction was like Penny. Stella trusted Derek to look out for her and her friends' safety. But anything else was still up in the air. He—

"Stella?"

She jumped out of her skin.

Derek sat on the roof, feet dangling over the edge. "You out here digging a trench?" he asked, nodding at her fervent pacing that cut a path through the fallen leaves.

"What are you doing? How'd you even get up there, in your condition?"

"This is my house, Stella. If I want to play on the roof in the middle of the night, I can. *You're* the one who's trespassing. And quit making me sound like a disobedient grandpa. My shoulder hurts, but I can still function."

"I live here now too. Not trespassing."

His smile flashed in the darkness. "Get up here."

"What?"

He gave her a flat look. "I watched you climb a twelve-story building. You don't get to use the stairs. *Get up here.*"

Stella grumbled, but his demanding tone sent a weird little pleasant feeling through her. *Nope, don't you dare. Shut it down.* She grabbed the porch railing and climbed until she straddled the roofline beside him, pushing *those kinds* of thoughts away.

From their perch, the perfect grid of symmetrical streets stretched to the Memorial. Stella looked away from the scar on the skyline with a pang in her chest. A small part of her wished she could do more. She'd played a role—albeit indirectly—in Pharmatrox rising to power. She'd been a cog in the Pharmatrox machine. But it was too late to fix the country. The only option was to escape and make sure Silas and her new friends got to safety.

But what about the Architect? whispered Death in the back of her mind. Finding the true Architect would get Penny off Stella's case. But even if she did find the Architect, what good would that *really* do? If the Architect held all the answers, they would have fixed everything by now—right?

If the Architect couldn't fix anything, why would I be able to?

Shutting off the deluge of analytical thoughts, Stella turned a wistful gaze to the sky. A swath of stars and the tendrils of the Milky Way dappled the velvet night.

"What are you thinking about?" asked Derek.

After a long moment, she answered. "For the first time in my life, I can see every single star in the heavens. It's the most beautiful thing I've ever seen. And then I look at the havoc we've wreaked on the ground. I see the darkness all around us. And I don't understand how some god or celestial being or whatever, who could create something as beautiful as what I see up there, could stand by and let us destroy what it made down here."

Derek nodded as he considered her words. "Everything that's happened since the Beginning—it's changed people. When faced with impossible choices, you learn who you really are. What you're truly capable of." His eyes got a distant look in them for a moment, then his gaze snapped back to hers. "You learn what you're willing to do for those you love."

Heat crawled up her neck, and she looked back to the sky, her thoughts turning to Quentin, Tara, and Lawrence. Evie. Roberto. Silas. She flicked a glance at Derek, and her insides warmed. The roster of people she cared for welled inside her like a wave, ready to smash her wooden rowboat against the unforgiving shore.

"Tell me about your life Before," she said.

Derek pushed his dark hair back. "Did a stint in the service for a while, but the military life wasn't for me." He made a face. "Problem with authority."

"And because then you couldn't have the floppy hair or the almost beard."

"Right. And then I somehow ended up in the exact same job with an equally infuriating commanding officer in Malosi Olesa." He rubbed a tattooed hand over his mouth and shook his head, but she saw the smile that hid underneath. "Before that though, I worked odd jobs here and there. Security details, deliveries, construction. Helped repair some of the SubTran trains. Never stuck with anything for too long though."

"Why not?"

Toying with a loose shingle on the roof, he said, "I guess I was just wandering around, searching for something that didn't make me feel so damn alone."

Stella studied his silhouette as the peachy hue of early daybreak faded through the night sky. He cut a striking profile.

"I like to paint," he said.

The abrupt revelation took Stella by surprise.

"I never wanted to be an artist," he said. "I didn't want to turn my escape into something I relied on for my livelihood. Art is my refuge, not my means to an end. Not that I think professional artists are hacks. Just that I know I would be, if I were one. So I save my brush for when the pain is too great or my thoughts are too dark. And then I put it on a canvas."

"What kinds of demons are hiding in your darkness, Derek?"

He didn't answer right away. They watched as the sky deepened into strokes of fuchsia and ruby. Derek remained silent for so long she thought he wasn't going to answer.

In a small voice, he said, "I was on the ferry."

His words were a bucket of ice water upended over her head. She gripped the roof for support. "You—you said about the leaked newscast—"

"There was no leaked newscast." Derek turned to the Memorial with a look of mingled revulsion and shame. "I was there. I witnessed the Beginning. And I did nothing. I *ran*." His hands clenched into fists. "All I did was run away."

She placed a tentative hand on his arm, wishing she could siphon away his pain. His guilt. She knew what it was like to agonize over a past you could not change. To lie rather than face your own mistakes.

"It's what any sane person would have done, Derek. You can't blame yourself."

"No. You see, I *can*. *You* didn't run. You did something." He scrubbed a hand through his hair. "My sister and I took the ferry to work every day, and we always sat below on the main floor. But not that day. I'd had a tough week, coming off a night shift. I hadn't seen the sun in three months. It was my idea to sit above."

Stella gulped and clenched his arm tighter. "What happened?" She had the horrible sensation she was about to hear Derek's revolutionary spark.

"About halfway through the trip, a man—if you could call him that—stumbled to his feet. He had his hood up, so nobody paid him any mind. Nobody noticed what he was. But they wouldn't have realized anyway. He swayed and started making these guttural noises, like a wild animal." He gripped the shingles with white knuckles. "My sister got up to see if he was okay. That's when he attacked her. Bit right into her neck. And I—I just ran." He broke off and covered his mouth.

The woman in the blue pantsuit. Stella pressed her forehead against Derek's shoulder and held him as he shook. She knew the heavy weight of watching a loved one die and being unable to save them. She knew the shadows of cowardice. The shame of inaction.

Derek's face cracked, spilling out tears, and he touched Stella's cheek, light as a whisper. "Thank you," he said, "for doing what I couldn't."

Stella smiled, but it didn't touch her eyes. Her own shame rumbled inside her. The dust called to her in a velvet voice threaded with poison, and the tendrils of darkness wove through her mind in an inescapable maze. A hell she'd never leave behind.

She took his hand and placed it on his thigh, but kept ahold of it.

"That's why I want to help you," he said, squeezing her fingers. "You fight back. But me? I'm not like that." He ducked his head and stared at their intertwined hands. "I'm a coward."

That sentiment didn't sit right with Stella. "You've fought in the Faction with Mal since the Beginning. You stayed to fight when the guards overwhelmed us at the Spire. *You* pulled Quentin out of harm's way. None of that sounds very cowardly to me."

"I'm glad I did save the kid, because honestly, I really like that ball-buster." He withdrew his hand from hers and rubbed it across his face. "It kills me to say this, but if I'd known I'd get shot, I might have made a different choice. I'm not proud of that. And look at what I did with Rodney. Rather than standing up to him, I fell in line. Then I defected. I ran, again."

"You're fighting to free Silas though. That's not running away."

"But *I'm* not the one capable of saving him. You are. I'm not a hero, and I don't pretend to be. I *want* to make a difference in this war, but in the face of real danger, I get other people to fight my battles. Or I freeze. Or I run. But you're stronger than me, stronger than anyone I've ever met. It's people like you who will take down Pharmatrox and set our country to rights again. Not me."

Stella shrank away from his words. "Everything is too far gone, Derek. The only thing I can do—*we* can do—is save who we can and get out. And just because you need *help* rescuing Silas doesn't mean you're hiding behind other people. There's no shame in needing a team."

Wow, pot meet kettle. She was more comfortable with the idea of working with others than she had been previously, but she could use some work at taking her own advice.

"And you have made a difference. To me. Saving Quentin...I never could have forgiven myself if something had happened to him. He deserves a better life, and I want to give it to him." She cleared the emotion from her throat. "Speaking of, did Mal secure those extra seats on the convoy?"

Derek posted both hands behind him and leaned back. He didn't look at her as he said, "I promised you seats, and you'll have them. The convoy won't leave until you're ready, so there's still time."

"Still time for what?"

His eyes flicked to hers. "Time for you to change your mind. You could make a real difference in this war, Stella. You have the literal key to get into most of the troxy facilities and access their database and the network. Take them down from the inside."

"I'm just one person, Derek. One person can't take down Pharmatrox."

"I'm not asking you to do it by yourself. If Kev were here, we could have used the Faction to help us at the Spire." He made a frustrated sound, and his dark eyes settled on her in a hard look. "And I think we both realize that we need the Faction's firepower if we're going to be successful at saving Silas."

Stella bit her lip and didn't answer.

The sun had fully risen now, bathing them in the golden glow of dawn.

Derek blew out a breath and said, "We need to consider Mal's idea of working with Penny to get rid of Rodney. And with Rodney gone, we could lock down his detox serum supplier and make sure anyone who wants it can get it."

"You'd do that? Team up with Penny?" She'd barely come to terms with the fact that *she* was willing to team up with the woman who'd made her a user. But he made a good point about the detox serum...

"I'll do whatever it takes."

Something lodged in her chest. Derek would do anything to get Silas back, even if it went against his nature to run or freeze in the face of danger. She didn't blame him for being that way. Her reaction was always to fight, but after the dust settled, she ran too. She'd done that exact thing many times. Even now, with how she was fighting for Silas, all the while planning to flee after he was safe. Self-preservation and acting in her own interests are what had kept her alive, and it was probably the same for Derek.

But with the peek she'd gotten into his mind tonight, she couldn't agree with his self-assessment. Derek was no coward, and she'd help him to see that for himself. Somehow.

"Teaming up with Penny...that's a huge risk," she said. "Not just for me, but for all of us. Penny can't be trusted."

"Mal seems to think she can, and I trust him."

"Can we ask him to reconsider lending us some troops, or helping us out in another way that doesn't involve working side by side with the woman who's been trying to kill me for months?"

"We can ask again. But it might come down to a choice between working with Penny to make it happen or leaving Silas behind. And I don't think you want to abandon him."

Stella dug her nails into her jeans. No, she'd never work with Penny. But she'd never abandon Silas either. There was another way to do this. She just had to find it.

42

Penny

PENNY DUCKED UNDER THE hood of the Humvee and unscrewed the old, crusty glow plugs with a wrench. She'd spent the morning doing maintenance and oil coated her hands, arms, and clothes. But she enjoyed it; it took her back to the long summer days of working on the family farm and repairing tractors with her dad.

She screwed in the replacement glow plugs she'd found in a half-incinerated Humvee in Sector 11. The new ones were only in slightly better shape, but anything would be an improvement. The engine was drinking gasoline and misfiring, and with fuel limited, they couldn't afford to let any go to waste.

A week had passed since the spectacle at the fighting pit. To Rodney's fury, the family he'd been primed to murder had escaped. He'd sent patrols out looking for them, but Mal had assured her they would never be found. Since then, she'd immersed herself in work to keep her hands busy.

Things might be turning to shit at the Faction camp, but her efforts to hunt down Stella were proving fruitful. She'd found the little woodshed about a mile from Stella's camp, and she checked both locations regularly. A big blond guy lived there, but Stella had yet to return. Penny was patient though. And she was closing in. Soon, Stella would have nowhere left to run.

Penny was tightening the last glow plug when she felt someone looming behind her. She took her time wiping her hands off on a rag and inspected her work before closing the hood.

"You gonna say something or just stand there and stare at my ass?" she said, turning around.

Mal's eyes jumped up to hers. *Shit, was he really staring at my ass?* His large frame blocked out the late morning sun and cast his face into shadows.

"One of the hydroponic farms burned down."

Mal sure knew how to get her attention.

"What?"

"I don't understand what's confusing about that sentence. Do I need to write it down for you?"

Someone please give me the strength to not strangle this insufferable man. "How the fuck did it burn down?"

Mal crossed thick arms over his sculpted chest in a stance that screamed *powerful.* She'd stand like that all the time too if she was the size of an industrial refrigerator. "Don't know. Would have told you if I did."

"Perfect." Penny took a deep breath. "Which one? The Hayland?" *Please say no.* The hotel rooftop five blocks away housed their biggest garden, complete with a greenhouse for growing food during the rapidly-approaching winter.

"That's the one."

Penny slammed her hands on the hood of the Humvee and bent her head. "Is there anything left?"

"Still doing damage assessment, but doesn't look good. None of the crops survived."

Fuck. Penny paced the length of the vehicle and back. "Accident?"

"Found a can of accelerant and a flare, so I'd say no."

Fuck on a stick. The troxies could have found it and gotten up there somehow, and destroyed it to sabotage them. But after Rodney's stunt with the weapons stockpile, she wasn't so sure.

"When did this happen? And where were your guards?"

Mal's gaze darkened at the blame in her tone. "This morning after the guard change. Sanjali and Raph were up. But they said someone—a new recruit claiming to be sent by me—told them there was a last-minute schedule change and they were to patrol the armory instead. Could have been a troxy posing as one of us."

Or it could've been Rodney. The words hung unspoken in the air between them.

"How'd the troxies get someone past our defenses?"

Mal ran a hand through his hair and sighed. "It wouldn't be too hard. We gained some Pharmatrox defectors and civilians after that last battle. A lot of new faces in camp. One of them could be a mole."

Goddamn it. We have other farms, but will it be enough? "You need to keep a tighter leash on your troops and do a better job of screening them."

Mal stepped in front of her, interrupting her pacing. He stared down at her in that way he thought was intimidating but just made her want to punch his lights out. "You need to back the fuck off and not tell me how to do my job."

She squared up to him and poked him in the chest. "Because you *didn't* do your job, we're down a major food source. And winter is coming."

He glared at her hand, and she poked him again before fastening her hands safely on her hips where she wouldn't be tempted to swing at him. She liked pushing his buttons, but damn if he didn't know how to push hers right back.

"Does Rodney know about this?" *Did Rodney do this?*

Mal narrowed his eyes, as if he knew what she was thinking. "I didn't tell him, but word spreads fast. People are already blaming the troxies."

"I'll talk to him. And you've gotta stop getting up in my space, Mal." She pushed him back a step. "People can't see us talking. Like you said, word spreads fast."

Mal gave her a hard look. "Noted," he said, then turned on his heel and stalked off.

Rodney was holed up in his office, surrounded by his cronies and lots of drugs. The place was somehow even dirtier and smellier than the last time she'd been there. She hid her grimace as Rodney snorted a line of dust off the desk and turned his beady eyes to hers.

"Come to join the fun with your old friends?" He gestured to Callum and Toby, who lounged on the couch along the far wall. Callum waggled his fingers at Penny, but she looked right through him.

"Heard something I thought you'd want to know," she said to Rodney. "The Hayland farm is gone. Burned down."

She didn't know what reaction she had expected, but it certainly wasn't the one she got: *laughter.*

Rodney's cackles ended in hacking coughs, and he pounded his chest with a fist. He wiped a tear from his eye and said, "Oh, Penny. I thought for sure *you* would see through my 'smoke screen.'" He burst into hysterics again, beating his palms on the desk.

I fucking knew it. Damn him.

"You burned down the farm?" She needed to hear him say the words.

Rodney's fingernails had grown long, and he'd sharpened them into lethal points. He clacked them on the desk as he spoke. "Some of the guards I had stationed around the Hayland caught a man sneaking in to steal food and farm supplies. They brought him to me, asked me if they should kill him. But it gave me an idea."

Rodney has his own guards stationed around camp? I wonder if Mal knows. "Why'd you do it?"

Rodney planted both hands on the desk and pushed to his feet. "Because it keeps the people *angry*. Anger, passion, rage—that's the lifeblood of this revolution. And that's where Kev is wrong." He pulled his black-bladed lucky knife out of his belt and slammed it into the desk with each point he made. "He isn't willing to do whatever it takes to win the war." *Slam.* "He doesn't want to rid the world of the troxy filth. In fact, he *embraces* some of them as his own, like that big fucker who leads my army." *Slam.*

A strange protectiveness surged through her at the mention of Mal. She didn't like the glint in Rodney's eyes.

"But *I'm* willing to do all of that," he said. "Purging the troxies is the only true victory. And that can't happen if the people lose their passion. So I set a little fire to remind them who the enemy is and what they're capable of."

Even though his eyes were absent of black veins, Rodney had turned—in more ways than one. He'd gone too far. It wasn't just one innocent family's life on the line; he was endangering *everyone* by torching one of their largest food sources. She wanted to beat his head against the wall until he saw sense. He'd always been a slimy, self-interested, bloodthirsty man. But the dust amplified those traits. And now he had power—and a taste for getting more of it. And goddamn it, he had the means to make it happen. She looked around the room filled with his followers. Their numbers grew by the day.

This has to end.

"Where's the man who broke in?" she asked. "Did you kill him?"

Rodney chuckled. "Of course not. Not yet, anyway. That's up to him." A nasty smile split his face. "The bastard *negotiated* with me. I was feeling generous, so I offered him a job. Could be useful."

Innocent or guilty of the crime of stealing, the man didn't deserve whatever twisted arrangement for indentured servitude he'd been forced into. She stood to leave—she knew where Rodney kept his victims—but almost forgot. She was playing a role.

"Brilliant move, seizing on an opportunity like that. Wish I'd thought of it myself. That's why we need you." The words burned her throat.

The bastard fucking *smirked*. "Means a lot coming from you, my girl. Means a lot."

Penny nodded and ducked into the hallway, forcing herself to walk, not run, to the lower-level storage rooms reserved for prisoners. She peeked in the window of the metal door. Ten people huddled in the dark room lit by a single flashlight. And one of them—

One of them, she recognized.

She twisted the doorknob. Locked. *Obviously.* Mal should have a key, but Rodney might not trust him with that.

Several footsteps and loud, familiar voices sounded down the hall—Rodney's goons were headed her way.

She abandoned the prisoners for now until she figured out how to free them without rousing suspicion. As she walked away from the room of likely innocent civilians, her resolve hardened.

She found Mal in the war room where he normally planned their battle strategies. He wasn't alone—four of his soldiers sat around the table with him. They all glared at her when she entered.

"Get the fuck out," she said to the soldiers. "Mal, you stay."

Mal stood and crossed his arms. He probably did that so often because they were tired from dragging his knuckles on the ground all the time. "Did you enjoy that? Treating me like one of your dogs?" he said.

Penny made an irritated sound. "Could you sit down, please?" She prodded him toward the chair he'd just vacated. "I can't talk to you when you're towering over me like that." He gave her a look, but he sat. She stayed standing so she was closer to his eye level.

"Don't get offended," she said. "Everyone needs to think I'm Rodney's loyal second. But yes, I did enjoy it, since you asked."

"What do you want?"

"Found out what happened to the gardens." She filled him in on everything Rodney had said.

When she finished, Mal pushed away from the table and rummaged in one of the lockers behind him, then slid a magazine into a hand gun and shoved it in the back of his pants. He went for a pair of knives next.

"What are you doing?" she asked.

Mal didn't look at her and continued assembling his personal armory. "Getting those prisoners out. Then I'm going for Rodney. This needs to end."

Slamming the locker shut, she said, "He'll kill you, Mal. I saw it in his eyes. You come at him, you're dead. But you're right. This has to end." She gave him a meaningful look. "And we'll end it. When the time is right. When we have a *plan*." She offered her hand and he shook it, sealing their deal.

Rodney was a dead man walking.

A strange expression flitted across Mal's face before he turned away. It looked almost like respect.

43

"Okay, Turi. I can finish one more folder before I go completely cross-eyed."

Stella propped her feet on a creaky wooden chair. The only light in the library came from the tangerine sunlight filtering through the skylight as the afternoon faded into evening.

"Is your CLEO still dressing like a grunge-punk princess?" Derek asked, gesturing vaguely with his sandwich.

"She thinks it matches her 'rebel' persona."

Derek made a sound of agreement and went back to the city maps he was perusing.

After their talk on the roof last night, something had shifted between them. Laying himself bare like that, owning up to his flaws...Stella saw him in a whole new light.

So she'd invited him to the library. His knowledge from working in security and construction would be instrumental in planning the Spire break-in. She didn't mind him watching as she swiped through invisible files. His presence was companionable, not intrusive.

While she and Derek planned, Quentin and Tara scouted for food and supplies. At Quentin's insistence, he wanted to "go outside and play like the teenager that I am," and Tara had agreed to accompany him. The two made a trip to the workshop every day to drop off a care package for Lawrence. Stella couldn't blame Lawrence for wanting to stay away, but she regretted being the reason that she'd—hopefully only temporarily—broken up the three musketeers.

After hours of study, Stella had the Spire's blueprints memorized—mostly. Derek sat back and crossed tattooed arms corded with muscle across his chest. *Why am I noticing that? It's only* Derek. Before the Beginning, she'd dated around but had never gotten serious with anyone. Work had always come first. *And who has time for dating during the fucking apocalypse? Focus.*

Derek tapped a finger to his chin. "Do you see anything that could be a service entrance or a loading dock? When I drove freight trucks, the warehouses were always busy places. That could be a good place to sneak in. Blend in with the crowd."

Stella scanned the blueprints. "Yes, around the left side toward the back. From there, we could—"

"Stella?" Turi materialized beside her, and Stella jumped at her sudden appearance.

"Yeah?"

Turi squinted at the blueprints hovering in the air. "These floor plans aren't right."

"What's going on?" Derek asked, standing and leaning a hip on the table beside Stella.

"There's an entire floor missing from these blueprints," said Stella, repeating Turi's words. "Between the nineteenth and twentieth floors. Turi cross-referenced them with a satellite scan of the Spire, and the two don't match. The Spire is one floor taller than this blueprint indicates."

"An *entire floor* kept off the books?"

"This has to be the hub of their secret experiments. The Phoenix Trials. It's the perfect place to hide things they don't want anyone knowing about. Silas has to be there. The detox serum too."

Derek's eyes were bright and alert. "How do we get in?"

Turi zoomed in on a portion of the blueprint. "Special access elevator here. Your Helix Key or guard's access card should work."

Stella relayed the information to Derek.

Derek nodded in thought. "Mal is coming by the house in four days for his usual check-in. We can ask him again about lending us some troops. In the meantime, we keep learning as much as we can about the Spire. Gather some supplies, practice training with Tara." He dropped a hand on Stella's shoulder. "We'll be prepared this time. I promise."

She smiled at his touch and turned back to the blueprints, wishing there was a way she could let him *see* them for himself. In fact, she and Derek made a perfect match; Derek needed her to view the blueprints and describe them, and she needed his insight to make sense of what she was looking at.

Stella's head throbbed from hours of staring at the grid of glowing blue files. And from withdrawal. Her stomach roiled and her hands quaked. Time to call it a night. The Pharmatrox guard patrol would be coming within the next two hours anyway.

As Stella packed up, Turi popped into her view. "You might want to see this."

Stella jerked upright, and Derek's hand flew to his knife on the table. "What? What is it?"

"Turi found something."

Derek relaxed with a sigh. "I really hate that I can't see or hear her. You've been gasping and lurching around, and I always think we're about to be attacked."

Stella snorted. "Sorry. I'll try to keep the theatrics to a minimum. Turi, what'd you find?"

"This file pinged for the word 'troxapine' and it got a hit for being recently opened."

"Who opened it?"

"Dr. Ingrid Hansen."

Stella leapt out of her chair, toppling it over.

Derek jumped up, scanning for a threat. Then shook his head. "Damn it. Fell for it again."

But Stella barely heard him. Her eyes were glued to the file, Dr. Hansen's name in the "recently viewed" status bar. *Dr. Hansen. She's alive.*

"Can you tell where she accessed it from?" asked Stella, her mind racing. "Has she had any other network activity? Can we ping her Patch?"

"Her IP was hidden, so I cannot determine where she accessed this file. Her Patch is offline, but I'll alert you if that changes."

So Dr. Hansen also found a way to avoid being tracked by Pharmatrox.

"What's happening? Who are we pinging, Turi?" Derek stared intently at an empty chair.

"Turi's sitting on top of that bookshelf." Stella pointed in the opposite direction. "It's my mentor, Dr. Hansen. I thought she might be dead. But she's still out there, fighting against Pharmatrox. Maybe she infiltrated the Spire or another Pharmatrox facility. Maybe she could help *us*. From the inside."

"I like the sound of that. But I'm guessing there's a problem or else you would have already contacted her."

"Her Patch is offline."

"But you know for sure she's inside the Spire?"

"Well...no. It's just a hunch. It would make sense for her to come here if she escaped New York. It's what a lot of people did. It's what *I* did."

Derek scratched his jaw. "Unless it's someone else using her credentials. If Rodney's people captured her on the road, they could have stolen her Patch and tortured the information out of her. Even some of Kev's followers might be capable of that."

At his words, the room spun and Stella pressed a hand to her forehead. In an instant, Derek was there, clasping her arm in a steadying grip. "I'm sorry, that was insensitive. I shouldn't have said that."

Stella gave him a weak smile. "It's okay. The fact that someone with her credentials viewed a file recently is a positive sign, but I won't get my hopes up. Our plan should still be to infiltrate the tower on our own, with the Faction as backup." *Mal has to say yes. I can't bring Penny into this. Won't.*

"What was the file she viewed?" Derek asked. "Seems a little weird to be researching when the world is falling apart."

"That's what *we're* doing," Stella said, spreading her fingers and opening the file.

It contained a series of video clips featuring the same person—Evie. *What the fuck?* Stella clicked play.

Evie sat in front of a green screen background in a makeshift studio, set up with bright lights and mics. She shifted in her plastic chair and shuffled a stack of papers. A young woman with a dazzling smile sat across from her, a clipboard poised on her leg. Stella recognized her as the Pharmatrox media coach and the woman who had coordinated the photo she'd taken as a favor to Dr. Hansen.

"Okay, Evie, let's take it from the top. You're doing great. Just ignore the cameras and lights." The woman gave her an encouraging smile.

"Thank you for speaking with me today. Tell us about the latest and greatest from Pharmatrox. What can we expect from this new product?"

Evie's forehead glistened, and her notes trembled in her hands. "It's simple," she recited. "You take one pill every week, and it boosts your immune system. You'll never get sick again. There's nothing like it on the market currently. It's extraordinary. The government has bought our entire initial run, to be distributed to every household at no charge. It's all approved by the Leader."

"And no side effects too? That is pretty remarkable. Okay, now get ready for a hardball question, Evie. You've got this. Just remember the tips we practiced." The woman cleared her throat and continued in a reporter voice. "But what about the Pharmatrox scientists who claim this drug is more dangerous than you're letting on?"

Evie glanced at the papers in her lap. "Nothing more than a few disgruntled former employees. We're making history at Pharmatrox, and they're upset to be left behind. Troxapine is perfectly safe. It's—" Evie broke off and shook her head. "I'm sorry, Alana. But I can't say this. I can't *do* this. Can't you get someone else who's better trained?"

Alana scribbled a note on her clipboard. "The Leader wants the nation to hear from the architect behind Pharmatrox's revolutionary pharmaceutical solutions. You want to disobey a direct request from the Leader?"

"But *this*"—Evie shook the papers—"isn't the drug I designed. This isn't what I wanted."

"Honestly, Evie—"

The video cut off.

This isn't the drug I designed. This isn't what I wanted.

Stella paused and rewound the footage. She watched again. And again.

...straight from the architect...

Evie's words from that day on the ferry came back to her. *I have that TV interview coming up this week. It's supposed to drum up some good PR so we can get funding for some of our more...robust projects.*

Stella blinked at the hologram.

Evie.

Evie was the Architect?

And this was proof that Pharmatrox knew troxapine had issues before they'd distributed it. But they'd silenced the whistleblowers and planned to smooth it over with a PR stunt. *Dios.*

"Stella, you've been staring into space for ten minutes." Derek grabbed her by the shoulders and forced her to look at him. "What the fuck is going on?"

In her peripheral, she noticed another file pinned to the video.

"I'm still figuring it out. Hold on."

She clutched his arm, her tether to reality. The file was a proposal for a drug designed to have calming effects and suppress the amygdala, while boosting the immune system. A cure for chronic anxiety and communicable diseases.

But the title of the proposal was dionazole, not troxapine.

And the name in the byline was Dr. Evelyn Luanne Markson.

Stella's jaw unhinged. She blinked away the holographic rendering and looked into Derek's eyes.

"My best friend—Evie, Silas's sister, *that* Evie—was the Architect."

"*What?*"

The words rushed out of her in a shaky voice. "She came up with the idea for dionazole, and somehow Pharmatrox used that to create troxapine. And they probably tampered with her original formula for dionazole too."

Derek sank into a chair, a notch in his brow. "Maybe that's why Pharmatrox captured Silas—they think he knows something or can further their goals in some way."

"Silas doesn't know anything. Not even *I* know anything, and I worked there." Evie's last words tolled in her mind. *There's a lot of things I never told you.* "Evie was my best friend and yet...it feels like I hardly knew her."

"One last thing before you get distracted, boss," Turi chimed in from her perch on the bookshelf.

A virtual note was pinned to the file, typed by Dr. Wanda Chun. Stella read it aloud.

Troxapine, at first, worked as intended. The users became docile and easy to manipulate. The second batch appears to have been tampered with. Whoever ingests it adopts erratic behavior. After a period of time, they rot from the inside out, resulting in death.

However, I have discovered some rare exceptions to this. Certain individuals experience heightened senses and other desirable traits as a result of this bad batch. I've sent orders to have them rounded up and transferred to the Spire for the next phase of the trials. The Leader will be interested in this.

Derek shifted to sit on the table in front of her, eyes narrowed. "I thought the Leader was a Pharmatrox puppet..."

A dark pit formed at Stella's center. "Me too. There was also a rumor circulating that it was a collective effort of some directors acting as one person. This is the first indication I've seen that the Leader is a real individual with a real agenda. Pharmatrox is trying to recreate specific results, something the Leader wants. But what?"

"Somehow, I felt better thinking the Leader was a fake figurehead." Derek leaned back into the circle of ruby-red light pouring through the rotunda, face creased in thought. Twilight approached, and they'd have to head back to Maple Street soon.

Stella found herself standing almost between his legs. When had they gotten so close? She sat in the chair beside him instead.

"Who would've thought those little packets of powder would bring the world to its knees?" Derek traced the woodgrain of the table with a pensive look. "Feed the people a drug they don't need, get them addicted to it. All for the purpose of power, control. But control was the one thing they lost." He took his knife and twirled it in contemplation. "I lost control too."

She knew what moment he was reliving. The contents of his patient file flashed in her mind. Death's voice whispered to her. *When will it be your turn to lose control, Agnes? And who will you hurt when you do?*

Stella shook off the unwelcome words. "Whatever you might have done while under the influence of the experiments, that wasn't *you*, Derek. None of it is your fault."

"I could do more though. If I could remember anything else from my time at Oakwood, maybe it could help us rescue Silas. Or end Pharmatrox. Or do *something* useful besides sit around with an empty head!" He slammed his fist on the tabletop. When he looked up, his face fell open in a wide-eyed look of terror. "Stella, what if I've done things—horrible things—but I can't remember?"

"We've all done horrible things," she said in a small voice. "But that doesn't make us horrible people. *Or* cowards. We are not the sum of the worst things we've done. We do what we have to do to survive."

The shadow of a smile crossed Derek's lips. "Enduring hardship does tend to make us more wise, doesn't it?" He placed a hand on her shoulder, his thumb tracing the scar that slashed across her chest, and held her gaze for a charged moment. "Thank you for not giving up on me. For giving me a chance."

"We all deserve a second chance."

He lifted an eyebrow. "Even Penny?"

Stella swallowed, her mouth suddenly dry. "Jury's still out on that one."

44

A FEW MORNINGS LATER, Stella dragged herself downstairs to Derek's kitchen and pulled out the essentials to make coffee. She didn't have the energy to build the fire and boil the water, but she'd be worse off if she didn't have any coffee at all.

Her rations of dust kept her functional, and Death had mostly faded. But she much preferred Death's nonstop monologue to the insomnia, shakes, and splitting headaches. Caffeine barely put a dent in the migraines and certainly didn't help with the insomnia, but she didn't have much choice.

I could ask Derek for more dionazole...

At her insistence, Derek had used the vial of dionazole from Mal to finish his detox cycle, with the promise of getting her more as soon as possible. But she didn't want him or Mal getting caught stealing and thrown in the fighting pit. She'd stretch out her last baggie and take the serum once Silas was safely beside her. If she failed...The abyss within her yawned.

If she failed, there'd be no redemption for her. In a drug or in anything else.

"Dark thoughts for six a.m.," she muttered.

Goose bumps dotted her bare legs, and she rooted around in the coat closet for something warm to wear over the tee shirt she slept in. She pulled on a soft plaid flannel that hit her mid-thigh. The mornings were getting chillier and held the promise of fall, but the afternoons could get warm. She paused when she heard footsteps thumping down the stairs.

A shirtless, sleep-rumpled Derek stumbled into the kitchen—*dios, those tattoos*—ruffling a hand through his messy hair. She'd seen him without a shirt before but had been a bit distracted by his bleeding gunshot wound at the time. Her gaze lingered on the intricate black lines and whorls tracing up both of his arms and meeting across the planes of his chest. His wound was looking better, but could use some more recovery time.

Derek froze when he saw her. His eyes traveled the length of her bare legs all the way up to her face. "My shirt looks good on you."

Stella's thoughts scattered like confetti. She grabbed the first one that flew by. "I assumed it belonged to the dead guy hanging from your flagpole."

He snorted.

"But I do feel better knowing it's yours."

He smiled at that and pulled on another flannel from the closet, leaving a few top buttons open.

Her brain started working again once his distracting body was no longer on display. "How's your shoulder?" She put down her coffee fixings and approached him. "Any sign of infection?"

"It's sore and the stitches itch like hell."

"We can take those out soon. Lawrence—" She broke off. Not for the first time, she missed his reassuring presence. At the Outpost, he'd been their caretaker, their cook, their medic. Their protector. Tara and Quentin seemed to be doing okay, but she could tell they missed him too. "Lawrence might have something for the itching and the pain," she finished in a voice that was stronger than she felt.

"It's manageable. Don't worry." He tucked a strand of hair behind her ear, his fingers brushing her cheek. She leaned into his touch. Then hesitated when she realized what she was doing. *Who* she was doing it with.

Maybe it's the exhaustion making us both delirious.

"Morning!"

They sprang apart like shrapnel, Stella bumping into the center island behind her. "Quentin? What are you doing up so early? I thought teenagers were supposed to sleep the entire day away."

"Does that sound anything like me? There's much too much to do. Buildings to climb. Pop-Tarts to eat." He noticed Stella and Derek standing awkwardly far apart. "Intimate moments to interrupt." He grinned, waggling his eyebrows at Derek. "Looking a bit disheveled, Derek. And your shirt is unbuttoned. Did Stella have anything to do with that?"

All the blood sprinted into her face. "You—I—we were just—" She stopped. *Joder.* It was too early for this. She pointed at Quentin. "Help me build a fire. Or don't. I don't care. Just stop talking. Derek, fix your shirt."

She took the coffee things and hurried into the living room before anyone could comment on her undoubtedly red face, but not before she saw Quentin elbow Derek's side and Derek grab him into a noogie.

Boys.

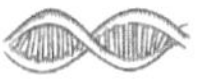

An hour later, coffee in hand and granola bar in belly, Stella sat in the living room, with Quentin and Derek taking stock of the supplies they'd gathered over the past few days from old troxy facilities, abandoned homes, and several stores.

Everything was organized into piles: weapons, tactical clothes, dry food, tools, medical supplies, and miscellaneous, which included things like duct tape, rope, and whatever doodads Quentin had begged her to keep.

Derek examined a vest and tossed it into the pile. "Mal should be here in a few hours. He'll tell us we have way too many clothes and not enough weapons. He tends to favor the strategy of going in with guns blazing."

"I thought he wouldn't help us because it was too much of a risk with Rodney in charge," she said.

As far as Quentin knew, Mal and Rodney were just friends of Derek's. His involvement with the Faction was still...undisclosed.

"He might not be able to lend us any people, but it's worth asking again. And he could help us strategize." Derek eyed her as she untangled a ball of rope. "Still haven't changed your mind about working with her?"

The damn knot was impossible. And she didn't need to ask who Derek meant. She couldn't get Penny out of her head. "I'm looking into other alternatives." But she had no other ideas.

She'd put off thinking about it, focusing solely on planning the break-in. Between that and her discovery of Evie's involvement with troxapine and dionazole, Dr. Hansen's credentials showing up, and the revelation that Pharmatrox had sabotaged Evie's original project—there was too much rattling around in her brain. But now that they were nearly ready, she couldn't avoid it anymore. They needed firepower and backup for their plan to work.

Derek, thankfully, didn't press her on it. Quentin, however, had a question. "Working with who?" He dug through his knickknack pile until he found a deck of cards, which he began shuffling.

"Don't worry about it," said Stella.

Quentin shrugged. "Hey, Derek, I've got a fun game we can play." He bent the deck, primed to launch the cards.

Derek pointed a stick of beef jerky at him. "Do it and I'm eating all of your junk food, twerp."

"Boys, play nice," Stella said, looping the rope into a neat coil and adding it to the pile.

The front door banged open, footsteps pounding down the entryway. Tara appeared, sweat-covered and panting. "Please tell me Lawrence is here."

Stella rose and exchanged a look with the guys, both of whom shrugged. "He's not in the workshop?"

Tara rested a hand on the wall as she caught her breath. "No. I waited for a few hours, but he never showed."

Lawrence wouldn't disappear without a word to Tara or Quentin. A whisper of suspicion breathed on her neck.

"Do you know where he might've gone?" Stella handed her a glass of water, and she drank deeply as Derek and Quentin approached, faces pinched in concern. "Maybe he went on a supply run."

Tara wiped her mouth and shook her head. "I was bringing him stuff to make sure he wouldn't have to do a run on his own until I could convince him to stay here with us. Yesterday, he said he wanted to set up his own hydroponic farm inside the workshop to grow plants during the winter. He mentioned going back to the Outpost to clean out the garden and do a harvest. The workshop doesn't look like it has been touched since yesterday."

The dark feeling inside Stella wound its fingers around her heart and squeezed. "Do you remember when I first came to the Outpost? He talked about the Faction supplies and how much he envied them. Do you think he might have gone to one of their farms? And—" She couldn't even say it.

Tara's eyes widened, and she shouldered her metal baseball bat. "I'm going after him."

Stella shared the same sentiment. If Lawrence was a Faction prisoner, he could end up in the fighting pit. It didn't sound like Rodney exercised much discretion about who he killed or why. And if Lawrence wasn't a Faction prisoner, he'd already been missing for a day. He could be anywhere.

"Wait." Stella threw up a hand, and her gaze snapped to Derek. "Derek might be able to help. He...knows some people." Stella didn't want to admit it, but Penny could help in this situation. She'd seen Lawrence during the raid on his camp and could positively identify him.

Derek ran a tattooed hand across his face, his expression grim. Stella made *tell them* motions.

Tara parked her hands on her hips and stared Derek down. She hadn't warmed up to him yet. "Well?" she said.

"I'm ex-Faction. Broke from them around the same time Stella stumbled into your camp."

Tara grabbed Derek by his shirtfront and hauled him close. "I knew there was something wrong with you, you *maldito mentiroso*."

"That's what I said when I found out," said Stella.

"And *you*"—Tara rounded on her—"don't even get me started, *chula*. You knew what he was and you *brought us into his house*?"

Derek showed her his palms. "It's a long story, and we can fill you in on the details later. But I might be able to help. Mal should be here soon, and we'll figure it out then."

"Mal?" Tara looked at Stella.

"He's the general of the Faction's army," she said.

"You expect me to trust *you*, trust the Faction, the diablos who did *this*"—Tara held up her arms hashed with scars—"to me?"

Derek's expression darkened. "I'm sorry for what you've been through."

Tara held her bat in a tight grip, but at least she wasn't swinging.

"If Lawrence got caught in a Faction farm, Rodney will have him in the stadium armory," Derek continued. "And if he's there, Mal will know. We'll figure it out. I promise you that."

"Your promises are as worthless as your apologies." Tara turned on her heel and stomped out of the room.

With both Silas and possibly Lawrence's lives now hanging in the balance, Stella had a choice to make. A choice that scared the shit out of her.

Be afraid, but don't sit around in your fear was something her father always told her. *"If you wait until you feel ready or prepared, you'll spend a lot of your life waiting instead of living.*

"So be afraid, mija. Feel that fear. But don't let it hold you back."

When Stella caught up to Tara at the foot of the stairs, Tara whirled, anger etched in her face.

"I want to find another way to save Lawrence and Silas without the Faction, but there's no time," said Stella. "This is the only help we're going to get."

Tara narrowed her eyes. *She's thinking about it. That's good.*

"I know we don't know Derek that well," she continued, "but he's kept his word to me so far. There's a lot you don't know, and I swear you'll get the full story. But Lawrence needs you. He needs *us*. We'll get him back. *I* promise you that."

"That punk-ass Jonesy better be telling the truth," Tara growled as she stomped upstairs.

Joder, I just agreed to work with Penny. But if it saved her friends, it would be worth it.

Or maybe I just signed my own death warrant.

45

A FEW HOURS LATER, a knock sounded at the front door. Mal had arrived.

"I'll get it," Derek said, disappearing down the hallway.

Stella caught Tara's eye. She wasn't happy about working with the Faction, but she was willing to hear Mal out. "It's going to be okay." Stella squeezed her arm.

Quentin bumped her shoulder and said, "I'm sure Lawrence is fine, T."

Heated voices came from the hall. Something wasn't right.

"Stella," said Derek. "Could you come here?"

Stella unfolded herself from the couch and padded down the hallway—

But ducked behind the front door and yanked Derek with her, slamming the door in their visitors' faces.

"*What the hell is Penny doing here?*" she whisper-shouted.

Derek looked pissed. "I don't know. It was just supposed to be Mal."

"Fuck. I don't want her near the others."

"Don't want who near the others?" Tara asked from the end of the hall.

Stella pointed to the front porch. "Mal is here. He brought the woman who trashed the Outpost."

"I, for one, would love to lay eyes on her." Tara tapped her metal bat against her boot. "But I'm with you. Quentin shouldn't be part of this."

Quentin's head popped around the corner, his expression indignant. "Why can't I be in the meeting?"

"Because the woman who wrecked our camp and almost killed us is standing out there," said Stella as she towed him toward the back door. "But you were still in your tent, so maybe she hasn't seen you yet. She doesn't know that I'm involved in this little meeting, and there's no telling how she'll react. If she sees you and associates you with me, you could be in serious danger."

Quentin dug his heels in and squirmed out of her grip.

Tara grabbed his other side and said, "Stella and I can hold our own, but you need more training before you're ready to fight off the likes of her."

Quentin tossed his bony elbows around. "You guys aren't my *moms*. You can't tell me what to do."

Tara snorted. "Yeah, we're your big sisters, so listen the fuck up, Quent—"

Stella cut Tara off and held Quentin by the shoulders. "You have the right to make your own decisions. So I'm begging you. Please stay outside for this one. It's for your own protection."

Quentin huffed and grabbed his deck of cards from the counter. "Fine. I'll play fifty-two pickup by myself." He went into the backyard, making sure his mutinous muttering was audible.

Stella deflated once he was safely outside. Tara nudged her. "It was the right call. Thanks for putting him first." Then she twirled her bat up to her shoulder and said, "Let's meet this lovely woman."

Stella steeled herself and called to Derek. "Let them in."

Derek entered the kitchen first, a question in his eyes. She smiled, but it felt a bit crazed. Mal followed and nodded to her.

And then Penny was walking into the room.

Stella's stomach tried to crawl up her throat. The fiery look on Penny's face matched the flames of her wavy red hair, and she bared her teeth in a feral smile. Her hand flew to the sickle at her belt, but Mal barred her with his massive arm.

"Don't."

Penny sunk her nails into his bicep. The man didn't even flinch. "She's the Architect, Mal. The one I've been hunting. The one who *did this to us*."

"You got any proof of that?" asked Mal.

"I saw her picture in a newspaper."

"And did it specifically call her out by name as the creator of troxapine?"

"It didn't have to. The meaning was clear, it—"

"Do you think it's possible you're so desperate for someone to blame for the state of our country and for whatever terrible things you've done that you latched onto the first scrap of 'evidence' you came across?"

Stella's mouth popped open. Who was this man who could talk like that to *Penny*? Penny never stood for anyone going against her. It's why she made such a formidable leader of the Marauders.

But then Penny did something unanticipated.

She *backed down*.

Penny put her sickle in her belt and crossed her arms, but her eyes seared into Stella and held the promise of blood. "I'm not finished with you." She turned her attention to Derek and Tara for the first time and sized them up. "Malosi says you might be willing to help us with a little organizational restructuring."

"I don't give a flying fuck what you want," Tara said to Penny, then stepped up to Mal. Their height difference would have been comical, but Tara's fury was bigger than the towering Samoan man. "Our friend went missing yesterday. We think he might have tried to steal hydroponic supplies from the Faction. Do you know anything about that?"

Mal glanced at Penny, and something passed between them.

"Big dude—not as big as Mal, of course, no one is as big as *him*—blond-ish hair, darker beard?" asked Penny.

Tara's eyes widened. "Yes, that sounds like Lawrence."

"Lawrence." Penny snapped her fingers. "Knew that guy was familiar."

Stella paled and cut Penny off before she could say *why* he was familiar. "He's alive? You know where he is?"

"Rodney's got him locked up," said Penny. "He decided it would be a good idea to burn down the whole farm and blame it on the troxies. Fucking moron. He cut Lawrence a deal—help expand the farms, and he won't hunt down his loved ones, aka you guys, and murder you."

Stella's stomach bottomed out. "How would Rodney even find us?"

Penny shrugged. "He has spies everywhere. Or he'd torture it out of him." She glanced at Mal. "But I don't see why I should risk my own skin to free your friend."

Mal smashed his teeth together. "Penny, we talked about this. We need them. They'll help us take out Rodney, and with Stella's credentials, we can access Pharmatrox hangars and weapons caches. Stealing is a lot easier when we have a fucking key. Shit's hitting the fan, and we can't afford to turn our backs on help when it's offered to us."

He balled his hands into fists and stared Penny down. "Now, I thought you and I had reached an accord, but if you can't keep your fucking word, then I suggest you walk out of this house right now before I put a bullet between your eyes, because goddamn it, Penny, I've had it with your shit. You're either on the team or you're not. So pick a fucking side and shut the fuck up."

By the time he finished, the two looked like they were about to rip each other apart.

Tara gave a low whistle, and Derek gawked at them.

"Do you want Rodney dead or not?" asked Mal.

Penny's hand curled into a fist. *Mal might be in for a knuckle sandwich.* "Yes."

"Good. Me too. Glad I don't need to shoot you. You're the only one who can get close enough to him for this plan to work." Mal crossed his arms and spoke to the room. "If we work together, we have a good chance of springing Lawrence and overthrowing Rodney in one go." He focused on Stella. "With Rodney gone, you'll have whatever backup you need for rescuing Silas."

Stella's eyes flicked to Penny, fuming beside Mal. "What's to stop Penny from slitting my throat?"

"I'll personally guarantee your safety," said Mal, eyes glued to Penny. "If she moves against you or does *anything* I don't like, I'll kill her myself."

"Me too." Derek's intense stare bored into Penny.

"Thanks, guys, but your 'guarantees' won't matter if she knifes me in the hallway while you're all occupied," said Stella.

Penny sneered. "At least you realize how easy it would be for me to kill you."

Mal scrubbed a hand through his curly hair. "Penny, for fuck's sake. What did I just say? You've picked your side. And Stella is on that side. So *shut the fuck up.*"

This time, Penny did rear back her arm to hit Mal, but he grabbed her wrist and pulled her into him. "Do it and see what happens."

The tension between them sizzled, but it wasn't all rage and violence…Maybe she *could* trust Mal to keep Penny in line. At the very least, Stella was interested in hearing his plan.

Tara rolled her bat against her leg as she watched the exchange, then said, "With Rodney dead, who will take over leadership of the Faction in the Capital?"

Stella had been wondering that too. And she didn't think she'd like the answer. Mal scratched the stubble on his jaw and glanced at Penny.

"She will."

"No," said Stella.

"*Fuck* no," said Tara.

"Mal, don't you think—" Derek started, but Mal silenced him with a gesture.

"Look. We can talk about the details later. I'll still be in charge of the troops, the battle plans—the war, essentially. My soldiers are loyal to *me* and not to her. And she knows that." He cut a hard glare at Penny, who rolled her eyes. "But a fair amount of people approve of Penny and trust her leadership. Between the two of us, we can head up the war efforts here until we come up with a better long-term strategy. But, Derek"—the big man turned imploring eyes to his friend—"if it's not me and Penny who lead, who else is there?"

Derek leaned over the counter, palms flat on the surface as he absorbed Mal's words. When he nodded, Mal clapped him on the back.

"So what's our assassination plan?" asked Tara. "Puñeta, there's a sentence I never thought I'd say."

"We—"

The back door banged open and Quentin ducked inside, chest heaving. His mouth started going a mile a minute. "I know you kicked me out, but there's a turned out there—one of the slow, dumb ones, not those rabid things—but I don't have a weapon or anything, and I'm getting better at flinging cards, but I don't think I've gotten to the point where I can throw them with lethal severity yet, so if—" He cut off, face the color of spoiled milk.

"I'll take care of it." Derek moved to go outside, but Quentin was frozen. Staring at Penny.

And Penny stared back, the same blank expression on her face. The malice melted off of her like hot wax from a candlestick.

"Quentin?" Penny whispered. "You're alive?"

"Penelope?" He flew across the room and flung himself at Penny. And she hugged him back, burying her face in his hair.

Penelope? Hostia, what is going on?

"You look so different. This world has changed you." Penny touched Quentin's cheek. Her eyes darted across his face, connecting the dots of his freckles. "I...I thought you were killed in the fire. Mom and Dad—" She broke off and held him to her chest.

"I jumped out the window in your bedroom before the fire took the house." Quentin's eyes were far away as he relived unseen memories. "How did you escape? Where have you been?"

Penny's face plummeted.

And Stella knew. *Penny's not just his dead sister.* The pieces of the puzzle clicked into place with a resounding boom that echoed through her bones. The ghost of Death's laughter cackled in her ears.

"It was you," Stella said to Penny. "The user who burned his house down and killed his entire family—that was you."

46

Penny

HER LITTLE BROTHER'S EYES were as big as silver dollars. *He's alive. I didn't kill him. He's here, he's real—*

"What? You're a user?" Quentin asked, backing away from her.

A hole formed in Penny's chest, its ragged edges tearing at her as her world came crashing down around her.

"Not anymore—"

"You killed Mom and Dad." His small voice pierced into every dark place in her soul.

"I wasn't sober. I was hallucinating—"

His brow notched in a defiant look that he'd only used on their parents before. "And *you're* the one who's been after Stella? Who sent the turned to our camp?" He stood between Stella and the Black woman who looked ready to stab her. He clutched Stella's hand and Penny's heart *cracked*. "You almost killed us. Almost killed *me*. Except now you're sober."

"Quent, I—"

"No. I don't want to hear it." Quentin brushed past her without a glance and disappeared upstairs.

This can't be happening. Everything she'd done since *that day* had been because she had nothing else to live for. The only thing that kept her going was her thirst for revenge. Vengeance. Making the troxies suffer as much as she suffered. But now...Quentin was alive. Her parents were still gone, and that was a guilt she'd never shed. But her little brother, her whole *world*—he was still here. And he hated her. Hated who she'd become. What she'd done.

A strangled sound pierced the silence, and she was shocked to discover it had come from her. Her hand went to her chest. It felt too tight, the room too hot and close, her breaths coming too quickly.

Stella had been there for her little brother when she hadn't. She *could* have killed Quentin with her stunt on Stella's camp. If she'd known, she never would have—

A steadying hand fell to her shoulder. Mal's hand. "Penny..." His normally stoic face had softened into a look of concern. Concern for *her*. She couldn't take it. Suddenly, she was aware of everyone's eyes on her.

"I'll do whatever you want," she said. "Tell me what the plan is later." With that, she dashed out of the house. She ran and ran, but she couldn't outrun the memory of the disdain on her little brother's face as he looked at her, his hand latched onto Stella's.

47

"How is he?" Stella asked.

Tara threw herself onto the couch beside her with a sigh. Stella tossed her a pillow, and she stuffed it under her head. "He still won't talk. Won't eat."

Quentin had barricaded himself in his room all day after...Penny. Stella couldn't imagine what was going through the kid's head. His recent life had been nothing but turmoil and trauma, with few people to rely on.

She'd tried to pry him out of his room, but he wouldn't budge. But if she'd found out that a close relative she'd thought dead was actually walking around in the world murdering people, she'd probably lock herself in a room too. Quentin was a tough kid and he would get through this. Stella would make sure of it.

"Are we sure he's still in there?" asked Derek from where he sat on the floor beside Stella. "Apparently he can escape out of windows."

Tara propped her socked feet on Stella's lap and said, "He's in there. I made him verbally confirm it or else I said I'd kick the door in." She blew out a breath and buzzed her lips. "His *sister*. Puñeta. I don't know if it's better or worse for the kid that she's alive. We need Lawrence back. Quentin needs him."

"We'll get him back. Tomorrow." Stella gripped Tara's ankle, her mind far away. "I owe him that much, and more."

"Are you ever going to tell us what happened between you two?" asked Tara.

Derek slid an elbow in beside Stella's thigh and rested his head on his fist. The close contact felt...natural. Comfortable. She huddled into her flannel shirt—er, well, Derek's flannel shirt—and inhaled his calming scent of sage and sandalwood. She hadn't changed out of it since that morning. She liked the way his eyes lingered on her when she wore it.

"Lawrence can talk about it when he's ready," she said. "But...well, we've crossed paths before. And he had every right to react the way he did."

"Oooookay. That's not cryptic at all," Tara said, tossing her feet to the ground and stretching.

"Tara, wait. There's something else." Stella bit her lip. She wanted Tara to say yes, and she wasn't sure if she would. "Part of my deal with Derek was to get extra seats on a convoy headed to the Canadian border. I got seats for all of us—you, me, Lawrence, and Quentin. If you want them."

Tara's eyebrows shot up. "The border? You mean, we'd be able to get out of here? Out of the country?" Tara turned to Derek, steel in her eyes. "Is this for real?"

Derek nodded. "Convoy will leave whenever you're ready."

"I...I don't know what to say." Tara's eyes shone, and she pressed a hand to her mouth. "Stella, that's...that means a lot. That you would even think to do something like that for us." She pulled Stella into a brief but tight hug. "This doesn't mean that I won't still beat your ass in sparring matches if you're not practicing." Tara swiped at her face and plastered on a serious look. "I'll talk to the boys about it. Once we're all together again. Tomorrow."

"Tomorrow," agreed Stella.

"Guess I better get some rest." Tara glanced between Derek and Stella, a slight lift to her brow. "Goodnight, you two."

When Tara's footsteps had faded upstairs, Derek rose to sit on the coffee table across from Stella, their knees bumping. Her eyes traced over his shoulder muscles bunched under his tee shirt, tight and tense. Interlacing his hands between his legs, he stared at the floor.

Stella nudged his knee with hers. "What's going on in there?" she asked.

Derek exhaled in a gush. "This is crazy, right? Nine months ago, we were just going about our daily lives. And now, we've planned an entire assassination and a coup." He wrung his hands and bounced a knee.

"Having second thoughts?"

"No." His voice wavered. "No," he said again, stronger. "It's just...if I fuck this up, there will be nowhere to hide. Rodney will know we were the ones behind it even if we don't get caught. Mal's the general, I was Mal's second, Penny is Rodney's second. We're at the top of the list for potential assassins. I..." Derek twisted the silver ring around his pointer finger. "Fuck, I'm scared."

Stella brushed her fingers across his hand. "Me too. But our plan is solid. Even I'm confident in it, and I'm scared shitless of Penny going off-book and killing me to satisfy her own twisted vengeance."

"She won't be anywhere near you, and Mal will keep her in check." Derek twined his fingers with hers, and a pleasant feeling rose in her at the protective undercurrent in his voice. "We just have to focus on our part—getting Lawrence out."

"Let's go over it again, one more time." She knew the plan, but the comfort of repetition eased her anxiety.

"Tara will cause a diversion with a stolen troxy cargo truck—we'll get it tomorrow on the way over—and stage an attack. Come to think of it, the noise might churn up a few turned to come out and play, which wouldn't be the worst thing. Mal and Penny will go for Rodney and swap out his detox serum with morphine, while Mal's soldiers subdue Rodney's followers. You and I will go for Lawrence. Mal's guys will be on security detail, and they'll slip us the key. Then we'll hop in Tara's truck, stash it somewhere, and hike it back here."

Stella shifted in her seat. "I can't believe it took us all day to come up with that. It feels...easy? Not enough?"

"We've got a strong team. Good under pressure and excellent improvisers. Even Penny." He swept a thumb across her wrist. "So you're still going to Canada?"

Stella withdrew her hand under the guise of smoothing her hair. "I promised Evie I would get Silas to safety. But let's get through tomorrow first. I can only think about one insane heist-slash-assassination at a time."

The fire reflected off the planes of Derek's face, his high cheekbones casting his expression into shadows.

"You're still with me, right?" she asked. Was this too much for him? Did he not want to help with Silas anymore since she wouldn't stay and aid in the Faction's war efforts?

"Silas is a good man. I won't abandon him." He leaned in and stilled her hand where it fidgeted with her Patch, pulling it back to her lap. "And if you want to stick around and consider how else you could help in the war, I'll be by your side. I won't abandon you either."

And for once, Stella believed him without question.

48

S TEALING THE PHARMATROX TRUCK had been the easy part. Easy, but Stella had still almost gotten her head blown off.

In the wee hours of the morning, she'd crept downtown into Sector 8, where Mal's intel said there was a Pharmatrox armory with cargo trucks in the basement garage level. With Tara and Derek's help, she'd taken out a patrolling guard, donned his gear, and infiltrated the building using his credentials. She didn't want to use her Helix Key or contraband Patch, in case Pharmatrox picked up on her credentials' proximity to suspicious activities—like trucks getting stolen—and decided to track them. She and Mal each had a radio, but they were only to be used in an emergency to decrease the risk of any communications getting intercepted.

She'd taken out a few guards in the garage and hopped in the truck no problem. Until a guard she hadn't noticed snuck up beside her and almost blasted the door off with a volt rifle. Although she'd subdued him, her hands had shaken on the steering wheel the whole drive up the ramp. Her hit of dust that morning had barely taken the edge off; she was getting used to a lower dosage, but her body always hungered for more.

Stella now used her Patch's jammer to disengage the truck's GPS and tracking beacon, and threw open the passenger door for Derek and Tara.

And Quentin, apparently.

Tara held him by the back of his shirt and glared, while Derek stood there with a dumb smile on his face.

"What the hell are you doing here?" Stella's glare matched Tara's. "And Derek, why are you *smiling*?"

"I told you to duct tape him to a chair, but you two wouldn't listen." Derek pulled himself up into the truck and crouched in the middle between the seats.

Tara shoved Quentin ahead of her and followed. "Let's go," Tara snapped. "Back to Maple Street."

Quentin jutted out his jaw. "I know where you're going, so I'll just sneak out again."

"And what if we try Derek's idea?" said Tara.

"Guess I'm hobbling through the street with a chair stuck to my butt."

"The hell you are, tomatito—"

"Let him come," said Stella. "Better to know where he is than have him show up at the wrong time." She tossed him the radio. "You're in charge of that."

She glanced at him out of the corner of her eye as she drove through the neutral zones toward the stadium. The twerp had a self-satisfied smirk on his face. But a darkness weighed on him in the sag of his shoulders and the circles under his eyes that hadn't been there before he'd learned about Penny.

"You have to do what we say," she said. "This is going to be more dangerous than what we did at the Spire."

"I know. I heard you scheming in the kitchen all day yesterday."

Tara poked him in the arm. "You were in your room."

"I was listening from the top of the stairs. How do you think I knew where to find you?"

Derek snorted and Stella sighed. *Figures.*

Quentin patted his backpack. "Brought some things that might help. Flares, in case the turned show up. More flares in case we want to do some good old-fashioned arson. Extra rope, bolt cutters, a flashlight, and this airhorn thing I found in the garage, if we need to make a ruckus."

Stella grunted. "That's actually a good idea. Give the horn and flares to Tara. And T, try not to destroy the truck if you can help it. It wasn't fully unloaded, so there's some boxes in the back. Could be something useful."

"Noted."

When they arrived near the outer perimeter of the stadium, Stella pulled over, and Tara switched into the driver's seat as they unloaded.

"You good?" she asked Tara.

Tara nodded. "If you guys aren't out of there in an hour, I'm bringing in the cavalry."

"What's the cavalry?" asked Derek.

"A herd of turned, probably. I don't know yet, but don't make me do it. Just get in and get out. Quentin, what is it that Stella's always telling you?"

"Don't get eaten."

"Don't get eaten. Good boy. See you in an hour."

The truck rumbled toward the Faction's supply cache in a nearby brick building. In a few minutes, Tara would begin revving the engine and rustling up their distraction. Mal and Penny would move as soon as Rodney sent troops to investigate the disturbance, while Derek and Stella, and now Quentin, went for Lawrence.

All they had to do now was wait.

49

Penny

PENNY ROSE BEFORE DAWN. Not that she'd slept at all. Her anguish at yesterday's events had only intensified, and with the sunrise came a familiar feeling: rage. Rage at herself for destroying her family, her life, and her relationship with her little brother. Rage at Pharmatrox for their insatiable quest for power and control. Rage at Rodney for feeding her bloodlust. Rage at Stella for being the sister she couldn't. The sister she could *never* be again.

Penny readied her supplies in the small ground floor office that was her private living space. A small cot was shoved in the corner beside a rickety shelf, and a table and chairs sat next to a locker that held her weapons and gear. She rifled through her bag for the vials of morphine. Rodney would be starting his detox cycle today, so they had to do this *today*. He wouldn't detox again for a few weeks. She clenched her hand around a tiny bottle, knuckles white.

Rage was the only thing that had kept her alive these past nine months, and it was rage that would save her now. She embraced the feeling. Used it as fuel. As much as she hated Stella for her involvement with the troxies, she'd never raise a hand against her. For she'd seen the look in Quentin's eyes when he'd grasped Stella's hand. It was the way he used to look at her when they were kids. Adoration. Acceptance. *Love.*

And she'd never take that away from him. She'd already robbed him of so much. She owed him a debt she'd never be able to repay. Freeing Lawrence would never redeem her in Quentin's eyes—in any of their eyes—but it was a start. She didn't know how to earn their forgiveness, and she wasn't even sure she wanted it. She certainly didn't deserve it. But Lawrence meant something to her little brother. So did Tara. And so did Stella. So she would make sure they were all safe and could continue on with their lives. Far away from her.

Penny slipped the vials in her jacket pocket and put a few extra knives in her belt. She wasn't taking her pack—too cumbersome, not to mention suspicious.

Rodney's office contained a constant rotation of his inner circle, so she'd have to hope her sleight of hand was good. Mostly, she was relying on them to be too distracted with boobs and booze to pay attention to her rooting around in his desk. Rodney would send troops to investigate Tara's diversion, and he'd make sure to command them himself. He wanted people to see *him* giving the orders, not Mal. *Narcissistic asshole.* His own self-righteousness would be what killed him.

After a soft knock at her door, it creaked open. Mal paused with his hand on the knob. Dark stubble was growing in along his jawline, but his hair on the sides sported a fresh shave, leaving his curls long on top.

"Not used to you knocking," she said and twitched her head for him to come inside.

He shut the door and leaned against the wall. "How are you? After yesterday."

She snorted and returned to polishing her knives. "You think I'm mad at you for yelling at me? I'm a big girl. I can take it."

"That's not what I was referring to."

The hole in her chest ached. "I don't want to talk about that with you."

"Fair enough. Tell me this—are you able to do your job today, or do we need to wait?"

Penny shoved a knife into its sheath and said, "I'm fine. I'm focused. Satisfied?"

"And you won't harm Stella." It wasn't a question.

"I'll keep my hands to myself."

His eyes raked over her, and the memory of their argument at Derek's house flashed in her mind. Bodies flush, his big hand wrapped around her arm.

And she wanted to rage at *him* for the way he made her blood simmer.

"See that you do." He checked his watch. "Ten minutes. Be ready." He left her alone to finish preparing.

Ten minutes later, the alarm sounded.

50

"To arms! Breach at the northern gate!"

A flood of people poured out of the stadium, heading directly into Tara's distraction.

"Time to move," said Stella.

In the confusion, she, Derek, and Quentin blended in with the crowd and circled to the stadium's south entrance. Stella and Derek wore sweatshirts with the hoods up. Nobody would recognize her from the fighting pit, probably, but it wasn't worth the risk. Quentin stuck close to her side, a black toboggan covering his bright hair. With all resources diverted to dealing with the imminent threat, only a pair of guards remained behind.

"Shit," said Derek. "They're Rodney's guys. I'll handle it." He approached the guards clutching their junky rifles. "Got a meeting with Mal," he said to one of them.

"Thought you defected," said the guard with a hooked nose. "Rodney's orders to shoot you on sight."

"So why am I not dead?" he asked.

"Call me curious."

Derek glanced at Stella and yanked her hood off. *What the—?* "Found the troxy that escaped from his pit, and one of her friends. Think Rodney might be interested in that?"

The other guard's jaw dropped, and the first guard blinked. "Hell yes."

He unlocked the gate, and in one swift motion, Derek disarmed him and slammed the rifle into his face, knocking him out. Stella took out the second guard with a punch to the temple, then they dragged the bodies inside.

After Stella pulled her hood back on, she said, "Didn't realize outing me was part of the plan."

"Had to improvise," said Derek, pressing his back flat against the wall. Quentin copied him, his gangly little shadow. "I'd never let them hurt you."

"Next time, I get to punch someone in the head," whispered Quentin.

"Sure, kid," said Derek, leading them inside.

People rushed around the circular hallway that ran the circumference of the stadium, grabbing various weapons. Someone shouldered into Derek with a gruff "Watch it" as they made their way quickly to the basement storage rooms.

"Do you have the key?" asked Stella.

Derek smiled and flashed her the keys in his palm. "Guy that bumped into me was one of Mal's. And so are they." He nodded to the guards stationed outside of a metal door. "Raph, Sanjali."

"Derek." The two stepped aside to let them pass.

Everything was going according to plan so far, and that made Stella nervous. *We're almost there. Just need to get Lawrence and our part is done.*

Quentin eyed the grenade clipped to Raph's belt. "Is that real?" He reached a finger to poke at it, and Raph jerked away.

"*Yes*," said Raph.

"Can I have it?"

"No!"

"Quentin, stop pestering him," said Stella.

After Derek unlocked the door, they filed inside. Quentin shined his flashlight around the room. Five people huddled inside, dirt-crusted and thin.

None of them were Lawrence.

"Mierda." Stella's hand slipped off the slimy, damp wall. "He's not here," she said to Derek.

Death hissed in her head. *Failed. You failed again.*

"Fuck. Are you sure?"

"Yes, I'm fucking sure." She fought to keep the panic out of her voice and cut a glance at Quentin. "Could Rodney have—" She didn't want to finish the sentence. Couldn't.

Derek went outside to speak with Raph and Sanjali. Quentin held the flashlight, his face blank. If anything had happened to Lawrence...

Stella ushered the five people outside, pulling Quentin with her. "Up the stairs, down the hall, there's a gate on your right."

The prisoners didn't need to be told twice. They shuffled up the concrete stairs and disappeared into the chaos above.

Derek rejoined her, frowning. "They said Rodney threw some people in the pit recently, but none fit Lawrence's description. Last night, Rodney's guards locked a guy in the main arena. Chained the doors shut. Sanjali thinks it might've been Lawrence."

"Quentin, get your bolt cutters," she said, heading for the stairs.

"Aye, aye." Quentin held them aloft.

They ran through the crowd to the first set of arena doors. But there weren't any chains.

"Fuck." Derek threw a shoulder against the metal doors. Locked. "Let's try that way."

They ran in the opposite direction of the crowd to the next set of doors. Same thing. Locked, but no chains. As Derek slammed into the doors again, something jangled from the other side.

"Derek...what if they're chained from the *inside*?"

Derek's hand curled into a fist, and he looked like he wanted to try punching his way through.

"I have an idea." Quentin perked up from behind them. "I'll climb in from the outside, cut the chains, and let you guys in."

"*Climb?*" Derek gaped at him.

"I'm a good climber. And this baby has plenty of handholds. It'll be easy." Quentin looked to Stella, ardent tenacity lighting his expression. She could not deny him this, and really, he was their only chance at saving Lawrence now.

"Okay," she said. "Give me the radio in case we need to reach Mal. If you're not on the other side of this door in—"

Quentin screwed up his face as he considered. "Fifteen minutes."

"—fifteen minutes, I'm coming out there to—"

"—give you an atomic wedgie," finished Derek. He punched Quentin's shoulder. "Go get 'em."

Quentin ducked his head and scurried off, while Derek and Stella huddled in the small alcove by the door.

"I can't believe you're letting him do this," said Derek.

Stella shrugged. "He climbed an air traffic control tower just fine."

Derek's eyes bulged. "He what?"

"It's a long story," she said as the crowd continued flooding past. "Rodney is sending a lot of people to deal with our distraction."

"He likes swinging his dick around. Mal has more loyal troops than Rodney, but Rodney's people are fucking crazy, so unfortunately that evens things out. Crazy does count for something."

"Mmm." Stella picked at a hole in the concrete wall as she counted the minutes.

The radio crackled from her belt loop, shattering the tense silence. Stella's hand flew to Derek's shirtsleeve, and she grabbed the radio.

Mal's voice. "We have a problem."

51

Penny

*T*ODAY, THIS ENDS. No more Rodney fucking things up for the resistance or lording over people in his reign of terror. No more useless bloodshed.

No more.

Today, she'd be rid of this demon.

Penny stepped into the hallway, where Mal waited for her. Hidden in the shadows, they watched Rodney's guards file down from his office. Other people came out of their rooms and tents that lined the circular hallway on the main floor, grabbing weapons and looking around in confusion.

A few seconds later, Rodney himself descended the stairs. His greasy hair was slicked back, his gaunt face more skeletal than usual. He must have used a lot this past cycle for him to deteriorate so quickly. The vials of morphine were a reassuring weight in Penny's pocket as she watched the loathsome man step into a leadership role that was never meant to be his.

"Somebody's doing something naughty on our northern border." Rodney's voice carried through the cavernous hallway. "Kill them. Don't bother bringing them to me." Someone handed him a volt rifle, and he slung it over his shoulder. "If anyone happens across my *general*, tell him I have it handled. And that if I see him, I'll shoot his fucking balls off."

"Nice," rumbled Mal.

Rodney led his guards—about fifty people—through the hall toward the north entrance. Other stragglers took up arms and joined him, but many did not. Those who remained behind battened down the hatches and prepared for an attack.

Once Rodney was out of sight, Penny and Mal moved.

When they got to his office door, Penny paused. A few voices came from within, but she had expected that. "Watch the door," she said. He put a hand out to stop her, fixing her with an intent gaze. Adrenaline buzzed through her.

"You can do this."

"I *know*," she sneered. But she'd never admit how his words of confidence spiked inside her.

She went inside, the messy office in its usual disarray. Eight new faces looked up as she entered. Some of them sported black eye tattoos on their arms. A few with glazed-over eyes went back to what they were doing, mainly drinking and snorting dust. But the rest of them...they were concerning. Watchful eyes, twitchy movements. These were users with heightened senses and augmented abilities, like she'd been.

"Rodney sent me back," she said to the room. The twitchy users regarded her with suspicion. The others ignored her. "He forgot his lucky knife." *What a superstitious fuck.* She went to the desk—fortunately, it was off to the side and would shield what she was actually doing.

The drawer was locked, but Rodney wasn't as clever as he thought he was. She popped open another drawer and lifted the false bottom to grab the key, then unlocked the drawer and swapped out the five vials of detox serum with the morphine. Rodney's regular serum supplier had gone dark recently, and his stash was running dangerously low. He might have a hidden stockpile somewhere else, but he would use what was in his desk first. Hopefully.

Penny held up one of her extra knives to show the room she'd gotten what she came for and put everything back in its place.

But then Mal walked inside, and she frowned. His posture was too straight, and he looked pissed...

Rodney ducked around the larger man, his black-bladed lucky knife held to his kidney.

Callum, Toby, and five of Rodney's regular inner circle filtered in behind them, eyes gleaming. Not turned, but pretty fucking close. One more hit, and they'd be over the edge.

Fuck.

"I knew you two were up to something," said Rodney. "Your little charade didn't fool me. I see the way you look at each other when you think no one is watching." He gave a low chuckle and pushed Mal farther into the room, using his massive body as a shield. "What are you up to, Penny?"

One of his twitchy followers pointed a finger at his desk.

"Ahh. So you've been keeping tabs on me. Tracking when I go on a detox cycle. Smart." Rodney snapped his fingers, and the user unlocked the desk drawer, pulled out a vial, and tossed it to Rodney. "You think I hadn't thought of that? That someone would try to poison me?" He laughed again, digging the knife into Mal's back until he flinched.

Penny's hand drifted to the knife at her belt. If she could get a clear shot at Rodney, she could throw it through his beady fucking eyeball. But that would leave them in a room full of his followers, his blood fresh on her hands. And if any of them turned, that blood would be her death sentence.

"That's what I have taste testers for," said Rodney. "But I couldn't let you know that. You, the one person most likely to kill me. But you were never here often enough to see me detox. Always running around playing with *him*." He jerked the knife and Mal inhaled sharply.

She locked eyes with Mal, and he nodded slightly. He was fine, but she needed to hurry.

She took stock of her options. She had three knives and her sickle. Mal had a gun at his hip and a knife in his belt and boot. Her eyes landed on a side table. Another huge bag of dust sat open, calling to her.

"Normally, you'd be right about my detox cycle," continued Rodney. "But not today. No, I switched things up. Took a bit *more* than usual, just in case some red-headed bitch decided to make a move against me."

The bag of dust was within reach. So close. One sweet hit, just enough to give her the speed and ferocity to take out Rodney and his followers. She could detox right away with the stolen vials in her coat.

She swallowed, her attention fastened to the dust as the rest of the room faded away.

The memory of Rodney's voice snaked through her mind. *"We always kill those who deserve it."*

Just a taste. Just one hit. As the dust sang its siren song, her hand turned white around the hilt of her sickle.

After the fire, Penny swore she'd never succumb to the dust again. Penelope was the user who'd killed her parents and almost killed Quentin. Penelope was everything she hated about herself: weak, selfish. And Penelope was *dead*. Penny was different. Better. *Stronger.*

Penny would never go back to being Penelope. Not ever again. Not even to rid the world of this piece of human filth. This was Penny's fight—*her* fight.

She ripped her gaze away from the dust.

Rodney smiled, pleased with himself. "I've been waiting *months* for you to try, Penny, my girl. You think I don't know how you feel about me? I've seen the way you look at me with such disgust. Such contempt. You think you could outsmart *me*?"

Just one more inch to the right, you scumbag.

Rodney shook his head and sighed. "Take her."

Callum advanced, clawed hand outstretched, and the rest of Rodney's followers closed in.

Penny snatched the vials out of her pocket and held them high. "One more step and I'll smash them."

Rodney held up a hand. "Hold."

Everyone stopped. Even Callum. *Oh, so he* can *listen to instructions. Fucking weasel.*

"You took a big dosage? Sloppy, Rodney," she said. "Very sloppy. Your serum supply is limited, and you're *hours* from turning. I can see it in your eyes. In your sallow, disgusting *face*. No matter what putrid garbage you spew to your followers about how you're special and you'll never turn, I know you fear it."

Rodney's tongue darted out to lick his lips, eyes shifting between her and the serum.

"So take one more fucking step and I'll smash your salvation to pieces."

Rodney's lip curled and he threw his head back, cackling. "Oh, the lies! Do you hear the lies this woman is weaving?" He made eye contact with each of his followers. "I've used more than any of you, and I haven't lost myself. The dust has made me *better*. The highest-evolved version of myself. And you all can have it too." He nodded to the giant bag of dust, and his followers' eyes snapped to it.

"Take it and see," he said. "And do not be afraid! You're my loyal followers. If you turn, I can bring you back. The serum will bring you back. *We* are the future of this country. *We* alone are the ones who can destroy the troxics."

Is this the vitriol he saves for his inner circle? Making himself out to be some kind of fucking prophet? She knew he was delusional but didn't realize he'd crafted himself a fucking *cult.*

Rodney pointed to Penny. "Our enemies must be eliminated."

Fucking hell. The room exploded into action, users launching at her, at Mal, at the dust.

Mal elbowed Rodney's gut, but Rodney sliced a good cut up the side of his ribcage before Mal disarmed him. That didn't stop Mal; he was tougher than that. Without pause, he shouldered Rodney aside and fired off shots.

Rodney wriggled and swung something around—a volt rifle. *Shit.* He blasted a few volts, some hitting his own people, and the smell of burnt flesh filled the air, choking. Mal slammed Rodney's arm against the wall until he dropped the weapon, then kicked it out of reach.

After Penny decapitated one of Rodney's goons, Callum launched at her, and she swiped her sickle across his torso. He hissed and lashed out with clawed hands, cutting her arm.

The room filled with snarls at the scent of her fresh blood.

Half of Rodney's users had turned, while others were near to turning. They attacked each other, ripping at flesh, dark blood dripping. Some circled her, black eyes leaking obsidian tears.

Penny shoved Callum away and sliced through a few turned, then glanced at Mal, who spoke into their emergency radio with one hand while he held off Rodney with the other. She took aim with one of her knives and threw, grinning when it sunk hilt-deep into Rodney's upper back and he howled.

"Kill the bitch!"

Shrieks and hisses filled the room as the eleven—*eleven, fuck*—turned closed in. Toby, Callum, and Rodney were the only ones who were still themselves, and the cowards hung back to watch the show.

Penny gripped her sickle. *I'll give them a fucking show.*

The door burst open behind Mal, *more* of Rodney's followers piling into the room. *Shit, they must have been waiting outside.*

Mal threw himself against the door, but even his bulk couldn't keep the sea of people from pushing in. "There's too many!" he shouted.

Between her and Mal, they could handle eleven turned and three users. But with more users—and probably turned—shoving their way in and Mal unable to assist her, there was no other option. They had to run.

Fuck. We failed. It's over.

Penny grabbed a decorative paperweight from the desk and hefted it at the window, shattering the glass and leaving a jagged opening. Swishing her sickle, she fought her way to the window and beat back the encroaching turned.

She glanced over her shoulder as she ducked a claw. "Come on, Mal!"

"Not yet." He pinned her with a hard glare, face slicked with sweat and blood as the door undulated behind him. "I can hold them." He flicked his gaze to Rodney. "Finish this."

Rodney paled. He lunged for Mal's gun, and Mal kicked him in the stomach, but Rodney managed to get the weapon, firing into the room as he lost his balance. One bullet whizzed past Penny's ear, and she spun to the floor until she heard the click of the gun running out of bullets. She'd taken out five turned, and the six remaining ones rotated between attacking her and fighting each other.

But she only had eyes for Rodney.

This is my only chance to kill this shithead. Her rage fueled her as she cut through the wall of turned until only Callum and Toby were left, guarding Rodney. Mal strained against the door, but he held his position, veins popping out of his arms as he braced them on either side of the small entryway. He couldn't let go of the wall to radio Stella and Derek for help or else he'd lose his hold and the door would burst open.

They were on their own.

Penny unleashed a slew of attacks at Callum, Toby, and Rodney to keep them distracted from Mal. She threw two knives, one in each hand. One skewered Toby in his pudgy belly, and he fell face first. A *ping* sounded as Callum swiped aside the other and lunged at her with a long knife. He was skilled, but she had rage on her side.

She threw a metal chair at Callum and bowled past him, charging for Rodney. When she reached him, she tackled him and they rolled, struggling for position, until they slammed against the wall, Rodney on top. He grinned down at her with ugly teeth and raised his black-bladed knife.

"I knew you had it in you. I knew you'd never take a back seat to me. A valiant effort." As Rodney brought the knife down in a vicious stab, she pushed his arm to the side and headbutted him in the face, feeling the satisfying crunch of bone. He shrieked, his nose showering her in dark blood.

"You talk too damn much," she said, then rolled them, reversing their positions.

He bucked underneath her, and she punched him in the bleeding mess of his ruined nose. He screamed, clawing at her face with bloody, slippery hands. Fending him off and stretching, she grabbed his knife that sat a few feet away. When she looked down at the vile man, he hissed and spit blood at her as he bared his teeth and snapped his jaws. He knew what was coming for him. And he would not beg for his life.

Good. Because I don't want to fucking hear it.

She clamped her hand around Rodney's throat, and a harsh laugh burbled between his lips. As he looked at her with watery eyes finally shattered by black veins, clarity washed over her. She would rid the world of one more monster.

"See you in hell." Penny shoved the black blade under his chin. Once. Twice. Again.

Rodney's screams drowned in blood. He gurgled a laugh, and his last words rasped out in a slow hiss. "That's...my...girl."

Wiping the blood from her hands, Penny slumped against the wall. She thought she would feel relieved. The only man she'd ever feared was finally gone. But the darkness around her heart tightened its grip.

Another dead body. Add it to my list.

"Penny!" Mal's warning pulled her back into the room.

"You bitch!" Callum hissed, launching at her.

They both went down as he fell into her, and she slammed the bloody knife into the side of his face, raking it through his cheek, and punched him in the gut.

Penny was the only one who got up, Callum whimpering and bleeding at her feet.

Surrounded by black blood and bodies, she looked across the room at Mal, straining to hold the door closed.

Done. It's done.

Now to avoid getting eaten so they could deal with the rest of their problems.

52

"IT'S BEEN FIFTEEN MINUTES. Hasn't it been fifteen minutes?" Stella fidgeted with the radio.

Rodney caught them. Mierda.

Mal had radioed with the news. He said he and Penny had it handled and they should keep going for Lawrence, but she and Derek should be ready for trouble. *How comforting.*

And now Quentin had been gone too long.

Derek glanced at his wrist. "It's been twelve minutes."

"You're not even wearing a watch."

"I'm good at estimating."

Stella pushed off the wall. "I'm going to check on him."

Derek hauled her back into the cover of the alcove as a large group of people hustled past them toward the suite level. They looked ragged and half-starved. Derek eyed them with a dark look.

"Who are they?" she asked.

"I don't know. A lot has changed in the short time since I defected. Rodney has really fucked things up. But that all changes today."

She settled against the wall beside him to wait. A headache pounded inside her skull, drowning out her thoughts. About five minutes later, chains rattled from the other side of the door.

"Quentin?" She placed her palm to the cold metal.

More rattling, then a loud *creeeeak* as the door pushed open, revealing Quentin on the other side.

Quentin shouldered the bolt cutters with a cheeky smile. "Nothing like breaking and entering. Or, entering and then breaking, I guess."

Derek plopped a hand on his head with a smile, and they slipped inside.

"You were two minutes late," said Stella as they jogged down the hallway and into the arena. A chill swept over her as she remembered the last time she'd been here. *Jeering voices. Snarls. Decaying bodies. A sea of red masks.*

The pit was quiet this time. The stage was empty, the helicopter perched in the brown grass awaiting repairs.

Then she saw him. A lone figure knelt in the dirt, chained to the railing, as he fiddled with a wooden lattice and PVC pipe.

"Lawrence!" She sprinted down the concrete stairs and launched onto the field, running to him.

"Stella?" When he looked up, Stella's heart ached. A split lip wept blood into his mangled beard. Dirt and sweat crusted his entire body, his shirt torn and hanging off of him. His ankles were lashed together and chained to the railing above. His eyes widened as Derek and Quentin came up behind her. "How did you..."

"Later. We have to hurry."

Quentin and Stella took turns cutting through the chains. They'd freed Lawrence's left leg when glass shattered far overhead.

"Almost there," said Quentin as he sliced through metal.

Aggravated squawks and wails sounded from the stands above. When Stella turned to look, she saw Penny and Mal climbing out of the broken window of a suite. *What the...?*

They jumped to the level of seats below and raced down the stairs as a swarm of turned clawed through the window behind them.

"Shit," said Stella.

"Shit," Derek agreed.

Lawrence rubbed his wrists and stretched his legs. "What's the prob—oh. Yeah, shit."

"Can you run like hell?" Stella asked him.

Lawrence ditched his torn shirt and nodded. "I didn't come this far to get eaten now."

"Penny! Mal!" Derek waved, and the two barreled down the stairs and leapt over the railing, the turned chasing at their heels.

Quentin stiffened at his sister's appearance and stepped closer to Stella's side.

"What the hell happened?" asked Derek.

"Later!" Penny was covered in blood, and Mal bled from his side, sweat drenching his tank top. "This way."

Penny led them through a locker room entrance, and once they were all inside, she nodded to the dented row of lockers. "Mal, if you could?"

With a grunt, Mal ripped the lockers off the wall and dropped the hunk of metal in front of the door. Bodies slammed into it from the other side, rattling the hinges.

Quentin's jaw dropped. "Dude. *Duuude.*" He held out a fist. Mal bumped it, his lips twitching.

"That won't hold. We should go," Mal said and motioned them all toward the exit.

When they reached the door, Quentin snipped the chain and they tumbled into a deserted hallway.

Pointing to the left, Derek said, "North gate that way. Tara will be waiting."

Tents were pitched along the sides of the hallway where the Faction members lived. Some poked their heads out at the noise as they jogged past, but quickly hid again when they saw Mal and Penny. Mal nodded to a few of them.

Minutes later, the group reached the gate, where several armed guards approached. Stella tensed and gripped her machete, but when Mal clapped one of the men on the back, Stella's stress level ratcheted down a few notches.

"Good job holding the gate," he said.

Outside, Tara's truck screeched to a halt. "Get in, losers!" she yelled, throwing the passenger door open. "Don't have much time. The noise rustled up some turned."

Mal jerked his head at Stella and the others. "I think your ride is here."

Quentin and Lawrence ran to the truck, but Derek and Stella lingered. "Can you handle this on your own?" asked Derek. "We just blew up a fucking powder keg."

"We'll take out the turned before they hurt anyone," said Mal. "Luckily Rodney was crazy enough to chain the doors shut, so the ones in the arena should stay confined while we pick them off. My guys are taking care of Rodney's soldiers who got swept up in Tara's brilliant distraction. Was a good way to find out who's in his pocket. Was also helpful that some of them decided to brand themselves with that ugly eye tattoo."

Stella studied Penny, who had been uncharacteristically quiet. "And what of Rodney?"

Penny's eyes never left Quentin as she watched him climb into the truck. "I took care of it," she said, sliding a black-bladed knife into her belt.

Mal lifted a hand as if to place it on Penny's shoulder, but switched at the last second and clapped Derek on the back. "I hope I can count on your help in rallying those we have left. It's up to us to push the troxies out of the Capital. Take out their HQ, if we can, and contact Kev in Chicago."

"That's something we can discuss." Derek's eyes found Stella's, then snapped back to Mal. "Tomorrow. Let me take Stella and the rest home."

Mal nodded and extended a hand to Stella. "Thanks for your help today. Quentin and Tara too. When you want my troops for backup, you'll have them. And I'll personally help as well."

She shook it, his large hand swallowing her own. "Thanks, General."

Mal grunted. She thought it was a laugh. Glancing at Penny again, still frozen and silent, she said, "Penny, I—" Her throat tightened. "Thanks. For getting us in here to help Lawrence."

Penny blinked, coming out of her daze, then nodded and stalked down the hallway.

Did I just thank *the woman who's been hunting me down for months, the one who made me a user?*

The prison break-slash-assassination and hiding the stolen cargo truck had taken most of the day. It was late afternoon by the time they got back to Maple Street, and the crew lined up for cold showers. Indoor plumbing was functional, but since Pharmatrox had cut power to the grid everywhere except for their own select few facilities, the water heater wasn't.

But as covered in dirt and sweat as she was, Stella didn't care so long as the shower was wet. When it was her turn, she gathered a clean set of clothes from her room and went into the hallway.

Lawrence came out of the bathroom, clothes wadded in his arms. Stella froze. *Shit, shit, shit. I'm not ready for this conversation.* His cracked lip looked painful, but his hair and beard were scrubbed clean. When he saw her, his hands tightened around his clothes as the silent seconds ticked by.

"We should talk." The words croaked out of her dry throat.

"Agnes." Lawrence's voice was thick like honey, and Stella flinched at the sound of her name.

"That night—" She stopped, Death's laughter filling her ears. How many times had she relived *that night*? How often had she feared this very moment? *Best get on with it.* "Evie knew she was dying. She sacrificed herself so you and I could live. She knew Penny would kill us all unless I did what she asked. I didn't want to kill her. She was my best friend, Lawrence. I loved her too. I—"

He closed the few steps between them and touched a fingertip to her gold pendant. His eyes were a depthless, murky mystery. "I believe you."

A relieved sob tumbled out of Stella's chest, and she said, "Why do you believe me now?"

He ran a hand through his beard. "I've thought about that night every day. I blamed myself for not fighting back. From where they'd hauled me to the woods, I couldn't see or hear very well. All I saw was you holding a knife, and then my friend was dead." A tear escaped and he brushed it away. "After getting to know you, seeing how you risked yourself for Tara and Quentin—and for me too—I know you're not like Penny. Evie told me stories about you. How you were always looking out for her. She was as headstrong as they come, and so if she had her mind made up that she was going to sacrifice herself for us, I believe that she didn't give you a choice."

Stella's tears dripped onto her chest and ran the length of her scar. "I'm so sorry. For the pain I've caused you. For bringing Penny to your camp—then and now. For everything."

Lawrence placed a hand on her shoulder. "Quentin trusts you. Tara trusts you. It will be...difficult for me, but I will work on trusting you too. You saved me from a life of miserable servitude today, and that's no small thing."

Stella squeezed his hand, afraid she might burst from the tension building inside of her. "Thank you," she said with a watery smile and stuffed herself in the bathroom before the dam holding back her sobs broke.

After they'd eaten a hearty dinner of instant meals and canned goods from the stolen truck's cargo, Stella and Derek sat on the couch while Quentin played cards with Tara at the kitchen table. Lawrence had already retired to the room he now shared with Quentin; he'd agreed to stay permanently.

Whenever Stella thought of Lawrence, the guilt remained, but it was the dull ache of healing rather than the writhing mass of self-loathing. It would take more than Lawrence's forgiveness for her to be able to forgive herself, but it was a start.

"No, that's not a straight flush." Tara tapped the cards on the table. "You're missing the eight, tomatito."

"There's an eight! It's right—oh." Quentin scratched his head and eyed Tara's cards. "Hey, T, look at Derek and Stella canoodling on the couch. Don't you want to make some sort of derogatory comment?"

Tara snapped her head toward Derek and Stella while Quentin's hand slid toward her cards.

Stella shrugged and showed Tara her hands. Derek chuckled softly. He was close enough that his breath tickled her ear. "No canoodling here," she said.

Meanwhile, Quentin grabbed an eight from Tara's cards and put it with his. "See! Told you I had an eight."

Tara narrowed her eyes and snatched the card back, bopping him on the head with it. "Cheater. This isn't Go Fish."

Stella was pleased that Quentin was acting like his normal self, but he refused to talk about Penny, and that worried her. Maybe he just needed more time to process.

"Okay, bedtime," said Tara. "We've got an early morning of strategizing with your favorite boy, Mal."

Quentin smiled, stars in his eyes. He'd found a new hero. "You just don't want me to keep beating you at poker."

Tara scoffed. "It's called beginner's luck. Come on. Bed." She motioned for him to go upstairs, and he made a show of dragging his feet. At the end of the hallway, Tara paused, her expression a mix of amusement and reproach. "Don't stay up too late," she said to Stella and Derek, then left them alone.

Stella rested her head on the back of the couch and stared into the fire, Derek a warm and reassuring presence beside her.

"That's the first time she hasn't insulted me or called me Jonesy," Derek said, leaning back and interlacing his hands behind his head, his shirt rising and exposing a stripe of torso.

Stella ripped her gaze away. *His face. Look at his* face.

Cabrón, it's a nice face.

And also not a good place to look if she didn't want to be distracted. She stared back to the fire.

"Lawrence means a lot to her," she said. "Helping us get him back was a good mark in your favor."

"Of course I helped." He shook his head. "*I* should have stopped it all sooner. Between Mal and me and his army, we probably could have. But Rodney was such an insidious threat that we didn't know it was too late until it was *really* too late." He angled toward her, eyes bright and intent. "Thank you for helping us. For trusting me."

"Thanks for keeping your word." She smiled, but wrung her hands in her lap. It had been over a week since Silas had attacked her at the Spire. And in that week, they'd accomplished so much. But it wasn't enough. There was still so much to do. How much time did Silas have left?

Derek traced a fingertip down her arm to her fidgeting hands, and she stilled under his touch. "What's troubling you?"

"Just thinking about Silas." *And about how you're a failure*, whispered Death. She cringed away from the swirling voice that was everywhere inside her head. Always blaming. Always accusatory.

"With Rodney gone, we have more resources at our disposal. It will be okay."

"You always make the impossible sound easy." A smile tugged at the corner of her mouth.

"Things are always easier with you."

Derek's low voice sparked something within her, a long dull ember flickering with new life. She didn't know what to say and thankfully didn't have to flounder for a reply because a knock sounded at the door.

"I'll get it." She was in the hallway before Derek had a chance to say anything else that made her insides turn to Jell-O.

She huddled into the warm flannel—*Jesus, it still smells like him*—as she opened the door.

To Penny.

She blinked, her brain sending signals to *run*, but her feet remained frozen in place. "Uh, hi," she said, stepping outside onto the porch and shutting the door behind her. "What is it?"

Penny had cleaned off the gore of the day and was dressed in a black tee and black jeans. But for once, Penny looked unsure. Her face stripped bare of malice, scorn, rage...of everything that made her Penny. She tucked a lock of hair behind an ear and asked, "Is Quentin here?"

Stella nodded. "He's in his room."

Penny bit her lip. "Would—can I—do you think I could talk to him?"

She wasn't used to a Penny who stumbled over her words. *Something about seeing Quentin has changed her. She's different than the woman who hunted me...but how much different? And is it enough to trust her alone with Quentin?*

"That's up to him. But I'll ask." Stella studied Penny for a moment. "You killed Rodney today. That's a big step for you." She didn't know how to get the woman to open up, and she wasn't sure if she wanted to know what was inside. But she had to get a glimpse of what was going on in her mind before she'd allow her anywhere near Quentin.

Penny looked at the street below with a cold expression. "Rodney taught me the harsh realities of this world—kill or be killed. He taught me how to survive." Her hands tightened on the porch railing as she added, "But sometimes I feel like it cost me my humanity."

She and Penny had made some hard choices since the Beginning. It was a slippery slope—doing things she wouldn't normally do, in the name of survival or because she didn't have another choice. She kept telling herself that killing Evie had been a mercy. But now that she knew a detox serum existed, the guilty gremlin clawed at her conscience. Maybe Evie could have been saved if she'd been able to hang on a few more months.

Maybe survival had cost Stella her humanity too.

You could kill Penny, right now. Kill or be killed. Death's voice was a velvet caress, her boot knife a heavy weight in the side of her shoe. But Stella didn't want to kill her.

She had thought death was the only way to stop Penny. But now, Quentin was Stella's salvation. If not for his presence, she had no doubts that Penny would have killed her by now, Architect or not. And Quentin had saved Stella from herself too. Because of him—and Tara and Lawrence—she didn't want to use anymore. A pebble of warmth pulsed in her heart. It felt like a lifetime since she'd had someone she could confide in, someone she could trust. And it was all because that squirmy kid had fallen through her ceiling.

From the look on Penny's face now and how she'd helped them at the stadium, it was clear Quentin had brought a small part of Penny back to herself.

Quentin was Penny's salvation too.

"Please." Penny's mouth pressed into a tight line. Her eyes steadied on Stella, imploring. "Survival means nothing to me if my little brother hates me."

Stella nodded slowly. "I'll get him."

53

Penny

P ENNY TAPPED HER NAILS against the porch railing as she waited. The old paint chips peeled off in her fingers, and she flicked them onto the sidewalk.

Rodney was dead. Rodney was *dead*. She could no longer blame him for her choices, for the darkness and the pain she carried. Rodney had been the perfect scapegoat. Blaming him for fueling her bloodlust had been easy. Even easier when she'd *embraced* that bloodlust. Had craved it. Needed it.

But now, she saw the bloodlust and hatred of Rodney for what it was: a veil. A smokescreen. Something to hide her true feelings and failures behind so she could keep putting one foot in front of the other and not fall apart.

It had taken looking into the eyes of her little brother as he flinched away from her in that arena that morning to realize that she was glad for Rodney's death, but she was still falling apart. She was the only one left to take responsibility for her choices. For ruining her own life. Rodney had helped in that, certainly, but she'd been well on her way to disaster before they'd met.

Behind her, the front door creaked open, and Quentin poked his head out, peering at her suspiciously as he stepped outside. He'd grown about an inch since the Beginning. He'd be taller than her soon, if he kept growing.

"Hi," he said.

"Hi." She couldn't breathe.

"Stella said you wanted to talk." He crossed his arms and stuck out his jaw, and unshed tears burned in her eyes.

"You look just like Dad when he was fighting with the tractor," she said before she could stop herself.

Quentin snorted, a crack forming in his icy exterior. "I went a few bouts with that tractor myself, so I understand his frustration." Then the cold mask fell back in place. "Why are you here?"

"I—" Why was she there? She needed to see him, to look at him and know and feel and believe he was real. *Alive.* But she couldn't pour her heart out to him. He wasn't ready to hear it. And she wasn't ready to spill it. "I came to ask if it would be okay if I helped with the next part of your plan. The Spire break-in and rescuing Stella's friend, right?"

Quentin frowned. "Why would you want to help? You've been trying to kill Stella for months."

Damn it, but the kid was blunt. Just like her. She had to appreciate that.

"Heard Mal was joining you, and I can't let him have all the fun," she said. Quentin gave her a stony stare, but a dimple flashed in his cheek. She could work with that. "I want to help you. Stella and I have a...history. But you're my brother. I'd do anything for you."

Quentin squinted at her. "Even team up with someone you hate and not slice and dice her?"

"Even that."

Quentin scrutinized her for a minute more. Then he shrugged. "You can come."

A thrill went through her. *I can't believe it. He said yes.*

"But I don't want you near me or Stella. You stay with Derek or Mal where they can watch you."

As fast as her hope had flared, it snuffed out.

"See you tomorrow for the planning session, I guess," he said. "And don't show up here again unannounced. It makes Stella nervous. And...and I'm not ready to talk to you yet."

The door was shutting in her face before she could say anything more.

Penny hiked back across the city. At sunset, she reached the stadium, nodding to Mal's guards stationed on the perimeter.

After Quentin had left that morning, Mal and his troops had eradicated the turned in the stadium, and she had given a little speech to calm everyone and drum up morale. She didn't remember what she said. Something to the effect of "Rodney's dead, I'm in charge now, the war is still on, no more using the dust." She'd made the call after discussing it with Mal. The dust was her way to control people too, but after Rodney's leadership and the dregs of humanity that had flocked to him, it left a bitter taste in her mouth. She didn't want to be anything like that man.

As for Rodney's followers and sympathizers, few remained in the Faction camp. Didn't mean they couldn't cause problems, but she wasn't worried. Many had branded themselves with the black eye tattoo, so they'd be easy to spot. Especially now that the dust was outlawed, it would be even easier to single them out because they'd be the ones using.

And turning.

She swallowed the thought as she headed toward her room. She had a good idea of which Rodney sympathizers to keep an eye on. She wouldn't force them to detox—she'd never force a drug on anyone again. But if they wouldn't detox and they kept using, she'd eliminate them before they became a threat.

Mal favored kicking them out of camp, but she disagreed. They'd turn eventually. And when they turned, they'd kill someone. Eat them. She didn't want to be responsible for unleashing that nightmare on some innocent person when she could have prevented it.

As for being in charge of the Faction, she didn't want the responsibility. Shit was so fucked in the Capital that she barely had time to think beyond the next twenty minutes, let alone plan for the future and strategize an entire *war*. And the last thing she wanted was to work side by side with the giant, brooding Malosi. But there was no one else to lead. She'd had enough of standing on the sidelines, watching Rodney destroy the resistance. *I'll be damned if I let it fall apart under me too.*

But there was still one glaring loose end. When she and Mal had cleaned the bodies out of Rodney's office, one had been missing. Callum was not among the fallen, and no one had seen him around camp. The slimy eel was hiding somewhere. Waiting for his moment. He'd be back. She wasn't afraid of him, but he *could* pose a threat if he was able to gather Rodney's remaining followers.

Penny blinked, confused. On autopilot, her feet had carried her to Mal's room. She'd never visited him here before, but she knew where it was. *But why the hell am I here?* She shook her head and turned to go, when the door opened behind her.

"Penny?"

She glanced over her shoulder and caught a glimpse of Mal's chiseled body—the guy was fucking *ripped*—as he froze, shirt in hand. The tattoo on his arm swirled onto his pec and accentuated his...everything. Her eyes snagged on the bloodstained bandage plastered across the ridges of his abs.

"You want to come in, or did you just come here to stare at me?"

Penny snapped out of her daze—*what the fuck was that, anyway?*—and squeezed past him into his room, *very* careful to avoid touching him. His room was set up much like hers, spartan with meager belongings. A creased paperback book lay open on the cot, and his shelf was well organized. She leaned against the table and studied the hell out of the cracks in the concrete floor as Mal pulled his tee shirt on.

He waited. She appreciated that he didn't push her as she wrangled her thoughts. Eventually, she said, "So I'm in charge of the Faction now? Just like that?"

"Seems that way. There will be a...transitional period. I've sent a message to Kev. He'll no doubt approve of it."

"I'm surprised you'd trust me to lead."

"I figure it's a shared responsibility with me and Derek, if he wants it. But you're the only other person here who commands any amount of respect from these people, even if much of it is fear-based. You can change that narrative over time, if you want to. And it will help that I'm your general. That will provide some consistency and stability." He studied her face, her tense posture. "But that's not what's really bothering you."

She tapped her boot on the ground and chewed the inside of her cheek. "I went to see Quentin."

Mal nodded. Waited again. Where there used to be contempt on his face, there was now...something else. Something softer. He was a hard man, but his edges were malleable. *I wonder what caused that change?*

"He hates me," she said. "He hates me, and he has every right to."

"So fix it."

"I can't fix it."

"You can fix it."

"No, Mal, I can't fucking fix it. I killed our parents. I fucking trauma-tized him. I'm surprised he even talked to me when I went over there. He accepted my help with the Spire break-in, but he wants nothing to do with me." She pushed a hand through her tangled hair. "He should wish I was dead too."

Mal stepped up to her, close enough that his legs brushed hers. "The fact that he *did* talk to you tells me he doesn't hate you, and that you can fix it. This is not broken beyond repair."

"What do you know about it?" she snapped. The idea of fixing things with Quentin terrified her almost as much as him never speaking to her again. She sighed. "I just...I want to fix it, but I don't know how. And what if it doesn't work? What if...what if I lose my little brother all over again?"

Mal reached out a big hand and tipped her chin up, thumb sweeping over her jaw. She felt too hot, too exposed under his intense gaze. "You will not lose him. You are the most stubborn woman I have ever met, and I know you won't give up on him." He gripped her chin between his thumb and pointer finger. "So *fix it*."

The timbre of his voice rumbled all the way to the tips of her toes.

"I'll fix it," she said.

54

THE SPIRE SAT AT the end of the road, its reflective panels disguising it to look like every other building—blocky and squat. A squadron of guards patrolled the perimeter. Clouds hung in the night sky and obscured the bright moon.

After three days of planning, which included Mal using Stella's Helix Key to siphon weapons and supplies from Pharmatrox warehouses, they were ready.

Today, Stella would bring Silas home.

A distant rumble vibrated the air as a fighter jet streaked overhead toward the south. When an alarm sounded, several guards piled into an armored truck and sped off.

Stella tapped her Patch and viewed a video feed from a raid drone, seeing Pharmatrox guards fighting back a line of red-masked Faction members. Mal was busy keeping the troxies distracted and far away. She blinked away the feed and rubbed her sweaty palms together, longing for the dust. But no. She could make it through this. For Silas. She could detox with him, once he was safe.

Derek sidled up to her with a reassuring smile. Quentin was hiding in a smashed storefront; Penny and Lawrence somewhere else. Everyone was in position.

Right on cue, the stolen Pharmatrox cargo truck trundled into a nearby alley, and Tara waved to them. One by one, Stella and the others slunk through the shadows.

Sticking her head out the driver's side window, Tara said, "All aboard."

Quentin and Lawrence stowed away inside the now empty food and supply boxes in the canvas-covered truck bed. Derek slung a rifle across his back and climbed atop the truck, clad in an all-black outfit that rendered him invisible against the black metal roof, courtesy of Mal's supply of guns and tactical attire. Stella touched her own Glock strapped to her leg, grateful to have bullets again.

Cutting a glance at Penny, Tara motioned Stella to come closer and said, "Todo bien?"

Stella gave her the OK signal. "Sí, tía. Adelante."

Tara nodded and shifted the truck into gear.

Stella felt Penny's eyes on her like the ghost of a touch. The two took their positions under the truck, gripping the metal frame and hooking their toes through the loops intended for a spare tire.

A wave of unease at their proximity overcame her. It felt unnatural being so close to someone who had been her enemy for so long. Who still might be her enemy. Stella's hands trembled. *Just one more day before detoxing. I can do this.*

She swallowed her apprehension and gave the bottom of the truck a solid kick, then they rolled out of the alley toward the Spire.

Stella clicked the key fob, and the invisible perimeter bubbled around them. Her hands began to sweat as she heard the guards asking Tara some questions. Yesterday, Stella had used her Helix Key to alter the delivery logs to include their truck. The Pharmatrox armory they'd raided also had a few extra guard keycards, which Tara now showed to the perimeter guards. Stella didn't know what kind of access levels it had, so she still needed to steal one from these guys to activate the elevator later.

They circled the truck, boots crunching in the fine gravel, but one of them paused beside Stella. She held her breath as she withdrew his access card from his belt with a delicate pinch and stuffed it in her pocket.

After a few seconds, the guards gave the all-clear and the truck lurched forward. The diesel fumes nearly choked Stella, and she swallowed her cough.

As planned, Tara drove around back to the loading dock. A set of three guards directed her as she backed into the open bay, and the garage door went up with a clatter.

Muffled voices came from inside the loading dock, and the canvas curtain scraped back. A garbled shout, then a thud.

Penny and Stella locked eyes from underneath the truck and sprang from their hiding places. In the time Stella had dispensed with her single guard, Penny dropped both guards on her side.

Muted sounds of fighting came from inside the building. The truck was backed flush against the open garage door, and magnets locked onto the truck's docking mechanism—a troxy design to prevent deliveries from being raided. It could only be unlocked from inside the warehouse. Pharmatrox restricted access, so not even Stella's Patch could get her in. They couldn't help until someone opened the door for them.

"Incoming," said Derek. He fired two silenced shots, and two of the eight approaching guards fell where they stood.

Back to back, Stella and Penny whirled in tandem, taking out the guards. Derek finished off the last one with a clean shot through the forehead, and everything was still.

"Goddamn it." Tara leaned against the shattered window of the truck, blood pumping from a wound in her shoulder. "Just clipped me, but it won't stop bleeding. Stella, help me tie a tourniquet." She tore off the bottom of her shirt, and Stella assisted.

"You sure you're good?" Stella asked as she tied the tightest knot of her life.

"Never better, tía. Let's get your boy."

Penny watched with an expression that looked...impressed.

Derek, ever practical, dragged the bodies of the fallen guards under the truck and removed their gear. A few seconds later, Quentin poked his head out of the loading dock's side door and paled at the blood on the pavement, but beckoned them inside.

Endless rows of shelves and pallets stacked to the ceiling of the expansive warehouse. It took up four floors in the back half of the tower. Shiny white containers wrapped in plastic lined the walls and glimmered in the fluorescent light.

A glaring red light blinked from the terminal near the back door. *SECURITY ALERT* blazed on the screen, but when Stella swiped the guard's stolen keycard, the red light turned green and the warning message vanished.

She tapped her Patch, and it connected to the tower's network. The security feed pulled up in a glowing blue hologram, and she navigated to the warehouse's camera.

"Turi," she said. The blue holographic woman appeared in her peripheral, the Spire's expansive network bringing her to life. "Patch in that video loop we talked about for the warehouse camera and the external one. Overwrite the saved footage."

"Hell yes, boss." Turi winked and then dissolved.

Now that their tracks were covered, Stella tapped her Patch off and blinked back into reality.

Derek's eyes combed her for signs of injury, but she waved him off. Tara and Derek donned the stolen guard uniforms and adjusted their rifles, while the rest pulled on lab coats from the nearest shelf and hid their knives and handguns beneath their clothes. A lab coat wasn't the best choice of disguise for Stella, but she was the only one with a legitimate Pharmatrox ID. If there was trouble, she might be able to talk their way out of it.

"Okay, Stella," said Derek as he secured his guard vest. "Where to now?"

"The restricted access elevator that will take us to the hidden floor." Stella handed Derek the Helix Key. "This way."

They split off into separate squads to be less conspicuous. Stella led the way with Quentin, Tara following as their guard. The second group, led by Lawrence and Penny with Derek as their guard, followed twenty paces in their wake. The hairs on the back of Stella's neck bristled at the thought of Derek and Lawrence alone with Penny. But it had been the only way to get Quentin to agree to the plan, and Stella didn't want to force the kid to sit this one out. As she'd already learned, he did not listen to those kinds of instructions.

The inside of the tower was a stark contrast to the outside, with shiny milky-white glass and tile coating every surface. Even at the late hour, the tower buzzed with activity—troxies flitting from room to room, orderlies pushing carts of supplies down the hall at reckless speeds, and guards clomping on heavy-booted feet.

Stella swept down the hallway, following the memorized path through the maze of corridors. Her heart pounded in her throat, and she glanced over her shoulder. Derek and the others were half a hallway behind her.

As Stella waved the guard's access card over a small pinhole in the wall, a panel slid back to reveal the elevator. They piled inside, and Stella looked for Derek one more time. He gave her a wry smile.

But then a group of troxies in white lab coats spilled out of the intersecting hallway into Derek's group.

"What's this?" said one of the troxies.

Icy talons of panic plunged straight into Stella's chest and snatched her breath away. She caught one last glimpse of the fear painted across Derek's face as Tara dragged her into the elevator.

The doors slid shut behind her like a death sentence, entombing them in silence.

55

TIME STALLED FOR A beat, and Stella couldn't breathe.

She sagged into the corner. *Derek. Lawrence. They have them.*

Hands dropped on her shoulders, pulling her out of her panic. Tara peered into her eyes with a solid resolve.

"Remember the mission." Tara squeezed Stella's upper arms. Stella was speaking to the former Army officer now. "Remember why we're here. Derek and Lawrence took this risk willingly. They knew what could happen. They're all smart—even Penny." Tara paused to consider. "Maybe *especially* Penny. They'll make it." Tara held Stella in place until she nodded.

Tara was right. Derek and Lawrence could handle it. She ignored the fact that she had to rely on Penny to have their backs.

When the elevator doors slid open to the hidden twentieth floor, Stella straightened her coat and stepped out.

Silent.

Empty.

The corridor stretched endlessly in both directions, the glaring ceiling lights reflecting off the shiny white walls and floors. Stella felt like she was encased inside a marble.

"Where is everyone?" Quentin whispered. Tara shrugged.

Stella winced at her squeaky boots as she walked down the eerie quiet of the corridor. She tried to walk with a purpose in case they came across any troxies, but with each step, her confidence in the mission leached out of her.

How could she think they were prepared to do this? Just a handful of inexperienced people, taking on a company cunning enough to take over an entire country's government. The more she thought about it, the more ridiculous she felt. Derek's panicked face flashed in her mind. Every fiber of her being wanted to charge downstairs and go to him.

But if Silas was here in the Spire, she had to find him. And what if Dr. Hansen had found this place too? Maybe this was where they manufactured and refined the detox serum. There could be an endless supply hiding behind one of these doors. She had to try. She'd never be able to rest, not until she knew the truth. It was this resolve that carried her deeper and deeper past the point of no return.

As they continued walking, a piercing wail ripped through the thick silence.

Stella raced down the hallway, the others stumbling in her wake. The cry sounded again, from behind one of the doors at the end of the hall. She slammed the access card against the reader and ripped the door open.

The space was a small observation room with a simple desk. Compared to the modern grandeur of the rest of the tower, this section was primitive. Only two folding chairs faced the giant window of one-way glass punched through the craggy cinder block walls. The viewing room was a fortress, with walls of solid concrete and a reinforced steel door.

Through the window, a white medical room set up with clinical precision stared back at them like a movie on a screen, crisp and clear. A trio of troxies huddled around a metal table in the center of the room.

A man's body lay supine upon it. Flaccid, bruised skin hung from scrawny bones, his eyes burrowed in dark, hollow circles. But his sunken cheeks rattled with the irregular intake of breath.

The man was still *alive*.

One of the troxies shoved a needle in the man's floppy arm.

Then the man screamed. He arched his back so fiercely Stella thought he might snap in two.

Her lips trembled as she placed a fruitless palm against the glass. *It's true. Everything from the Phoenix Trial case notes, everything Derek said about Oakwood. All of it. It's all true.*

The man thrashed and snarled as the surrounding troxies rushed to restrain him, but then his scream abruptly cut off, and he turned his skeleton eyes to where Stella and the others stood hidden behind the one-way glass. A horrific smile serrated with broken teeth twisted across his gaunt face.

Stella jerked back and motioned for Tara and Quentin to follow. She headed down a hallway off the main corridor into another wing.

"Stella, what the hell is going on in this place?" asked Tara.

Stella shook her head and swallowed the hollow feeling inside her.

"There's another window. A *big* one." Quentin pointed at the other end of the hall, where more glass carved out a huge section of the wall. The monstrous window looked into another small office with a viewing window into a room bigger than the last one.

But the horrors it held were far worse.

About twenty metal tables stood in two rows. Each table had its own body. Some were covered with white sheets like old furniture. Some bodies sported scars ripping their torsos like zippers. Some were so bruised it was impossible to determine their natural skin color.

A wall of medical devices and equipment crowded the far side of the room, where a white cylindrical machine caught her eye. *Is that…? No, my gene editing simulator is in the New York lab.* And her machine was oriented horizontally, not vertically like this one.

Stella watched on as a troxy weaved her way between the rows of tables, her back to the one-way glass. She paused at one of the bodies with a torso scar and sliced open the incision with a scalpel from a tray of tools.

Nausea roiled in Stella's stomach.

The troxy thrust her gloved hand inside the chest and clutched the heart, then inserted a syringe directly into the tissue and waited. The body on the table convulsed, then lay still. The woman shook her head and marked something off on her digital clipboard.

No. No more.

Stella kicked open the office door and burst into the medical room, the hinges exploding into bits. Antiseptic and an underlying sweet note of decay permeated the air. On the opposite wall, Stella's reflection stared back at her from another pane of one-way glass.

The troxy woman proceeded as if she hadn't been interrupted, her back to them. She removed the soiled gloves and stood before another table, the supine body atop it covered by a white sheet. She tapped her digital clipboard and flicked a syringe.

"Stop!" shouted Stella. She gripped her machete in an iron fist, poised to snuff out the troxy's life—but then she saw the reflection of the woman's face in the far wall and the ruby ring glinting on her finger.

Stella's weapon clattered to the ground.

"Dr. Hansen? What—what are you doing?"

56

Tara and Quentin gaped at Stella. "You know this woman?" asked Tara.

"She's..." *My mentor.* But the words caught in Stella's throat. What the hell was going on?

Dr. Hansen's lips parted in a familiar smile. "I wondered when you would figure it out."

Stella's brain tripped. "Figure what out?"

"I left you a trail of breadcrumbs to follow, and you did it excellently," said Dr. Hansen. "The successful Oakwood break-in, files that stood out to you, ones that pinged higher in your search results—I arranged it that way. I hope you read everything."

She knows about the Oakwood break-in? "Why...why would you do that? Where have you been? How did you get out of New York? I thought you were *dead*."

Dr. Hansen pinned Stella with a serious look. "I want you to understand what we are doing. I want you to *see*."

We? But Dr. Hansen had always been staunchly against the other departments, especially experimental pharmaceuticals...hadn't she?

"This is what I've been preparing you for your entire life."

"My entire...Dr. Hansen, we met when I was eighteen. How could you..." Stella stared at Dr. Hansen, who gave her that warm, familiar smile again.

Open your eyes.

The tapestry of Stella's life, woven from so many tiny threads, finally came into clarity, and she saw the whole picture. She saw why Dr. Hansen, a renowned and undoubtedly busy scientist, would take a personal interest in a promising but otherwise unremarkable college student. Why she'd converse with her for years and offer career advice, guidance, and encouragement. Why she'd vouch for that student and offer her a flashy, high-paying job right out of school at one of the most powerful companies in the world. And why she'd want to work closely with her mentee and be involved in her daily life.

The world faded into a shadowed blur. Dr. Hansen's mouth moved, and Stella knew what she'd said, the words that had locked everything into place, but she only heard a distant, high-pitched buzzing sound.

Stella stared into Dr. Hansen's ice-blue eyes framed by short silver hair. Quentin's hand clamped onto her upper arm was the only thing keeping her tethered to the present as she became acutely aware of her surroundings again, pixel by pixel, and reality faded back in.

Tara's face, creased in confusion. Quentin's eyes, wide as dinner plates.

"I'm your mother, Agnes," Dr. Hansen repeated.

"My mother...?" The word felt foreign on her tongue. "My mother is dead." Her mother wrote journal entries about first dates with handsome Spanish mechanics who enjoyed Hemingway. She *couldn't* be the same woman who was her role model. And the woman who supported horrendous experiments. *No. Por favor, no.*

A sad smile picked up the corners of Dr. Hansen's mouth, and dropped. "I'm afraid that's not all. I'm the Leader."

Stella reeled. This was all too much, too fast.

Tara eyed the woman, arms crossed. "I served in the Army for years and never knew who my 'commander in chief' was. You mean to tell me you're the one to blame for the current state of our country?" Tara looked unimpressed.

"Pharmatrox asked me to be the Leader shortly after you were born, Agnes," said Dr. Hansen—Ingrid. Stella could not think of this woman as her mentor; Dr. Hansen no longer existed. Dr. Hansen was a *lie*.

"Intense weather changes, famine, and the sky-high price of fossil fuels had destabilized our country," said Ingrid. "The president was a fascist fool, entirely unfit for office. The government was on the verge of collapse already, and then the Sickness came. People were dying, and someone needed to step up. Pharmatrox was adamant that I cut all family ties before assuming the role of Leader. I accepted, even though it meant you would never know me. I wanted to make the world a safer place for you—and to do so, I had to leave. You were too young to remember, and your father promised to uphold the story that I'd died of the Sickness."

"I don't understand." They were the only words Stella could muster.

"This company is my *life*, and I fully believe in its ability to do good, but some do not," said Ingrid. "I didn't want for you to live a life I had forced you into. If you wanted to join Pharmatrox, I wanted it to be *your* choice, and not because your mother was the Leader."

Stella's blood ran cold with the betrayal, the violation. Her mother's journal entries that she'd read thousands of times were really written by Dr. Hansen. Her entire *life* was a lie.

"But now that you've joined us, and you've come here of your own volition, you're ready to hear the full truth," said Ingrid. "And then you can claim your legacy. You can join me in earnest. Think of how much we can accomplish together."

"We worked together for years, Dr.—Ingrid. And we *did* accomplish many amazing things. But this..." Stella stared at the butchered bodies on the table. "I don't want this to be my legacy."

Ingrid's smile gained an edge. "Perhaps you'll change your mind."

A body on a nearby table twitched, and the sheet fell from its face. A familiar profile lay exposed in the harsh fluorescent light.

Hot bile rose in Stella's throat, and she choked. "Silas! Is—is he—?"

Silas's eyes fluttered and his breaths rasped. Then she remembered the syringe. Ingrid's finger on the plunger. "What did you do to him?"

Ingrid touched Silas's shoulder, a fond smile lighting her face. "He's important. I need him—*we* need him."

She looked at her friend, breaths shaking his barrel of a chest. "Why?"

Ingrid smoothed Silas's hair from his forehead, her ruby ring glittering in the harsh light. "Silas shares some of your same immunology factors. An interesting hybrid. Troxapine does not affect you two in the way that it affects others. And it affects Derek differently as well. Others in our care have similar features, experiencing immunity to certain effects and enhancements in other traits.

"It's my job to find out why, so I can create the desired effect: total obedience. I'm confident that by using dionazole to test new versions of troxapine on the same patients, we can refine the formula and create an iteration that works uniformly for anyone. And I have a few ideas for how to harness the more...aggressive characteristics troxapine induces."

Stella shook her head in denial. *Exactly like Silas said all those years ago. We're just rats in a cage to the troxies.* It was all too impossible to comprehend.

Stella's childhood fantasies shattered before her eyes. This woman was a total stranger to her. She wasn't her mother, and she wasn't her beloved mentor. The woman who had written the journal was gone.

"What happened to you?" Stella whispered.

Ingrid cast her a glacial look, all hard lines and ice-chip eyes. "There is only one way to face the dangers of a dying planet with depleting resources: a strong head of state and a united people. One voice, one collective mind working together for survival. Unity Is Strength. No person is an island. We are all 'a piece of the continent, a part of the main.'" The familiar words tickled something in the back of Stella's mind. "Pharmatrox trusted me. They gave me the chance to unite everyone as one unit singularly focused on the advancement of our country."

"You talk about fascist fools, and yet you are one," snapped Tara. "Your 'Unity Is Strength' bullshit is why racially motivated crimes were at an all-time high before the Beginning. You're the reason it's dangerous for me to just be myself. People don't want your fucking unity platform. Do you know how many Pharmatrox scientists have defected to the Faction? I'm sure it's more than you and your cronies want to admit."

"If they do not support us, it's best they leave," said Ingrid. "We have no room for disobedience in the world we are building."

Tara frowned. "And yet you allow the Faction to continue existing when your superior military could bomb them off the face of the planet? It doesn't make sense."

"We need every *body*. Each person is a clue, a piece to the genetic puzzle. We don't want to eradicate the Faction—we don't want to kill *anyone*. Every single person could hold the key to uncovering unique genetic markers and perfecting the troxapine formula. We need *everyone* if we're going to create a perfect, obedient mind."

The scope of Ingrid's plan dawned on Stella, and her blood ran cold. "You're building an army. After the Sickness, people left the country in droves. Rats abandoning a sinking ship. You need an army to keep people from fleeing, to control the population, so you can turn outward and advance your delusional agenda to the other nations. You want to make us all *mindless robots.*" Stella slapped a hand to her face. "Hijo de puta, Silas was right."

Ingrid's smile evaporated. "We need you, Agnes. You, Silas, Derek, people like you—there are others out there, we just need to find them. We need to study you so we can perfect troxapine. It will unite us, assure we never get sick, make us stronger than we've ever been. Join me. With your brilliant mind, we can accomplish so much *more.*"

Stella took a step back. "I'm not *helping* you, Ingrid." She gestured to the rows of bodies. "I've seen what you've done in the name of science. I know the evil that goes on here. Pharmatrox—they've *brainwashed* you. You and countless others. Can't you see that?"

"Oh, but Agnes." Ingrid's cold smile lanced through Stella. "You've already helped. So much."

"What?" Her throat tightened.

Ingrid's gaze flicked to the white cylindrical machine, the one Stella had noticed before. "Your simulator is the base model that was instrumental in creating our own—the one we use to find the genetic markers of our perfect test subjects."

Stella's pulse rushed in her ears. "The project you had me working on—the pregnant woman with the unnamed genetic mutation—was that a lie too?"

"The woman was never pregnant—she was a user I was studying." Ingrid dragged the sheet back over Silas's face with a thoughtful expression. The fabric puffed over his mouth in time with his irregular breaths. "Your work has been crucial in tinkering with the troxapine and dionazole formulas and running test simulations. Of course, we still require actual human test subjects to assure the formulas function within the body."

Pharmatrox had everything they needed to make an even more devastating version of troxapine. And Stella had handed it to them on a silver platter.

Ingrid's device, the rounding up of innocent people for her experiments—none of it would have been possible without Stella's work. Stella thought she'd been doing *good*, helping people. But Pharmatrox had stolen her work and perverted it, twisted it for their own nefarious purposes. Just like they'd done to Evie.

Stella's hands shook, but not from withdrawal. From *rage*. "I always thought you were on my side, but it was all an act to keep me working as your happy, oblivious little minion. You *sicken* me. I'll never join you."

At her last words, Ingrid's eyes turned from ice to stone. She snatched a scalpel from a tray and jerked Quentin to her side, holding the blade to his jugular.

"Hey, watch it—" Quentin squirmed, but Ingrid's arm tightened around him.

"I'm afraid I must insist." Ingrid pressed the scalpel until a bead of blood welled underneath its slim edge and rolled down Quentin's neck.

Stella drew the gun strapped to her leg and pointed it at her mother. Her mentor. The woman who'd taught her *everything*.

It had all been a lie. A duplicitous, manipulative *lie*.

Tara followed suit with her weapon, and Ingrid's mouth dipped.

"Step away from him." Stella's finger itched on the trigger. Just one gentle squeeze and it would be over, it would—

The one-way glass behind Ingrid shattered in a rain of glittering shards—but the shots didn't come from Stella.

Bullets shattered the other side of the window, and a flood of troxy guards surged inside.

57

T HE GROUP SPUN INTO action. Tara fired into the incoming guards, Quentin on her tail.

"Take that, troxy bastard!" Quentin ducked and weaved, slashing guards with his knife.

Stella looked up from the fight to see Ingrid dodging the melee and wheeling Silas's gurney away.

"Tara!" Stella shouted.

Tara blocked Ingrid before she could reach the hallway, and after a brief struggle, Tara punched her in the nose and she collapsed.

More bullets pinged off the broken glass behind them, and Stella slumped in relief when Lawrence and Penny hopped through the ruined window. Penny thrashed open throats with her sickle as she fought her way to Quentin's side, while Lawrence bashed in helmets with a guard's billy club.

But where's Derek?

Stella swallowed her panic. She needed to help Silas first. As she raided the nearby cabinet and stuffed medical supplies in her pack, her eyes raced over the medicine names. Acetaminophen. Troxapine. Adrenaline. Penicillin. *Yes! Dionazole.* She grabbed the full supply of everything but troxapine and a handful of syringes, then shoved through the guards and stuck a needle in Silas's neck.

"Adrenaline," she said to Lawrence, who guarded the unconscious Silas. "It might take a minute to take effect, through that mystery cocktail of drugs in his system." *If it even works at all.*

"Let's move!" said Tara as she shot cover fire into the crowd.

Ten guards trailed in their wake as the group sprinted for the elevator. Penny shoved Quentin into the elevator ahead of her, blocking his body with hers. Lawrence hefted Silas over his shoulder and kicked the gurney away, Tara right behind him.

Down one of the intersecting hallways, Stella heard a familiar shout.

Derek. Magnetic steel cuffs clamped around his wrists, and a big guard hauled him away.

"Derek!"

She fired her Glock and clipped the guard's shoulder. Derek drove an elbow into the man's abdomen, grabbed something from his belt, and ran toward Stella.

"Thanks," he said as he waved the oblong device over his manacled hands. The cuffs popped open and he ditched them.

"Let's move it, Stella girl!" Tara shouted from the elevator.

With the guards thundering down the hallway toward them, closing the distance, Stella and Derek charged the remaining few feet, baseball-sliding as the elevator doors hissed shut behind them.

A hush filled the small space. Nobody moved.

Silas's gasp tore through the silence, and he flailed in Lawrence's arms. Wild eyes rolled around, and Lawrence held him tight as he thrashed.

"Silas, it's me! It's Aggie." Stella held his face in her hands until she saw recognition alight in them. When he stilled, Lawrence set him on the ground.

"Agnes?"

The horrors of the past, of the Beginning, melted away with just the sound of her name, from the mouth of someone she had thought forever lost to her. A wrenching sob broke from her chest as she pulled her best friend into a tight embrace. He was okay. Alive. *Evie, he's alive.*

Quentin cleared his throat, looking at the ceiling and holding out a pair of gym shorts and a tee shirt from the bag concealed under his lab coat.

Silas looked at the white sheet wrapped around his waist and laughed. Stella's heart ached. "Thanks...?"

"Quentin." Quentin kept his eyes glued on the ceiling, a fine blush creeping across his cheeks.

"Thanks, Quentin." Silas pulled on the clothes and ditched the sheet. "A little tight, but better than running around with my dangly bits bouncing around." He flashed a grin and got a chuckle out of the others, the tense atmosphere in the elevator easing slightly.

"We'll do formal introductions later," said Stella, eyeing Penny, who was posted up in the corner with her arms crossed. A tinge of guilt slithered up her spine. She had secretly hoped Penny would be...eliminated in the crossfire. But Penny had surprised her. She'd actually helped them and was vital in their escape. *I have no idea what to make of that.*

When they reached the second floor, Stella pulled the stop button. Lawrence bashed the square light panel in the ceiling with his billy club and shifted it to the side, creating a hole.

"They'll have guards posted at the bottom waiting for us," said Stella. "There's a maintenance ladder in the elevator shaft. It should have a separate entrance at the bottom. We'll climb down that way. Derek, Lawrence—give me a boost."

They climbed through the hole and regrouped on top of the elevator car, Quentin pulling a flashlight out of his bag and clicking it on. The light caught an iron ladder built into the opposite wall less than ten feet away.

"We'll have to jump." Tara looked at Silas with concern. "Are we sure the recently reanimated is up for it?"

"Let's do it."

The adrenaline gave Silas's smile a manic edge. Something about the version of troxapine coursing through him must have lent him extra alertness and dexterity for him to be so mobile already.

Stella eyed him, but nodded. With a running start, she leapt from the edge. She landed hard against the metal rungs of the ladder, the breath punching from her lungs. After her own wobbly descent, one by one, they all filed to the bottom.

"This way." Stella headed toward a small metal door in the corner that opened into an underground maintenance access hallway. The grimy concrete chute was lit by exposed light bulbs and ended in a pair of rusted metal doors.

Doorways peppered the sides of the hallway, remaining shut even as the group thundered past. Wild shadows danced on the walls, cast in the dingy yellow light of the murky incandescent bulbs, and the smell of old exhaust and diesel fumes permeated the cold air.

Looking over her shoulder, Stella was relieved no one was pursuing them. As the group ran, she felt like she was on a treadmill, the exit never drawing any closer.

Suddenly, alarms blared throughout the building, but the hallway remained deserted. *Just a few more feet.* Hope flared in her chest as they neared the end.

They were twenty steps from the exit when the guards came.

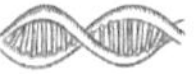

"Stella!"

As guards poured into the hall, dividing the escaping group in two, Quentin drowned in a sea of black uniforms. Lawrence, Tara, Penny, and Quentin were surrounded.

"Derek, get Silas out of here!" said Stella as she took on the guards.

"But what about y—"

"Do it!" she yelled as she shot her last bullet in a guard's face. She didn't wait to see if Derek listened.

Penny pushed Quentin behind her, but Quentin shifted away and closer to Tara. Out of bullets, Tara swung her rifle and beat them back, but each time a guard fell, another took his place.

One grabbed Quentin's wrist and jerked the knife out of his hand.

"No!" Stella shouted, caught between three guards.

Penny's gaze snapped to Quentin. "Fuck." She slammed an elbow into a guard's throat and tackled another, but it was too late. Quentin was already being dragged down the hallway, kicking and squirming.

An inhuman yell erupted out of Penny, and she disarmed a guard, spraying his remaining bullets into the crowd. But it wasn't enough. More guards took their place, swarming like flies to a corpse.

Stella lunged to join Penny, but a hand on her elbow stopped her.

"We have to go. More will come." Derek towed her toward the exit. "We can't save him if we're captured too."

Stella shrugged him off and threw herself into the fracas. As guards packed the hallway in a confusing, thrashing mob, she could barely discern one body from the next.

A flash of bronze hair.

She snatched at the familiar sight and caught an arm, dragging it with her as she ran for the door. Shouldering open the exit, she burst outside where the others awaited her. Derek twisted the Helix Key into a port beside the door, and a deadbolt slid into place.

Stella turned to smile at Quentin behind her.

But it wasn't her freckled friend.

It was Penny.

Devastated, Stella sank to the damp ground.

They'd done it. They'd saved Silas and escaped the Spire. And they'd learned more about the truth of Pharmatrox than anyone ever had. An impossible feat.

But it had come at a terrible price.

Quentin. Her stomach twisted with the wrenching realization of the horrors awaiting that sweet boy at the hands of the troxies. At the hands of her *mother*. The discovery of her mentor's manipulation weighed heavy on Stella's heart. Her whole life had been a fabrication. An elaborate scheme by her own mother. And she had fallen for it.

Defeated, Stella held her head.

Derek crouched in front of her and tilted her face up. "Hey." She snapped her tear-filled eyes to his. "This isn't over. We're getting him back."

Lawrence stood beside him. "There wasn't anything we could have done. Derek is right. We can't help them if we're prisoners too."

Derek held out a hand. She grasped it and he hoisted her up, and Silas threw a lanky arm across her shoulders. He'd lost weight, but he was still a sizable man. He smiled and she felt less empty. "Where are we?" Silas asked.

"About five blocks from the Spire," Stella said. "Our escape route was an underground access tunnel used to usher in cargo trucks of prisoners under the radar."

"What are we going to do about Quentin?" asked Tara. She, like the rest of them, looked tired and haggard. But a light of fierce resolve winked in her eyes. Lawrence threaded her arm through his with a look of matched tenacity.

Ingrid would waste no time in using Quentin for experiments. *The clock is ticking—fast.*

Stella opened her mouth to answer, but it was Penny who replied. Her brow pulled taut in a hard look of determination.

"We get him back—no matter the cost."

58

"DEREK, PASS ME THE circuit board and the transmitter," said Stella.

Derek looked blankly at the radio pieces on the table. "Ah yes. A beebooper and a whatsit."

Stella rolled her eyes and pointed to the parts she wanted, and Derek handed them over. In Derek's garage, Lawrence had set up a temporary workshop and apothecary. She and Silas were repairing extra radios for Quentin's impending rescue mission, while Derek occasionally helped but mostly organized his mess of a tool box.

Silas had been quick to volunteer for her little project. Over the past couple of days, his memory had started to return in patchy pieces as the dionazole flushed the troxapine from his system. He nudged Stella's shoulder and gave her a companionable smile, but it did little to lift her spirits.

Their search for Quentin had stalled. Ingrid wouldn't keep Quentin in the Spire because they knew how to get in, so he had to be somewhere else. Penny, Mal, and his soldiers searched the eastern and southern sectors, while Stella and the rest covered the northern and western with the Faction's help.

Researching in the library would be useless, since the only reason Stella had discovered anything at all had been because Ingrid had planted it. Stella listened in to troxy transmissions and drone footage on her Patch, but it was too much data to sift through. She hoped Penny and Mal were having better luck. They were due for a check-in tomorrow.

Ample afternoon light flooded through the open garage door, and a cool breeze drifted inside. After a few minutes, Silas asked, "How come every time that red-haired woman comes near you, you look like a cat that got thrown in a tub with a toaster?"

He surprised a snort out of Stella and earned a chuckle from Derek, but her blood ran cold at the reminder that she'd saved Penny instead of Quentin.

"I do not," said Stella, popping off the back of another radio and gutting its insides with a little more force than necessary. She clenched her fists to hide her hand tremor. It had been nearly constant for the past day. Her head felt like someone had taken Thor's hammer to her skull, and a cold sweat coated her body.

She hadn't taken the detox serum yet. Her last baggie of dust held one hit, a burning brand in her pocket. Now that Quentin was lost...what if she needed the dust's extra dexterity in order to save him?

You didn't need dust to save Silas, said Death. *You'll find any excuse to keep using.*

Deaths words formed a vice grip around her throat, and she swallowed.

"Yes, you do," Silas said, picking up a part and sliding it into place with expert hands.

"I second that," said Derek, who popped the hood of the stolen troxy van and began his own tinkering.

Stella shifted from foot to foot. "I don't trust Penny, but I know she'll do anything to save Quentin. We need her help to make things right." She braced both palms flat on the work table, sweat rolling down her spine even in the cool air. "I'm beginning to think things will never be right again."

Derek rested a hip on the van's bumper. "What do you mean?"

Stella faced them, throwing up her hands, and let loose the question that had been tormenting her for days. "So we rescue Quentin. Then what? Our country is still like this! Pharmatrox has all the power, and they're running barbaric experiments on people. And it's *my* fault."

Silas frowned. "How is it your fault?"

Derek shifted against the van, a curious lift to his brow.

Tara and Quentin were the only ones who knew of Stella's role in aiding Pharmatrox. She hadn't wanted to overwhelm Silas until he'd had some time to adjust. But mostly, she had no idea how to explain, or what she planned to do about it. Rage and betrayal had blinded her to feeling or doing anything else.

"My machine," she said. "The one I designed to simulate DNA edits and treatments. Pharmatrox is using it to collect and map the genetic information of prisoners to isolate which civilian targets they want for their experiments, and to help them refine the troxapine formula. I saw it for myself. It's in the Spire. The dust, these experiments—it's *my* technology. Even though Evie—" Stella choked on the end of her sentence.

Me cago en la leche, I haven't told him about Evie yet. She'd been too swept up in her own issues.

"Ah, Silas? I have to tell you something about your sister." Her dry throat clicked as she swallowed.

Silas's expression brightened at the memory. "Is she okay?"

Stella shut her eyes. She couldn't bear to look at him. Derek slid his hand into hers and squeezed.

"Evie...didn't make it. I'm so sorry." She'd tell him the full truth about her death one day, but not today.

Silas held his head, a look of anguish painted across his face. "When I didn't see her with you, I knew something bad must have happened. I hoped…" He shook himself and placed a hand on Stella's shoulder. "I'm okay." He blinked as a thought occurred to him. "What of Ivan?"

Stella's heart clenched. It was the first sign Silas had shown of remembering his partner. "I haven't seen him, but that doesn't mean something bad happened. He could still be holed up in his apartment."

Silas rolled a screwdriver across the workbench, a notch in his forehead. "He'd mentioned going to Canada before Containment. Maybe he's there." Silas scratched his head. "But you had been about to say something about Evie?"

Stella blanched. "She—well, ah." *Say it. He needs to know.* She cleared her throat. "She was the Architect. Her original idea was for an anti-anxiety medication. Dr. Hansen—Ingrid manipulated it as a tool for mass mind control."

Silas stared at her, his forehead puckered. "My *sister* created troxapine?"

"Sort of. I never knew either. I don't think anyone did."

Derek pulled on the back of his neck and said, "Shit. I'm sorry, Stella. But none of this is your fault. You were lied to. So was Evie. How could either of you have known Ingrid would use you like that?"

She nodded, but the words rolled off of her. No amount of platitudes would abate the guilt crashing over her in waves.

But Silas…he was looking at her as if seeing her for the first time. Wide-eyed, open-mouthed, as the wheels of his mind turned. The circuit board he'd been holding slipped out of his hand and clattered on the table.

"I know," she said, rubbing her forehead. "It's a lot to take in."

"No," said Silas. "I mean yes, but that's not it. Agnes, *you're* the one we've been waiting for—the one with the power to end this, to take down Pharmatrox. It's not the Architect who could save us all—it's you." A distant rushing sound filled Stella's ears like a steam engine picking up speed. "*You* designed the bones of the machine. *You* can destroy it."

Stella laughed at the ridiculousness of it, but trailed off when she saw Silas's face. The shaft of sunlight pouring through the door illuminated clever eyes set in a serious visage. No hint of drugs—or uncertainty—clouded his gaze. Derek nodded, understanding dawning on him too.

"Oh god. You're serious." She held her head in her hands, fearful it would fly off and hit Silas like a dodgeball. "They already have the designs. They'll just recreate it. Destroying the machine does nothing but cause a temporary delay."

"You've also been in their security systems, haven't you?" asked Silas. "When we were playing with passcubes and designing Sara Ellis's Patch?"

"What of it?"

"I've designed robust security systems and data architecture like Pharmatrox's. But *you've* been deep into their system's structure. You've even done some of their security updates. I have the road map, but you have the majority of the directions. Between the two of us, we can hack their system and take down the network from the *inside*. They probably have backup servers in a separate location, but that data is severely crippled if the network is destroyed beyond repair."

"This is good," said Derek. "No network means no comms, no access to their servers. An enemy who can't coordinate is much weaker. If we take out the main head at HQ and decentralize them, another one may grow in its place. But if the heads can't access information and can't talk to each other…"

"We can pick them off one by one," finished Silas, his eyes taking on a frenzied glint. "And they'll have no way to know we're coming for them. Aggie, if you show me the designs for your machine and its software, we can write a virus for that too. We can render the machine and the network inoperable—*permanently*."

Stella rolled a radio antenna in her hands. Derek was right. Had been right all along, but not for the reason he thought. It wasn't her Helix Key or her credentials that would turn the tide in the war. It was *her*. Her mind, her experience, her work. Nobody else knew how that machine functioned, and she didn't know where to find any IT department defectors. Between her and Silas, their skills would be enough to emulate even someone of Roberto's high caliber. And with Derek's help in determining battle strategy, Pharmatrox's physical security measures, and building layout, plus Mal's troops and knowledge of Pharmatrox military capabilities, and hell, even Penny's ruthlessness—

"Hostia, we could really *do* this," she said, her hand tightening around Derek's. She didn't remember grabbing it.

Pulling her close, he brought his other hand to her face, thumb sweeping across her cheek. Silas watched the exchange with a smug expression.

"So you're not running to the border?" Derek asked. "You'll stay and fight? Help us reclaim the Capital?"

She fought back a smile of her own. "I'm not running to the border *yet*."

Derek beamed, the biggest smile she'd ever seen from him, then wrapped an arm around her and pulled her into his chest. His lips touched her forehead, and she felt his smile. "Thank you, Stella."

Silas tugged on his earlobe. "Can I ask about this 'Stella' business? Do I have to call you that?"

Stella extricated herself from Derek, but smiled at the feeling of him against her side. "I needed a new name when I joined Penny's crew. After...after I lost Evie, I didn't feel like myself anymore. The choices I made took me further and further away from the person I was, so I chose the name Stella—for you, in a way. Your favorite beer. The Marauders and I were ransacking a convenience store, and I saw an advertisement for Stella Artois. *Stella*, I remember thinking. *She is how I will survive this.*" She finished with a weak shrug.

"No matter what you've done, you'll always be my Aggie." It was Silas's turn to hug her.

Tears burned behind her eyes, and she pulled away and dug in her pocket, then slapped the baggie on the table, white powder glimmering in the golden afternoon light.

"Derek, where's the dionazole?" Stella's voice sounded far away to her own ears. The cage of darkness in her mind rattled its chains. Death swirled inside her. *You won't do it. You're too weak.* "I'm ready."

Derek rummaged in the back of the van and returned with a small vial and a syringe. Fear bubbled inside her like hot acid, and she gripped Silas's arm with sudden dread.

"What if I detox and I just...can't handle life without the dust? I don't have any more of it. I can't escape into sweet oblivion again."

Derek gave her a sharp look. "You don't need the dust. You never did."

Silas nodded his agreement and clasped Stella's hand. "Life is waiting beyond the darkness of oblivion, Aggie. We just have to be brave enough to seek it. I am." He inclined his head to Derek. "Your new friends are. I know you are too."

Stella's vision swirled into a dark tunnel with Silas at the epicenter.

Open your eyes.

She rolled up her sleeve, eyes wide open. "Do it."

That night, Stella tossed and turned in bed, assaulted by her past. Evie. Dr. Hansen. Quentin. Sleep dashed out of her grasp. The dionazole was clearing her system of troxapine, but it would take time. The air in her room felt too hot and close, the walls too confining. Her mouth tasted of stale vomit, cottony and dry.

She needed fresh air, so she rolled out of the sweat-soaked sheets, pulled on some clothes, and went downstairs.

Someone was already there.

"Derek?"

The cold tile bit into her bare feet as she joined him in the kitchen. He wore a tee shirt and sweatpants, his hair messy. He flashed a smile, but his gaze was contemplative, like that night on the roof. Had it really only been two weeks ago?

"Can't sleep?" he asked.

She held out her hand to show him how it shook. "Detox is a bitch. But I'm getting through it. You?"

He shook his head, his eyes haunted. "I often dream of the ferry. My sister. It always ends the same. Her blood on my hands as I run away." He tightened his hand around the glass of water he held and pushed it toward her.

She took a long drink and swished it around. "I have dreams like that. Of Evie. Do you think it ever gets easier? Dealing with...what we've done? Everything we still have left to do?" She sighed and sagged against the wall behind her. "I'm so damn tired. I wish there was *someone else* to do this. Someone else who could shoulder the responsibility of taking down Pharmatrox HQ. I just—" She broke off, shaking her head.

"It's really brave of you, you know," he said. "Not just detoxing, but sticking around to help with the war. You're different now that you know the truth. It's lit this fire in you." Derek ran a tattooed hand over his mouth, and his lips quirked. Her fingers itched to touch him, to feel that smile against her skin. "Well, you've always had an inner fire. It's what drew me to you in the first place. But whatever happened in that room with Dr. Hansen, it changed you. And you're stronger now because of it."

Derek stepped closer, posting a forearm on the wall above her. Stella leaned in but stopped short of touching him. Bringing his other hand, rough with calluses, to her face, he dragged his thumb across her cheek. "You don't have to run away," he said. "Not anymore. Not ever again."

"You don't have to run either," she said. Her fingertips ghosted across his chest, his tee shirt soft against her skin.

A sad smile tugged at the corner of his mouth. "It's all I know how to do."

"I'm pretty good at it myself. But I'm choosing to stay now. Would you...consider staying? With me?" She wasn't entirely sure what she was asking, just that she didn't want him to leave.

"I'm finding there aren't many things I'd say no to, if you're the one who asked me."

A river of feelings flooded over her. Whatever complicated pasts they both had, this man—he understood her. Two people fighting against their instincts to run at the first sign of danger or to think they couldn't make a difference. In all of her imaginings of what came next in this brutal world, she'd always stood alone. Or maybe with Silas. But now, things had changed. She had Tara. Lawrence. Quentin. And looking into Derek's eyes now, she knew.

He'd be with her until the end too.

Her fingers curled into the collar of his shirt, and he dipped his head—

"Glad to see I'm not alone in the no-sleep club."

At the intrusion, Stella blinked, and Derek sprang to the other side of the kitchen.

Tara strolled in and rummaged in a cabinet. "Don't mind me. Just getting a snack. Carry on with the smoldering looks and heavy touches," she said, laughing into her box of crackers as she went back upstairs.

Derek scratched the back of his neck. "Guess we should try to get some sleep." But the heat in his eyes suggested anything *but* sleeping.

Stella cleared her throat and smoothed her hair. It was getting long. She'd have to decide soon if she was going to shear it again or let it grow. *Yes, think about your hair and not the attractive man watching your every move, looking absolutely devastating.* "I'll see you tomorrow."

When she fell back asleep in the wee hours of the morning, it was the first time she didn't dream of Evie.

She didn't dream of anything at all.

59

Penny

PENNY PICKED HER WAY through the woods toward Maple Street, blending into the trees. Invisible. Alone.

Well, except for Mal beside her.

"Stop being so loud," she hissed. "You'll attract every turned in the goddamn city."

A muscle in Mal's jaw flickered and he said, "I'm silent and you know it. You're upset about Quentin. You've been in a rage ever since he was taken."

Quentin.

Penny flinched. The name was a dagger to the heart. She seethed as she stormed through the woods.

"Now who's being loud," Mal said from behind her. She whirled and shoved him.

"*Yes*, I'm 'in a rage.' I'm fucking pissed that I keep endangering my little brother." She shoved Mal again. Anger felt good. "I'm *incensed* that he won't grow up in a normal world with a normal life." Shove. "And I didn't even get the chance to fix things with him before he was snatched by the fucking troxies."

She moved to shove Mal again and he caught her wrists. Eyes glinting, he backed her up against a tree and pinned her hands above her head.

The planes of his body pressed against hers all the way down to her boots, and it made her chest heave with fast breaths as she stared him down. Or, well, up. *He's so fucking tall.*

"Let me go."

"Are you done?"

She wriggled against him. *Damn, those hands are strong. And the rest of him. Jesus.* She clenched her teeth. "Get off me."

"Good. Push me again, and you lose your walking privileges. I'll throw you over my shoulder and carry you like a sack of potatoes the rest of the way. Don't fucking tempt me." He released her and walked ahead, not looking back to see if she followed.

"Pompous ass," she muttered as she rubbed her wrists where he'd touched her.

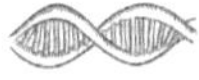

It was evening when they arrived. Derek's house was blanketed in blackness to match Penny's mood, but the faint glow of firelight and flashlights flickered from inside.

They joined everyone in the living room. The one they'd rescued—Sid, or something—wasn't around. The group looked haggard, like they hadn't slept.

"Any luck?" Derek handed her and Mal a glass of whiskey each, and they sat on the couch.

Time to put on a brave face.

As Penny cradled the drink in her lap, Stella eyed her from across the room, fidgeting with the knife hilt in her belt. She probably didn't even realize she was doing it.

Penny took a sip and sighed. "Seriously, Stella. If I wanted to kill you, I would have done it already. You showed me your proof that you're not the Architect, and I believe you. So stop squirming."

With Stella's Helix Key, they'd gotten a few extra Patches from one of the Pharmatrox armories, and Penny had used one to view Evie's proposal for dionazole and the mock interview recording. It was strange to think that she didn't have to feel a burning hatred and betrayal now every time she looked at Stella. Stella had a lot more reasons to hate Penny now than Penny had to hate her.

Mal stiffened beside her, ready to grab her and prevent her from launching across the room. She rolled her eyes at him. On with business. "We're just here to report. I found Quentin."

Tara sat bolt upright, looking ready to wrestle a grizzly bear. *Excellent. We can use that.*

Derek grumbled. "You should have led with that, Penny."

"Whatever. Dr. Hansen is keeping him in the cathedral. It's a goddamn solid concrete structure, and its walls are impenetrable. It looks like she's setting up for Pharmatrox HQ 2.0."

"There's a shit ton of high-grade security," said Mal. "But not the obvious kind. Proximity sensors hidden in the trees. Reinforced steel doors behind the original wooden ones. Bars on the windows that align with the stained glass designs. Probably cameras around the gargoyles and other things we can't see."

"So there's no way in or out?" said Stella.

"From what I've gathered, Dr. Hansen likes to make an emphatic point," said Penny. "I bet if we show up, she'll come out to play."

"What about guards?" asked Lawrence.

Penny snorted. "I know Stella can handle a knife and a gun. I taught her myself. And you all are more than capable."

"Once we get in—assuming we even *get* that far—how are we supposed to know where to find Quentin?" said Stella.

"If I were Dr. Hansen, I'd make a big scene," said Penny. "You know how I used to like putting on a show."

Derek put another log in the fireplace and said, "So where exactly is she keeping him?"

Penny's face went flat. "It's a church, Derek. Don't be daft. What's the most important place in a church?"

Everyone gave her matching blank looks. Penny never had been interested in religions, even before Pharmatrox had banned them for being too divisive. But she at least knew the basics.

Penny sighed and massaged her temples. "How am *I* the holiest one of this group?" she muttered. "The *altar*. The big, fancy, ornate table-like structure at the front? The place where all the seats are pointed? That's your main stage. I'm not leaving Quent—" She cut off her sentence with a wince. *Dammit, I can't even say his name without losing my shit.* "Look, if you have a better plan, let's hear it. If not, we're doing this my way. So discuss. I'll wait." She slugged her whiskey and slid the empty glass onto the coffee table.

The others sat in a tense silence for a few seconds before Lawrence finally spoke. "What do you think?" His face mirrored Stella's tight expression.

"So we blast our way in and hope for the best?" said Stella. "That sounds...suicidal. Even with the Faction's help, will we be able to get past the cathedral's security?" The question was aimed at Mal.

He leaned forward on his elbows and said, "With the added gear from the Pharmatrox armories, we'd be able to put up a good fight against their guards and breach the perimeter."

Lawrence rubbed his beard in thought. "It's our only chance. I say we do it."

Penny smiled. "That's one vote for Team Penny."

"Don't call it that," snapped Stella.

"Do what?" Stella's friend staggered into the living room. He scratched his stomach and took a swig from Derek's offered glass of water. "What's wrong with you?" he said to Stella. "Looks like you ate one of those really rotten toadstools Lawrence tried to make us eat yesterday."

"Penny found Quentin," said Stella.

The big man choked on his drink, eyes bulging. He coughed and pounded his chest, then said, "What?"

"She is apparently no longer interested in decapitating me. Officially. And she and Mal have a plan."

Penny straightened in her seat. "*Penny* has a plan. Mal just has the big guns."

Mal crossed his arms with a grumble. "The big guns that you *need* for your plan."

As Stella relayed the previous conversation to her friend, he stared into the fire and nodded to himself.

"Agnes, we need to tell them," he said.

Agnes? Must be her name from Before.

"There's no good option here, Silas."

Ah, Silas, that's right. Oddly Biblical for these times.

"Tell them and maybe we can come up with a better plan together," said Silas.

Tara frowned and looked at Lawrence. His expression matched hers. "Stella, want to fill us in?" she asked.

Derek was the only other one who didn't look confused. *Good to know these people have as much issue communicating effectively as Mal and I do.*

Stella rubbed her forehead and said, "We have a plan for how to take down Pharmatrox IIQ, and maybe even the other satellite facilities across the country."

Penny blinked. "I think you should have led with *that*." She shrugged. "I'm interested. Let's hear it."

"I know a lot about their security systems and the machine they're using to develop and test troxapine." Stella gnawed her lip and cut a glance at Silas. "I designed the machine. But that wasn't its original intent."

Penny shot to her feet. "You—you—" She couldn't even think straight. *I was right. This* is *her fault.* She clenched her sickle in an iron grip. She didn't remember removing it from her belt.

But as she looked at Stella, she saw her own reflection. A woman who had fallen to the dust and had wanted to give up—but had stubbornly held on and pushed through addiction to face the raw realities of the life she had made.

Penny wanted to see Stella as evil like Pharmatrox. But now that she wasn't the Architect and was actually a troxy *defector*…Things were never black and white. Good versus evil. Stella had made hard choices that resulted in death and destruction, just as Penny had. Their methods and motives were different, but the outcomes were the same. And now, Stella wasn't claiming to be a white knight, the savior of the world. She was just a woman who wanted to do the right thing. To clean up her mess.

Penny understood something about that feeling. It was a feeling she had never been brave enough to do anything about. Until now.

Decision made, Penny returned her sickle to her belt and reclaimed her seat. "We still need to get to the 'plan' part of your plan."

The group looked at her like deer in headlights.

"What? Surprised I want to help and not kill you on the spot? Me too. Talk, before I change my mind." Penny crossed her ankles in a deliberately relaxed posture, even though every muscle in her body pulled taut. If they really could destroy the entire company and win the war, *that* would bring her the justice she had been seeking for so long. It had to.

Mal surreptitiously slid his arm across the back of the couch, as if ready to latch onto her should she change her mind. "Back off," she murmured. He gave her a lazy smile and did not move. *Asshole.*

Pacing in front of the fire, Stella said, "Pharmatrox needs the network in order to execute their plan for mass mind control—monitoring everyone through their CLEOs, broadcasting propaganda, controlling the flow of information, storing their data, communicating, and coordinating their army. We take down the network, we cripple them and take control of HQ. And we destroy my machine."

Penny frowned, but it was Lawrence who spoke. "That's not a plan, Stella."

"Still working on that part. Now that we know about the cathedral...I never saw that building in any of my research, so they must have kept it off the books like the Spire. They're hiding something there besides Quentin. My machine is too bulky and complicated for them to have moved it this fast, but it's possible it could be there too." Stella paled. "Or somewhere else entirely."

Great. She has no fucking idea.

"Sounds like we need to split up," said Derek. His brow furrowed as he glanced at Stella, face tight with worry.

That's interesting. Der-bear's got a little crush.

"We should hit both simultaneously," said Mal. "We'll only have one shot at this. They'll know we're coming for the Spire, so we've already lost the element of surprise there."

"I'll go to the cathedral," said Stella. "I need to end things with Ingrid myself. Personally. Silas, you should go to the Spire. How's that virus we were working on?"

Silas nodded, but wrung his hands. "Devastating. It will render the machine and the network irreparable. A polymorphic boot sector virus and wiper malware, if you want to get technical. But..." Silas's voice trembled like leaves on a tree during a storm, thin and fragile. "I'm not you, Agnes. I'm not like any of you." He flapped a hand at the room. "I don't *do* stuff like this. I'm a computer guy. I don't infiltrate the secret headquarters of our fascist rulers and hack their security systems. That's *absurd*. I know I came up with the idea yesterday, but now that we're all talking about it, it sounds ludicrous. Impossible."

Stella took a deep breath and closed her eyes. When she opened them, they were focused on Penny. "That's why Penny is going with you."

Penny blinked. *Now* that's *interesting.* She tapped a finger to her lip and shrugged. "I'm in," she said, putting on an air of casual disinterest, but inside, she was boiling with anticipation. *I have to get inside that tower. This is my chance for vengeance. For absolution. To burn the whole thing down.*

"You're—?" Silas spluttered and slapped a hand to his face, letting it slowly drag down his cheek. "You wanted to kill Agnes until about five minutes ago. I should trust you to have my back in enemy territory? Do you think I'm an *idiot*?"

"I don't think you want me answering that last bit," Penny said, propping her feet on the coffee table. "The chance to personally see this pestilence of a company dismantled beyond repair? Hell yes, I'm in."

Mal inclined his head to Stella. "The Faction is behind you all the way. Whatever you need, you'll have it."

"Things have settled since...Rodney?" Stella asked.

"Many of Rodney's followers either left or are dead," said Mal. "We're not as divided as we once were, but things are...tumultuous. I have my loyal band of soldiers, and more weapons now, thanks to you. We'll go with Penny and Silas to the Spire while the rest of the troops draw the troxies away with another fight somewhere else. Force them to fight a war on three fronts."

"I have a thought," Tara chimed in. "Mal took me on a walkthrough of the Faction's armory to see what we're working with. They've got a helicopter. It's a busted hunk of junk. The guns are completely blown to shit, the doors don't close, the controls don't work. But it'll fly. I'll be flying with no gauges, blind as a goddamn bat. But it's got just enough fuel and ammo to make a difference. I can help you bulldoze through the defenses at the cathedral and then go pick up Silas and Penny at the Spire's helipad for a quick escape."

"You can fly?" Derek looked at her, impressed.

"I went to aviation school for a bit before I decided on the infantry."

"An aviation school dropout?" Penny said. "Great. I feel very safe."

Tara glared. "Jump off the building, then. It makes no difference to me."

"Enough," said Stella. "It's better than we could have hoped for. Mal, Penny—when do you think we can be ready?"

Mal rubbed his chin and studied Derek. "If Penny and I have some help training the troops and planning another battle in, let's say, Sector 16, we could be ready in three days."

Derek gave a low whistle. "Okay, challenge accepted. I'm at your disposal." He turned to Silas. "I'll go over the Spire blueprints in detail with you and upload them to a Patch."

"Good." Stella placed a hand on Silas's shoulder. The man had been nonstop wringing his hands since she told him Penny would be his partner in crime. "Do you think you can do it, Si?"

Silas massaged his temples and kept shooting glances at Penny. "Fine. Okay. But, Stella, we'll need to spend the next seventy-two hours practicing with one of those extra Patches. And I mean, *constantly*. I don't want to get caught unawares in the Spire's network. So you need to show me the ropes and everything about how to navigate once I'm in."

"We'll be able to communicate with our Patches before you kill the network, so I can help you if you get stuck," said Stella. "And I could use some extra practice with everything too."

Silas's face turned a more normal color of brown rather than spoiled-milk pale. "You ready to be my teacher, for once?" He bumped her with his elbow, but his smile didn't quite reach his eyes.

Bastard is scared shitless, and rightly so.

"Great. We're in agreement," said Penny. "We split up. That always works out spectacularly for people in the movies, right?" Her tone dripped sarcasm. "Anyway, it's the best we're going to do. Let's get to it."

Stella tensed like she wanted to argue, even though it was her plan.

"And Stella?" Penny said.

"Yes?"

"Save my brother. Or I *will* decapitate you."

60

"I**S EVERYONE CLEAR ON** their part?" Stella surveyed Lawrence, Tara, and Derek beside her. Her nerves jangled like wind chimes in a hurricane. She touched each of her weapons for the hundredth time, the dionazole a reassuring weight in her pocket. If Ingrid was experimenting on Quentin, he'd need it.

They nodded to her, adjusting their volt rifle straps. Mal had resupplied them with ammunition, but not enough to matter if they were swarmed by guards or turned. Volt rifles weren't the best choice in close combat, so everyone also had a bullet rifle, just in case.

"We'd better hope Silas, Penny, and Mal can do *their* parts, or this is all for nothing," Lawrence said.

The cathedral straddled the hilltop in its gothic grandeur like an enormous horned spider as bright moonlight cast elongated shadows on the front lawn. The cathedral was a *fortress*, just as Penny had suggested. A small squadron of Faction forces hid in the tree line behind them as backup, but it didn't feel like enough.

Derek nudged her, concern tugging at the corners of his mouth. "How are you feeling?"

Her stomach heaved, but she managed a smile. "Like shit. But I'll survive."

Since taking dionazole, Death had fully dissolved into the depths of Stella's mind. Her heart ached at the thought she'd never see Evie again. The shakes, sweating, and vomiting had yet to abate, but she'd get through it. She'd already lived through worse.

"Everything go okay with the helicopter?" she asked Tara.

Tara nodded as she scanned the perimeter. "Hidden in the woods about two miles from here with some guards. There's a Humvee to take me there when it's time. Limited fuel and ammo, so we need to make it count." She patted the radio strapped to her hip.

Silas and Penny had one to let her know if and when they needed a ride, and Lawrence had one too in case their group got separated.

Stella's stomach churned as she thought of Silas breaking into the Spire without her. With *Penny*. Silas had picked up navigating the network quickly, but he wouldn't know exactly what he was working with until he logged in at the Spire.

Stella gulped and clutched her volt rifle. Silas knew what he was doing. And Penny would keep him safe. She had to trust that.

Lawrence branched off to the left while Tara went to the right, keeping close to the shadows of the trees. They all wore Pharmatrox armor and had the fobs that would allow them past a perimeter—as long as they were attuned to the right frequency. But Ingrid knew Stella was smart and had to anticipate that Stella would find the cathedral. And if Ingrid still wanted a chance at swaying Stella to her side, she wouldn't kill her or her friends.

At least, Stella thought she wouldn't.

This plan relies a lot on hopes and dreams. But there was nothing to be done about it. They had to go—now.

When Stella moved toward her position, Derek stopped her. The look on his face had her heart shooting into her throat. He brought a tattooed hand to the back of her neck and pressed his forehead to hers, and she breathed in his scent of sage and sandalwood. A moment of calm before the raging storm ahead. "Be careful," he said.

"I'm always careful." She gave him a brief grin.

"Hardly," he scoffed, and headed after Tara.

Stella joined Lawrence, her steps and heart a bit lighter, but she faltered as she approached. It felt wrong waltzing in the front door, but Penny had assured her that playing into Ingrid's hands was the only way to gain entry to the cathedral. It felt more like they were live bait though.

A few minutes later, the front door creaked open. Light spilled into the fog and illuminated a single figure on the stairs. Three others joined it. Then five. Then ten.

Then *more*. Too many to count.

The doors burst open, and an army of turned poured onto the lawn. Some crawled on deft hands and feet, predators circling for the kill. Others ran in jerky and stunted movements, unpredictable and fast.

Even with the Faction troops, they were wildly outnumbered.

Stella launched into the fight. Bodies dropped around her as the Faction emerged from the trees, firing volts and bullets. But with Stella and her friends surrounded and in close quarters, they couldn't risk taking too many shots.

These turned were different than any she had faced before; they had the black eyes, but were less feral. Some moved with fluid grace and struck with precision. Others fought with brute strength, using rocks and debris as deadly weapons.

She realized with a twist in her gut that this was her mother's doing. What Dr. Hansen had dedicated her life to. A manufactured, obedient army capable of destroying in droves.

Tara bashed a turned's skull with the butt of her rifle, while Stella impaled two on her machete. She looked up, and her stomach plummeted when she saw a slew of Pharmatrox guards rappelling down the side of the cathedral and joining the fight. *Carajo.*

Derek sliced through turned with a long hunting knife until he reached Stella's side. "Too many," he said, stabbing another torso.

Stella's hand twitched toward her gun, but she resisted. She didn't want to accidentally shoot a friend. But with guards now in play…

"We need to make a break for it," Lawrence shouted over the snarls of the mutant army and the meaty thuds of weapons on flesh. "Get inside and bar the doors."

Tara's raven curls glistened with fresh blood, and her teeth shone white through the gore on her face. "With me." To the twenty or so Faction members, she said, "Keep these fuckers away from that door."

The group gathered behind Tara as her bullets pummeled the battlefield, clearing a path through Ingrid's army. The swarm of turned erupted in chaos, the loud sounds stirring them into a frenzy.

Stella and the others sprinted toward the safety of the cathedral.

They burst into the narthex, scrambling to slam the door. A set of metal doors reinforced the ancient wooden ones, but without the locking mechanism engaged, there was nothing to hold them shut.

"Grab that!" Stella waved an arm at the display case across the large entryway.

Lawrence and Derek dragged it in front of the door while Tara unloaded the rest of her bullets into the turned clogging the doorway. But it barely made a dent.

The doors undulated as a mass of bodies surged against them, and fingers and hands groped their way through the opening.

"We've gotta hurry," said Stella to Derek, who leaned against the wall, leaving a bloody handprint.

Lawrence spared a sheepish look at the black stains his boots smeared across the floor and said, "Something feels very wrong about tracking blood inside the supposed house of God."

Stella shoved the shiny steel doors standing between her and the sanctuary. Nothing. "God gave up on us a long time ago," she said. "We're on our own. See if there's a Helix Key port to open this door." Ingrid might not know about Stella's Helix Key or Sara Ellis's Patch, so her credentials should still be active and unblocked.

They dispersed through the long entryway corridor, searching the crevices for a hidden access point.

"Hey, I think I found somethi—"

With a sound like a soda can bursting, the main doors flew open and punched the display case into the opposite wall, an army of gray bodies pouring into the narthex and moving as one mass toward them. The Faction force spread among them, shooting and stabbing, but more turned had joined the fray.

Oh, hell. Maybe the turned from the city are flocking here.

"Go!" Derek shoved Lawrence and Stella aside. "Tara and I will handle this. We'll follow when we can."

Stella opened her mouth to protest, but Lawrence grabbed her and ran.

"I saw something on a statue," said Lawrence over the din of battle. "I think it might be a Patch scanner."

The statue, a small replica of Mother Science, guarded the sanctuary doors. A small button glowed in her mortar and pestle. Stella tapped her Patch and hit the button, opening a Helix Key port. When she twisted in the key, a cheerful chirp sounded in her head as the credentials were accepted and she and Lawrence tumbled into the cavernous space.

Once inside, the door sealed shut behind them with an authoritative *thunk-hiss* and blanketed the room in a weighty hush, the battle in the hallway silenced and forgotten. Stella dragged her hands across the wall, searching—

Carajo. "We're locked in. Or, I don't know how the fuck to open this door again."

"What? Can't you just use your Patch, or whatever?"

Stella shook her head. "I can't find a scanner or keyhole."

"Shit," Lawrence said, pulling at his beard. "Let's find Quentin first. We'll deal with that later." He grabbed one of the torches that lined the nave, and they advanced down the aisle toward the main altar.

Columns soared into the heavens of the vaulted ceiling, dozens of stained glass windows lining the upper parts of the walls, a hundred or more feet in the air. Shadows flickered across the alcoves, teased by Lawrence's roving torch. Chains crisscrossed the other doors far off to either side, and unease swelled inside Stella like an unwelcome, yet familiar, intruder.

Her hand itched toward her Patch. She wanted to talk to Silas, but they had agreed to only use the comms if they were in trouble. No news was good news.

As they approached the altar, their footsteps were the only sound echoing through the church's cavernous innards.

"Maybe he's not in here," Lawrence said in a hoarse whisper.

When a dark chuckle reached out through the thick blackness, Lawrence brandished his torch and whipped around, eyes wide. "Who's there?"

The torch caught the reflection of a pair of eyes perched on the pulpit to their right. He lounged atop it, one leg dangling over the edge.

"Quentin?" Stella's knees wobbled with relief. "Quentin, are you okay?"

Quentin didn't answer. Didn't move. As Stella and Lawrence slowed, Quentin tilted his head and smiled. But there was something wrong with his smile. Something off.

Something slyly sinister.

Fear doused Stella in a cold wash. Faster than a blink, Quentin whipped out a knife and threw it at Lawrence. He dodged, but Quentin headed straight for Stella, and they fell to the ground in a tangle of limbs.

"Quentin! It's me!" Stella held him away from her as he tried to slash her throat with another knife. But his eyes were wrong too. They were the eyes of Silas when he had attacked her. This wasn't Quentin anymore.

Quentin was gone.

Lawrence grabbed Quentin and hauled him off. Or he tried to. In an acrobatic move unlike him, Quentin threw himself into a back handspring and landed in a crouch. She and Lawrence exchanged bewildered looks. They didn't know he could do that.

Quentin sprinted at them...but then halted, looking around in confusion. "Guys? Where am I? What's happen—"

Instantly, his face was wiped blank again, and he bared his teeth, charging at Lawrence.

Lawrence dropped the torch and blocked Quentin's knife, grabbing his wrist. He twisted and threw Quentin against the stone railing with a crash and yelled, "What's going on!" The torch rolled across the floor and threw oblong shadows in a blinding sunburst pattern.

"Ingrid must have dosed him with troxapine," said Stella, "but it's not working correctly."

Lawrence grappled with Quentin. "What do we do?"

"We—"

Rainbow glass exploded into the sanctuary as the rose window shattered, a volt of electricity sizzling into one of the tapestries hanging from a wooden balustrade. A few beats of silence as the flames crept toward a gas lamp sconce. Then a massive explosion ripped the air, flaming bits of fabric spewing across the aisle and igniting the other tapestries until all of them were engulfed in flames.

From outside, several twitchy bodies squeezed through the bars across the broken window.

In the light of the burning church, a familiar figure stood in the aisle.

All advanced toward Stella and Lawrence.

61

Penny

PENNY EYED THE SMOLDERING black glass tower from their hiding place in a nearby alley.

The windows on several of the lower floors were blown out, the fangs of glass glittering in the moonlight. Smoke leaked out of the jagged openings and crept toward the ground in a dark fog.

But the burning Spire wasn't the most troubling part. No, she was more concerned with the gang of users actively smashing windows and murdering people.

Several dozen users—some of them turned—clashed with a small force of remaining Pharmatrox guards that hadn't already abandoned the facility to fight Mal's forces by the riverfront. More users and turned trickled in from the surrounding streets, drawn by the scent of the dust and blood burning in the air.

Beside her, Silas fiddled with the strap of his rifle. On her other side, Mal gave a low whistle, and a team of four dozen red-masked Faction members packed the alley behind them. Looking at the sea of feral users and turned, Penny was grateful for Mal's presence. He exuded power in his armored vest and weapons strapped to every surface of his body. They all wore Pharmatrox armor and tactical gear, and she and Silas each had a small pack with extra weapons and supplies. Her thoughts strayed to the other half of their crew at the cathedral, and her heart thundered in her chest. *This had better work.*

Mal's brows lowered over honey-brown eyes. "What happened? It's a fucking free-for-all."

Silas grunted. "I'm guessing the users showed up when the troxies dropped the perimeter to meet your forces in Sector 16. It looks like some of the troxies evacuated." He frowned at the flames. "The ones who stayed behind could be destroying evidence in case they are overrun, but the users could have set the fires too," said Silas. "Hopefully no one decides to trigger the self-destruct codes."

Penny snapped her head to him. "The what?"

"Some bigger companies have an emergency protocol that involves flooding the halls with an immobilizing neurotoxin or sometimes a flammable gas. I've seen it in some of my own clients' systems. Some would rather burn it all down than let anyone get their hands on their secrets. It's always a last resort, but from the looks of it, the troxies might get desperate pretty soon."

Mal scratched his chin. "So what's that mean for us?"

"It means the building could burst into flames at any moment, or we could inhale the toxin and be trapped. And then the building could burst into flames."

Mal frowned. "Why didn't you mention this sooner?"

"Would knowing about it ahead of time have changed our plan?"

He has a point.

Silas scratched his head, considering. "If they haven't triggered the self-destruct codes yet, it means they're likely holing up in the secret lab and hoping their army can handle the disturbance. Good news is, that also means the machine is likely still in the Spire too. But we'll have to fight through the troxies to get to it."

"Excellent. Wouldn't want it to be too easy," said Penny.

Her mind went to a vision of Dr. Hansen, standing above an organized selection of gruesome bodies, a cold and calculating look flashing in her blue eyes. She'd seen that look before. In Rodney. Ingrid was the real danger. She shuddered at the thought of what that woman could be doing to Quentin.

Penny would do whatever it took to get Silas to that hidden floor.

"So what do we do now?" she asked.

Turning to his soldiers, Mal said, "Stick to the original plan. Draw the fight away from Silas and Penny. I'll get them inside." Then he turned to Penny. A strange feeling went through her at the weight of his attention. "Don't do anything more insane than usual."

"Don't tell me what to do." She smiled with fake sweetness and batted her eyelashes.

She saw the flash of his smile before he turned to his troops and yelled, "Let's do this!"

With overlapping shouts, the group charged out of the alley, weapons held aloft. Silas had a hard time keeping up, so Penny grabbed his arm and towed him along.

The Faction hit the Pharmatrox guards, users, and turned in a red brick wall of brute force. Gunfire chattered and blades scraped against bone, punctuated by shrieks and wails.

When a gangly turned set his sights on Silas, Penny yelled, but she was too far. He leapt, clawed hands outstretched, black eyes weeping obsidian tears down his wrinkled face—

Mal shouldered Silas aside and skewered the turned with a knife as long as his forearm, then sloughed the body off of his blade, hands covered in oily black blood.

Penny smiled. *Useful in a fight, he is.*

Mal shoved Silas toward the Spire's entrance as Penny dodged the various melees of users and turned fighting over vials of troxapine and bags of dust. When she caught up to Silas at the front entrance, they slipped inside. Penny turned with an exhale—

—and bumped straight into a solid bulwark of a man guarding the stairwell.

The user was even taller than Mal and Silas. He peered down his nose at them, his dust-sharpened eyes glinting in the flickering fluorescent lights.

He must be like Stella and me—the dust affects him differently too.

Looking them up and down, he twirled his knife across his knuckles. Beneath his rugged beard, his lips curled in a sneer.

Silas reached for his rifle, but the bigger man thwacked him across the face with the flat of his blade. Within seconds, a welt blossomed on Silas's cheek.

"None of that," said the man in a gruff voice, rubbing a hand over his shaved head and tugging his beard. He sized up Penny with an appraising gaze, then shifted his attention to Silas. *The weaker prey.* He pointed his knife at him, the tip dangerously close to his eyeball. "Who're you with?" the user asked, taking a menacing step forward.

"S-sorry?"

The user grabbed a fistful of Silas's hair and said, "If you're one of Malosi's vultures, I'll put your head through this wall right now!" With his dust-induced strength, Penny had no doubt the user was more than capable of following through. "I said, *who are you with?*" The user roared, flecks of spittle landing on Silas's face. He ripped his head back, priming to smash it against the wall.

But Penny whipped her sickle and hooked the user's wrist. Then she noticed the black eye tattooed on his forearm. She took a gamble and said, "We're with Callum."

The user released Silas like he'd just been zapped with a volt rifle. Then his bushy brows lowered over suspicious eyes as he peered at Penny. "I ain't seen you around camp before. I'd remember a pretty face like that." He reached a fingertip for her cheek, and she flicked her blade to his throat. "He did warn me about a red-headed bitch who was too big for her britches."

Fucking fuck. "Plenty of other bitches with red hair. Let us pass. Or maybe you'd like to explain to Callum why you were harassing the new recruits he put in charge of securing the fifth floor?"

When a shadow of fear flickered across the user's face, Penny gave him a sparkling smile, all teeth. "What's your name again? I'd like to let him know exactly who needs to have his head removed from his shoulders."

The user straightened and toed open the stairwell door. "Sorry for the trouble," he groused. "Can't be too careful."

Before he could change his mind, Penny elbowed Silas through the door and shut it behind them. Smashing glass and shrill cries echoed through the concrete stairwell from above like an unseen horror film.

She prodded Silas ahead of her. Derek had shown them an alternate elevator on the sixth floor they could use if the first floor was inaccessible. She wanted to get far away from Big User, fast.

"Penny...what the hell was that? Who's Callum?"

Penny's skin crawled. That rat bastard must have set up his own camp somewhere in the city. She should have stabbed him in the fucking skull, but she'd thought he'd bleed out. Stupid mistake. "Pray you never find out. Come on, pick up the pace."

They passed doors hanging off their hinges, portals into smoldering destruction. Blood and soot streaked the walls in a macabre mural. Troxies rushed between the offices carting boxes of papers and supplies, harried looks on their faces.

As they reached the fifth-floor landing, Silas paused midstep. Penny nearly crashed into him. Annoyed, she asked, "What is it?"

"I think I have an idea," he said, then ducked inside the fifth floor.

"Silas!" Penny snatched for his arm, but he slipped through her fingers. She grumbled and followed.

The soot-stained hall extended before her like the barrel of a shotgun, the fires burning low. Callum, the fucking pyromaniac, had always set fire to whatever he could get his grubby hands on. *Hopefully he decided to stay at camp and let his minions do his dirty work.* Despite the ruckus on the front lawn, this floor rang with an eerie silence.

"We're wasting time," she said as they inched down the hallway.

"There should be a supply of dust on this floor. It's one of the lower labs where they worked on refining it."

"Planning to get high?" Penny asked, scanning each door as they passed but seeing no sign of life within.

"No, but it could be used as a distraction in case we're overcome by a swarm of users or turned."

Penny grunted her assent. *Smart. Good plan.*

A crash sounded from a room down the hallway.

Silas turned to Penny, face pale with fear. "That's where the dust is."

Of course it is.

"Silas, your rifle," she said. He blinked, then fumbled with the large weapon strapped to his back. "Now hold it like Mal taught you." He choked up his grip on the rifle and nodded. His hands quaked, but it was good enough.

Penny took the lead and crept toward the din of destruction. She nosed the door open with her sickle, but Silas made a noise behind her and a heavy hand fell on her shoulder.

A slick, muffled voice drawled in her ear.

"Look what we've got here."

Spikes of revulsion shot through her as she turned around. Black veins threaded Callum's nasty green eyes, and the left side of his face sported thick, ugly stitches from the corner of his mouth to his ear, rimmed in red and pus. She could smell the infection from where she stood.

In an instant, Callum grabbed a fistful of her hair and yanked her close. "Thanks for the new pretty smile, Penny," he slurred, slipping a knife out of his belt. "Let me return the favor."

Faster than Penny thought possible for the lumbering man, Silas swung his rifle in an awkward attempt to smash Callum, but Callum caught it in an iron grip that belied his skinny stature. The distraction gave Penny enough time to duck away and draw her sickle. Callum jerked the rifle out of Silas's hands and propped it against his shoulder, then looked past Silas into the room behind him. "Find anything?"

"You betcha." Another man's voice, raspy as straw, came from the other room. "Got a whole case of dust in here."

Silas stepped forward, but Callum poked the rifle into his chest and speared him in place. He wagged a finger and grinned, teeth sharp and inhuman. "Get it and let's go." He turned his attention to Penny, and a thousand centipedes crawled across her skin. "Who's the big guy?" He shifted the barrel of the rifle underneath Silas's chin. Silas gulped and looked at Penny in terror.

Positioning herself closer to Silas, Penny twirled her sickle in one hand and drew her handgun with the other. Callum's beady eyes were bright with delight. The fucker was itching for a fight. She had to play this right or Callum would kill Silas just because he could.

"Do with him what you like," she said. "He's a troxy. Found him trying to escape. I persuaded him to show me where the dust is." She gave her sickle a loving caress and shot a sinister grin at Silas. He blanched at first, but then realization dawned on him, and he twitched his head in a slight nod.

Callum narrowed his eyes. "You don't use, so what you need it for?"

"Don't see how that's any of your fucking business." She pointed at the package of dust clutched in Callum's lackey's hands. "I'll be taking that, thanks."

"Seems to me you're outgunned," said Callum. "Why don't you take your boy here and run along? Would hate to start any trouble." His predatory smile implied the opposite.

"Told you, he's not mine." In a swift move, Penny pulled Silas toward her and held him from behind. She poised her sickle at his throat, but with the hand hidden behind his back, she gave him a reassuring pat. "I'll kill him myself, just to be rid of the trouble."

Callum sneered. "That's more like the Penny I remember. Jumping to blood as the first answer to any problem. Still the same."

Still the same.

His words sliced through her, and her hand tightened on the hilt. Was she still that same bloodthirsty Penny? She had thought herself above being a mindless killer, like Rodney. Like Callum. When she killed, she killed with purpose. She was *not* a monster—or so she thought. At the look of doubt in Silas's eyes, fear that she *would* actually slit his throat despite her reassurances, something inside of her shifted.

Silas, Stella, Quentin, all of them—they were afraid of her. Still. They saw her as the *equivalent* to this murderous man in front of her. In her mission to destroy Pharmatrox and absolve herself of the smothering guilt of killing her own family, she'd become the very thing she had always feared.

She would not be like Rodney or Callum, killing for sport. Killing to instill fear and gain a crew of followers that would fight for her. Killing for *control*. Not ever again. She wasn't that Penny anymore. She'd never been the sister Quentin deserved, but she could do better now. For him.

In Silas's ear so only he could hear, she whispered one word. "*Duck.*"

He ducked, and Penny launched at Callum. She grabbed the rifle and smashed the butt into his throat. Instantly, he collapsed, hacking hollow coughs, as she stuck a knife in his torso and kicked him in the face. He went limp, blood seeping onto the tile.

Without pause, she drew another knife from her belt and threw it at the bumbling user clutching the bag of dust. It skewered into his round belly. He looked at it in disbelief, then fell forward, blood pooling beneath him in a slow circle.

"Let's get the fuck out of here." Penny tossed the dust to Silas and reclaimed her knife from the user's torso, then wiped the blood on her jeans.

Silas peeked at her with an uncertain smile. "You had me worried for a second. I thought you might actually kill me."

Penny ran a hand through her snarl of red curls. "Sorry. Seeing Callum reminded me of someone I used to be. A nightmare version of myself."

Silas snorted, but turned it into a cough. Penny hoisted an eyebrow. "What?" she said.

"Well, from what I hear about your recent antics...if *this* Penny is a better version, then I'd hate to meet the *nightmare* version."

Penny fixed him with a hard gaze and said, "I hope you never have to do the things I did in order to survive."

Silas's eyes widened as he shoved her—*What the fuck?*—and she smashed into the wall as he took the brunt of Callum's surprise attack. The two men fell to the ground, Callum on top.

Will this cockroach not fucking die?

Silas struggled to regain a better position and managed to land a few blows to Callum's face, but Callum recovered and grabbed his arm. A band of steel cinched around Silas's wrist and clicked with a cold finality.

Still seeing stars from her collision with the wall, Penny couldn't make sense of the scene. When her vision cleared, her eyes locked on Silas's wrist *handcuffed* to Callum's.

62

QUENTIN ADVANCED DOWN THE cathedral's aisle through the smoke toward Stella and Lawrence, a group of ten turned—*Jesus, some of them have* guns?—on his flank. Thick smoke cloyed the air, the fire mere minutes away from catching the wooden balustrades lining the upper choir lofts.

A bullet ripped through the smoke, plunging into Lawrence's shoulder. With a grunt, he dropped to a knee, and Stella pulled him behind the pulpit as another shot pinged off the metal lectern. Blood welled from his wound, and she stuffed it with her bandanna.

"Lawrence! Stay with me!" Stella peeked around the lectern to catch a glimpse of the others, but ducked as more bullets pitted the stone floor.

As the flames engulfed the wooden balustrade that ringed the sanctuary, a new burst of heat filled the room, black smoke billowing into the ceiling.

Mierda, this is bad.

Stella dodged attacks and zigzagged as more turned poured through the window, dropping the hundred feet to the ground as if it were nothing.

From his position behind the lectern, Lawrence fired a few shots. "Watch it!" he yelled to Stella as Quentin swept her legs and disarmed her. She rolled with his attack and launched a hymnal at him, but he absorbed the blow as if he didn't feel it. Without warning, he pounced and they collapsed to the floor. In the struggle, she tossed him aside and sprang to her feet.

Before she could catch her breath, another dark shape slammed into her and drove her to the ground with the force of a freight train. She landed on her hip and felt the vial of dionazole in her pocket shatter against the concrete.

Hijo de puta. Now their only hope was to incapacitate Quentin or find more dionazole.

Dragging her knife through the turned's torso and positioning herself to protect Lawrence, she yelled, "Keep shooting!"

"I'm nearly out," Lawrence shouted as she held off another turned. In the distance, the air throbbed with a low hum that reverberated through Stella's bones. The fiery, smoky air felt alive, like it was rushing up to swallow them whole.

A turned sank her teeth into Stella's shoulder, and she screamed, her voice hoarse. Blood ran in hot rivulets mingled with sweat and soot as she kneed the turned in the stomach, but she latched on like a pit bull. More blood spilled, churning the turned into a cacophonous frenzy.

Stella flicked her fingers across the floor, looking for—*there*. Grabbing the Bible, Stella beat the turned over the head until she released and Stella scrambled away.

Dizzy from blood loss and smoke inhalation, Stella's vision blurred. The thrumming sound crescendoed, and her vision faded in and out as Quentin approached her through the haze. She staggered toward Lawrence. If she could get to a defensible position, she could use whatever bullets were left to—

Every window in the church exploded.

63

Penny

A MANIACAL LAUGH BURST from Callum's lips as he lifted his wrist cuffed to Silas's. Based on the veins in his eyes and his wild behavior, he was probably hours from turning. If he didn't die from his guts falling out. *How the fuck is he still conscious? Is it because of the dust?*

The sloppy black eye tattoo on Callum's forearm seemed to blink as he shook his arm. "And guess what? There's no key!"

Penny's stomach plummeted. Either Silas was chained to this madman for the rest of his life, or someone was losing an arm.

"Go!" said Silas as he scooted away from Callum. He slid the package of dust across the floor to her. "Get the hell out of here!"

"Shut up, Silas." Penny raised her sickle, but Callum pressed an evil-looking dagger to Silas's mouth.

"Hold it right there, Red," said Callum. Penny stopped. His tongue darted out to wet his lips. "This troxy of yours is going to show me where the rest of the dust is."

Quick as lightning, Penny threw her knife at one of the lights above Callum's head, and it exploded and rained down shards of glass. Taking advantage of his distraction, she tackled Callum, yanking Silas's handcuffed arm with them.

Silas flailed out of Penny's way as she latched her hands around Callum's throat. Callum tried to shove her off, but Silas leveraged his bulk and sat on his arm, holding him down, as Penny slashed her sickle across Callum's throat, again and again, until she was coated in his dark blood.

"Penny! I think you got him." Silas's hand on her arm brought her back to herself, and the bloody haze faded.

Dead. He's finally dead.

"Sorry," she said, then rifled through Callum's pockets.

Silas sat in a daze, transfixed by the pool of blood creeping across the floor.

"Damn it!" She took Callum's long knife and began hacking at his elbow.

Silas recoiled in horror. "What are you doing!"

Penny sawed viciously, and her hands slipped in Callum's blood. She dug her thumb into the tattoo of the black eye and gripped it tighter. "He wasn't lying. He doesn't have a key for the handcuffs. So unless you'd like to drag his dead body around with you..."

"So now I get to carry around *a dismembered arm?*"

"I could always cut off your arm instead."

Silas's jaw snapped shut. "Dismembered arm it is. Really wish we had Quentin's bolt cutters right about now."

Penny ignored the flare of guilt at the mention of her brother and cleaned her hands and knife off on Callum's shirt. Silas grimaced at the limb dangling from his wrist. The black eye tattoo wept tears of blood onto the floor in a quiet *pat-pat*.

"Thanks," he said. "I definitely couldn't have done that myself. Not without vomiting everywhere." His voice was strong, but he swayed on his feet like he might pass out.

The lights in the hallway flickered in warning.

"Come on," said Penny, steering them toward the stairs.

They stepped off the elevator and into a blinding-white hallway in dis-array, but Penny pulled Silas into an off-shooting hallway. Vicious snarls crept around the corner, and the walls vibrated from the violence contained within.

"I thought this was a *secret* floor?" said Penny.

Silas shrugged. "Escaped prisoners and science experiments gone wrong. The lights were flickering, so maybe the power surge caused cell doors to open accidentally? I'm not sure." He clutched the dust against his chest and looked at Penny with wide eyes. "I don't know what I was thinking. I can't do this." He pressed his back against the wall like he wanted to dissolve into it.

"You're the only one who can," Penny said, then inched around the corner and chanced a peek.

Users and turned tore at each other, at the ceiling and floor tiles, whatever they could get their hands on, their arterial blood spraying the walls. The contents of the labs and offices launched into the hallway, tossed by unseen troxies. Broken glass and broken bodies littered the floor. Piles of debris...

...and some stray human limbs in puddles of congealed blood.

Penny ducked back. Silas had sunk to the floor and was pointedly not looking at the arm attached to his.

Hauling Silas to his feet, Penny said, "Tara should be on her way to get us any minute. Let's finish this and get to the roof."

Silas nodded blankly with misty eyes, and Penny placed both hands on his shoulders, steadying her gaze on him. "You can do this, Silas. Think about Stel—Agnes. She needs you."

At the mention of Agnes, his eyes shone with a bright resolve, and he took a few stuttering steps into the hall, Penny close behind him.

The users and turned stopped fighting and stared at them with hungry eyes, blood dripping from their clawed hands.

Lowering into a fighting stance, Penny twirled her sickle and said, "Silas? Now would be a good time for your plan."

Silas tore open the bag of dust and emptied its contents behind him as he sprinted for the end of the hall. The users and turned leapt at the ground, licking the floor and inhaling as much of the drug as they could.

Penny dashed after Silas, and they dove inside the last office that had a window overlooking the lab she'd seen in their first break-in. After grabbing the nearby desk and barricading the door, Silas ripped books from the bookcase and hefted that on top of the desk.

"Those users are about to have the biggest high they've ever had, and we'll be right at the epicenter. Their reactions will be swift and explosive, so we don't have much time."

He blinked as he stared into the lab on the other side of the one-way glass, where several troxies roved aisles of metal tables with bodies atop them, tapping on their digital clipboards. They acted as if their tower wasn't getting ripped apart around them.

"Do you see Stella's machine?" she asked, her hand flexing toward her sickle. She itched to drag it across the throat of every troxy who was compliant with these experiments.

Silas only stared, his gaze locked on the troxies.

A body flew into the door of the office, leaving a person-sized dent in the metal, snapping them back to attention.

Silas pointed at a white cylindrical machine sitting to the side. It was bigger than a refrigerator, with a hollow middle. Inside the hollow portion, projections and holograms of DNA strands swirled and expanded, a troxy monitoring and recording the results. The troxies probably thought they were safe here in the lab with reinforced walls, while the users and turned slaughtered each other outside.

But they hadn't accounted for Penny. And she would kill them all.

"There's only eight of them," she said. Extra lab coats hung on hooks in the office, and she put one on, then tossed another to Silas. "Maybe you could just walk right up to the machine. I'll keep them busy while you do whatever computery things you need to do. Got it?"

Silas swallowed and bobbed his head as he pulled on the extra large coat, grimacing as he stuffed Callum's arm in the sleeve with his own. "Yep. Okay. Let's go." He tapped his Patch, and the connecting door to the lab beeped and swung open.

Sweaty and jittery, Silas edged his way toward the machine. She wished he didn't look so fucking guilty. She walked up to one of the metal tables and pretended to study the clipboard of notes beside the sheet-covered body, her sickle concealed beneath her coat.

Silas almost made it to the machine before someone spoke.

"You're not authorized to be in here." The troxy monitoring the machine, a short balding man, glared at Silas as he adjusted his glasses.

"Um, well, you see, I—"

"Security!"

Fuck.

Penny whipped out her sickle and drew her handgun. "Nobody do anything stupid." The troxies stared at her, open-mouthed. As one reached for a button on the wall, she switched out her sickle for a knife and threw it, spearing the woman's hand to the wall. Her shrieks filled the air as Penny said, "Anyone else feel like being a hero? No? Wonderful. Stay where you are. Silas, do your thing."

Silas stuck his hand into the holograms and made some weird hand motions, and then did other things that she couldn't see from her vantage point.

Her finger itched on the trigger. She *wanted* someone to be a hero, to take one step out of line so she could end them all. They weren't unsuspecting troxies like Stella; they *knew* what they were doing. This was the lab where troxapine was developed and refined, where they experimented on people, tested their organs, their genes, their flesh. Poked and prodded. Twisted and manipulated until there was nothing left.

None of those people deserved to walk out of that room alive.

One minute went by. Two minutes.

Silas was taking too long. Someone could have triggered a silent alarm or some sort of alert with their Patch that she couldn't see. Not to mention the turned they'd have to fight through in the hallway to get back to the elevator.

"You almost done?" she asked.

"I'm installing it now," Silas said, twisting his hand.

As he was typing on the holographic keyboard, the short, balding man lunged for Silas. Without hesitation, Penny put a bullet in his back. The man did not rise.

"I said *stay put*." She didn't lament the loss of life, just the waste of ammunition. But his move made the other troxies brave. A few rushed Silas and others ran for her. Some cowered under the tables and wailed for their lives.

A pudgy man huddled under the table closest to her. She grabbed his ankle and hauled him out.

"Please, no!" The man covered his head. "Pharmatrox threatened my family. Said if I didn't do what they wanted, they'd experiment on *them*. You have to believe me!"

Penny's grip on her sickle wavered. *Lies*, whispered Rodney's reptilian voice in the back of her mind. *We always kill those who deserve it.*

Other troxies advanced, throwing test tubes and medical equipment at her, faces painted with *fear*, not fury. Not anger.

How many of these troxies were like this poor, pathetic man in front of her? How many had been blackmailed and manipulated into doing things they didn't want to do? How many were like Stella? The piles of bodies Penny had racked up in her search for the Architect weighed heavily upon her. Maybe they hadn't all deserved the justice Penny had meted out to them.

What a great fucking time to grow a goddamn conscience.

She fired her gun into the ceiling. "Everyone, shut up!" The room went still. "You'll all get out of here alive if you just fucking *stay still*. The Spire is under siege anyway, so your fascist overlords won't blame you. They'll think this little lab break-in was courtesy of the chaos. Sound good? Great. Hands up, everyone. Put them on your heads. Yes, very good. Silas?"

"Coming!"

Forty-two seconds later, Silas jogged toward her. In a low voice, he said, "All done. Next time they turn it on, it's toast."

"And the network?"

"There's a terminal in the observation room I can use to upload the virus."

"Great. Let's hurry the fuck up."

Penny kept her gun trained on the troxies as they backed toward the observation room. When the door clicked and sealed behind them, she finally relaxed.

"I thought you were going to murder them all," Silas said as he punched a keypad and revealed a hidden hatch in the wall, then tapped his Patch and connected to the network.

"I thought about it," she said. "Didn't want to waste the bullets."

Silas gave her a look like he didn't believe her, but shrugged. He closed his eyes. When he opened them, his gaze was far away, focused on the unseen, waving his arms and making a pinching motion with his fingers.

Penny looked around the room. "Why are you flapping your arms like that?"

Silas's eyes refocused on her. "The Patch is an implant that uploads the CLEO and the network into my consciousness." His eyes shifted. "I'm standing in the center of a globe of tiny blue fluorescent lights." He brought both hands together, then pulled them apart and typed as if on an invisible keyboard. "Shit."

Sounds of violence from the hall grew louder behind the barricaded office door, and Penny passed her sickle from hand to hand. Guaranteed one of those troxies had triggered some kind of alarm after they'd left the room. Their time for delivering the virus was running out. "What is it?"

Beads of sweat formed on Silas's brow. "It isn't working. It's supposed to be pulling up a terminal so I can enter my own code, but it locked me out."

"Great. What do we do now?"

"Hold on, I'm trying to—oh Aggie, you sly devil." Silas smiled and rubbed his palms together, then spread his arms wide.

Penny waved and pointed to herself. "Hello, non-Patched civilian over here. What the hell is going on?"

"It's a passcube. Lucky for us, it's *my* passcube. It's the unbreakable one I used to teach Aggie how to code her own. She must have uploaded it into their system to practice, but someone found it and decided to use it. I only have ten seconds to crack it before the Patch automatically activates the self-destruct protocol."

"You—? Okay, whatever. Just hurry up."

Silas made a series of quick hand gestures, poking and twisting the air. The whole thing would have been comical if not for the screeches of users and turned. She shifted the barricade away from the door and glanced into the hall, seeing the black blood of the turned coating the white tile like tar. Half of the users and turned lay shredded on the floor, while the remaining ones tore at each other with their bare hands. One of them locked eyes with Penny in a wild black stare.

Heart in her throat, Penny ducked back into the office. "Silas? Let's speed this up." She wasn't scared of users or turned. She'd killed many before. But she'd never dealt with any who had used this much dust. She didn't know what they'd be capable of—and *that* scared her.

Silas finished with a flourish. "Done." He stared into space. Blinked a few times. Waved his arms again.

"Silas?" Penny didn't like the look on his face.

Silas's eyes were still focused on the unseen. "It didn't work. It's—*shit*!" Turning panicked eyes to hers, he said, "The Patch sent the self-destruct codes. We have exactly fifteen minutes to evacuate the building before it releases a neurotoxin. The troxies will be fine, they probably have gas masks locked away on every floor. But we've gotta get out. I solved the cube, but I can't access the network's source code from here. It led me to a dead end. A blue screen. A big fat hunk of nothing."

Oh, fuck. This can't be happening.

He swiped his hands in fast motions, staring into space. "It looks like someone recently changed the network's editing rights and restricted it to a particular terminal." He tapped his Patch. "Aggie? Are you there? There's only one terminal that can push updates to the network—and it's not in the Spire. Or it *was* here, but the location was moved recently."

Silas thrust a hand through his hair as he listened to Stella's reply. "I don't know," he said. "What should I do now? Hello? Agnes?" He jammed his hands through his hair. "Fuck. She's not answering."

Something slammed into the metal door as the lights flickered off, and Penny and Silas locked eyes. "Double fuck," said Silas. "We've gotta get out of here."

"We're on floor, like, nineteen and a half. How much time do we have?" she asked.

"Not much."

"Power's out, so no elevators. Think you can sprint up or down twenty floors of stairs in less than fifteen minutes?"

"Shit."

"Yeah, shit."

"Maybe Tara can hover by a window and we...jump into the helicopter from there? Tie a rope and throw it across? We have rope in our packs."

"Let's call her and see what she says. We'll start heading for the roof and duck off to a lower floor if we run out of time."

Silas nodded, but he looked like he wanted to throw up.

Penny opened the office door into a bloody hallway.

64

STELLA RAISED HER ARM against the spray of broken glass. The repetitive thrumming continued, and wind swept away the dust and smoke.

The stolen helicopter hovered on the other side of the barred windows, wobbling and swerving from side to side like a drunken bumblebee.

"Stella, Derek's on the radio!"

She ran to Lawrence's side, fumbling the device. "Derek! The windows just exploded, probably from the fire. Tara's covering us with the helicopter. Are you okay? Where are you?"

"*I'm* flying the helicopter."

"You're—*what*?"

"Tara's injured. Broken arm, maybe. We got overrun so we ran for it. Tara's manning the guns—or, well, she's firing her rifles out the broken door."

"Coño, this is a hunk of junk!" came Tara's muffled voice and the sound of bullets and volts.

"We've got some grenades we can drop too," he said.

"We're locked in. The windows are a hundred feet up, so we can't climb out. Can you break the door down? And how do you know how to fly a fucking helicopter?"

The two said "He doesn't" and "I don't" at the same time.

"I'm giving him directions, but he *needs to hold her steady or I'm gonna puke*," yelled Tara in the background.

"We'll get the door open, somehow," said Derek. "Hang tight."

The transmission ended in static, and she and Lawrence shared a dumbfounded look.

In her ear, Silas's voice Patched through.

"Aggie? Are you there? There's only one terminal that can push updates to the network—and it's not in the Spire. Or it *was* here, but the location was moved recently."

"Joder. It has to be here. She'd want to keep it close."

Before Silas could respond, something pummeled Stella in the side of the head, and her Patch lost its signal. Quentin swung again with a candelabra, but she ducked, ears ringing. As she fought, her mind sprinted through the possibilities.

Where would Ingrid hide the network's control terminal? She would never risk giving away its location, so it wouldn't be here in the sanctuary where she'd lured them. Stella would have to hack her way into the terminal and deliver the virus herself. Silas was a better hacker, so maybe he could talk her through it.

As she tapped her Patch to reboot it, twenty or more turned poured through the recently smashed windows, leaping to the floor. Tara tossed grenades through the barred windows and unloaded some shots into the horde, but the grenades didn't even make a dent against the sanctuary's steel doors.

Turned surged up the aisle like a wall of black water.

"Derek," Stella said into the radio.

"I see it. I have an idea. It's a very bad idea. Give me a few minutes."

She didn't know what that meant, but she kept fighting and Lawrence fired his few remaining bullets. The fire ate away at the wooden balustrade, smoke clogging the air and burning her eyes.

While grappling with Quentin, she managed to pull him into a chokehold, but he squirmed out. *Goddamn it.* She needed a chance to *think.*

Turned clawed at each other as much as they attacked her and Lawrence. *Ingrid still needs to refine the formula. This can't be what she wants. And I know the flaming cathedral was not part of her plan. She'd never want to destroy her new lab.*

Stella stepped out of herself and shifted into Ingrid's mindset. The loss of the wholesome mother in the journal entries was a searing hole in her chest that burned every time she breathed. She wanted to claw out the fake happy memories and throw them into the flames.

But the journal held the only clues she had of this twisted woman's mind.

*This is personal for Ingrid. Pharmatrox, the dust, these experiments—*they're *her real children. Precious to her.*

Stella shoved Quentin to the ground, but he rolled until he was on top, grabbing the radio from her belt and smashing it against the floor. *No!*

A knife pressed against her neck, and the look in Quentin's eyes was like a machine. Absent. Cold. All trace of the kid she knew, gone.

With one last surge of effort, Stella butted him in the face with her forehead. She felt the knife slide along her neck like butter as Quentin fell to the side, unconscious. It wasn't a deep cut, but it would need stitches.

As she racked her brain, she dragged Quentin behind the pulpit.

Something has to be meaningful to Ingrid. She left me, left papá for this. She did this for me. She wants me to take over.

Stella coughed as the smoke crowded her lungs. They had to evacuate. The balcony was inches from collapsing, flames eating up the dry wood.

Derek, where are you?

A turned with a rifle charged her and she took out his legs, disarmed him, and shot him with his own gun, then took the volt rifle attached to his back and fired both into the onslaught of turned.

The lifetime of conversations she'd had with Ingrid looped through her mind at top speed. Her first glimpse of the woman at NYU's career day. Late nights at the lab. Countless downloads after directors meetings.

Stella gulped. Ingrid's hands inside a body. Tapping on a clipboard. Flicking a syringe.

The revelation punched through Stella, leaving her breathless.

Her ruby ring. She still wears her wedding ring.

She still loves papá.

All of the relevant journal entries came flooding back to her. But one of them stood out.

I met a man at the bookstore today—Jay Monserrat. He walks up to me holding his favorite book, which is apparently For Whom the Bell Tolls.

A high place. High ground was safer. Stella had always believed that, even during her time living in the air traffic control tower.

"It's in the bell tower!" Stella shouted.

"What's in the bell tower?" Lawrence asked, grabbing a fallen volt rifle and firing.

"The network terminal, it's—"

The front of the cathedral exploded as something plowed through the thick sanctuary door, spewing stone and shards of metal.

Flames devoured the helicopter's metal skeleton as the blades continued rotating at a deadly speed, chopping through the turned, all of them dead or dying.

A familiar face appeared in the cockpit window. He held the radio to his mouth, his lips moving, and placed a bloody hand on the smoky glass.

"Derek!" The name tore from Stella's throat in a roar as she sprinted for the wreckage.

The helicopter blades whipped burning debris and acrid smoke in a toxic tornado. Beyond the wreckage, the entire front of the church was demolished.

Their escape route.

Stella shielded her face with an arm and helped a wounded Tara unhook herself from her seat. When Derek appeared, covered in dirt and bleeding from a gash on his forehead, he helped carry Tara, and Lawrence hustled over with an unconscious Quentin over his shoulder.

"The radio got damaged in the crash, but I think it worked enough to get a message to Penny and Silas," said Derek. "I told them we can't make it."

"*This* was your idea? You could have died!" Stella said as they hurried toward the giant hole in the front of the church.

The sounds of the battle from the front lawn filtered through the heavy smoke. A field of carnage swathed the narthex, bodies of turned and guards heaped in piles, torn to shreds by bullets, weapons, and claws.

"If you didn't notice, I crashed." Derek coughed and spat black goop. "So clearly, I didn't know what I was doing. I tried to shoot out the front of the church. Tried grenades. When that didn't work, I plowed through the door. It was the only thing strong enough to break through and not risk killing all of you inside."

Stella's hands worried over him. "Very resourceful, but never do that again."

A bright smile slipped through the grime on his face. "Hopefully I never *need* to do that again."

"You could have *died*," she repeated.

"But I didn't." Coughs wracked his chest and he spat again. "Where to?"

Her stomach churned at the thought that Penny and Silas now had no way to get a quick pickup from the Spire. Her Patch was still rebooting, so she couldn't contact him yet, but Silas was smart and Penny was ruthless. If Silas couldn't think their way out of the situation, Penny would fight them out. And they had Mal's support on the ground. They'd be okay.

"The bell tower," Stella said. "But Lawrence and Tara are injured, and Quentin's knocked out." She ushered them to an alcove. "I'm going alone."

"The hell you are," said Derek.

Tara slung her volt rifle to her front, favoring her injured arm. "Lawrie and I can handle this. We're both armed, not incapacitated."

A snarl came from the end of the hallway, and Stella spun, her heart in her throat. A handful of turned trickled through the broken windows. The remnants of Ingrid's army.

Tara took a one-armed aim with her volt rifle. "You said bell tower? Let's go."

65

Penny

I'M SORRY. YOU'RE ON *your own.*

The words careened inside Penny's mind like the metal ball in a pinball machine. She flicked the pegs in the hope that their reality would change, but the heavy orb of fate came crashing down and sank into the pit of her stomach with the weight of finality.

They'd been on the twenty-fifth floor's stairwell when Derek had radioed with the news before the transmission had cut off. But the weight in Penny's stomach knew the truth. They were probably going to die too.

I'm sorry, Quentin.

Something slammed into a door a few landings below them.

Turned—the ones Silas fed a whole package of dust to—snapped their jaws and poured into the stairwell. Drawn by the scent of dust, more had joined them. A veritable ocean of turned now swarmed mere feet below.

Penny ripped open the door to the twenty-fifth floor. "In here." They ducked inside a hallway, crammed with a tornado of activity. Troxies crisscrossed the halls, heading for exits, their arms full of whatever they could carry. "Try all the doors. Or if your Patch can open one...?"

Silas tapped his Patch, Callum's bloody arm bumping against his wrist. One of the door latches popped open, and they slipped inside just as screams and snarls echoed through the hall. His hand stuck to the knob, shaking. "Jesus, I'm not *equipped* for this."

Penny grabbed him by the shoulders. "Hey. You've gotten us this far. Now use that big brain of yours and get us out of here."

Silas took a deep breath and glanced around the room. The previous occupants must have already evacuated. It was a small lab set up with a table with a built-in sink, a desk, a fume hood, and various microscopes and test tubes. His eyes locked onto the sink-table thing.

"Penny, give me the ropes from your pack."

Penny's eyes widened. "Silas, this isn't exactly what I meant—"

"The ropes won't reach all the way to the ground, but it's all we have." A fierce resolve lit in his eyes, and after she handed him the rope, he began tying. "We have less than eight minutes to get out before we can't anymore. Because of the plumbing, these tables are bolted to the floor."

Penny cinched the rope around her waist and tied it around one of the thick table legs, as Silas had done, then shot a bullet at the floor-to-ceiling window. A spiderweb crack formed, and she punched out the safety glass.

Silas moved to edge over the side, but she stopped him. "I'm going first."

But before either of them could move, the lab door burst open, revealing growls and grasping hands, black eyes and bloody faces.

"Never mind," Penny said, pulling Silas over the side of the tower as a few turned plunged off the edge, grabbing for them.

Bracing her feet against the glass, Penny bounced down the building. Above her, Silas followed suit. At one point, his feet slipped, and he slammed face first into the windows.

As howls of the turned sounded from above like a distant pack of wolves, she shouted, "Try rappelling."

Silas nodded and bounced off the glass.

At the tenth floor, the rope pulled taut.

"Now what?" Silas asked, hovering beside her.

Penny charted their options. They had maybe six minutes left. She noticed a smashed window, the hole surrounded by glittering glass shards. It was about four windows away. They could make it, but they'd have to swing.

"Follow me." Penny tightened the knot at her waist and swung back and forth. As she picked up momentum, she threw her whole body weight toward the opening. Glass bit into her side, but she gained enough purchase to claw herself into the room. After untying the rope, she stuck her head outside.

Silas pumped his legs furiously, then swung toward the window, lunging for Penny's outstretched hand. Glass scraped across his arm, and she braced her feet on either side of the window to haul his massive body inside the vacant office. Once they were safely not dangling off the side of the building, Penny grabbed a wad of bandages from a nearby cabinet and thrust them at Silas, when a distant crashing sound came from behind them.

When Penny edged toward the window and peeked out, half of a lab table plummeted past her, banging off the tower and cracking windows on its way down.

"Good thing we untied—"

Silas flew across the room, pulled backward by the weight of the falling table, the rope still secured around his waist. He flailed and caught himself on the jagged window edges, digging his hands into the glass with gritted teeth.

The table pulled him toward the ground, his body arching backward, but Penny slashed through the rope with her sickle. It slapped against the floor and zipped out the window as Silas collapsed into the room, chest heaving. But then he was on his feet.

Penny looked at him. "Are you—?"

"Yes, I'm all right. Come on, we don't have much time."

Bleeding from his hands and arm, Silas fumbled the doorknob in a slick hand. Mercifully, the tenth floor was empty.

As they leapt down the stairs, shouts echoed upward. Around the turn of the fifth floor, they plowed into a bevy of bodies. Silas wheeled his arms, striking at anyone who got near him.

Men, women, and children, all with matching looks of wide-eyed fear and identical paper hospital robes. These were prisoners, not users.

The cell door locks must be included in the emergency evacuation proto-col, or they unlocked earlier during the power surges. White lab coats mixed among them. *Troxies.*

Penny's hand twitched to her sickle, but she abated. What if these scientists had been manipulated like the man from earlier, or like Stella? *Or Mal too.* It wasn't her job to personally judge every single troxy and dole out their justice. She had to rise above. She had to take out Pharmatrox at the source. *That* was her focus. *That* was what mattered. Ending the war and making sure her little brother never had to live in fear again.

"Silas, cool it. They're trying to get out too."

They pushed onward with the prisoners, but on the fourth-floor landing, a pack of users blocked the way. A burly man and a petite woman stood at the front, knives held in loose, confident fists. Their arms sported black eye tattoos.

"We're with Callum. Let us pass!" said Penny over the wave of people.

The woman's eyes settled on the dangling arm handcuffed to Silas's wrist and the tattoo of the black eye, and her face fell open in recognition.

Fuck. Can't avoid this fight.

"If you run into him, let him know I found something of his." Penny brandished her sickle. "He might want it back."

With a shriek, the woman lashed out, and the stairwell erupted in chaos.

Some prisoners cowered in the corners, but others fought and looked just as feral as turned. With only their bare hands to use as weapons, the prisoners tore at Callum's crew, ripping their nails across their flesh, biting into their necks and faces, tearing the ears from their heads. Blood sprayed and pooled on the floor in a slippery mess.

Silas reeled in horror, and Penny grabbed him from behind. He whirled, striking with his elbow, but she caught it in a deft fist. "It's me, you idiot. Let's go. If they want to fight, let them. I'm not dying for them."

Stricken, he rubbed a hand across his face. "I know the hell they've been through. I can't just leave them to die."

"What do you suggest! We're running out of time!"

He glanced around, then his eyes brightened as he saw something. He pulled the fire alarm and a blaring shriek sounded, amplified by the echo, red lights flashing.

Light and loud noises, two things turned hate—and these users are so close to turning.

Every user in the stairwell *screamed* and clutched their hands to their ears, beat their heads against the walls, and ran in circles, looking for an escape.

"Time to go," Silas shouted, shepherding the prisoners past the undulating mass of panicked users.

They burst outside just as a hissing sound filled the air behind them. What remained of the Faction's forces battled with users, turned, and Pharmatrox guards on the lawn.

Relief washed over Penny as she saw a familiar hulking figure.

"Mal!" Silas shouted over his shoulder as he barreled past. "When that neurotoxin is released, the wind will spread it. We should get as far away as possible."

"Copy that." Mal signaled his troops to follow, and they sprinted toward the street and the protection of the alleyways, the prisoners stumbling in their wake.

Behind them, an alarm bleated, and a white fog drifted out of the Spire's shattered windows. Penny threw herself into an alley, and Mal and Silas ducked in beside her. A thundering herd of prisoners and the Faction packed in around them to wait out the deadly fog.

Penny slouched against the wall. Silas looked like he wanted to keep running until he hit the ocean.

The wind was in their favor, and after a few minutes, Penny spoke. "Silas destroyed the machine," she said to the question on Mal's face. "The Spire is flooded with a neurotoxin that will either kill or incapacitate you, so I'd stay away from that."

"And what about the network? Is it destroyed?" asked Mal. Covered in the gore of battle, his intense expression was made all the more piercing.

Penny bit down on her lip. She couldn't say it. Couldn't dash his hopes.

Silas cleared his throat. "Ah, actually, we have a problem..."

66

S TELLA AND THE OTHERS sprinted to an alcove leading to a spiral staircase, Lawrence hefting the unconscious Quentin over his shoulder. Tara's feet slapped the metal stairs behind her, followed by the thunder of the hunt on their heels.

The tight spiral opened up into the grandeur of the bell tower, the stairs bracketing the perimeter to the top. The group sprinted ahead, making fast progress, but the turned were catching up.

Derek cross-checked a turned in the chest, then tossed him over the railing. "Go, Stella! We've got this."

Lawrence propped Quentin against the railing and nodded to Stella, arms braced and ready to fight, while Tara fired bullets into the turned.

Everything in Stella screamed to stay behind and help. But she trusted them. They could hold their own.

So she raced up the rickety stairs, sweat dripping, lungs heaving, and reached the top on shaky legs, the clang of weapons and snarls clamoring in the air.

A bronze bell dominated the landing. Too big to remove, the troxies must have decided to leave it in the tower. Stella dragged her hands across the surface, searching for a button, a divot, anything—*there!* A small switch at the bell's lip. She slid it to the side.

When her Patch pulsed to life, a pinhole opened in the bronze bell and a needle poked out. It needed blood to read the DNA-markers. Ingrid's blood.

Or Agnes's.

Mierda. What if this is a trap?

Pounding footfalls sounded behind her before a clawed hand tossed her against the stone wall, something in her side giving a painful shift. A turned peered down at her, beady eyes locked on the dried blood of her neck wound. Stella stumbled to her feet, hunched over in pain, and prepared to fend him off.

Tara one-arm shoved a body off the stairs as she and Lawrence approached the top. Derek brought up the rear, stabbing a turned in the neck and tossing it over the side.

"Did you find it?" Lawrence asked, whipping the butt of his rifle at another turned.

Stella aimed a kick for a turned's chest. "Yes, but what if Ingrid tampered with it? What if my blood sets off booby traps?"

"You're her daughter!" Derek said, elbowing one over the railing. "That has to count for something."

A million scenarios of how everything could go horribly wrong blitzed through her mind. "I could be poisoned, or it could trigger the self-destruct codes and send us all up in flames. We could *die*."

"We might die anyway!" Tara paused in her fight and locked eyes with Stella. "Do it, tía."

Decision made, Stella lunged for the bell and slammed her hand on the needle.

"Welcome back, Dr. Monserrat," said the cathedral's CLEO in her head. *I'm in. Hostia, I'm in.*

She was connected to the network. When she tapped into her Patch's comms to talk to Silas, a horrible screeching sound lanced her ears. *Carajo.* Her Patch's comms function must have gotten damaged in the fight. She was on her own.

The sounds of battle faded to a dull din as a glowing blue passcube appeared in the air.

She smiled and got to work.

Her hands moved in a familiar motion, completing the passcube in mere seconds. *Thank god for that extra practice with Silas.* Next, she pulled up the network's main terminal, which was only accessible from here in this tower, by someone of Ingrid's blood. She pulled up the malware she and Silas had designed and uploaded to her Patch. *Shit.* Some of the file had been corrupted from the damage. Her fingers flew across the holographic keyboard as she filled in the blanks with new code. *This better fucking work.*

Then she swiped to the final screen, and a password box appeared.

Ingrid's words from their confrontation at the Spire had been jangling around in the back of her mind for days. *Unity Is Strength. No person is an island. We are all "a piece of the continent, a part of the main."*

With shaking hands, Stella typed the words that would end the network and cripple Pharmatrox. An excerpt of the epigraph from her papá's favorite novel, *For Whom the Bell Tolls.*

No man is an island.

After pressing enter, her network connection severed, and the hovering blue text disappeared.

Stella gripped the edge of the bell in a sweaty hand. *It's over.*

Ingrid's corruption of the original quote curdled in Stella's stomach. *Does she think she's honoring papá's memory? That she's doing all of this out of* love? Ingrid didn't understand love. She wasn't *noble*. She wasn't the woman Jay Monserrat had met in the bookstore.

She was an aberration. A monster Stella should have destroyed when she had the chance.

"Stella!"

As she twisted around, a turned slammed into her, and she smacked her head against the bell. She stabbed him with her knife and he screeched, grabbing her by the throat and pulling the knife out of his leg. The blade aimed toward her face—

A spray of blood erupted and blinded Stella. She scooted away as Penny—*Penny?*—kicked the turned's head across the floor. His body collapsed beside her in a pool of black blood.

Stella stared at the headless body, uncomprehending, as Penny pulled her to her feet. Then Silas appeared beside her. His lips moved in slow motion, but Stella could only hear the staticky sound of a broken television. She looked from the headless body to Penny's concerned face. Concern for *her*.

Then the world snapped back to full speed with a crash of sound and color.

Tara tossed the last turned over the railing, and Lawrence and Derek held an unconscious Quentin between them.

Penny prodded the severed head with her boot. "This is a shit show," she said, then turned and winced. A knife hilt stuck out of her rib cage. Penny swatted Stella's hand and yanked it out herself, holding her side. "Fucker caught me at the last second."

Stella's thoughts tripped over themselves. "What...how...what are you guys *doing* here?"

"Later," Silas said, covering his face with his shirt to ward off the smoke. "Let's get everyone outside. The fire is contained in the sanctuary, but we should hurry. And we brought reinforcements."

67

AS THE SUN PEEKED over the horizon, it washed the scene on the front lawn in the blood-red light of dawn. The battle raged on, the Faction gaining an edge due to Mal's reinforcements. Heaps of dead bodies—users, turned, guards, Faction—littered the wide field.

The group reconvened near the tree line behind the Faction's line of defense.

Lawrence and Derek put the unconscious Quentin in the dewy grass. Concern etching her brow, Penny dug in her pack, withdrew a syringe of dionazole, and stuck it in Quentin's arm. His eyes fluttered, but he did not wake.

Stella cleared her throat and glanced at Penny. "Er—thanks. For keeping Silas safe. And for what you did in there—killing that turned."

Penny's artful brows pinched together. "It would have killed you." She stared at Quentin's slack face with a stricken expression. "*He* needs you alive."

"When he wakes up, there's no telling what his mental state will be. I don't know what kind of dosage Ingrid gave him."

"Is he going to be okay?"

"Yes," Stella vowed. "I stole more dionazole from the Spire, but we'll need a regular supplier."

Penny's mouth was a hard line. "We'll get it." She held a hand to the wound in her side, her black shirt wet with blood. Stella raised an eyebrow, but Penny shrugged her off.

When Derek sidled up to Stella, she ducked into his side. "Thank you."

He wrapped an arm around her and said, "You're the one who took down the network. We now stand a fighting chance against the troxies because of you."

"Let's save the victory lap for when we actually win," said Penny. "Ingrid is missing. There's still a battle going on." She squinted at the battlefield...searching. "Mal needs us. Let's finish this." She snapped her fingers at a Faction woman guarding the Humvee and pointed at Quentin. "Watch him. If *anything* happens, send someone to get me immediately." She eyed Silas. "You stay with him too."

"Yes, ma'am." The woman did an awkward salute, and Penny made a noise in her throat.

"Don't call me that. And no saluting. This isn't the troxy fucking Army." Penny jerked her head at the rest of the group. "Blades are best. We don't want to accidentally fry or shoot Mal's—*my* troops in that melee. Let's go."

They plunged into the fight, the meaty sounds of weapons against flesh, feral shrieks, zaps from volt rifles filling the air. Stella strayed to the edge of the battle, Derek beside her, as she cut down a path of turned and guards. Despite their injuries, Lawrence and Tara fought at her back, chopping through opponents like trees—Tara one-armed, with her left fixed into a quick sling.

A small group of guards, faces obscured by full helmets, approached from the ruins of the burning church. The guards looked...different than the ones that had descended into the fight earlier. These moved with a predatory grace, uniformly and in step.

At their center, a woman in a crisp white lab coat marched toward them.

A cold feeling slithered inside Stella. Were...were *these* the first of Ingrid's elite soldiers? The ones that the new formula of troxapine actually worked on as intended?

Stella bashed her way through turned until she reached the group, yelling, "Ingrid!"

The huddle of guards stopped and split down the middle, revealing the woman they protected. "Ah, Agnes," said Ingrid. "My apologies for the fire; that was an unfortunate interruption. I had planned to discuss things with you in the sanctuary, but I had to divert my attention to salvaging my experiments and equipment."

Good to know she still cares more about her work than about me. Clenching her fists, Stella said, "Discuss things?"

"I wanted you to experience Pharmatrox's newest creations firsthand. And to offer you this." Ingrid held up a vial of dionazole.

"We don't need it—we already gave some to Quentin."

"The latest version of troxapine differs heavily from previous iterations. So we had to reformulate dionazole as well. I have it"—she shook the vial—"right here. And it's yours." Ingrid smiled. A cracked vase of long-dead flowers. "If you join me."

Stella gripped her weapons belt with both hands. "So this was your plan? You're trying to *buy* me?"

"I made you who you are. I trained you. I taught you. I made you *better* than me. And isn't that what every mother wants for her child? For her to be better, to have a better life?"

"You're not my mother."

Ingrid pursed her lips and slipped the vial into her lab coat pocket. "But I *was* your mentor. I'll ask you one more time—join me. Help me build a better society. Doesn't that little red-headed rascal of yours deserve a better world?"

With an unearthly yell, Penny sprinted at Ingrid, her knotted red hair whipping behind her. Stella hadn't even heard her approach.

The guards shifted into formation around Ingrid and fired volts at Penny, who danced out of the way. She favored her wounded side but fought them back with speed and aggression.

Stella searched the battlefield for familiar faces and shouted for them to join their fight. Derek, Lawrence, and Tara dodged the bodies to come to their aid.

Mal noticed and laid down some cover fire into the line of Ingrid's elite guards. A few dropped around Penny as she whirled her sickle, but not enough. And they didn't stay down for long, reclaiming their volt rifles and returning fire.

"Enough," said Ingrid. Her guards formed up around her as Penny circled behind them. "I'm disappointed, Agnes. Very disappointed." Shaking her head, she tapped her Patch. "Bring the helicopter." She tapped her Patch again. "I said bring the helicopter. Hello?" Her face went white with pure terror, and her eyes found Stella. "What did you do?"

A triumphant grin spread across Stella's face, and she wiped the gore from her forehead. "*No man is an island*, Ingrid."

Rage and fear warred across Ingrid's face as she realized the depths of what she'd lost. She let out a wordless yell and turned to her guards. "Get me out of here."

Her guards pounced, taking up the fight with a new fervor.

One lunged for Penny, but she rolled to the side, landing in a low crouch. Mal was at her back, firing volts into the guards, to no avail. *They must have some special new armor that diffuses the electricity.* Mal realized it at the same time and tossed the rifle aside, taking aim with his gun instead.

Lawrence and Tara made a dynamic fighting duo, each watching the other's back as they whirled in unison.

From behind her, Derek said, "I've got two on this side. You good?"

Stella grunted as she kicked a guard and slashed her machete at his neck. "Bastards are hard to kill."

She glanced at the larger battle happening near them. The Faction was overtaking the troxy guards and turned, forcing them closer and closer to the burning church. They were still in this. They still had a chance to win, even with Ingrid's elite squadron.

While Mal reloaded his gun, a guard cross-checked Penny in the chest, and she fell backward. She took the short black-bladed knife from her belt and scooted away from the approaching guard, but even from a distance, Stella saw the seed of fear in Penny's eyes.

The guard thrust his knee onto Penny's chest and held the volt rifle to her forehead, a knife pressing into her throat.

All fear, all indecision, melted away. Stella aimed her gun at Ingrid's head with a steady hand. "Stop. Call off your guards."

Stella had never wanted to kill Penny, but she'd wished for her death many times. But that had been the leader of the Marauders, the vicious hunter. This Penny...She was different. She'd risked her life for Silas. For all of them. And they wouldn't have gotten this far without her. She was Penelope, Quentin's sister. A woman desperate to make up for her mistakes. Stella knew how heavy the weight of the past could be. Penny didn't deserve to die.

Ingrid turned and arched an eyebrow. "You'd kill your own mother to spare this woman? This *creature* who hunted you for months and murdered countless others?" The guard pressed the knife against Penny's throat, blood welling under the blade.

With his bulky frame, Mal plowed into the guard, ripping his helmet off and beating the man in the face with it, again and again. Penny grabbed the fallen volt rifle and fired it at the guard's exposed head, frying him instantly.

Stella locked eyes with Ingrid.

"You're no mother to me," Stella said, then pulled the trigger.

The bullet hit Ingrid dead center in the forehead—at the same time a black knife point burst through the middle of Ingrid's neck. A river of blood poured from the wounds and bloomed across her pristine white lab coat.

Penny pushed Ingrid's lifeless body aside, clutching a bloody knife.

"Didn't mean to steal your thunder." Penny inclined her head to Stella, voice breathless. Blood pumped from the wound in Penny's side at a steady pace, and she coughed up blood. "I could use a sit-down."

She stumbled and Mal caught her, scooping her up into his arms. He bellowed for reinforcements. Now that the Faction had the larger battle under control, they jumped in to finish off the elite guards.

Finally, it was over.

Stella poked her machete in the ground to steady herself as the adrenaline leaked out of her and her withdrawal symptoms multiplied. Derek appeared at her side, and she leaned into him, wrapping an arm around his waist.

Penny stirred against Mal's chest and coughed again. "Quentin?" Her eyes were glassy, her skin too pale.

"Let's get her to the Humvee," said Stella.

68

Stella injected the new version of dionazole into Quentin's arm from where he sat propped against the Humvee's tire. And waited.

Drawing her into his side, Derek said, "He'll wake up. Give him some time."

She nodded, chewing her lip. "He needs a new dionazole formula. Ingrid said she had the supply with her."

Derek traced soothing circles on her back and said, "We'll check her guards. Some of them had tactical packs."

Beside them, Silas stared at the burning church with a blank expression. "What happened with the helicopter?"

"Ask him." Tara pointed to Derek, who gave a sheepish shrug.

Silas blinked. "I figured there was some kind of problem, but didn't anticipate an...inferno."

Stella eyed Derek. "You sacrificed yourself. For me. For all of us."

Derek snorted. "It's not self-sacrifice if I'm still alive."

She nudged his shoulder. "That's not how it works. You put yourself in a life-or-death situation. And you *chose to fight*. You didn't run." She grabbed his shirtfront and forced him to look at her. "So don't tell me you're a coward. Not ever again."

Derek touched his forehead to hers, his lips quirking. "I suppose I can agree to that."

Silas shook out of his stupor and asked, "Is the network destroyed?"

Plastering a hand against the side of the Humvee, a bone-deep exhaustion seeping through her, Stella said, "It's done."

Silas pulled her into a hug, shaking with relief. "We took out the machine. It will be a while before they make another one, if they even can, now that their data is confined to some inaccessible server farm somewhere."

"You were right all those years ago," Stella said. "Maybe now we can rebuild and do things the right way."

Silas nodded, but he still watched the flames. She suspected he may never explain the full depths of the horrors he'd experienced. She gave him an extra squeeze.

A gasp split the air, and Quentin awoke, wide-eyed, arms flailing. "Stella? Tara?" His eyes locked onto something behind Stella.

Mal had opened the passenger door and slid Penny into the backseat. Quentin leapt up and Stella grabbed his shoulder. "Penelope? What happened?"

"Woah, hey," said Stella. "Slow down. How are you feeling?"

Quentin wriggled out of her grasp and elbowed his way in front of Mal to Penny's side. "I'm fine."

Penny shifted her gaze between all of them and landed on Quentin. She touched his face and whispered between lips speckled with blood, "I'm sorry, little brother."

Quentin squeezed her hand and cast a wild look around. His eyes found Stella. "Do something!"

Penny looked at Stella. All the anger that had tightened the lines of her face vanished as she clung to life with gritted teeth. The complicated tangle of emotions Stella felt toward this woman swirled inside her, but a glance at Quentin's heartsick expression was all it took to make her decision. She took a knife out of her belt. "Penny, you still have your lighter?"

Penny's chest rattled as she chuckled. "Always." She dug her silver lighter out of her pocket.

Stella flicked it on and heated the thin blade of her knife until it glowed. Mal tightened his hand on Penny's thigh as he realized her intent.

"I'll do it," he said in a gruff voice. He wrapped an arm around Penny's waist to hold her still, and she gripped his massive bicep in white-knuckled fingers.

"Do it," Penny hissed.

In a swift movement, Mal lifted her shirt and pressed the blade to her side. She groaned, biting into his shoulder, eyes fluttering.

"Can you clean her wound and handle the stitches?" Stella asked Mal, who nodded. She raised an eyebrow at the way he held Penny close to his chest and the...blistering look on his face.

"I'll help too." Quentin scurried to the back of the Humvee and rooted through the medical supplies.

While Quentin and Mal worked on Penny, Stella turned her attention to everyone else's injuries. Her own could wait—the cuts on her neck and torso, her likely broken, or at least bruised, ribs, countless others she didn't remember.

"How's your shoulder?" Stella asked Lawrence.

Lawrence grunted. "I can manage. Tara needs some stitches though. And a better sling."

"Way to tattle on me, Lawrie." Tara brushed Stella off as she advanced with a first aid kit. "I'll handle it myself."

Putting an arm around her, Stella said, "Thank you." She rested her head atop Tara's.

Tara gave her a hip bump and a wink. "Gonna have to be more specific, tía."

"Thanks for not kicking me out that day I first stumbled into your camp with a bleeding Quentin in tow. For teaching me your style of fighting." Stella cracked a smile. "For being my friend." She directed her words to the larger group. "Thank you all. I could never have done this without you."

"At least you finally admit it," said Tara with a slight smirk. "No hay de qué. Don't be a dummy. I love you, Stella girl. I'll take care of me and Lawrence." Snatching the first aid kit, she pointed to Stella and Derek. "You two tend to each other."

Stella and Derek went to get more medical supplies from the Humvee. Her hands trembled as she sifted through the bandages and sutures. The adrenaline had vanished as the events of the night caught up to her. Derek clasped her hands, and she finally looked at him. Understanding alighted in his gaze.

"This can wait," he said, twining his fingers through hers. "Come on."

Stella's boots felt heavy as bricks as they approached Ingrid's body.

Ingrid's face twisted in an eternal expression of surprise, blood dripping from the corner of her mouth. Stella's hands curled into fists. Killing Ingrid had never been part of her plan. But it had been the right choice. The *only* choice.

Standing in somber silence, Derek asked, "Are you okay?"

She should feel something, right? *Anything.* This was the woman whose words she read every day in that journal. The woman who had coached her throughout her entire career.

But all she felt was emptiness. Emptiness, and overwhelming relief.

I made you who you are. I made you better *than me.* Stella may never know the extent of how Ingrid had corrupted and manipulated her. The unknown secrets writhed in her mind, forming a new speck of darkness. But Derek's arm fastened around her shoulders held off the storm clouds gathering on her horizon.

"I'm okay." Stella stared into Ingrid's glassy blue eyes, all trace of her mentor gone. She took the first deep breath she'd taken in months.

The reality of what they'd accomplished swelled inside of Stella. Pharmatrox was gutted, crippled. The Leader was dead. They'd made a huge step forward for the resistance.

This battle was over, but for Agnes, the war was just beginning.

69

Back at Derek's house, Stella was the last one to take a cold shower. She struggled into her jeans, damp skin and injured ribs a hindrance, but she was grateful to be clean. The stitches across her neck tugged, and she inspected them in the mirror. Another scar to match her others.

They were all gathering in the living room in a few minutes to plan for what came next. It was well after midnight and they were exhausted, but the meeting could not wait. She wished she could crawl into bed and sleep for an eternity.

No rest. From one battle onto the next. Until it's done.

Stella scrubbed her towel over her shaggy hair and went across the hall to her room, where Silas lounged on her bed, snoring like a chainsaw. She tossed a pillow at him, and he startled awake.

"Levántate, cabrón," she said. "You don't have to go to the meeting, but this twin mattress is *not* big enough for both me and your massiveness to sleep in."

Silas stuffed the pillow under his head with a sly smile. "I thought you might be moving into *someone else's* room."

Something glowed deep in the pit of her belly. "Derek's just a friend."

"Yes, and I look at the big, muscly, delicious Malosi like I just want to be his *friend*."

She snorted. "Already told you. Mal's only got eyes for one person, it seems. But neither of them acknowledges it."

Silas gave a wistful sigh. "Both too stubborn. They're oddly perfect for each other."

Stella tucked herself onto the mattress beside him in what little space remained. "How are you feeling?"

He shrugged. "Fine. A bit fuzzy and pukey, but nothing major. I'll be glad to be done with those injections. I hate needles."

Stella pulled him into a hug. "If you ever need to talk about what you went through, I'm always here. I'm so sorry for everything."

Silas held her at arm's length, frowning. "You saved me, Aggie. And Evie's death was not your fault." Earlier, she'd explained her true role in Evie's death. She'd felt like vomiting the entire time, and it had taken her twenty minutes to get the whole story out. "You're the only one still blaming yourself for that. Even Lawrence seems to have accepted it, from the way he's stopped looking at you like he wishes he had laser beams for eyeballs. It's time to forgive yourself. Let it go." He squeezed her shoulder.

Her eyes burned, and she put her hand atop his. "I'll try."

When a knock sounded against the doorframe, the glowing feeling returned. Derek leaned against her bedroom door, hands in his jeans pockets. His dark tee shirt clung to every dip and curve of his muscles, his tattoos prominent against his light tan skin.

Her voice was raspy when she said, "What's up?"

"Waiting for you," said Derek.

Silas slapped his hands on his thighs and stood. "That's my cue. See you kids downstairs." He gave Stella a thumbs-up behind Derek's back before disappearing.

She stood and smoothed her shirt, suddenly forgetting what to do with her hands. "You were waiting for me?" she prompted.

Derek pushed off the doorframe.

Mierda, am I even breathing?

The wall bumped against her back. "Yes. I've been waiting for you for a long time."

Then his hands were in her hair and his lips were on hers.

His touch was soft at first, and she made a frustrated sound, knotting her fingers in his shirt and crushing her lips to his with a desperate need to know and taste and feel that he was *alive*. All the tension and fear that had been roiling inside her since they'd first gotten separated at the cathedral poured into her kiss. He returned it with the same edge of urgency. Not caring about their friends waiting below and the conversations that carried up the stairwell, she held him tight against her.

His mouth parted in a smile under hers. "Finally," he said. He rested a warm hand behind her neck, and she breathed him in.

A cough came from the end of the hall, snapping them out of the moment. She and Derek whipped their heads to see Quentin on the landing, grinning. "I found them!" he shouted down the stairs. "*Snogging.*" Tara's laughter was the loudest.

Stella's cheeks flamed, while Derek slipped off his shoe and threw it at Quentin, who ducked, still beaming, and scampered downstairs.

"Duty calls," said Derek. He motioned for her to go first, and he followed.

Stella's face felt hot when she took a seat on the living room floor. Tara, Lawrence, and Silas occupied the couch, while Penny and Mal posted up on either side of the fireplace, both standing with their arms crossed and wearing matching serious expressions. Stella stifled a smile and bumped against Silas's leg, and he waggled his eyebrows in response.

"So now what?" said Quentin from where he and Derek sat atop the center island in the kitchen. They'd found a few vials of the new dionazole in Ingrid's pockets—enough to give Quentin a good start on his detox—and he seemed to be doing fine.

Stella gaped at him. "What, was this not enough adventure for you?"

He shrugged. "I kind of got used to running for my life. Now I'm going to get flabby and out of shape without some evil pharmaceutical corporation chasing me down and trying to off me every five seconds."

"I can chase you around with Stella's machete, if you like," said Derek. "Keep you on your toes."

Quentin gave Derek the finger, and Derek pulled him into a headlock.

Stella spoke up. "The network and the machine are destroyed, and Ingrid is"—she swallowed—"dead. But Pharmatrox is not yet ousted as a threat. They can still regroup. Rely on old forms of communications like radios."

Mal nodded his agreement. "Pharmatrox has some kind of succession plan in place. They wouldn't leave the chain of command up in the air, especially in a time of crisis. But I'm sure their list of successors has changed for security reasons, due to defectors and the like."

"Has anyone been able to contact Kev in Chicago?" Derek asked.

"I sent a small team to deliver the message and scope out the situation," said Mal. "It will be a while before we hear back. We have time to make contingency plans for how we want to handle the Pharmatrox satellite facilities. In the immediate, we should secure the Capital and eradicate or subdue all Pharmatrox presence." Mal rubbed a tired hand across his face and added, "But that will be a task for tomorrow."

"What do we do about the users and the turned?" asked Lawrence.

"We'll raid Pharmatrox facilities for dionazole and other supplies," said Penny. "Mal has—*we* have people doing that right now, before any other opportunists can step in and fuck things up. We'll rehabilitate the users who can be saved and…eliminate the ones who can't."

"I can help," said Lawrence. "I've been tweaking some recipes for herbal remedies to help with withdrawal as the dionazole kicks in. I'll set up a garden here with some of the Faction's hydroponic supplies."

"Any assistance would be great," said Penny. "Everyone in this room should now consider themselves a part of our advisory council as we rebuild. We'll help the civilians any way we can, and make plans for how to reintegrate troxy prisoners back into society. Maybe I'm getting ahead of myself, but it's not too soon to start taking care of our people. Quentin, Lawrence, and Silas—I thought you might be interested in heading up those efforts."

Quentin's face lit with enthusiasm at being singled out, but he stifled it quickly, his eyes darting away from his sister. He seemed to be acknowledging Penny's existence now, but Stella hadn't talked to him about it yet.

"Tara, Derek," continued Penny, "with your military knowledge and fighting skills, Mal and I could use your help with battle strategies and fighting on the frontlines, if you're willing." When Penny looked straight at her, Stella stifled a flinch. "Stella, we'll need your insider Pharmatrox knowledge when it comes to weeding out all of the facilities—both here and across the country."

Stella had only just stopped jumping every time Penny said her name, but the two had a long road to travel before forgiveness was in the cards.

"I don't know how much help I'll be since my Patch is useless," said Stella. "Since the network's down, none of their locks or security protocols will function, but they might have manual backups. So I'll see what can be done."

"I'm in," said Tara.

Derek nodded his agreement and clapped Mal on the back. "Looking forward to being your number two again, Mal."

Mal rolled his eyes. "You'll always be my number one pain in the ass."

"Glad to have a hand in reigniting that bromance," said Penny. "Let's call it a night. Mal and I need to get back to the stadium to take stock of our losses and see what we're working with." Her eyes found Stella again, then shifted to Silas. "Thank you. It's because of you two that we have a chance of winning this war."

It felt weird to be *thanked* by someone who had been hell-bent on her death for months.

She wasn't sure she'd ever get used to that.

70

Penny

PENNY AND MAL STEPPED onto Derek's front porch. The wound in her side flamed with every movement, but the quick cauterization had kept her from bleeding out. If she moved too much, her stitches tugged. Beads of blood dotted her tee shirt, but the black fabric hid them well.

"Um, Penelo—Penny?"

She turned at the sound of Quentin's voice. He stood in the doorway gnawing his lip, hand frozen on the knob. In a blink, he darted in and threw his arms around her. She stifled a groan at the impact, but squeezed him tightly, ruffling his bronze hair.

"I'm glad you're okay," he said as he stepped away and back inside.

"Hey, Quentin?"

He paused, a look of uncertainty puckering his brow.

The words dried in her mouth. "I'm sorry—for everything. I know an apology will never make up for the things I've done. I don't deserve your forgiveness. But I'll spend the rest of my life trying to earn it." Her voice cracked, and she cleared her throat. "I love you, kid."

Quentin's eyes glimmered, and he gave her a firm nod. "Um, bye. Bye Mal." He waved and shut the door.

I'll take it.

She couldn't help the silly grin that spread across her face as she and Mal headed back to the stadium. The battle at the Spire had drawn most of the turned to the opposite side of town, so there weren't many to disturb them as they walked. But she stayed on alert for any stragglers.

She and Quentin had a long way to go to reclaim their relationship, but the fact that he hadn't slammed the door in her face was a good sign. She didn't know how to begin earning his forgiveness, but she'd start by winning this war for him and making sure he never wanted for anything. It might even mean befriending Stella. Her insides twisted at the thought. She'd had it out for the woman for months, and her knee-jerk reaction was to reach for her rage. But now, she and Stella were on the same side. Allies was easier to stomach than *friends*. She assumed it was the same for Stella too. Allies, she could do.

"Seems like the kid is warming up to you," said Mal. "He was beside himself when you were injured. I'm not sure how much you remember." His jaw tensed and his hands flexed at his sides, as if he recalled the way it felt to touch her, feel her blood on his hands.

She remembered it too. But her thoughts lingered on the way Mal had cradled her against his body, woven a protective arm around her, sewn her stitches with gentle hands.

She stopped and faced him. "I remember everything."

He halted, inches away. His eyes grazed over every inch of her, carving a flaming path. He reached for her—

A turned screeched a few streets over, and more took up the cry in a chorus of howls.

Mal dropped his hand and cleared his throat. "We should get back."

Penny nodded and they jogged away. She shook off the lingering heat. What did she want to happen? *Why* did she want it to happen? The man drove her insane most of the time with his standoffish attitude.

After a few minutes of running in silence, Mal spoke. "You're going to take over the weekly strategy meetings."

Penny frowned. "Why? I hate meetings."

"If you want to be taken seriously as the leader of the Faction's presence here, you need to get to know the soldiers, and let them know *you*. Show them why you deserve to lead."

She made a sound in her throat, but he was right. If she was going to lead, then she needed to fucking *lead*. Thinking of the troops as her troops instead of Mal's wasn't an easy transition, but she'd get used to it. They still had a whole-ass war to win. They'd accomplished so much, but it was only a matter of time before the troxies regrouped. And she needed to make sure they were culled before that could happen.

"And..." Mal fell quiet.

She glanced at him out of the corner of her eye. A muscle flicked in his jaw. "And what?"

"And getting...involved with each other is not a good idea. I'm your general."

She skidded to a halt. "*Involved?*"

Mal huffed in frustration. "You want people thinking you fucked your way into a leadership position?"

"Oh, because *that's* the only way a woman could become the leader?"

Mal crossed his arms. "Of course not. You know that's not what I mean. But people talk out of their asses and say stupid shit. I don't want the transition to be more difficult for you."

"While I appreciate your noble effort to protect my delicate lady reputation, I don't give a fuck what anyone says. I don't need your protection either. And I *don't* want to get 'involved' with you. Get over yourself, Mal."

An unreadable expression crossed his face before Penny turned away.

She pushed their pace faster. They'd already spent too long outside in the dark. But as she ran, she remembered the feeling of Mal's skin against hers, how it felt to be held by him.

And she knew it wasn't something she'd soon forget.

Fuck.

Epilogue

S TELLA PULLED HERSELF ONTO the roof of Derek's house, surprised to see she wasn't alone.

Against the backdrop of the rosy sunrise, a dark silhouette cut a
prominent figure. She clambered across the shingles and settled next to
Derek, and he draped an arm across her shoulders and tucked her into
his side. Over the past few weeks, she'd gotten more comfortable with
allowing herself to *feel* the full spectrum of her emotions. To fully live in
the moment. For so long, she'd been singularly focused on saving Silas,
on seeking redemption, that the guilt and duty that drove her were the
only emotions she'd had room for.

But now, she could afford a brief respite and settle into herself and her
new friends.

"I'm glad you're here," she said.

Derek tucked a flyaway hair behind her ear. She'd decided to let it grow
out and return to her natural dark color. "Where else would I be?" He
kissed her softly, and she smiled under his touch.

Her life felt normal again. Well, not *normal*. Nothing would ever
be normal. But instead of crippling fear and unending dismay, she felt
acceptance. *Quentin's goofy smile.* Camaraderie. *Lawrence giving me a
chance.* True friendship. *Tara saying she loves me.* Loyalty. *Derek sticking
by my side.* These people had become her home. Her refuge. Her *family.*

It had been a lifetime since she'd felt safe enough to build that kind of community.

She didn't have to run anymore—from herself, from the Faction, from Pharmatrox. No, she was bringing the fight to the troxies. By manipulating her for her whole life, Ingrid had assured Stella's position as a leader in the resistance.

"So your mission leaves tomorrow?" she asked, but she already knew the answer. She'd been dreading the day for weeks.

Derek nodded. "Mal wants to get an early start. We're taking a few units to scout the nearby Pharmatrox facilities and round up the troxies so they can't cause any issues. We'll give them the chance to join us, leave the country, or hole up somewhere in the suburbs and let us fix things. Penny also wants us to help or, ah, take care of any users in the area. If they want dionazole, we'll give them what we have, but we need to find a new supply soon. Hopefully those facilities have some. Tara is coming too."

Stella had just finished her own course of dionazole last week, and she was feeling more like herself again. But the dust would always be a seed of darkness that had forever taken root inside of her. She might have kicked the habit, but she'd never leave the addict behind. It would always be a part of her. She wasn't ashamed of it. Tara's words from their rooftop sparring session came back to her. *If we don't learn how to carry our darkness, it'll fester inside us. All we can do is learn from it, and do better.*

And remember to let the light in every now and then.

Stella shifted beside Derek, and he pulled her closer. "I'd tell you not to worry, but I know that's impossible," he said. "And besides, you'll be busy."

Stella grumbled. "Silas is relentless. He's been making me practice my coding. I hate it and I hate him."

"You *love* coding."

Stella sighed her assent. "I *do* love it, but damn him, he doesn't have to be such a dick about it and remind me every two seconds that he's the best teacher I've ever had. Anyway, he's convinced that Pharmatrox has a hidden server farm they could use to rebuild the network, and he's probably right. But don't ask me where to find it. He's planning an elaborate way to hack it, or something. I don't know. He gets pretty unhinged when he's excited and starts talking really fast. I should take notes next time."

Placing a gentle fingertip to her cheek, Derek said, "You smile more when he's around. I'm glad we got him out of there." He dipped his forehead to hers. "Thanks for taking a chance on a 'douchey-looking stranger on a motorcycle.'"

"Is someone up here quoting me?" Quentin scampered out of Stella's bedroom window and onto the roof beside Derek, who reached to ruffle his hair, but he wrestled away. From below, Lawrence and Tara stuck their heads out of the same window.

"Oye, tomatito!" Tara hung halfway out and glared at Quentin while Lawrence held onto her belt loops. "If you fall off that roof and break a leg, you'll also find my foot up your ass! How you gonna run from the turned with a broken leg, huh? What does Stella always tell you?"

"Don't get eaten." Quentin blew raspberries at her. "Okay, *Mom*, I'll be careful. Jeesh."

Lawrence chuckled. "Tara, you know the kid has sticky limbs like a tree frog. He'll be fine." He looked pointedly at his hands preventing her from falling out the window. "Are *you* trying to break a leg and get eaten?"

Silas wedged his head out of the neighboring window, perplexed. "Why are you people always on the fucking roof?"

A pebble of warmth glowed in Stella's heart at the sight of him.

As the vibrant colors of the sunrise reached their zenith and the light of a new day painted the ruined city in swaths of gold, the darkness Stella had been wearing like an armor since the Beginning cracked and shattered. Evie's death, Silas's capture and torture by Pharmatrox, her obliviousness to the insidious evil of her former employer, her own role in Pharmatrox's treacherous empire, Ingrid's betrayal—she'd carry those scars for the rest of her life. But they didn't have to be sinking anchors fastened to her soul. They could be reasons to do better. Reasons to keep trying. Reasons to keep *living*.

She wished Evie could be there. She pictured her friend, round-faced and smiling, sitting beside her as she watched a new day trickle over the horizon. Stella rested her head on Derek's shoulder and hooked her arm through Quentin's.

"I think you should start calling me Agnes."

Leave a review

I hope you enjoyed the beginning of this rowdy crew's journey. Your reviews mean the world to me! If you could take a few minutes to post a review on your favorite site, I'd be forever grateful.

See you in the sequel...

Review on Goodreads

The (steamy) journey continues...

Thirsty for more steamy moments?

Penny and Mal's story continues in **The Lies That Hide Within**.

Coming soon!

Sign up to be notified about the release date:

Order your special edition hardcover

Want a special edition hardcover of The Darkness All Around Us to add to your bookshelf?

The special edition hardcover includes:

- Naked cover art by @lucielart

- Digital sprayed edges

- Dust jacket

- Bookplate signed by the author

- 2 additional art prints by @lucielart

Order your copy here before they're gone!
Very limited supply available.

Acknowledgments

When I first had the idea of Stella and Quentin, I never imagined I'd finally get to the point of publishing their story and putting it into your hands.

This story has changed and evolved so much from the very first scene I ever wrote. I sat down to write with absolutely no idea of what was going to happen. I just knew I wanted to write a book, and Stella and Quentin would be the stars.

After years of trying and failing, I finally finished a draft in 2021. That was only the beginning.

Seeking outside help to get my manuscript to where it is today was the best decision I ever made. It's because of my editors Cameron (Cee) Montague Taylor and Nadara at Nay's Notations that my book is better than even I thought it could be.

Cee's brain and ideas were instrumental in telling this story the way I wanted to and in doing the characters justice. And Nay helped to polish my prose and keep all of the scenes rolling along at just the right clip. This book would not be what it is without their assistance, and I'm a big ole ball of weepy gratitude. If you're looking for a developmental editor and a line/copy editor, I cannot recommend them enough.

Thank you to my character artist, Lucía, who did the special edition naked cover and the two character art pieces that come with it. She is responsive, creative, and absolutely a joy to work with. Many thanks as well to my cover artist Trif Book Designs who worked tirelessly to make my cover absolutely perfect (and dealt with my plethora of emails).

A huge thanks also to my beta readers, Madison and Amanda. You read a very early version of my book and had a hand in shaping its future, so thank you for helping me to get to this point.

Thanks to my Street Team, my ARC readers, and anyone who took the time to write a review of my book. You're the real rock stars. Reviews and early reads and support are so important, and it means so much.

Thank you as well to my fellow author pals for always being open to answering my questions and connecting me with the right resources and the right people.

I'm so grateful to my friends, family, and my partner for always supporting me, cheering me on, and for being understanding when my brain is elsewhere and my head is in the clouds. Your unending patience and love mean everything to me.

Finally, a huge thanks to my parents. My special edition books would not be possible without them. They're the ones packing the boxes and sending them out, since I live in a very remote location where shipping books is not financially feasible. Thank you, Mom and Dad, for always making my dreams come true.

And thank you, dear reader, for going on this journey with me. You took a chance on a new author, and I hope you'll stick around for what I have in store—it's going to be a wild ride.

Until next time,

Meg

About the author

Megan Boley is a dystopian and urban fantasy author. She loves writing stories with badass women and a healthy dose of plot twists. If she's not plotting the triumph (or demise) of her next set of characters, you'll find her at jiu jitsu or reading on the beach.

Instagram: @meganboleyauthor
Tiktok: @metal_meg
Website: megboley.com

www.ingramcontent.com/pod-product-compliance
Lightning Source LLC
Chambersburg PA
CBHW061853310726
48972CB00004B/1008